DELUSI[...]

To Rose Marie —
a great mother in law

Terry Lewis

Pineapple Press, Inc.
Sarasota, Florida

For Bruce and Mary Ethel Hinchliffe

Inquiries should be addressed to:

Pineapple Press, Inc.
P.O. Box 3889
Sarasota, Florida 34230

www.pineapplepress.com

Library of Congress Cataloging-in-Publication Data

Lewis, Terry, 1951–
    Delusional / Terry Lewis. – First edition.
        pages cm
    ISBN 978-1-56164-604-3 (pbk. : alk. paper)
    1. Psychological fiction. I. Title.

PS3562.E9765D45 2013
813'.54–dc23

                                                    2013011574

Design by She' Hicks
Front cover art and design by Carolyn Novak, TC Novak Designs, LLC
Printed in the United States of America

ACKNOWLEDGMENTS

When I began my research for this novel, I went to my friend and fellow judge Stew Parsons, who for many years was the general counsel for Florida State Hospital. He advised me to get in touch with Ellen Resch, the clinical program director at the facility.

It was good advice. Ellen suggested books and articles to read, took me on a guided tour of the facility, arranged for me to shadow psychologists and speak to patients, and graciously answered my many questions. A special thanks to her and the other staff members, including Hospital Administrator Diane James, for allowing me a glimpse into their world.

I am grateful to the many people who read earlier drafts and provided valuable comments: Fran Lewis, Angie Barry, Pat Looby, Ellen Resch, Pam Ball, Russ Franklin, Tom Lager, Michael Whitehead, Liz Jameson, Pat Murphy, Karen Huber, K.H. Schneider, Meredith Fraser, and Charlie Wilkinson. Of course, you wouldn't be reading this if the publisher hadn't agreed to take on this project and see it through. So my thanks to David and June Cussen, Kris Rowland, and the other fine folks at Pineapple Press for making the editing and publication process a pleasant one. And finally, to my agent, Evan Marshall, a true gentleman, thanks for your optimism and encouragement.

"As for me, you must know that I shouldn't precisely have chosen madness if there had been any choice."

—Vincent Van Gogh, 1890

I am not God, and I've never claimed to be God either, despite what it might say in those reports. They twist my words, you see, because it suits their purposes. What I actually said is that, on occasion, God speaks to me. And that's very different. Communication with the creator of the universe is not the sign of a mind out of touch with reality but of a soul in touch with the cosmos.

It is true that I have, over the years, suffered from mental illness. I don't deny it. The illness has not, however, adversely affected my intellectual capacities. My ability to perceive, to analyze, and to understand complex subject matter is well documented. I have uncanny recall of minute details over a span of many years, and my powers of concentration are, I dare say, exceptional.

My sensory powers as well have been sharpened, not dulled, by my illness. When my senses have not been deadened by drugs, I can hear whispered voices twenty yards away and smell a woman's perfume from across a large room. If anything, my problem has been sensory overload. Sorting, organizing, and interpreting the information and stimuli that constantly bombard me can sometimes be difficult. At times I feel like a switchboard operator with too many incoming calls.

Maybe my interpretation of things has at times been inaccurate. I'll admit that. But we all construct our own realities, don't we? And how do we know that the majority's perception is the true reality? History is replete with great thinkers who were labeled madmen because their way of perceiving and understanding the world around them was radically different. Yet they were later proven to be correct.

So, before you dismiss my account as the ranting of a madman, ask yourself this: How could this supposedly crazy person present to you, in extensive detail, in cogent and literary prose, the events that have led us to this point? And if my narrative seems a bit rushed at times, or incomplete, you must understand the urgency to get this story down quickly, before I am discovered, before they can drug me into incoherence—or worse. Remember as well that the truth is sometimes symbolic, and I may have to lay it between the lines. That is the core of myth, is it not?

All I ask is that you keep an open mind and judge for yourself. Measure my words for logic and for truth. Compare them to your own knowledge of the people and events. You will find, I am confident, that what I shall tell you here is not only deeply disturbing but factually and emotionally accurate as well.

***

You want to know about the murder, of course, but first, a bit about myself. This is, after all, my story, and you should have a proper context in which to understand the events, an anchor against the winds of diversion and distortion.

My name is Nathan L. Hart. I was born in Arlington, Virginia, ten years from the date—and at the exact time—that Richard Nixon, sitting in his office across the Potomac, told the nation, "I will resign the presidency, effective noon tomorrow." Most people consider this an interesting coincidence but nothing more. I don't believe in coincidences.

My father was a spy, a covert operative for an agency so secretive it had no official public identity, referred to by its members as simply the Unit. Of course, I didn't know he was a spy to start with. He told us he worked for the State Department as an analyst. He took occasional trips out of the country for conferences or as part of a diplomatic or trade delegation, he would say.

But I started noticing the clues, putting them together: the magazines left on the end table, slightly dog-eared to a particular article; the arrangement of foods in the refrigerator; whether he fully closed the door in the den or left it slightly ajar; the positioning of the salt and pepper shakers on the kitchen table each morning. They became his way of secretly communicating with me, grooming me to perhaps one day work beside him. He never came right out and said it, of course. In fact, when I broached the subject, he denied his involvement and discouraged all conversation on the topic. But I knew, and my father's reticence simply confirmed it.

My mother was an elementary school teacher, a beautiful woman of grace and charm, and extremely pious. She made sure that my brother and I received the proper religious and spiritual guidance. I took my Bible studies and my religious education seriously, but by the time I was fifteen or sixteen, I had begun to feel confined, cramped by the dogma of one particular sect of one particular religion. I was offended by the sanctimonious conviction of church leaders that there was only one way to salvation, and I began to explore other religious traditions and spiritual ways. Eventually, with an open heart and mind, my focused, internal search resulted in direct communication with God.

I bring this up now only because it plays an important role in the story. As I told you, God speaks to me on occasion. And the message is not always one of benevolent guidance from a loving God, either. Sometimes the sentiment is quite the opposite. And this makes sense, don't you think? If God is all-knowing, omnipotent, the creator and ruler of the universe, then why does he allow bad things to happen unless that is his will? I say that God is both good and evil. If you think about it, that's the only way it could be. There must always be a balance. It is, I believe, through the very acceptance of this intertwined and inseparable duality that I have been given the gift of divine insight, of intimate communication with God.

And when you are able to perceive, to understand on such a higher level, as I am, it is natural—almost inevitable—that those who are not similarly blessed will be skeptical. Many will be jealous, angry, and perhaps fearful. They might even label you insane, call you a murderer.

***

On the night that Aaron Rosenberg was killed, I was residing in Sunrise Cottage, the halfway house located on the grounds of the hospital. I was awakened around ten o'clock by the sound of footsteps on the front porch, followed by the creak of the front door opening and closing. I didn't think much of it at first, figured it was one of the residents trying to sneak in after curfew. But when the wood plank floor in the living room groaned under the weight of two sets of footsteps and I heard someone at the back door, my alertness level bumped up a notch.

An interior door opened, followed by another. Someone said something, but I couldn't make it out. Then I recognized the whispered, insistent voice of Andy Rudd, chief of security at the hospital: "Get back in your room." One of the doors closed again, and the footsteps made their way down the hallway, stopping in front of my room.

The door flew open, the overhead light was flicked on, and two psychiatric aides rushed through the doorway. They were holding seat cushions from the living room sofa in front of them as makeshift shields—a common technique when dealing with someone who might be armed with a knife or similar weapon. Rudd walked in behind them. I knew then that this was not about a broken curfew.

Was I startled? Yes. Did I panic? No. Indeed, I find that I am most calm in a crisis, when those around me are not. And I could smell the mix of fear and excitement on the men. I could see the tension lines in Rudd's face. Although I was prepared for an attack, that seemed entirely unlikely, so I lay there unmoving.

Rudd smiled at me. "Hello, Nathan," he said, looking around the room quickly before bringing his focus back to me. "Would you mind putting your hands where I can see them?" His tone was polite but all business.

I brought my hands out from underneath the sheet—slowly so as not to cause the men to panic—and placed them by my sides. "Hello, Andy," I said. "Kind of late for a visit, isn't it?"

Rudd motioned for me to stand. I did. Though I was dressed only in my underwear, I felt no embarrassment or self-consciousness. I was used to every level of physical and mental humiliation that comes with being a patient in a mental hospital. I had long ceased to care about such things.

"You been running or something, Nathan? You're sweating like a pig."

I said nothing.

He looked around the room as if to take its temperature. Then he told the other two men to check the bed, which they did, thoroughly. Satisfied that there was no weapon there for me to grab, he directed me to sit on the bed, then pulled up the small chair from over in the corner, placed it in front of me, and sat down. He was about three feet away now. While the other two men began a detailed search of my room, Andy leaned in a little closer to me. "Where's the knife, Nathan?"

"What knife?"

"You know we'll find it eventually."

"What knife?"

The man leaned back in his chair and shook his head slowly, as if disappointed by one of his children, then leaned forward again. "Have you seen Dr. Rosenberg tonight?"

"No."

"Been to his office?"

"No."

Rudd shook his head again. "No good, Nathan. We got an eyewitness, a custodian named Raymond Curry. You know Raymond, don't you? He knows you. And he says he saw you running out of Rosenberg's office with a knife in your hand. So, I ask you again, where's the knife?"

"He's either mistaken or lying," I said without hesitation. "I haven't been in Rosenberg's office in weeks."

Rudd leaned back in the chair again and frowned. Andy Rudd made a pretty good physical impression with his large, square shoulders and strong jaw. He kept his prematurely white hair trimmed close and had an erect military bearing, all of which diverted attention from a rather sizable beer belly. To the uninitiated, he could seem quite charming, I'm sure.

I could smell the cheap aftershave, however. I could see the cold malevolence behind the blue eyes. I sensed the lies, sitting just behind the straight white teeth, biding their time, waiting to come out. As he stood there, doing his best to project a cool, professional image, I couldn't help but recall a less flattering one.

It was July fourth of last year, and I was returning from a party the staff had held for the residents in the main cafeteria. As I passed by the shed where they keep some gardening equipment, I heard noises from inside, whispered voices. Slowly, carefully, quietly, I crept around the side and up to the back door, which was slightly ajar. I angled up to the opening, careful not to be seen, and peered inside. The first thing I could make out was the face of one of the patients.

Belinda Crayton suffered from acute clinical depression and had since she was a teenager. She attempted suicide twice and was hospitalized at Florida State Hospital on three occasions. It seemed that she masked her emotional and spiritual vulnerability with a larger-than-average physical frame and a hard countenance. That evening, her rather large frame was bent forward from the waist, her hands gripping the front of a garden cart for balance. Her dress was up over her waist, her panties down around her ankles.

Andy Rudd stood directly behind her, his hands resting lightly on each side of her waist and his pants down to just above his knees. His thrust was forceful and rapid, and as he did so, he seemed to look directly at me, though I am sure he could not see me. His face glistened with sweat and contorted with the strain, the line between pleasure and agony hard to draw.

This was the image that came to my mind that night as Andy Rudd looked at me. Strange, but it made me extremely relaxed. So, yes, when Andy later described me as being very calm that night, he was entirely accurate. When he said I was pretending to be asleep, however, that was a lie.

It is also correct that I asked him if Rosenberg was dead, though the sinister interpretation some have given the question is not accurate. The question was a very normal, natural response under the circumstances, don't you see? It didn't take a genius to figure out that these men had not busted into my room in the middle of the night to tell me good news. When Andy started asking about Rosenberg and about some knife, well, I just naturally assumed the worst.

My memory of the details, I confess, is fuzzy, dulled and distorted by the drugs I had been given, but I remember that I was extremely calm—until they pulled out that needle. You can understand that though, can't you? I knew that I was going to get a dosage way out of line. And it's humiliating, like a dog at the vet, being held down for a shot. So, yes, I became agitated. Wouldn't you under those circumstances?

But contrary to the reports from that night, I was never out of control. Never.

***

My skin begins to tingle and my stomach knots involuntarily. I place the pencil down on the pad, rise, and move quickly to the side of the window, then peer out. It has been less than forty-eight hours since my escape from the hospital, and already my senses have begun to sharpen, the effects of the drugs weakening. I had heard the truck coming, had sensed its presence and direction several seconds before it turned in to the parking lot. Now the light from its headlamps filters through the window blinds of the motel room.

The truck eases into a slot at the end of the building. Two men, both dressed in work clothes and baseball caps, get out. One of them, the driver, turns a beer can up to his mouth, drains its contents, then crumples the can and tosses it into the back of the truck.

"You got the key?"

"Shit, no. I thought you had it."

"Damn it, Chris, I told you . . ."

"Just kidding," the passenger says, pulling out something from his pocket and holding it up.

"Son of a bitch," the other man says as they both disappear into their room, the door closing behind them.

I stand there, looking at the closed door for several seconds, then scan the rest of the parking lot, peering into the shadows. I can hear the soft buzz from the light at the back of the lot, the distant sound of traffic, the night chatter of the animals in the nearby woods, and my own steady heartbeat. I detect no movement, nothing that seems unusual or out of place.

Everything is quiet again, still. Satisfied that there is no immediate danger, I walk away from the window and toward the table. The clock by the bed reads 2:35 A.M.

The heating unit by the window kicks in, stirring the still, stale air that smells of cigarette smoke and pizza. Perhaps I should try to sleep. I know I need it. It is a valuable weapon I must use if I am to succeed. But I know it is useless. I have been unable to sleep more than a few minutes at a time, and then, it is a fitful, restless sleep plagued by weird dreams. Part of the problem now is this room. Bad choice from a security standpoint. Second floor. Only one door in and out. I feel much too vulnerable here.

I take a cigarette from the pack on the table, retrieve the matches from the sweatshirt on the bed, and light up. I take a deep draw, hold it for a couple of seconds, then exhale with a great rush. I gather up the empty bag of chips and the candy wrappers, wad them up into a ball, and shoot it like a basketball over to the trash can in the corner. It hits the rim, bounces against the wall, and falls into the plastic container. Perhaps it is a good omen. I sit back down in the chair, pick up the pencil, and begin to write again.

CHAPTER 1

I was shooting eight ball with a small-time drug dealer when I learned I'd been appointed to represent Nathan Hart. The drug dealer, a man named Wayne Colson, was a former high school classmate from Miami, a fellow flag football player on our city league team a few years back, and now an occasional client. We were at the Rajun Cajun, a seedy little joint on West Tennessee Street that had cold beer, decent food, and a small room in the back where you could find a game of poker most nights.

It was a little after 4:30 in the afternoon, not a busy time normally at the place, but there was a respectable number of customers there, taking refuge from the sweltering Tallahassee heat. Four college kids in soccer outfits were sharing a pitcher of beer and a platter of wings at a corner booth. A couple of bikers, both with long hair and beards, dressed in their uniform of jeans and black leather, were shooting pool at one of the other tables.

I chalked up the end of my cue stick while walking around the table, planning my next shot. Then I bent down, eyeing the projected angle. My hair fell forward and I stood, pushing it back with my hand. When I leaned over and it fell forward again, I let it be. A film of perspiration clung to my arms and beaded up on my forehead. I drew the stick back and forth a couple of times, then struck the cue ball softly, directing it against the six ball, which cooperated by dropping into the side pocket. The cue ball traveled the length of the table, rebounding gently against the end rail, setting me up nicely for the next shot.

"Damn," Wayne muttered.

I was in a rhythm now, hesitating only a couple of seconds before setting up, then sinking the five ball and quickly lining up on the eight. "Corner pocket," I said, pointing my stick. I stroked the cue ball firmly, which connected with the eight ball, sending it where I had pointed.

Wayne pulled a twenty-dollar bill from his front pocket and tossed it on the table. "You a damn pool shark, Stevens," he said in a voice like gravel.

I picked up the twenty and stuffed it into my shirt pocket. "Just lucky," I said. "Want to go again?"

My client was a big, burly fellow with short, wavy hair, a dark mustache, a perpetual five-o'clock shadow, and an affected aura of malevolence. He wore black pants and a black shirt, open at the throat to reveal a chest full of hair and a large gold medallion. His eyes, sunken deep in their sockets, were two small, dark slits. He focused those slits in my direction then, muttering something about my having obviously wasted my youth in some pool hall. I didn't contradict him.

"You already got most of my money in legal fees. You got to hustle me too?" He frowned at me but made no move to put up his cue stick.

I twisted the chalk on the end of my cue stick absently while I considered his rhetorical question. My fee had been steep but the result very favorable—an acquittal on a sale-of-cocaine charge, despite the fact that the police had him on tape making the sale to a confidential informant. The C.I., a weasel by the name of Jerome Dixon, in exchange for a lesser sentence on his charges, had agreed to set up his supplier, Wayne. Not the best of witnesses.

People don't particularly like drug dealers, but they don't like snitches either. The jury apparently concluded that Dixon was simply not reliable, that he had tried to manufacture the deal with Wayne to get himself out of a jam. They walked my client on the charge.

Wayne had been extremely happy with the verdict and very grateful at the time, convinced of my brilliance and unconcerned about the fee.

As time passed, though, this changed to a grudging acknowledgement of my skills, then to a conclusion that any fool could have gotten an acquittal in the case and the corresponding resentment at having to pay a fee at all. That's the way it is with most criminal defendants—and why you get your fee up front.

"You got a bargain," I said finally. Wayne grunted, which I took to be reluctant agreement. I waved my stick in the direction of the table as a silent repetition of my challenge to another game.

He sighed in protest but said, "All right."

I grabbed the long-neck Budweiser from the shelf and took a swallow, then started to retrieve the balls from the pockets and roll them toward one end of the table. Wayne rubbed both of his hands on the powder block, then spread the powder over his cue stick while I racked the balls.

I was just about to break to start the next game when the front door opened and the sunlight from outside streaked into the room, filtering through the haze of cigarette smoke that hung in the air and bringing with it a gush of the sauna outside. The air-conditioning unit, already straining in its effort to keep the place somewhat cool, groaned in protest. The only windows in the place were small, up high, and very dirty, so the little bit of natural light that came in when the door was opened attracted the attention of the patrons.

So did the woman who came in with it.

The tall redhead stood just inside the entrance for several seconds, adjusting to the relative darkness as the door closed slowly behind her. Then she spotted me and walked over, her low-heeled pumps sticky against the gummy floor. She glanced at the beer on the shelf, then at Wayne, then back to me. "I figured you might be here."

"Hello, Jan," I said to my secretary, straightening up and holding my cue stick in both hands across my body, ignoring the implied criticism. "Looking for a game of eight ball?"

She frowned. "Hello, Ted." She held up the folder in her hand. "Strictly business, I'm afraid."

"Too bad," I said, and the silence stretched between us.

"So," she said, finally, "must not have taken long with your violation of probation hearing this afternoon. What happened? Client enter a plea?"

"No, but he should have. Judge Rowe called my case first. The hearing didn't take long. Then Rowe hammered him. He likes to do that, you know, set an example with the first case, give the others watching something to think about."

Wayne shook his head. "I know that's right."

I looked over at my companion, then back to my secretary. "You remember Wayne, fee-paying client and master pool player?" She nodded toward Wayne, who nodded back. "Anyway," I said, "I got through a little early, didn't feel like going back to the office." Looking at the file folder in her hand, I added, "But it appears that the office has found me." I hung up my cue stick in the wall rack. "You practice up a little, Wayne. I'll be back in a minute."

I grabbed my Bud and motioned for her to join me at a nearby booth. "Come into my office," I said as I lowered myself into the seat. She did likewise. "You want a beer?" I held mine up in the air.

"A little too early for me," she said, a hint of disapproval in her tone. I shrugged. I valued my secretary's judgment. She had saved my professional butt on plenty of occasions. But caring about the approval of others was a notion I had pretty much abandoned as of late. And Jan, who was not shy about speaking her mind, also knew when to keep her opinions to herself.

"What you got for me?" I asked, pointing my chin at the file folder Jan had placed on the table.

She pushed the folder over. "New court-appointed case. Paul suggested I bring you the paperwork on my way home."

I arched my eyebrows but said nothing in response. Nor did I make a move to open the file folder. Indigent defendants were normally represented by the public defender's office, but when the office had a conflict—where there were codefendants, for example—the court drew from a list of private attorneys to obtain representation for the accused. It was called the conflict list, and I was on it. It didn't pay much, but it was steady and the kind of in-the-trenches trial work that kept me grounded. Such appointments, however, were routine, not the kind of thing to prompt my partner to have Jan chase me down to tell me about it. "So," I said finally, looking in the direction of the folder on the table but still not picking it up, "what's the case?"

"The murder of that psychologist at Florida State Hospital," she said, looking down at the folder. "They've charged one of his former patients." She looked up at me. "Nathan Hart."

I stared at her for several seconds in silence. I knew about the case, of course. It had been a big news story the previous week. The psychologist had been stabbed multiple times in his office. A janitor who happened upon the scene saw Hart standing over the body, covered in blood, knife in hand.

I also knew all about Nathan Hart. He had been charged several years earlier with the brutal murders of his parents and brother. He claimed the family had been attacked by a contingent of CIA, Mossad, or other intelligence operatives, and that he was the only one to make it out alive.

Two of the three psychiatrists appointed to the case agreed he had been legally insane at the time of the crime. The third thought he was faking. Hart pled no contest and was placed on probation for life and committed to the psychiatric hospital indefinitely. He later came to regret his decision to plea and accused the prosecutor on the case of having tricked him and his lawyer. At the hearing on his motion to vacate the plea, he had threatened to kill both his lawyer and the prosecutor and their families.

I knew all this because I had been the prosecutor on his case.

"You are kidding, right?"

The expression on my secretary's face told me she knew the backstory. She shook her head slowly. "Nope."

I frowned. "Well, that won't last too long. I'm surprised the State or the P.D. didn't pick up on it and advise the judge at the time. When Hart finds out about it, he'll be sure it's some conspiracy. He'll be screaming to get me off his case."

Jan shook her head slowly again. "The subject did, in fact, come up. Not only did Mr. Hart not want you off the case, he insisted you remain as his lawyer."

CHAPTER 2

*W*hen my partner signed a long-term lease a few years ago for the private parking spaces on College Avenue, I considered it an unnecessary and extravagant expense. But when the cost of a parking ticket tripled, I began to see it as a wise investment. I now consider it an essential convenience and a birthright of partnership.

A little after 8:00 in the morning, I pulled into one of those parking spaces and opened the door to my Honda Accord. The air outside, already heavy and suffocating, rushed at me, swallowing the air-conditioned space in seconds. Ah, yes, welcome to the Sunshine State. I locked the car and headed across the street.

Our offices were located in the narrow, three-story Rose Building. It was an attractive structure: dark red brick accented with finished concrete around the windows and a generous facade of marble and mahogany around the French doors at the entrance. Just to the right of that entrance was a sculpted, long-stemmed rose set into the pink and gray marble. It was the only tangible reminder of the women's apparel shop, called simply The Rose, that had previously occupied the space for more than fifty years, hence the commonly used name for the structure.

I had nothing to do with whatever taste was evident in its appearance. Paul had purchased the building a couple of years before I joined him in practice and spent a small fortune renovating the space, supervising every detail. He still maintained sole ownership. The firm simply leased the space from him. The look of the place, both inside and out, was consistent with the small, boutique law firm image my partner had wanted to project: unique, fashionable, and expensive.

Boutique is not a word people would normally associate with me. I'm more of an off-the-rack, department-store type of guy. I've never quite understood either what prompted Paul to think I fit into his grand vision for the law firm when he asked me to join him. Indeed, in many ways we are opposites.

Maybe that's one of the reasons things seem to have worked out. We give each other balance. He has dragged me, kicking and screaming, into the bottom-line, expanding-client-base, business aspect of the practice of law. I have kept alive in him the essence of being an advocate for the client—the lawyering aspect of this profession. You play to your strengths for the good of the team, right? And despite the odd-couple aspect of it and my occasional complaints, I don't think I could have asked for a better law partner—or a better friend.

Adrienne, our receptionist, was already at her station when I came through the door. "Good morning, Mr. Stevens."

The young woman was smart, pretty, and had an overly positive attitude that I tried to overlook. The sunshine smile and sing-song voice were a little much for so early in the day, certainly before I'd had my coffee, but I didn't have the heart to hurt her feelings. "Good morning," I replied, returning her smile with one of my own, if not with the same level of enthusiasm.

As I headed toward the stairs and my office on the second floor, she called out to me. "Mr. Stevens."

I stopped and turned to face her. "Yeah?"

"Mr. Morganstein is waiting for you in his office." She looked down the hallway in that direction. When I didn't respond right away, she added, "He said you had a meeting this morning at eight o'clock?" She looked up at the clock on the wall, then back to me. "He asked me to remind you when you came in."

"And so you have." I stood there for a moment, considering whether to go on up anyway, just on principle. "He always has better coffee anyway," I said, then headed down the hallway, the clicking of my heels on the hardwood floor sounding ridiculously loud.

Paul glanced at his watch when I came through the open door of his office, but it was the only hint of criticism of my tardiness. I gave him a mock salute in return. He had been sitting at his desk, reading papers, and now he stopped to study me as I walked wordlessly over to the side buffet, the aroma of roasted coffee beans pulling me like a magnet. His coffee *was* always better. I poured myself a cup and sat across from Paul at the desk. I noticed the half-eaten almond croissant next to him. "So much for your diet," I said.

He shrugged and patted his stomach with both hands. "Life's short." Then, as if to confirm his defiance, he picked up the croissant and took a bite. He settled back in his seat, then adjusted his bow tie. "How are Beth and Annie?"

"Fine," I said without looking up, the catch in my throat betraying my discomfort with the subject.

He looked at me closely for a few seconds. "Everything okay?"

I looked back at my partner for a moment as he took another bite of croissant, his nonchalance an affectation. Paul had a mother-hen quality about him that was both endearing and annoying at the same time. His question was more than the simple one on the surface. It was like a multiple-warhead missile, able to hit several targets with one launch. In fact, I wasn't sure things were okay, but I didn't know why. Couldn't put my finger on it.

"Sure," I said, taking a sip of coffee with my own dose of affected nonchalance, fighting back a nausea growing in my stomach. "Beth said she needed the space, so I gave it to her. She says she's ready to come home."

Paul pursed his lips. He took off his glasses, wiped them with a cleaning cloth, and put them back on.

"Anyway," I said, eager to change the subject, "how's the law firm of

Morganstein and Stevens doing, Mr. Managing Partner?"

Paul pushed the wire-rimmed glasses up on his nose a bit and leaned back in his chair, then went right in with a summary of firm finances. It was more information than I wanted, but, bottom line, we were doing quite well. "And," he said, "I picked up a new lobbying client this week, the State Association of Public Defenders."

I was impressed and said so. And it made sense, really. Paul had been the chief assistant at the local office for several years and a de facto assistant to the paid lobbyist for the association.

"Theo brought in a new client this week too," Paul said, picking up the croissant. "An auto accident case involving a family from his church. A cement truck ran a red light, plowed into them. Looks like pretty clear liability and lots of damages."

"That's good," I said without much enthusiasm. Theo was Theodius Williams, our new associate of about a year. He had come on board when I got suspended, our longtime need for another lawyer having thus become urgent. He was a smart, young lawyer with a good court presence, but he was a little too eager for my taste and a bit of a kiss-up, especially to Paul. It seemed to be working, because my partner sang his praises every time the subject came up.

Eventually he got around to asking about the Hart case. "What's it look like?"

"Well, I've only had the case a few days, but I've read the probable cause and talked to the prosecutor."

"Who's that?"

"Maxine Chrenshaw."

"Oh, yeah. She lives in Chattahoochee, doesn't she?" When I nodded, he added, "Good lawyer. Reasonable." When I nodded again, he said, "I'm sorry. Go ahead."

I cleared my throat and gave him the basics. The victim, Dr. Aaron Rosenberg, was head of the clinical program at the hospital. A custodial worker found his body while making the rounds about 9:45 p.m., saw

Hart standing over him. Hart ran out and was later found in his bed, in his underwear, sweating like crazy. Clothes matching what the killer wore were found in the washing machine down the hall from Hart's room, blood on them. A cigarette lighter found at the scene was similar to one Hart had been seen with.

"Whose blood on the clothes? The victim?"

"Probably, but they haven't finished the lab work.

"Prints?"

"They lifted some at the scene but no comparison reports yet."

"They recover the murder weapon?"

I shook my head. "Not yet. Obviously a knife or knifelike weapon of some sort."

"Hmm. . . ." Paul ran a hand through his thinning hair.

"The suggested motive was that he felt like Rosenberg sabotaged his bid for conditional release. He threatened to kill the victim about three weeks before the murder. And, when the security folks come to his room that night, tell him it's about Rosenberg, he asks, 'Is he dead?'"

Paul winced. "Ouch." He took a sip of coffee and placed the cup back in its saucer, the cling of the china the only sound in the room.

"I'm wondering if maybe I should decline the appointment," I said finally.

Paul arched his eyebrows and was silent for a few seconds. "Why?"

I ran my fingers through my hair, feathering it back, looking at my partner. The answer, I thought, was obvious. Nathan Hart had been a small, frail-looking twenty-year-old when he took a baseball bat and butcher knife to his parents and younger brother. But evil has no age criteria. It is limited only by the mental and physical capacities of its host. I had prosecuted the man for murder, vigorously. He had threatened to kill me and my wife and daughter.

"Listen," I said, "getting death threats from criminal defendants comes with the territory when you're a prosecutor."

"Public defender too."

"Anyway, the threats by defendants against me were no big deal. I used to tell them to get in line. But a threat to my family . . . well, that's a different matter. And this guy—I took him seriously."

Paul said nothing.

"I didn't think that he'd ever get out of the hospital, quite frankly, and I knew that the slightest violation of probation could send him to prison for the rest of his life. Indeed, I expected he would mess up somewhere along the way. And now that he has, I'm being called on to defend him." I shook my head slowly. "I'm not sure I can do it with the zeal that the code requires."

My partner gave me a frown and leaned forward, forearms on his desk. "Fondness for a criminal client is not only rare but irrelevant, Ted. You represent him to the best of your ability, regardless of your personal feelings, period. It's all part of being a professional."

I nodded but said nothing.

"Of course," Paul said, "if you, in truth, feel that you can't provide a client with proper representation because of some personal considerations, you are obligated to remove yourself from the case." His emphasis on the words "personal considerations" and his tone of voice suggested, however, that to do so would be an admission of some lamentable moral weakness.

I knew what he was thinking: Notorious client equals high-profile case, sure to draw media attention. The added twist of the former prosecutor serving as defender would make it an even more compelling story. You couldn't buy that kind of advertising. The fact that it might make me a little uncomfortable was a minor obstacle. I was being manipulated, and we both knew it. Besides, he had a point.

I shrugged again. "Well, I'll talk to him, see how it goes."

After a couple of seconds Paul said, "Ralph Evans died a couple of years ago, you know."

I frowned. Ralph had been Nathan Hart's lawyer.

"Keeled over with a heart attack in the courthouse parking lot," Paul said. "Fairly young guy, fifty-six." Paul looked beyond me then, and I wondered if he was thinking of his own father's death from a heart attack at about the same age and his own risk factors. As if reading my mind and to show he was not concerned, he took the last bite of his croissant.

"Assuming you stay on the case, you have any preliminary alternative theories or suspects?"

"Too early to tell. Maybe robbery. There was a report that evening of an unknown man who ran away from security when approached. This was about nine-thirty. The door to the office building had been propped open, so access would have been possible for such a person—or for anybody, for that matter. And the victim's wallet was on the floor with the cash gone."

Paul nodded.

"Of course, maybe the victim didn't have any cash in his wallet to start with. And he had an expensive watch that wasn't taken. Plus, Rosenberg would probably have called security if a strange man wandered into his office at nine-thirty at night."

"What are the chances that Rosenberg had no cash in his wallet, though? Everybody carries some cash."

It was my turn to shrug.

"And cash is liquid and untraceable," he said. "A watch is neither." He waited a moment, then continued. "And if he would have called security for a transient, wouldn't he have done so for a patient?"

I couldn't argue with the logic of his observations. "Maybe Rosenberg didn't appreciate the threat," I suggested. "After all, he dealt with weird people every day."

"And that's just the other psychologists," Paul added, smiling. "Might explain the cigarette lighter found under the desk. Could be the robber dropped it."

"Could be," I agreed. "Certainly could have been left behind by the killer." Neither of us commented on the fact that the lighter could very well have been Hart's. Probably was. "There's another problem with the robbery theory, though," I said.

Paul looked up expectantly, "The nature and number of the wounds?"

"Exactly. This was personal."

"Or the killer was crazy."

"Or both."

Again, neither of us mentioned the obvious, that Hart fit in both of those categories.

"Better question," I said, "is how do we explain that our client was found at the crime scene, presumed murder weapon in his hand?"

Paul paused for a few moments. "He's guilty?" he offered.

"I think the prosecution has already claimed that theory."

My partner shrugged. "Okay. Well, how about Hart was there, but he didn't kill the psychologist. He finds Rosenberg on the floor. He bends down, gets blood on his clothes, picks up the murder weapon, which has been left behind by the real killer. Just then, the custodian comes in and our man panics. He runs out, hides the weapon, puts his clothes in the washer, then gets in bed and pretends to be sleeping when security shows up."

"And if he denies being there?"

"Then he'd probably be lying," Paul suggested. "Or delusional."

"If he wasn't there, the custodian is mistaken, or Hart is being framed. I suspect this will be the theory most popular with our paranoid schizophrenic client."

"Well, you know what they say: Just because you're paranoid . . ."

"Doesn't mean they're not out to get you," I finished for him.

Paul smiled and pushed his chair back from the desk a little. "Either way, sounds like an interesting case." He stood. "And, Ted, if you end up staying on the case, how about having Theo help you on this one?"

The flush in my cheeks was instantaneous. "I don't need any help," I said, my words coming quickly and tinged with a hint of defensiveness. I felt compelled to add, "Thanks anyway."

My partner folded his hands in front of him. "Of course, you don't *need* help," he said, "but it wouldn't hurt, and Theo could use the experience." He saw my frown and kept talking before I could respond. "He's good but he needs seasoning." Paul held out his hands, palms up. "And he really admires you, thinks you're one of the best trial attorneys around."

"Somebody give me a shovel. It's really getting deep in here."

"No, really. He would love to work with you on this case. You can get him to do the grunt work. If it goes to trial, let him do the minor witnesses." He hesitated a couple of seconds, studying me. "What do you say?"

It was all bullshit, of course. Theo wasn't dying to study at the foot of the master, as Paul suggested. My partner wanted our young associate to get some experience and maybe keep an eye on old, loose-cannon Ted at the same time. Given the demographics of Gadsden County and Florida State Hospital, he was probably also thinking it wouldn't hurt to have an African-American lawyer on the team. Not that it was at all likely to go to trial even if I stayed on. This case had plea written all over it.

Truth was, my reluctance to bring Theo in was based on the fact that I was a little jealous, a little resentful at the way the young upstart had wiggled his way into my partner's good graces so easily. My insecurity was clouding my judgment. I had to admit, as I thought about it, that it certainly wouldn't hurt to have a little help, someone to do the grunt work, as Paul put it. And to refuse the offer seemed to confirm the insecurity I was trying to ignore. I looked at my partner for several seconds before responding.

"What the hell."

CHAPTER 3

*F*lorida State Hospital is located in the town of Chattahoochee, about an hour west of Tallahassee. Coming in from I-10, the drive takes you through rolling hills, with farms dotting the landscape. Once inside the city limits, you pass down tree-lined streets of modest but well-kept houses and lawns and small churches. On the outskirts of town, to the west, is the Apalachicola River, whose banks rise up an incredible three hundred feet above the water. The downtown area runs for about two and a half blocks on Highway 90, with a few businesses and restaurants on the side streets. The quaint, picturesque little village looks like it belongs more in the mountains of North Carolina than in Florida.

The hospital itself is a village within a village, complete with its own fire station, medical hospital, post office, laundry, security force, and several on-campus residences. In 1833 the federal government built an arsenal on the site, a fortress against Indian attacks, complete with a maze of underground tunnels that led down to the river. In 1876, the one-time arsenal became Florida's first hospital for the criminally insane, and today it remains the primary forensic psychiatric facility in the state, with more than a thousand patients.

The town and the hospital have enjoyed a symbiotic relationship over the years. Practically every adult resident has at some time worked at the hospital or had a family member who did. The townspeople have embraced the institution and its residents, comfortable with their presence downtown, some working part-time jobs, some attending their church services. Of course, these are the good ones, as the townspeople put it, high-functioning, according to the psychologists. The few, the proud, the only slightly crazy.

I made the trip in less than the normal driving time but was still running about ten minutes late for my scheduled appointment when I turned in to the main entrance. Following the directions I'd been given, I easily found the building and parked. I took a last bite of donut and sip of coffee, then scrambled out of the car and headed up the walkway. The woman at the large desk just inside the entrance looked up as I approached and gave me a big smile.

"Good morning. May I help you?"

She wore a dark blue suit with red and white trim on the collar and cuffs and a small American flag pin on the jacket's lapel. I was tempted to salute but thought she might not understand or appreciate my sense of humor.

"Good morning," I said, smiling as well. I was willing to give courtesy a chance this morning even if I didn't feel like it. "I'm Ted Stevens, here to see Frank Hutchinson."

Miss Patriotic looked over at the large clock on the wall, then back to me. She frowned slightly as she said "Yes, Mr. Stevens, you had a nine o'clock appointment, I believe." A moment's hesitation, during which I could feel the courtesy resolve weakening. "Did you have difficulty finding us?" She was offering both mild chastisement and a way to save face.

I was having neither. "No, not at all."

My answer seemed to frustrate the receptionist a bit, and she responded by twisting her verbal dagger a little deeper. "Well, Mr. Hutchinson has been waiting for you," she said, with the emphasis on waiting, then looked over at the clock again. I gave no response, and she picked up the phone on her desk. "Let me get him for you." Her smile was still there, but it had lost its luster. She spoke into the receiver for a few moments, then told me that Hutchinson would be right out.

I ignored her suggestion to have a seat and instead walked around the reception area, taking a closer look at the paintings on the wall. A couple of minutes later, the general counsel for the hospital entered the reception area from the hallway off to the right. Frank Hutchinson was a short, pudgy man of about forty. His hair was thick and dark brown, and he wore it long, drawn tight into a small pony tail. He was wearing jeans, a tan and blue plaid shirt, and a dark blue tie, loosened around the collar. He extended a hand toward me and smiled.

"Hey, Ted. Long time, no see."

"Yeah, Frank. Good to see you." I returned the smile and grasped the offered hand. It was sweaty.

I knew Frank slightly from when he had his own law office in Tallahassee and I was with the State Attorney. He'd had a general practice, did a good bit of criminal work. Hutchinson closed his office a few years back to become general counsel for the hospital.

"Sorry I'm late," I said. "I had a little difficulty finding the place." I looked over at the receptionist, whose face registered a mix of puzzlement and annoyance.

"No problem," Hutchinson said. "I had plenty of stuff to keep me busy. Here, come on down to my office and we'll get you fixed up." He motioned with his head back toward the hallway from which he had come, then started off in that direction. I followed him.

The walls in the hallway were the same paneling-and-plaster combination as in the reception area, but the wood floors gave way to worn beige carpet. The odor of mildew was slight but unmistakable, the kind endemic to older buildings and not altogether unpleasant. Hutchinson's office was at the very end, a corner office with two large windows on each exterior wall, a high ceiling, and oak floors.

Inside, I took a mental inventory of the man's office. The matching cherry desk and credenza looked expensive, and the computer system on the credenza was state of the art. The desk was cluttered with books, legal periodicals, framed photographs, various writing implements, and several stacks of documents. A couple of computer magazines were stacked on the corner of the credenza. The walls were adorned with a half dozen certificates and a couple of the same landscape prints I had observed in the reception area. The one bookcase that stood between the two windows was jammed with more books, periodicals, and stacks of documents.

"How's Paul?" Frank sat behind his desk and motioned for me to have a seat as well.

"Good. He's doing good, as usual," I said, plopping down in a chair. The silence expanded between us until I said, "You like this general counsel bit? Does it suit you?"

Hutchinson looked off into the distance for a couple of seconds, as if considering the question for the first time, then turned back to face me. "Yeah," he said, finally. "I miss the trial work sometimes. I hardly ever get into court with this job." He looked off again momentarily. "But the folks here are good to work with, and the hours are a lot more regular than private practice. Plus, Chattahoochee is a great place to raise a family."

"You got kids?"

Frank smiled. "Two girls. One sixteen, the other fourteen." He pointed to a family photo on his desk. I picked it up, looking.

"They're adorable," I said. "But I thought you said two daughters. There are three here."

"The other one's my wife, jerko." He smiled. "Why do you think the girls are so good looking?"

"They obviously take after their mother," I agreed. "Your wife, she's a psychologist here, right?"

I returned the photograph to the desk. "Yeah, that's how I ended up here. She was commuting from Tallahassee, and when the general counsel job opened up, well. . . ." Hutchinson went on for a couple of minutes, extolling the virtues of small-town life. Then he seemed to grow self-conscious, abruptly changing the subject back to business.

"I've got everything you asked for: complete medical files plus administrative files. You also wanted to talk to his treating psychologist, view the crime scene, and meet with Hart, right?" I nodded. "What do you want to do first?"

I shrugged. "Whatever. Maybe take a look at the crime scene?"

"That's fine. Come on. I'll go with you, then I'll set you up in a room with the medical records. You mark the ones you want copied and I'll have someone take care of that. While you're reviewing the records, I'll see if I can find Dr. Whitsen, his psychologist. She's hard to tie down sometimes." I thought I detected a hint of disapproval in his voice.

"That'd be great, Frank," I said as I fell in behind him.

Outside, the clouds had parted and the August sun was beginning to burn off the morning moisture, making things a bit steamy. The air was still, thick, and smelled of mulching leaves. Although the large oak trees offered some relief from the rising heat and humidity, within seconds my shirt was sticking to me.

I followed Frank down the brick walkway that cut a path up the middle of a large expanse of Saint Augustine grass. I noted the flowers bedded along its border and around the trees, and the finely pruned shrubbery next to the buildings, and I gave voice to what I had thought when I first drove through the entrance. "This looks more like the campus of a small college than it does a forensic psychiatric facility."

Frank smiled slightly. "Well, they try to make it as normal as possible, you know." He waited a second. "I don't think anyone would mistake the folks walking around to be college students, though." He looked then in the direction of two men coming toward us.

"Patients?"

"One of them is, the one on the right . . . and actually, we call them residents. The other is an employee. You can tell by the ID on his pocket."

I was wondering why they didn't call people who were at a hospital for treatment "patients" but didn't ask him about it.

"So, the patients . . . residents," I corrected myself, "can just roam around anywhere?"

Frank looked straight ahead as he answered. "Not all of them, of course. Our forensics are kept very secure. But you have to remember, we have a lot of civil commitments as well, many of them voluntary. And the ones you see walking around? That's usually a long time coming. Free, unescorted movement around the campus is something that is earned."

We waited at the edge of the street as a panel van with several residents and staff in it drove by, then we crossed the street. I looked over at my companion. "Tell me about Rosenberg, Frank. What was he like?"

Hutchinson hesitated a moment. "He was our treatment program director, in charge of all programs and the staff who work in them. He had been here about fifteen years. Started as a staff psychologist and worked his way up the ranks." We had made it to the entrance of the next building now. Hutchinson opened the door and led me down a hallway to the right, stopping about halfway in front of an office I took to be Rosenberg's. Frank opened the door and I walked in.

I was disappointed to see that the room was empty except for the furniture. I had hoped to be able to sift through some of Rosenberg's personal items, get a feel for the man. I looked over at Frank, who seemed to read my mind.

"We boxed up his stuff," he said, by way of explanation. "Life goes on, you know. We haven't had the maintenance folks in yet, though, to clean up the place."

My eyes were drawn to the rather large stain on the carpet, to the side and behind the desk. "You still have them on premises, the boxed-up items? I'm especially interested in calendars, address and phone books, that sort of thing."

Frank pursed his lips together and ran his hand over the top of his head. "Don't know for sure. I can check with Barbara." To my questioning look, he added, "My wife. She was the one who went through his stuff, separated the purely personal from the work related. She probably gave the former to the family and distributed the rest to other staff as appropriate—whatever the police didn't take."

I was wondering why his wife would be the one to go through the victim's things, and Frank must have read my mind again because he said,

"She was like second in charge, I guess, and is acting treatment program director now."

"Will she get the job?" I had been walking around the room but now stopped and looked over at my host.

He frowned. "She probably would have a pretty good chance if she wants it, but I'm pretty sure she doesn't. It's not that much more money and mostly administration. She would rather be more directly involved with the patients."

I started to remind him they were supposed to be called residents but didn't. I took a seat in the chair and pulled it up close to the desk, imagining the victim on the night of his murder.

"Okay, so I know his rank and serial number, but really, Frank, what kind of person was he? Was he well liked? Did he have enemies? Did he have particular habits, passions, pet peeves, personality flaws?"

Frank looked over at me. "Does this mean that you are thinking of something other than an insanity defense?"

"Is that what you think, Frank, that he was insane at the time of the crime?" I paused for a second. "You know, a lay witness who is familiar with a person can testify, can give an opinion as to sanity. It's an exception to the general rule."

"I know that," he said, his tone a bit indignant. "Trust me, you don't want my opinion."

"Oh, but I do, Frank. What is your opinion?"

Hutchinson hesitated only a couple of seconds before saying "The man is crazy but not legally insane. He knows the difference between right and wrong. He just doesn't care."

I scrunched my eyes together, looking at him closely now. It was not the answer I had expected. "So, what's he doing here?"

"The truth? Because he killed three members of his family, and he fooled enough people into thinking he was legally insane at the time. But you already know that, don't you? You prosecuted him. You never thought he was crazy, did you?"

It was true, of course, but I was in a different role now and had to be careful what I said. There was also Frank's implied question: How could I represent him now? I shrugged neutrally. "Perhaps I was one of those he fooled."

Frank grunted, a begrudging acknowledgment of the reality of my situation. "Ever since he was admitted here, he has tried to manipulate the system to get himself released. My file cabinet is filled with letters, administrative complaints." Frank waved his hand back in the direction of his office. "In a word, he is a sociopath. He can be very logical, very charming when he wants to be, but only when it suits him. He can also be a pain in the ass when that suits him better." The man's face was beginning to turn just a little red.

"That sounds like a lot of lawyers I know."

Frank looked over at me and smiled. The anger I had sensed a moment ago was gone. "You asked."

"I did indeed." I stood and began to circle the office, thinking. Then I pointed to a red button on the inside of the base of the desk. "Panic button?"

"Hooks up to security. You don't like the situation, you push that and someone's here within a couple of minutes."

"So," I said after a long pause, "you were about to tell me more about Aaron Rosenberg?"

Hutchinson looked up at the ceiling, then out the window, as if searching for the answer there. "Good guy. Good administrator. Ran a tight ship, a real stickler for the rules. I personally got along with him fine, as I think most of the professional staff did, but he did have people who disliked him. Sure, but who doesn't? I can't think of anyone, however, who'd want him dead—except maybe your guy."

I ignored the dig. "Family?"

"Married for about thirty years."

"Happily?"

"As far as I know. His wife, Betty Ann, is a lovely woman. They have two boys, both off to college somewhere."

"And his personal life? Hobbies, interests?"

"He was a golfer. Pretty decent." He paused. "Big FSU fan. Used to go to all the home football games and some away ones if he could. He and his wife had parties once in a while for the professional staff, but other than that we didn't socialize together."

I sat down again in the victim's chair. As Hutchinson started again with another family values monologue, I began to imagine the scene on the night of the murder, picturing Rosenberg at his desk, perhaps reading his mail or writing a report. If a stranger appeared at his doorway—or a patient—why didn't Rosenberg push the panic button? Maybe he didn't think the person dangerous. Or maybe it was someone he knew and had expected. A colleague? A lover, perhaps? I turned the chair around to face the bay window. Maybe the killer was already in the room, hiding behind those curtains, murder weapon in hand, waiting for the right moment.

***

The first blow is to the back of the neck. Rosenberg feels the searing pain amidst the surprise and the shock, not sure at first what has caused it. The second stab wound is to the neck again, or maybe the shoulder, as the killer comes out fully from behind the curtain. The victim tries to turn to face his attacker but is unable to as the blade comes down again, plunging into his back with a tremendous force that pushes him forward.

Struggling mightily, beginning to grasp the danger, the terrible reality of the situation, the victim manages to turn in his chair. Does he recognize his assailant? Does it matter? He knows that he must defend himself with every ounce of strength he possesses or he will die. He grabs an arm, but it is the wrong arm, not the one with the knife, and the blade finds its target again, plunging to the hilt with a sickening thud into his chest. And then again. And again.

Still, he struggles, unwilling to accept in his mind what his soul has already embraced. He is aware of the lamp being knocked over and then he falls to the floor, the blood, strength, and will flowing out of him quickly now. Helpless, he looks up into eyes that are as cold and black as deepest space, as his killer prepares to strike what will be the final blow.

***

Frank's hand on my shoulder brought me back to the present with a jolt. "What?" I said, before the meaning of his words registered.

"You got what you need here?" Frank repeated.

I stood up, looked around the room one more time, and wiped at the film of perspiration that had formed along my temples. "Yeah," I said, but as I followed him out of the office, the imagined scenario still lingered, hauntingly vivid.

CHAPTER 4

I read the next entry.

"Resident complained today in the cafeteria that he was being poisoned. He refused to eat his food and demanded an independent blood test. He was assured that the food was safe. He insisted on speaking to the director of the hospital. When told that was not possible at the time, he became very agitated and upset. He refused to leave the cafeteria when requested and when approached by two aides, he cursed them, threw a chair against the wall, and tried to run past them. He was secured and placed in the quiet room for observation. Resident later apologized and was released back into the general area."

I closed the volume and put it aside, then rubbed my eyes. I ran my fingers through my hair, pushing it back, looking first at my watch, then at the still rather large stack of unread volumes of medical records. As if on cue, the door to the small room opened and Frank Hutchinson poked his head through the doorway. "How's it going in there? You at a good stopping point?"

I looked over at the stacks of records, then back at the lawyer. "Hell, yes," I said as Frank moved aside and a woman entered the room. Instinctively I stood, which seemed to amuse her.

"Ted Stevens, Dr. Rebecca Whitsen." Frank bowed slightly in making the introductions. The psychologist was a petite woman. She was physically attractive, though she seemed to have made a conscious decision not to draw attention to it, wearing no makeup, very plain, loose-fitting clothing, and a pair of rather large, black-frame eyeglasses.

I sensed her confidence, though, a confidence not uncommon in those whose expertise is, by its nature, difficult to measure. The eyes that looked out at me from behind those eyeglasses were dark and penetrating. I had the feeling they were sizing me up—and finding me wanting.

We shook hands, and I felt something akin to an electrical charge combined, strangely enough, with a sort of magnetic pull. Instinctively, I disengaged quicker than normal and stepped back.

"Mr. Stevens." The psychologist was the first to speak.

"Dr. Whitsen," I said, matching her formality. We both looked over toward Hutchinson.

"I'm going to leave you two now. I've got to run to a meeting. Listen, Ted, take your time with those records. When you're done, clip the ones you want copied or leave us a note, and I'll take care of it. You can leave them right there. And, Rebecca," he looked over at the psychologist, "he's going to want to see Nathan after the two of you are finished." The request was unspoken but clearly implied.

"I'll take care of it," she said.

Frank gave us both a wave of the hand and was quickly gone. Lawyer and psychologist turned back to face each other. Whitsen looked at her watch, then spoke.

"I have a few minutes to spare but only a few, Mr. Stevens. You may want to prioritize your questions with that in mind."

The woman's smile was smug and condescending. Anger shot through me like a rifle bullet, but I managed to stay calm. "I'm going to need more than a few minutes, Dr. Whitsen." The woman looked at her watch again, then at me, irritation creasing her mouth into a frown. "Of course, if you prefer," I said, "I can schedule you for a deposition with a subpoena duces tecum for all appropriate records. Then we can take our time as I go over every detail of your education and your training, explore your work history, then question you at length about every session, every notation in the medical records and charts of my client."

Whitsen seemed to be considering this for a few seconds. Then the frown was replaced by another smile, though this one was less smug. "Yes, I suppose you could do that. But then all you would get would be answers to questions—and only that," she said with emphasis, then waited a moment to let the concept sink in. "Look, I'm not trying to be rude or give you a hard time, but Nathan is not my only patient and I have other things to attend to." She looked down the hall as if to illustrate where those other things might be, then looked back to me. "We don't really want to play this macho-cowboy-lawyer-versus-psychologist game, do we?" There was a long silence as we evaluated each other. Whitsen held out her hand again. "Truce?"

I decided I liked her directness. "Truce," I said, shaking her hand and feeling again that intangible magnetism. "But I'm still going to need more than a few minutes of your time," I added quickly.

She looked at her watch again, considering. "Some now, more later?"

I nodded. "I can live with that."

"Good." She pulled up one of the chairs and sat down. I did the same. She leaned forward a little, hands clasped together. "Now, what questions do you have for me?"

"Did you know that I was the prosecutor on Nathan's prior case, the murder of his family?"

"I am very much aware of the history between the two of you."

"Then you know that I'm not exactly his favorite person."

She gave me a small smile. "I would say that his feelings toward you are complicated."

Typical, evasive, psycho mumbo jumbo. I frowned. "Any idea why he would want me as his lawyer?"

"He has spoken to me about the situation, so yes. I am not, however, at liberty to disclose confidential communication." She hesitated a couple of seconds, then added, "But I'm sure he will tell you if you ask."

"I'm wondering if he is just trying to play head games with me."

She shrugged, held her hands out, palms up, but said nothing.

"I'm going to meet with him in a little while, and I'd like to know what to expect. I remember him from his case, but that was six and a half years ago. I've read some of his hospital records this morning, which were helpful, but records tend to be sterile."

She nodded.

"You've been his treating psychologist for about three months now, so I figure you could give me an overall impression of his progress, details of his current mental state, and maybe some suggestions on how best to approach him, how to handle him so I can get to the truth."

She pushed out her lips and nodded slowly. "Your recognition of the importance of this is a good first step, though handling him is not how I'd put it," she said, with air quotes around "handling him."

I raised my hand in surrender. "Poor choice of words, perhaps. I just want to make him comfortable enough to talk freely to me."

She nodded her approval, then leaned back in the chair, arms crossed over her chest. "It won't be easy. As you know, Nathan's diagnosis is schizophrenia, paranoid type, a common symptom of which is delusional thinking, often involving the belief that others are out to harm you in some way. The most innocent actions are perceived to have sinister motives. Other symptoms may include hallucinations, sometimes visual but most often auditory."

"Hearing voices?"

"Exactly. That's quite common. Nathan has exhibited both delusional thinking and auditory hallucinations from time to time since he was in his teens."

"You don't think he is faking his symptoms, then?"

The condescension crept back into the woman's smile. "Think about it. You might fake your symptoms to avoid criminal penalties, but once your case is disposed of and you find yourself committed to a psychiatric facility, how quickly do you think you would 'recover' from your mental illness?" Again with the air quotes. "The man has been here for almost seven years."

It was a good point, I acknowledged. "So, how do you cure it, schizophrenia?"

"You don't. The most you can do is treat it, try to manage it, like you would diabetes or high blood pressure. You try to control the symptoms with medications. There are a few proponents of what is called insight therapy, more along the lines of traditional psychotherapy, trying to find a cause for the illness, address it, and work through the problems."

"And you, Doctor?"

Whitsen hesitated a moment, then said. "I think you do what works. To the extent the illness is chemically caused, medications can be very helpful. But the truth is, we don't really know whether we are just masking the problem with some pretty powerful drugs that can have significant side effects. Plus, there is a tendency of some doctors to prescribe more for control rather than for treatment."

There was a harshness in the doctor's voice and anger in the dark eyes when she said this, but she quickly recovered. "Anyway, medications are helpful only if the patient realizes the importance of taking them. Otherwise, as soon as he is out of your sight and control, he'll stop. That's where traditional therapy can help. There are often triggers that can bring on an episode or make it more likely. Knowing what those triggers are and learning how to cope with them empowers a patient to find a complete plan of treatment tailored for him."

"So, how has Nathan been doing?"

"Very well, actually. He was, until the unfortunate events of July fifteenth, housed in Sunrise Cottage, which is the least restrictive residence on campus. He has real issues with delusional thinking and taking his medications, but we had been making real progress in both areas."

"He's still saying the Unit killed his family?"

She looked at me, assessing. "You realize that although he was charged with the murders of his family, he has never admitted it."

Technically, she was correct. Hart had pled no contest, neither admitting nor denying the charges. I was intrigued that she had made the distinction. "You think he didn't do it?"

"I think one should keep an open mind."

The look she gave me suggested I should heed this admonition myself but acknowledged that it was unlikely. "The point is, he thinks he's an innocent victim, and that's the basis on which I have had to deal with him."

"Point taken," I said.

The doctor abruptly stood. "I really do need to go now. I have a team meeting. But, come, you can walk with me and we'll continue our conversation."

I rose and followed after the psychologist, who had already made it to the door. "What kind of team?" I asked as we started down the hallway.

"Pardon?"

"You said you had a team meeting. What team?" We were now walking side by side at a pretty good clip.

She looked over at me. "From the time they are admitted to the hospital, all patients have a team who works with them, establishing goals and plans, monitoring and assisting them in their progress. A team consists of a psychiatrist, a psychologist, a nurse, a social worker, and a certified mental health professional who acts as the leader, the coordinator. Every week the team meets and discusses its assigned patients. At least once a month, the team meets with the patient as well."

We had made it to the end of the hallway and now exited the building. "Is Nathan Hart on the agenda for your team meeting?"

"Not today, but these are the same members of Nathan's team. We did an emergency conference on him right after the murder of Dr. Rosenberg He's not scheduled again until next week."

We walked in silence for several seconds until we entered a building, the apparent intended destination. Once inside, I said, "As the treating psychologist, you can't be an expert witness for either side, but do you have some feel for whether Hart may have been insane at the time of the crime or whether he's competent to proceed to trial?"

The psychologist stopped and turned to face me. "Nice try, Mr. Stevens." She gave me the faintest of smiles. "But you asked for suggestions on how to approach him, and I'd advise you to expect the unexpected. Nathan Hart is a very smart young man who, given the parameters he has established, can be very rational and logical. You would be wise to consider every possibility, no matter how absurd it may seem at first blush."

I nodded, though not sure I bought what she was saying.

"You should also remember, however, that he is still subject to delusional thinking. He is still paranoid. You may never gain his full trust nor ever know what he is really thinking. He may very well have undisclosed motivations that make sense only to him."

"So, keep an open mind, but watch my back."

She smiled. "That sums it up pretty well."

She began walking again and I moved right after her, noting that she hadn't answered my question. We stopped a few seconds later outside a room, and she turned to me again. "Perhaps later, after you have met with your client and formed your own impression, we can continue our conversation. Come, let me introduce you to Nathan's team," she said, opening the door and ushering me into the room.

Seated around a large conference table were several people. As introductions were made, I did my best to remember their names and roles on the team: Betsy Durham, a short, squat woman with brown hair, the registered nurse; James Washington, a large, dark-skinned man with a shaved head who seemed to me an unlikely social worker; Emily Potter, certified mental health professional and coordinator of the team. Not yet present, I was told, was the final member of the team, Dr. Hemal Kristamurphee, psychiatrist.

"Standard operating procedure," Whitsen whispered to me. "We're always waiting for the psychiatrist." Then she looked over at the social worker. "James, we probably have a few minutes before we get started here. Would you be so kind as to escort Mr. Stevens over to General Forensics and introduce him to his client?"

CHAPTER 5

*T*he additional security was obvious: a tall chain-link fence around the perimeter, razor wire spiralling along the top; metal detectors; security guards to check IDs, make you sign in, inquire as to your purpose, that sort of thing. But even so, it was nowhere near as secure as a jail.

You may be wondering, then, why my client was still at the hospital, seeing as how he was charged with first degree murder. There were several practical reasons for this. First, the sheriff didn't want him in his jail. Mentally ill people are generally considered high maintenance, requiring significant—and expensive—medications. They often decompensate quickly without proper dosages and careful therapeutic supervision, something the jail staff has neither the expertise nor inclination to provide. The prosecutor knows as well that a criminal defendant is much more likely to remain or become competent while in the hospital rather than jail.

The patients preferred it, for obvious reasons. Your freedom of movement is much greater, and your keepers are, for the most part, more empathetic. The food is generally better. And there is that other powerful motivator: cigarettes. You're allowed to smoke at the hospital. In the jail, on the other hand, tobacco products of any kind are contraband, the mere possession of which is itself a crime.

For some, it is more than just a habit. It is their lifeline to normalcy, a security blanket that helps them keep it together. You can see it in the way they smoke—the nervous, almost desperate pull on the cigarette, as if all the relief they need is in that small nicotine stick. The more sophisticated also know that nicotine acts as a suppressant for several medications, reducing their effectiveness. For them, smoking is a surreptitious way of noncompliance, a small act of resistance or rebellion.

The reason I bring this up is because when I first caught sight of my client, he was smoking a cigarette out on the patio behind the building. I waited inside and watched through the window as James went to get him.

"Nathan, you have a visitor," Washington said as he approached the man. He stopped just behind him. "Your lawyer's here." Hart was sitting in a dark green plastic chair under the shade of the overhang. He was facing away from the door and did not turn when James spoke. Instead, he took a drag on his cigarette, inhaled, and then blew the smoke up toward the sky. It was brutally hot and there was not even a slight breeze. The still air was heavy, like a thick blanket, and it kept the cigarette smoke hovering just above him.

A half dozen guys were playing basketball—or something resembling basketball—over in the corner of the back fenced area. James then moved beside Hart. "Your lawyer's here, Nathan," he said again, as if Hart had not heard him the first time. Nathan flicked the ashes of his cigarette onto the concrete below, took another long drag, and inhaled. He blew out the smoke again before turning to stare at the social worker for a couple of moments. He said nothing and made no move to get up but instead looked past him toward the ball players.

James's face screwed up into a frown. He shifted from one foot to another. "You want me to tell him to go on back? That you don't want to see him?" He was getting tired of playing this game. When Hart gave no response after a couple of seconds, he said, "Okay." Then he took a couple of backwards steps, lingering there for a few more seconds.

My client took one more long pull on his cigarette, down to the filter. Then he dropped it on the concrete. He stood, still looking past the metal fence with the razor wire on top. The guys playing basketball had stopped their game now and were staring in the direction of the patio, waiting to see what would happen, maybe hoping for some incident. Nathan crushed the butt under his foot, turned toward James, and said, "Let's go."

***

Nathan Hart didn't much look like a murderer. He was short and slight of frame and had a disarmingly boyish face. Without the scraggly mustache and beard, he probably could have passed for a college student, maybe even high school. The grin he gave me seemed more impish than menacing. His large brown eyes were slightly unfocused, jittery, hinting at the madness within.

The memory pushed itself to the forefront then, unbidden and unexpected: Nathan, from across the courtroom, those eyes red with anger, glaring, his voice chillingly calm, saying he would kill me, but not before my wife and daughter died in front of me. He had actually called them by name, Beth and Annie.

The thought of it now caused my stomach to tighten and my heart to race as he stood before me, arms crossed over his chest. I willed the calm to return. "Nathan," I said, extending my hand to him.

He unfolded his arms and grasped my hand, more firmly than I expected. "Ted." He stepped back, his arms folded across his chest again, stroking his beard between his thumb and forefinger.

I waved my hand in the direction of the small library table. He nodded and sat in one of the chairs. I took the one across from him. His face was passive, calm, though his eyes darted around the room. His hands were folded in his lap. I started pulling files and a notepad from my briefcase as I spoke. "I am told that, when given a chance to have another attorney appointed to your case, you requested that I remain."

"That's right."

"Why?"

He gave me a small smile. "It is a bit ironic, don't you think?" He paused a moment, eyes darting around the room, then back to me. "But

I don't believe in coincidences, Ted. When they told me you had been appointed as my lawyer, I knew it was a sign."

"I see."

"I know we've been on opposite sides of things in the past, but I never held a grudge. You were just doing your job."

"That is true," I agreed. "I was just doing my job. But death threats against me and my family? That seems a little like a grudge to me."

He waved his hand in dismissal. "Just blowing off steam."

The casual tone in his voice was unconvincing, but I tried to match it. "I'd hate to see you if you were actually mad then."

He frowned.

"If you file any more post-conviction motions in your case, or if you go up for a conditional release hearing, I may be called as a witness against you."

Again, the wave of a hand in dismissal. "That's not my concern at this point. Besides, after you take a closer look at my prior case, I truly believe that, rather than opposing my post-conviction motions, you will advocate that I be cleared of all charges, past and present."

I frowned. "I haven't decided for sure whether I will continue as your lawyer, but if I do, it will be to defend you on the current charges, not to re-open the old case."

He smiled again, a knowing smile that reminded me of his psychologist. "But don't you see? The two cases are related. If you do your job properly, you will see that. And despite your protestations to the contrary, you have already decided to take my case, or you wouldn't be here. You see, Ted, our destinies are inextricably intertwined. They have been for some time. You sense it too, don't you?"

"Well, actually, no," I said, "I think that's all bullshit." Perhaps a little too direct for the psycho, but there it was. "After all, you don't really know much about me."

He held up his hand. "To the contrary, I know a great deal about you."

I sat back in my chair, motioned with my hand for him to proceed.

"Your full name is Edward Kenneth Stevens. You grew up in Miami, attended Florida State University law school, were with the State Attorney's Office for several years, and earned a reputation as a tough but fair prosecutor. You were, in fact, an up-and-coming star of the office when you handled my case. You left the office to become a partner in the law firm of Morganstein and Stevens, where you have handled several high-profile criminal cases and are generally considered a good trial attorney, though a little too willing to sail close to the wind when it comes to the rules."

He raised his eyebrows then, looking for a response, but I maintained a passive mask. "You were suspended from the practice of law for ninety days a while back for substance abuse and misrepresentations to the court. You have been married for twelve years and have one daughter. Your wife sued for divorce a couple of years back, but she dismissed the case."

He looked at me expectantly, obviously pleased with himself. When I didn't respond immediately, he continued, "Judging from the slight hint of stale cigarette smoke about you, the puffiness around the eyes, I suspect you spent some time in a bar last night. This suggests that the substance abuse problem is still with you, no doubt an attempt at self-medication of some psychological issues, probably stemming from some unfortunate circumstances of your childhood. Don't they all?" He grinned, hesitated a few seconds. "I could go on."

I didn't know whether to be pissed or alarmed, but after a few uncomfortable moments of silence, I realized that, in a bizarre, twisted way, I was somewhat impressed, though I chose not to say so. I didn't want to encourage his Sherlock Holmes–Sigmund Freud routine.

Apparently taking my silence as approval, however, he noticeably puffed up, and the grin broadened into a smile. "Even in here," he said, waving his arm around, "they give you access to computers. It's amazing the information you can find on the Net. There really is little privacy left for any of us anymore." After a couple of beats he added, "Of course, I also have keen powers of observation and intuition as well."

Again, I chose not to encourage him with a response. I straightened my files and pad in front of me, laid a pencil on the pad. "Very well, then. Let's talk about what the State has and doesn't have, discuss some options on how to proceed, possible strategies, that sort of thing."

He stroked his beard and nodded for me to continue. I quickly summarized the key evidence against him, as well as some weaknesses in that evidence. He interrupted me a couple of times with questions or comments, but for the most part sat there quietly, nodding occasionally, sometimes looking past me as if distracted or bored.

"Okay," he said when I was done. "What's next?"

I explained to him that everything he told me was privileged. I couldn't disclose it to anyone without his permission. "Certainly, I prefer that you tell me the truth, the whole truth, but the choice is yours. Tell me as much or as little as you want. Just understand that you may hamper my ability to help you if you give me inaccurate or incomplete information." I waited a few moments for his response. When he said nothing, I asked, "Okay?"

He was silent for several more seconds as he looked out the window toward the basketball players, then finally turned to me. "People say I'm paranoid, Ted, but I'm not. Not really. I'm just cautious."

I gave him a nod of neutrality.

"For the most part, I like what I know about you. The substance abuse thing and the anti-authority attitude—those are good things from my perspective, and I like the vibes I've gotten so far today. I understand you may not see it yet, but I feel that in a way we are kindred spirits. I have a sixth sense about such things, you know."

I wasn't sure how I felt about this particular vote of confidence, but I nodded for him to continue.

"So I'm going to cooperate with you fully, trust you with information, with my thoughts and ideas. I can only hope, for both of our sakes, that you will not betray that trust."

The calm manner and tone of his words masked the implied threat, making it all the more chilling. The once jittery and unfocused eyes locked on to me with laserlike intensity, boring into me. Beads of sweat popped out on my forehead. I wiped at them with the sleeve of my shirt and shook off a subtle foreboding that formed like ice in my gut.

"So," I said, "what do you remember about the night Dr. Rosenberg was killed?"

He looked around the room quickly, then back to me. He leaned forward and in a lowered voice said, "I remember I went to bed about nine-thirty that night or a little after. I was real tired for some reason and fell asleep quickly. Next thing I know, Andy Rudd and his goons are busting through my door." He leaned back in his chair.

Andy Rudd, I knew, was the head of security at the hospital. I waited a few beats to see if there was more, but he just sat there, looking at me. "You don't remember going to Rosenberg's office that night?"

"I didn't go to his office."

"They have an eyewitness who saw you there, standing over the body." I pulled a paper from my file. "His name is Raymond Curry, a custodial worker at the hospital."

"I know Raymond. I don't think he would intentionally lie, so he must be mistaken. He has to be, because I wasn't there." He looked around the room again for a brief couple of seconds. "I'm being set up, Ted."

"Okay," I said after a few moments of silence between us. "I'll bite. By whom?"

"The Unit, of course. And you can bet that Uncle Robert has coordinated things."

"Ah, yes," I said. "The Unit."

One of the documented symptoms of my client's schizophrenia was the delusion that he, his father, and his uncle had been members of an ultra secret espionage organization known simply as the Unit. He maintained that the attack against his family had been launched by this group, a response to the fears of its leaders that he was about to disclose its secrets. He had narrowly escaped death, he maintained. His parents and older brother had not. His uncle, he claimed, had been an active collaborator in the plan to kill his family and frame him for the murders.

Nathan frowned when I said nothing else in response. "I know," he said, "the first thought is, why would they go to such trouble? I had just been turned down for conditional release, after all, and was still confined to a mental hospital. I was no immediate threat to them even if I did get out. My credibility quotient was . . . is . . . non-existent." He grinned. "On the other hand, talk about paranoid! The Unit leaders are walking, talking poster children for paranoia."

"I see. So discrediting you even more than you already were was the motivation to frame you?"

He either missed the sarcastic tone completely or ignored it. "Precisely. I suspect, though, that they didn't initiate things, but rather took advantage of a situation that ironically dropped into their laps. They saw an opportunity and they took it. I'm pretty sure somebody on the inside was involved, perhaps acting for the Unit, or more likely for their own purposes."

"Who do you think is the inside person or persons?"

He reached into his pocket, removed a small scrap of paper, and slid it across the table to me. "No particular order of priority," he said.

I unfolded the slip of paper and went down the list quickly. For a paranoid schizophrenic, his pool of suspects was not as large as I might have expected—but large enough: Andy Rudd; Frank Hutchinson and his wife, Barbara; Rebecca Whitsen and James Washington; and Donnie Mercer. Mercer was a fellow patient who said he had seen Nathan with a cigarette lighter similar to the one recovered from the crime scene.

I looked up. "Why Donnie Mercer?"

He leaned forward a bit, pointed with his finger to the name on the list, and lowered his voice. "There are several residents of this fine institution who are vicious enough to have murdered Dr. Rosenberg, and Donnie is one of the few clever enough, bold enough, to have planned and carried out such a sophisticated scheme of murder and frame-up. He was assigned to Sunrise Cottage, so he would have access to my room and my clothing and could easily have left and returned without being detected, certainly as well as I could. He's approximately my size and body type, and, like me, he wears his hair long. If he was dressed in my clothes, especially the Yankees cap, Raymond could have easily mistaken him for me."

This was the most logical and rational thing my client had said so far.

"And," Nathan added, "Donnie lied when he said he'd seen me with the cigarette lighter. I never use a lighter, only matches."

"What about Whitsen and Washington?"

"I don't want to think they're involved, but both had ready access to my medications."

I gave him a frown.

"I was being drugged—I mean, more than usual—and these weren't the usual anti-psychotic medications. This was something different, some sort of hallucinogen, maybe LSD or PCP. Rather than stopping the voices, these drugs made them stronger, somehow more persuasive."

I asked the obvious question. "Why would anyone give hallucinogenic drugs to a diagnosed schizophrenic?"

"Exactly. They wouldn't, not if their aim was treatment or even simply management and control of the patient, which is the primary reason they give us those so-called anti-psychotic drugs anyway. No, they wanted to throw me off balance, to control my mind, to destroy my memory and my credibility. I tried to tell them, days before the murder, that I was being poisoned, but nobody would listen."

"Uh-huh," was all I could manage.

"And since nobody took a blood sample from me after the murder, that evidence has been lost. You think that was coincidental?"

When I said that it could be, he repeated that he didn't believe in coincidences.

"The very fact that I have no memory whatsoever of even seeing Dr.

Rosenberg that night suggests my innocence. Don't you see? Surely, even if I was being drugged and subjected to mind control, I would have some memory of such an event, even if the details were fuzzy. I would certainly remember if I had killed the man, wouldn't I?"

"I would think so," I assured him, though I thought I was again glimpsing the madness beneath the façade of rationality.

"Besides, despite what they say, I had no reason to murder him. Correct me if I'm wrong, but the prosecution's theory is that I killed Rosenberg because I believed he sabotaged my conditional release from this place."

"That's the theory, and they have witnesses who will testify that you threatened him."

Nathan shook his head.

"It's not true?" I asked.

"Oh, yeah, it's true. The twit had been real encouraging when I made the application. At my hearing he said he recommended it. But he folded like a cheap suit on cross-examination, admitted he couldn't guarantee that I would take my medication without close supervision."

He hesitated a moment, looking out the window, then turned back to me. "Was I disappointed? Yes, deeply. Did I say things to Rosenberg, make threatening remarks? I can't deny it. But that was just frustration and anger, with him and with the whole system. That's completely normal. Eventually I did calm down. I was cooperative with staff, and I made no further threatening comments. All of this is documented in my daily charts." He looked at me now for a couple of seconds. "If the denial of conditional release had been my motive, why didn't I kill him right away? Why did I wait three weeks?"

The word premeditation rose to my lips but stayed there. "So how did you and he get along generally?"

"So-so," he said, turning his hand one way, then the other. "We never got a rhythm really. But I didn't hate the guy. I didn't want to see him dead."

I gave him what I thought was a neutral nod, then asked him about the others on his list. He gave me the specific reasons for each of the other entries, and I promised to check out each one. Then I shifted gears a bit. "In the next few days, a psychologist I've hired will come to see you. He . . ."

"Oh, no, you don't," Nathan interrupted. "You're not going to question my competency or my sanity, are you, Ted?"

"Well, Nathan, I . . ."

"No way," he said, interrupting again. "Haven't I spoken rationally? Isn't it obvious that I understand the charges against me? That I can assist in my defense? You have no grounds to even file such a motion."

His voice had risen and his face was contorted in anger, his eyes blazing into me. He was gripping the sides of the chair as if to anchor himself, to force himself to remain seated, and I could feel the electric charge of tension in the air around him. I looked past him to the glass wall divider that separated us from the security officer just beyond. I looked over at the pencil that lay on my legal pad, within easy reach of my client. An image popped into my mind, of Nathan grabbing the pencil and plunging it into my throat.

I forced myself to breathe normally and forged ahead as calmly as I could. I explained to my client that while I personally agreed that he seemed competent, the circumstances—specifically, his present commitment to a psychiatric facility—made an evaluation almost mandatory. "The State might even request it if I don't to make sure it would not be grounds for appeal."

With what seemed a great effort, he regained his composure. He put his hands on the table palms down, as if preparing to push himself up. "I guess I can see the point, Ted, and if it's got to be that way, then I'll comply. But I can tell you it will be a waste of time. Your psychologist will say I'm not competent. Theirs will say I am. There will be a hearing, and the judge will find me competent." He sighed. "Waste of time."

I shrugged and held both hands out in front of me as if to suggest agreement. He gave me that boyish grin again, the calm having now returned. There was something else too, a vulnerability suggested in his posture, in those large brown eyes of his. Whether it was real or a mask, I didn't know. I had to admit, though, that despite the warning whistles going off in my head, I had, somewhere along the way, decided to stay on the case. I couldn't tell whether he was sane or insane, delusional or lying to me, or whether he might just be telling the truth.

And that intrigued me.

It was that image of him with the pencil through my throat, though, that returned to me as he was being led off down the hall. Despite his disarming appearance and regardless of his guilt or innocence on the current charge, I would do well to remember that the man was a cold-blooded murderer—and very dangerous.

CHAPTER 6

*Y*ou may think this a bit silly, but I've always had this fear, irrational as it may be, of being confined to a mental hospital as the result of mistaken identity. I was thinking about this as I headed toward the exit and noted that the guard who had been at the station when I first came in had been replaced. I suddenly had this image of him blocking my way and saying, "Where do you think you're going?" I say I'm a lawyer, just visiting my client, and that I need to get back to my office. And he says, "Sure, you are, but first, why don't you try on this white jacket?"

So I was glad to see that James Washington was waiting for me in the lobby, that I had someone to vouch for me and get me past security. He offered to walk me to my car. I assured him I didn't need an escort and didn't want to put him out, but he just shrugged. "It's on my way anyway." We walked side by side in silence for a while. It didn't seem like he was inclined to break it, so I did. "How long have you been at Florida State Hospital, James?"

He turned and faced me as we continued walking. The social worker was tall, though a little shorter than I, and about thirty pounds lighter, with broad shoulders. His head was shaved, which made his rather large ears seem larger. "Oh, about a year, a little less." If he was annoyed that I had used his first name, he didn't show it.

"You from around here?"

"Baltimore, originally, but I've worked mostly in the Northeast."

"I thought the accent was a little different." When he didn't respond,

I continued. "How did you end up in Chattahoochee?"

He waved to a staff person who passed on the other side of the street, then turned to me and said, "I've worked in mental health facilities most of my life. I have a sister who lives down here, in Valdosta." He shrugged. "The idea of sunny Florida seemed appealing after all those New England winters. I applied, got the job, and here I am."

"You like it okay?"

He continued walking for a couple of seconds before he finally said, "Yeah. This is a good facility. People are friendly. The pay is less than I'm used to, but so is the cost of living."

Okay, I was thinking, *enough of the small talk.* "Listen, James, maybe you can help me. I'm trying to get a feel for this case. You're on Nathan's team. You have regular contact with him. What's your impression of him?"

Washington continued looking straight ahead but answered my question without hesitation. "Nathan is smart. Real smart. He's also very manipulative. When he's on his medications, he does well and can actually be very charming. Especially with the female staff," he said, smiling. "Now, would I trust him out on his own? Well . . ."

His opinion of Whitsen was very favorable—smart and insightful, able to establish a rapport, a connection with the patients. Yes, she was a bit unorthodox, but that was a breath of fresh air as far as he was concerned. His admiration was so effusive it brought to mind the lyrics of an old country song—"It's hard to be humble when you're perfect in every way"—but I just nodded. After all, I had sensed a little of that charisma or magnetism myself in the few minutes I had spent with the psychologist.

We were in a parking lot by then. He stopped and turned toward me. "Well, here's where I'm parked." He was standing beside a 1963 Chevrolet Impala, white with red trim.

"This yours?"

"Yeah," he said, a bit of pride in the voice.

"Very nice. That's a real classic and looks like it's in great shape."

"Yeah, I guess." The way he said it suggested it was not the first time someone had made a fuss over the old car. "You going to be all right?"

"Sure," I said, "but one final question, if you don't mind." He didn't respond but his face seemed receptive. "What can you tell me about Dr. Rosenberg?"

He looked off into the distance for a few seconds, then turned to face me. "I don't like to talk ill of the dead, but Dr. Rosenberg was not considered to be a very good psychologist . . . or administrator. He had a bit of a mean streak."

I thanked him for his candor, and as I watched James drive away in the classic Impala, I was left to contemplate the contrast between his unflattering evaluation of the victim and that given to me by Frank Hutchinson.

***

On the drive back to Tallahassee, I reflected on my initial interview with my client and my impression of him. When I prosecuted his case, I knew only what I had read about him and what I had observed from across a courtroom. I had never been in the same room with him alone. There were many legitimate reasons for me to be wary of him, to be suspicious of what he told me and of his motivations. But there was something about him that seemed sincere. And despite what he had done, I couldn't help but feel a bit of empathy for him, maybe even a bit of protectiveness. I wondered if he had the same effect on the psychologists who had examined him.

And if you accepted his premises—if you stayed within the parameters of the delusional world he'd created—he sort of made sense. There was just something a little off kilter about him, like a slightly off-course vessel that seems to be speeding along quite nicely until it runs right onto the rocks. The question was, could I separate the useful from the useless?

His obsession with the Unit was distracting, as was his insistence that he had been drugged, but his observations about Donnie Mercer seemed reasonable. There wasn't much meat behind his suspicions of Whitsen and Washington, however, just the fact that "they had access to my mind and my medications." Frank and his wife made the list because of a rumored affair between the wife and the victim. Maybe nothing to it, but it was a plausible motive for murder. His reasons for listing Andy Rudd were interesting and potentially more helpful. Rudd, he said, was being investigated for sexual misconduct with patients, an investigation that Rosenberg had pushed and in which Nathan was a witness.

My first call on the way back was to Joe Jensen, the forensic psychologist I had retained to evaluate Hart.

"Hello, Ted." There was an easy, relaxed tone in the voice, and I could envision him sitting in the recliner in his office, shoes off, feet up, some test results or other document propped up on his rather large tummy.

"Hey, Joe."

"Whatcha doin' with that gun in your hand?"

"Huh?"

"It's Hendrix , Ted. I was finishing the line for you."

"Huh?"

"Never mind. What's up?"

I confirmed that he had scheduled the evaluation and told him I needed a report ASAP. There was silence on the other end for a few seconds. "I'm pretty tied up right now, Ted. It may take a few weeks to do it right."

"Can you just half-ass it and get it done quicker?"

The psychologist chuckled into the phone. "Certainly. Or if you like, I could give you my opinion now, save a lot of time and money."

"How about you give me something quick, like a first impression, then take your time writing the report? I need to know what I'm dealing with before I start going too far down the rabbit hole."

"Have you met with him yet?"

"Just did."

"What do you think?"

"I'd rather not say at this point."

"That bad, huh?"

"No. Just want to get your take on him first. Then I may have specific questions."

There was another long silence before he responded. "Okay. I'll have something preliminarily in a couple of weeks. Will that work?"

"Perfect," I said. I thanked him, then disconnected.

My second call was to a number in Panama City. My daughter answered on the second ring.

"Hello. Petronis residence. Annie Stevens speaking."

So formal, so grown-up sounding. "Hi, Pumpkin."

"Hi, Daddy." The change in tone, the complete lapse in formality, was instantaneous, and it filled my heart with joy.

"I must say, Ms. Stevens, that your phone etiquette is quite impressive for one of your age."

"Huh?"

I translated. "That was a very good telephone greeting. Very polite. I'm proud of you. Did Mama teach you that?"

"Uh-huh," she said with pride in her voice.

"So, sweetie, what have you been doing today?"

"Well, Grandma took me shopping for school clothes."

I listened as my daughter gave a blow-by-blow account of their trip to the mall, describing each and every item in detail. "Wow," I said when she finished. "You are going to be the prettiest third grader in all of Tallahassee." When there was no response on the other end of the line, I continued. "So, are you getting packed for the trip back home?" Again the silence. After several seconds, I prompted again. "Annie, you still there, honey?"

Finally, the confusion evident in her voice, she responded, "Mama said I would be going to school here."

Now a longer silence grew between us. I must have misunderstood.

"What do you mean?"

I could almost hear the shrug in her voice now. "That's what she said."

Trying to quell the rising panic and anger and keep it from my voice, I said "Can you put Mama on the phone a minute, sweetie?"

"She's not here."

"How about Grandma then?"

"Just a minute."

I waited for what seemed to be an eternity. Finally I heard the voice of my mother-in-law. "Hello, Ted."

"Hey, Liz." I didn't waste time on pleasantries. "Where is Beth?"

"She went over to Pensacola to pick up something for Jimmy, something for the restaurant."

"Why is my daughter telling me that she will be going to school in Panama City instead of Tallahassee? What's going on over there?"

The long silence on the other end confirmed my fear. "Well, I'd rather you talk to Beth about this, Ted." Then she lowered her voice to continue, "Especially with you-know-who right here. I don't think any final decision has been made. We're all just trying to look out after her best interest, you know. I thought you and Beth had talked about this."

My mother-in-law was a genteel woman who avoided confrontation if she could. But she was also a manipulator, just like her daughter. I had little doubt that whatever plan had been concocted, whatever devious action had been taken behind my back by my wife, neither Liz nor her husband, Jimmy, had been in any way innocent bystanders. And she knew that Beth had not spoken to me about it. I debated for several seconds what to say in response. Fighting hard to keep the anger from my voice, I finally said, "I'm coming over right now, Elizabeth, and I expect Annie to be packed and ready to go with me." I paused for a couple of seconds. "That," I said with emphasis, "is what is in her best interest."

I disconnected the phone and put it back in its charger. I looked around quickly to make sure the traffic was light enough and that there were no state troopers around. Then I slowed my car, got over to the left-hand side, and crossed the grassy median. Within seconds, I had changed my direction and was heading west on I-10, toward Panama City.

***

Beth had gone to Panama City at the beginning of the summer to stay with her parents and had taken Annie with her. She thought I had been unfaithful to her—again. It wasn't true, but my previous indiscretion and the fact that I had lied about some innocent but suspicious-looking circumstances gave me zero credibility, further tearing whatever trust had begun to grow back. It had taken an ardent denial by the supposed paramour to thaw the ice a bit. She was still concerned about the lies but had agreed to try and work things out. But, she said, she needed to be away from me for a while.

This was not an ideal arrangement for a lot of reasons. Aside from the obvious logistical problem of the distance, I distrusted my in-laws and their influence over Beth. They had never liked me, never approved of me. Of course, the fact that Beth was three months pregnant when we were married did not start me off on the right foot with them. And my subsequent infidelity had not helped. Beth's lies and exaggeration about abuse had just made it worse.

Surprisingly, though, they seemed to be sympathetic to my efforts at reconciliation. They were old school about such things. If you had problems in your marriage, however bad, you did your best to work them out. You stayed married if you possibly could.

It seemed to help. Beth and I talked by phone often. We had several sessions with a counselor in Panama City. Things got better, it seemed. I was invited for the weekends and for the full week over the July Fourth holiday. Finally, Beth agreed to return to Tallahassee and give us another try at the end of the summer. She had enrolled Annie in a summer camp in Panama City, and they were enjoying the visit with her parents and extended family. They would be back, she said, before school started.

At that time I saw no ulterior motive at work on the part of my wife or my in-laws. Our reconciliation was fragile, perhaps, but we had been getting along well, or so I thought. In hindsight, I realized now that she had become a little distant toward the end of the summer, but there was nothing to suggest that she had changed her mind about returning to Tallahassee. Now, as I passed the city limits sign, I was wondering why I hadn't seen it coming.

I took the last swallow of the Bud I'd gotten at the convenience store on Highway 231 and placed the empty can in the beverage holder. I knew it wasn't a great idea to show up at my in-laws' house smelling of booze, but I needed to take the edge off. I unwrapped a piece of gum, put it in my mouth, and started chewing furiously. I tried Beth's cell phone number again, and again I got her voice mail. This time I didn't leave a message.

The Petronises' home was a sprawling Mediterranean on the bay in Bunker's Cove, an older, upscale neighborhood close to downtown and dotted generously with huge, moss-draped live oaks. I negotiated the route by instinct rather than conscious choice, taking little note of the familiar landmarks and street signs.

I pulled into the circular driveway and parked behind my father-in-law's Ford 250 pickup. At this time of the day, Jimmy would normally be at the restaurant, overseeing preparations for dinner. I figured his wife must have called him home. I saw my mother-in-law peek out the front window, then disappear behind the curtain as I headed up the walkway. Before I could ring the doorbell, the front door opened and Jimmy stepped outside, closing it behind him. I took the extended hand and shook it, despite my inclination to do otherwise.

"I heard about your conversation with Liz." His voice was even, his manner relaxed. "Let's you and me discuss this outside."

"Don't bullshit me, Jimmy. I'm serious. I'm here to get my daughter. Don't try to get in my way."

"Calm down, Ted. No need to get excited and upset Annie" He

looked behind him at the closed door, then back to me. I reluctantly followed him out into the driveway. We stood at the tailgate of Jimmy's truck. "Ted, you're a good father and I know you want what's best for Annie. Why don't you wait until Beth gets back and you two talk about this?"

I could feel the anger rising in me, threatening to envelop me completely, but I kept it under control. "Just go get Annie. I told Liz to have her packed and ready to go. Now go get her. When we are both back in Tallahassee, Beth can give me a call, or better yet, she can come home to Tallahassee, and we'll talk then."

I started to go around my father-in-law, but the big man moved to block my path. "Do you really want Annie to witness this, Ted? Do you?"

I was considering my choices and the repercussions when the police car turned in to the driveway. At first I was mad because I figured Liz had called them and Jimmy's job had been to stall me until they could get here. But I also knew that my in-laws had no legal grounds to keep my daughter away from me. Even with the Petronises' considerable influence in this town, the law, both natural and man-made, was on my side. Jimmy would have to acknowledge that I was the father, and the cop would make them hand Annie over. I just had to stay calm, play it cool.

"Hey, Dave," Petronis said as the officer got out of the patrol car and began walking toward us. *Oh, great,* I thought. *He knows the guy by his first name.*

The officer tipped his head slightly in Jimmy's direction. "Mr. Petronis." He looked at me with mild suspicion. He had probably been given the story with a little spin from Grandma, I imagined. "What seems to be the problem?"

I dove right in. "The problem, officer, is that I have come to pick up my daughter, but my father-in-law is giving me the runaround."

Dave, who was about the same height and weight as I, looked at me for a long couple of seconds, eye to eye, evaluating what he had just heard. "And your name is, sir?"

"Ted Stevens."

"You live here in Panama City?"

"No, I live in Tallahassee."

"And your daughter's name?"

"Annie Stevens."

"How old is Annie?"

I wanted to ask why any of this mattered, but I answered, "She's eight."

Dave looked over at my father-in-law. "What's going on here, Mr. Petronis?"

Jimmy gave him a short summary of the situation, factual but with his own spin, of course. Dave nodded several times patiently and politely. "I'd hoped it wouldn't come to this," Jimmy concluded. "He is the child's father, Dave, but she and her mother, our daughter, have been staying with us, with his agreement. The parties are having marital difficulties. Best to let the courts sort it all out, don't you think?"

"The mother is here?"

"Not at the moment, but she should be home within the hour."

The officer waited several seconds before replying, looking first at me, then back at Petronis. "Well, I mean, without a court order giving the mother or you custody, Mr. Petronis, or some obvious emergency, you've got no choice but to hand her over. He is the father."

My heart soared at those words. Apparently the man knew the law and was willing to enforce it.

But just as quickly it sank when Jimmy said "Well, as a matter of fact, Dave, I do have a court order, signed this morning by Judge Simmons, which gives our daughter sole temporary custody of the child." He pulled out a paper from his shirt pocket and handed it to the cop. He looked over at me. "Sorry, Ted, but Beth didn't know how you'd react. She felt like she needed some insurance in case you were not reasonable."

The anger boiled inside me. "You son of a bitch. Y'all have been planning this all along."

"That's not true, Ted."

I stepped toward the man, but the officer quickly got between us. Face to face with me now, the officer sniffed the air. "Have you been drinking, Mr. Stevens?"

"No," I said, and the lie smelled as strong as the beer.

"Mr. Stevens, you need to stand over there," he said, pointing to a spot toward the rear of the truck. I complied reluctantly and the officer resumed reading. When he finished, he handed it over to me to read. Then he addressed Petronis. "Why didn't you show me this right away, sir?" He sounded a bit annoyed.

"Like I said, I had hoped it wouldn't be necessary."

I read the document quickly, the archaic language cruelly familiar.

"This Cause having come before the Court on the Verified Petition for Custody and the Ex Parte Motion for Emergency Temporary Relief, and The Court having considered the motion and being otherwise advised in the premises, it is hereby Ordered and Adjudged that the motion is granted. Temporary custody of the minor child, Ann Elizabeth Stevens, shall be with the Petitioner, Elizabeth Arden Stevens, until further order of the Court. The Respondent shall have such visitation with the child as the Petitioner deems reasonable. Such visitation shall be arranged through a third party."

The signature was illegible—a big R and a line, then S and another line—but the printed name underneath identified the judge as Ralph Simmons.

I looked up at the officer, who said, "I'm afraid he does appear to have a court order, Mr. Stevens."

By now, I had used up all of my calm, all of my cool. What I did next was neither rational, logical, nor smart, though it gave me immense satisfaction. I held the order out in front of me and ripped it in half, then in fourths. For good measure, I tore them once more and then tossed the pieces up in the air. The wind scattered them along the pavement.

"Now he doesn't," I said.

***

Even with the startling events of the evening of July 15th, and despite the vast quantities of anti-psychotic drugs they dumped into me, I was still able to analyze the situation with remarkable calm and clearness of thought. I may have been a little fuzzy about exactly what had happened, but of two things I was sure. One, I didn't kill Rosenberg. And two, whoever did was doing a pretty good job of framing me for it. The question was, who?

One of the suspects had to be my current psychologist, Dr. Rebecca Whitsen. I didn't want to believe her possible of such treachery. Indeed, I considered her the closest thing to a friend and ally I had in the place. On the other hand, I had to consider every possibility, didn't I? It would have been foolish to take any other approach.

Rebecca had been assigned to me for about three months, having taken over from Rosenberg, who decided he needed to devote more time to his administrative duties as clinical director. From our first meeting, I knew she was different, unlike any other psychologist I had worked with. When we were introduced and left alone, she looked around the room quickly, mild annoyance and suspicion on her face. "Hey, you want to go outside? We can get away from prying eyes and ears."

I had not paid much attention during the introductions, but now I looked up at the woman with renewed interest, taking in her physical features. She was wearing very plain, loose-fitting pants and a blouse buttoned to the top. Her hair was pinned up, inexpertly so that strands fell off to the side and in front, and she wore black-frame glasses that were too large for her face. Though she did her best to hide it, there was no disguising the sultry beauty and shapely figure. She was neither smiling nor frowning, but the dark eyes that looked at me from behind the glasses were intense, penetrating, seductive, maybe even a little hypnotic.

"Excellent idea," I said.

We walked outside and sat at a picnic table. She told me that she had looked through my records and knew that I was highly intelligent, "not like those other losers," she said, waving her hand dismissively in the direction of the building from which we'd come.

I was surprised. A psychologist didn't refer to patients as losers, even though it was true. I liked her honesty, her lack of concern with political correctness. I liked what she said next even more.

"The fact is, by all clinical standards, you shouldn't be here. You are not a danger to yourself or others." She paused as she looked around quickly, then leaned in closer. "The problem is, there is an unwritten rule that nobody talks about but everyone knows: The more serious the crime, the more in need you must be of long-term treatment in a secure facility. No matter how well you progress, no matter what your mental capacities, the more serious the crime, the longer your stay. And if it's real serious, like murder . . ."

"I didn't murder anyone," I said, surprised to have been brought in so quickly.

She shrugged. "Doesn't matter. That was the charge and about as serious as it gets."

I shrugged.

"My point is this: You're going to have to be realistic. If you ever hope to get out of this place, you're going to need someone who knows what has to be shown, the criteria for release, and how to document it. You need someone in your corner. If you'll work with me, meet me halfway, I will do everything I can to get you your freedom."

I asked the obvious question. "Why?" The others, including Dr. Rosenberg, had paid lip service to my eventual release, but it was not on their radar screen. They didn't believe in it. Was this new one any different?

"Let's just say I don't believe in unwritten rules, only what's best for my patient."

I looked at this unusual woman for a long time, wondering what to make of her us-against-them pitch. Perhaps she was just trying to sucker me. Perhaps I should have listened to the inner voice of skepticism and distrust that has protected me over the years. But, you know, sometimes the burden of constant vigilance can be too much. Sometimes you let your guard down.

I wanted to believe her. I needed to believe her. I maintained a façade of disinterest and distance for a while after that first meeting, but in fact she won me over fairly quickly, probably quicker than even she had thought possible, and I found myself opening up to her to an extent I would never have imagined.

In the weeks leading up to Rosenberg's murder, I noticed that she had begun to get more intrusive in her questions and comments, digging into things I didn't want to talk about. She became confrontational and sarcastic at times. But when I resisted, she would back off, relax, and put me at ease again. When I confided in her that I thought I was being poisoned, she was the only one who didn't dismiss it. She promised me that she would be on extra alert and would keep me informed of anything she discovered. Of course, I was now wondering if it might have been Whitsen all along who was slipping me the hallucinogens. Could I have been so blind? Had my training, my instincts, dulled by medications, abandoned me completely? Still, our relationship was such that I didn't attribute to her actions any sinister motive. And even after the murder, as I have said, I wanted to trust her.

To this day I'm not sure I could tell you why.

***

I sit up straight in the chair, looking around the room. In an instant, I realize where I am and what has roused me: the closing of a car door outside. Cursing myself softly for having fallen asleep, I push back from the desk, rise, and move to the window. The clock radio by the bed reads 5:45 a.m.

I peer through the parted blinds, taking in the parking lot. On the east end, an older man in a baseball cap is slipping into a silver Ford Taurus. A woman, probably his wife, is already inside, her profile visible through the window. A couple of seconds later, the car engine roars to life. The man backs out of the space, then exits the parking lot onto the highway. I look after them for several seconds, listening to the sound of the engine as it changes gears, moving on down the highway. Then I head for the bathroom and a shower.

At the bathroom sink, I look at the image in the mirror. The long black hair is now short and blond, the mustache and beard, gone. I had purchased the scissors and hair-coloring kit, along with other toiletries, at a drug store the day before, just two of several items so the cashier wouldn't remember anything out of the ordinary if someone were to ask her later.

Likewise for the man at the bus station in Tallahassee. Now the cops will think I made my escape by bus. By the time they discover the stolen motorcycle abandoned at the apartment complex and make the connection to me, my trail will be very cold indeed.

The man at the used car lot in Thomasville will recall a clean-cut man in khakis, plaid sport shirt, and boat shoes who said he was a grad student at Florida State. Didn't want anything fancy, just something to haul the occasional load of straw for the yard, maybe furniture, or a small fishing boat. There would be no reason for him to think that our transaction had anything to do with the escaped mental patient he had heard about.

The driver's license I handed him was that of Danny Coxwell, one of the hospital aides. A few days before my escape, I lifted his wallet, took only his driver's license, then managed to put the wallet back in his pocket without his being the wiser. I will probably have at least several days before he even realizes that it's missing, and then he won't know that I have it.

My lawyer's bank card was just as easy to steal, right during my trial as he sat next to me. What was a little trickier was figuring out his PIN. I would only have a limited number of attempts before the ATM rejected the card. But I've always been good with puzzles and codes. And this turned out to be not as difficult as it might have been. On the third try, I punched in the letters of his wife's name, Beth, and voilà! Visits to six different branches yielded a good bit of cash.

I must admit that I feel a little guilty about it, but Ted must understand I had no choice and, if he's honest about it, will admit that had he done his job better, it would not have been necessary. At any rate, I have more than enough to finance the operation if I am frugal.

I gather my things, put them in the cab of my recently purchased F150, and make my way to the motel office. The clerk looks me over, though not in a suspicious way, just curious. He asks if everything was okay with the room. I tell him yes, it was fine. I have already paid in advance so I simply give him the key. "Thanks," I say, then exit the office in a non-hurried manner.

Near the office is a pay phone. Yes, some places still have pay phones. I hesitate a moment. Maybe I should call my lawyer, let him know that it was nothing personal. Though we have had our differences, I think Ted did his best. It simply was not enough.

I step up to the phone, pull all my change out, and place it on the shelf. I dial his number, then put the amount of money in the machine as directed by the operator. The phone rings four times with no answer. The recorder kicks in with the directive to leave a message. So I do, then hang up, get into my truck, and pull out onto the highway.

CHAPTER 7

*T*he sun blazed in the cloudless sky, but the air was less humid than usual, making the heat bearable. There were plenty of kids in the park on this Saturday afternoon, playing flag football, tennis, and softball, or just hanging out on the playground. My dog, Bjorn, followed me to a clearing near one of the ball fields. As I held the Frisbee aloft, he jumped from side to side, the anticipation almost too much for him to contain.

I turned, brought the disk back and to my side, then let it fly. Bjorn was off like a shot, chasing after it. At about twenty yards out, having perfectly calculated the velocity and angle of descent, he jumped up and forward, clearing the ground a good three feet, grasped the plastic disk in his mouth, and landed in stride. The Doberman pinscher slowed, turned, and trotted back to me, the proud hunter returning with his prize. He dutifully released it into my outstretched hand, then jumped back, his eyes intent on the Frisbee, ready to do it all over again.

Bjorn's speed and agility at catching a Frisbee was a natural attention grabber, and after our second throw and catch, a half dozen or so kids had been drawn from their other activities and had gathered off to the side, watching us. They were timid at first, wary of the big dog perhaps. Gradually, though, they mustered up the courage to come closer.

"Hey, mister," one of them said, "can I throw it for him?"

I threw the Frisbee again and Bjorn chased after it, caught it, and began trotting back.

I looked over at the kid and smiled. I turned to the rest of the group and said, "If you can get the Frisbee from him, you can throw it for him."

It took a few seconds for them to process the challenge. Then a couple of boys ventured over next to me and began holding out their hands toward the approaching dog. One of them asked me, "What's his name?" I told them. "Here, boy. Here, Bjorn," they called, hands outstretched. Bjorn stopped about ten feet away. By now the other children had come closer, wanting to be a part of it all but not ready to be active participants.

Some of the more adventurous moved toward Bjorn, hands outstretched to grab the Frisbee. As soon as they got within a couple of feet, though, the dog deftly sidestepped out of their reach, turning to his side and looking back at the two boys, taunting them.

"Here, boy," one of them called, but Bjorn just stood there. The children giggled, hesitated, then en masse began chasing after the dog. Like a quarterback scrambling in the backfield, Bjorn darted and dodged, feigned one way, then went the other, easily avoiding the grasp of the children. It was great exercise for them all, including Bjorn, but the kids were the ones who gave out first, finally realizing the futility of their efforts.

I called out to Bjorn and he dutifully came over, still easily avoiding the kids, then released the disk to me. I picked one of the older boys, motioned him over, and handed it to him. Couldn't let the game end in total frustration for them. "Okay, one more throw, then my dog and I need to be going. So make it a good one."

The boy motioned the other children to give him some space, and they backed up. He then held up the Frisbee so Bjorn could see it, wound up, and threw it underhand in a nice motion. Pretty good throw. Bjorn was off after it. As he made another flying leap and catch, I turned and waved to the kids, then took off jogging after him. "Thanks for exercising my dog, guys. See you around." They all waved back. I heard one of them say that he wished he could have a neat dog like that. It made me smile.

Bjorn stayed close on my left side as I jogged to our home on

Randolph Circle. Beth and I had purchased the nondescript, ranch-style house shortly after we were married and had steadily transformed the modest structure into something with some real curb appeal, complete with the storybook, white picket fence and ivy on the walls. We had added a garage with bonus room, a nice large deck in the back, and elaborate landscaping. As Bjorn and I slowed to a walk and approached the small brick structure, though, I noted that it had a forlorn look about it. The grass needed mowing. The beds were badly in need of weeding. The house itself seemed sad, drooping. It missed its mistress, as did I.

Beth had been just out of college, a fiery, dark-haired beauty ten years my junior who was working as a bartender at the Silver Slipper when we first met. The Slipper was a local restaurant that hosted the monthly Tallahassee Bar meetings. I don't know if it was love at first sight, but I asked her out that night, and within three months I had asked her to marry me.

Perhaps it wasn't a perfect match, our visions of marriage not exactly aligned. To be sure, our relationship has been volatile. We have loved with intensity and fought with intensity. Despite some serious problems, though, I always felt that we would weather it all and grow old together. Despite recent events, I had still hoped we would.

I took Bjorn out back and filled his water dish—actually a large aluminum bucket—with fresh water from the spigot. He drank extensively from it, though he generally preferred one of the three fountains inside and outside the house. With the use of a doggy door, Bjorn had access to the house, though in good weather he seemed to prefer the backyard most of the time. Now he followed me indoors, his paws clacking against the wood floors. He went with me back to the master bedroom, watched as I removed my sweaty clothes.

"What are you looking at?" I asked him. Bjorn cocked his head in response to my words, staring at me intently as I stepped into the shower, then retreated to other venues in search of something of more interest, most likely his food dish.

I stayed in the shower a good twenty minutes, running the cool water over my head as you would a hard-boiled egg, with much the same result. I emerged somewhat cooler and ready to brave the heat again, at least for the short walk from house to car. I dressed, gathered my wallet and car keys from the bowl on the kitchen counter, and headed for the door. Bjorn, who had been sprawled out on the wood floor in the living room, stood up, alert now. He followed me to the door. "Okay, boy, you're in charge," I said, turning back to him. "I need to go into the office for a while."

He wagged his stub of a tail as if he understood, but he crowded next to the door as if expecting to come with me. I held out my hand, palm facing him, and said, "Stay." He did as commanded and sat back on his haunches, but his eyes pleaded with me. I looked back at him for a few seconds.

"Okay, okay," I said, opening the door and motioning him to go through. "You are one spoiled dog. You know that, don't you?" He didn't, of course, but at least he had the good manners to appear enthusiastic and grateful about getting to come along.

***

The Rose Building was quiet—and cool, thank God—when Bjorn and I stepped into the reception area. Although my dog was very good at staying at heel and otherwise obeying commands, I used the leash with him downtown just to be safe. Once inside the office, I released him from his leash and he immediately began to investigate the surroundings, sniffing the entire area very quickly. I checked my mail slot, then made my way up the stairs, Bjorn just ahead of me.

At the top, I started toward my office but noticed the light on in Theo's office. "Theo, you here?"

"No," came the voice down the hall.

"Smart-ass," I said under my breath as I walked toward his office. The door was ajar and I pushed it the rest of the way, then stood in the doorway, my hands resting on each side of the doorframe. Theo, who had been typing something on his computer, his back to the door, swiveled in his chair to face me.

"Hello, Ted." Theo had a deep baritone voice that seemed incongruous with his tall, thin frame. He looked at my dog behind me, interested but not concerned. "And hello, Bjorn." Bjorn pricked his ears at the sound of his name but knew not to enter unless invited.

Part of me was impressed that Theo had come into the office on the weekend. Part of me felt threatened by it. "Hello, Odious. It's reassuring to know I'm not the only one without a home life."

He frowned at the use of his nickname but didn't respond to my comment. Instead he asked, "How'd it go with Nathan Hart the other day?"

"Interesting. Creepy but interesting."

Theo looked at me expectantly, waiting for some direction from me. I had been reluctant to bring him on and still was, but as it appeared we were not headed for a quick plea in the case, I needed to find a useful role for my young associate. "You read through the file, my notes?"

He nodded.

"You got a minute to talk about it?"

"Sure," he said, leaning back in his chair.

Bjorn took it as a joint invitation and followed me in. He did not roam, however, but lay on the floor next to the chair in which I sat. I took a swig from the water bottle I'd brought with me.

"Our guy insists that this case and his previous one are related. Specifically, he thinks this secret organization, the Unit, is behind both murders. Why don't you get together whatever paperwork you can find on the original case, talk to the others involved, see if you think we missed something." I tented my fingers. "Check out the uncle and his possible connection to espionage. See if there's anything at all to support Hart's claim."

Theo looked at me, frowning. "You think there might be something to this Unit thing?"

I shook my head. "I think it's all delusional bullshit, but we need to do this, if for no other reason to appease our paranoid client." I hesitated a beat, then added, "Besides, always good to keep an open mind. You bring a fresh pair of eyes to it, an objective, neutral perspective."

"What about his list of suspects? You want me to follow up on them?"

I took another swig of water, reached my arm down, and began rubbing Bjorn's ears.

"Yeah, if this goes to trial we'll need alternative suspects and theories, and I'd rather have something other than a conspiracy by some secret organization." I removed my hand from Bjorn's ears. He raised his head up momentarily as if in mild protest, then lowered it again to the floor.

Theo smiled. He leaned forward, his forearms on the desk. "Great. Any particular turn around time you looking for?"

I shook my head. "No big hurry. The sooner the better, but we need to be thorough." As I spoke, I was looking past the young lawyer, focusing on a photograph of Theo in a cap and gown, his parents, I guessed, on either side of him. They all looked happy and proud. I stood and Bjorn got to his feet too. "Well, guess I better get to work. I got a brief due on Monday, and I've barely started." I walked to the doorway, paused there, and turned. "And, Theo, thanks for the help." The words didn't come easily for me, but they needed to be said.

The young associate waved his hand dismissively and said "Sure." But as I turned back again toward the doorway, I thought I noticed a small smile on his lips.

CHAPTER 8

*T*he building was a converted residence on Park Avenue, between Franklin and Magnolia, a two-story red brick with dormers and a portico. The sign out front announced it as the Law Offices of Denise Wilkerson. I pulled into a parking space in the side lot, turned off the car engine, and checked my watch. Just a couple of minutes before nine o'clock. Good. I would actually be on time for a change.

Just as I started to get out of my car, I noticed Kate Marston leaving the front entrance. Kate was a very competent lawyer and an excellent basketball player who could mix it up with the guys in and on the respective court. I hesitated. There could be several explanations for her presence, but since Denise handled nothing but family law cases, there was only one logical one. I weighed the social pros and cons of remaining in my car until she left and opted for directness.

"Hello, Kate," I said as I closed my car door.

Kate, who was probably weighing her social options as well, smiled grimly as she walked toward me. "Hello, Ted. Fancy seeing you here."

We shook hands briefly and both looked around the parking area. Before the silence became too awkward, she said. "Haven't seen you at the gym recently." She brushed hair away from her face.

"Haven't been able to get up there too much these days," I said, looking past her to the traffic going by on Park Avenue, then back to her. "I heard you're teaching at the law school."

"Yes, the firm of Bradford, Horton, and Waters decided it could get along quite well without my services." Her laugh had a sarcastic tone.

I nodded, very much aware that her severance from the firm was a direct result of Kate's decision to disclose to my partner certain documents that her firm had attempted to conceal during a case. Although the firm's senior partner had publicly praised her action, spinning it as the correction of an unfortunate oversight, privately he considered it an act of disloyalty. It wasn't long afterward that Kate left the firm. Paul had tried to talk her into joining us, but she had pointed out that to do so would create the appearance that her actions had been improperly motivated.

"Their loss," I said.

"Thanks," she said, smiling ever so slightly, sincerity now in her voice. "I appreciate your saying so." She touched me lightly on the arm. "How are you doing, Ted?"

"Fine. I'm doing fine," I lied, and Kate knew it. There was an awkward silence again, which was finally broken by my revealing the purpose of my visit to the office. With her words of sympathy and encouragement, Kate disclosed that she too was preparing to file for divorce, without offering any details. That was all right too.

"Well," I said, putting my right hand in my pocket. "I better go. Don't want to be late and start off on the wrong foot with Denise."

"No, indeed. Well, listen, see you at the gym maybe."

"Yeah," I said and watched as she got into her car. I walked several feet toward the entrance, stopped, then turned and waved as she pulled out of the lot.

The reception area was the former living room, more long than wide, with a brick fireplace on the wall to the right. A large area rug covered most of the oak floor. The earth-tone furniture and Native American art on the walls gave the room a Southwestern look. It fit the occupant. Denise had a spread east, off Highway 90, close to the county line, where she kept cattle and horses.

"Hello, Mr. Stevens. Nice to see you again." The large woman at the desk gave me a smile. She was sitting forward, her hands palms down on the desk, and looking at me as if all she did was greet people who entered.

"Hello, Roberta. Nice to see you too."

Her smile broadened. She turned her head toward the doorway behind her and called out. "Denise, Mr. Stevens is here." She turned back to me. "She doesn't really like the intercom system," she whispered, somewhat apologetically.

A couple of seconds later, Denise Wilkerson appeared in the doorway, holding on to the frame with one hand, a cup of coffee in the other. As usual, she wore jeans, cowboy boots, and a plaid shirt, but her usual long, curly mane was now short—very short. She grinned at the surprised look on my face. "Yeah, it's me," she said, running her fingers through her hair. "Got tired of messing with it," she said as further explanation. She stepped forward and shook hands with me. Her grip was firm. "How ya doing, Ted?" She had a scratchy voice that made you think of cigarettes and booze.

"I'm great."

She gave me an appraising look that suggested she thought otherwise, but "Good" was what she said.

"I like the new hairstyle," I said, and she waved her hand at me in dismissal, again suggesting her disbelief. "No, really, it looks great on you."

She stood a moment looking at me, trying to decide if I was bullshitting her and deciding she didn't care. "Come on back," she said, starting to turn, then added, "You want some coffee?"

"Nah, I'm fine," I said, admiring the view as I walked behind her.

Inside her office, Denise motioned me to one of the chairs across from her at a small oak library table. Behind her was an old rolltop desk. She sat in a matching oak chair with a brown leather seat. Its wheels squeaked when she rolled it up close to the table. She took a file from the corner of the table, placed it in front of her, and opened it.

"I read the documents you dropped off," she said as she began shuffling through the contents of the file, "and had a brief conversation with your wife's lawyer."

"And?"

"As Yogi would say, it's déjà vu all over again."

I shook my head slowly but didn't respond.

She put the papers down on the table, then leaned back in her chair. "Okay. You do family law, so you know the drill. Just like before, she's filed for divorce. She's also gotten a temporary custody order and a temporary restraining order against you."

"That's what really frosts my . . ." I hesitated, looking at Denise.

She smiled. "That's okay, Ted, you can say balls. I assure you I've heard a lot worse. Hell, I've said a lot worse."

"It's all such bullshit."

Denise nodded slowly, looking at the papers in front of her, waiting for me to calm down a bit. "I take it this was a surprise to you?"

"Completely."

She glanced down again, reading. "It really does appear to be mostly a rehash of the first time. The only new allegation of domestic violence is this thing about you punching a hole in the wall." It was a question as much as a statement, and she looked at me, waiting. When I didn't respond right away, she said, "Is it true?"

"Well, yeah, but it wasn't like she makes it out. I wasn't trying to hit her or anything."

"What were you trying to do?"

"We got into an argument. I don't even remember what it was about. She kept egging me on, provoking me. I tried to walk away—I really did—but she grabbed me by the arm. I shook loose, then I turned and slammed my palm up against the wall. Must have been weak Sheetrock."

"Was your daughter present?"

"Annie was there, but she was asleep in the other room. She never saw anything."

"But she probably heard it."

"I doubt it," I said, though not sure. "Besides, Beth was the one raising her voice."

Denise looked skeptical. She waited a long time before speaking again. "Last time," she said finally, "she took you back."

I shook my head. "Ain't gonna happen this time, Denise. I don't care anymore. I've had it. I want to file a counterpetition. I'm tired of her bullshit."

"If I recall, that's also what you said last time."

"This is different," I said.

She waited a beat, frowning. "Let's not rule out reconciliation quite yet. You're still feeling angry and hurt. Let's let things cool down a bit."

"She's trying to keep me away from my daughter, Denise, by making up lies. A person like that doesn't deserve to have primary custody, much less sole custody."

"You know as well as I do, Ted, that this is probably just a tactical move. It puts her in control of the litigation, puts you on the defensive, and gives her some leverage. But, in the end, it's a rare case where the parties don't eventually agree to some joint parenting arrangement, and if they don't, the judge often orders it anyway. Her lawyer will know that too."

I knew what she said was true. I'd even filed similar pleadings on behalf of clients. But it was different when you were on the receiving end. "Okay," I said, "so what do we do?"

She answered my question with one of her own. "What's your status with the alcohol? You still sober? Going to AA?"

I hesitated only for a moment before responding. "I'm off probation so I don't have any prohibition on drinking anymore." Denise arched her eyebrows but said nothing. "I have it under control."

I expected her to remind me that this was what I said last time, but she just looked at me for several seconds, then said, "Other stuff?"

I shook my head, hesitated a moment. "Not in a long time," I said, rationalizing to myself that time was, after all, a relative thing.

Again she gave me a long look that suggested her disbelief. "Listen, Ted. Don't blow smoke up my skirt. I don't want to get blindsided."

I was tempted to point out that she was not wearing a skirt but thought better of it. Denise tended to get serious about her cases and was one of the best in town at what she did. I had also not forgotten that she had withdrawn as my attorney once before. It was during my first divorce case, which was eventually dropped. Denise had insisted that I remain sober for the duration. I promised I would. I didn't. She quit. At the time, I was furious, righteously indignant at this act of disloyalty. I realized later she had been right and told her so. This was probably why she had agreed to see me now.

I felt bad about lying to her right off, but it was only a small lie and one that could be made true with a little time. And I never overindulged when Annie was with me. I could and would do whatever I needed to do to keep my daughter in my life. "I swear, Denise, it's not a problem."

Her eyes looked into mine as she sat there for several seconds, considering my words. I cursed myself silently for not telling her the truth. Maybe it wasn't too late. Finally, just before I was about to break down and confess, she gave a long, loud sigh that suggested she would play the game for a while anyway. "All right," she said, "tell me about this incident in Panama City."

I summarized the facts cleanly and as neutrally as I could, though I couldn't help but spin it in my favor. My lawyer expected as much, would have been suspicious had I not slanted it.

"You're lucky you weren't arrested when you tore up that custody order in front of the officer," she observed when I finished my narrative.

"I didn't violate any law."

"Since when does that insure against arrest?"

"Good point," I acknowledged. "But it sure felt good."

"I'm sure it did, Mr. Out-of-Control. That's the problem, Ted. You do what you want, what makes you feel good, without considering the consequences. You have to know that this will just play into their hands."

I hung my head. Yes, I knew. I would do better, I told her. I would follow her directions to a T. Denise looked skeptical, but she shrugged and said, "Okay then. I want you to henceforth stop all consumption of alcoholic beverages and illegal drugs. And I'm going to want regular UAs to verify. Something to show the judge."

My stomach churned, but I willed my face to be neutral. "Then I want her to have the same conditions and monitored by UAs."

Denise lowered her chin toward her chest and looked at me over her reading glasses. "You have a prior DUI. You were suspended from the practice of law and required to go to substance abuse counseling. Does your wife have such a history?"

There were things I could have said: The DUI was reduced to reckless driving with alcohol conditions as part of the probation. All substance abusers don't go to counseling. But I said nothing.

"And they better come back negative," she said, still giving me that sharp look. I nodded. "Stay out of bars or anyplace that serves alcohol, just to avoid the appearance that you're drinking or hanging out with the wrong people. I want you to be the poster child for responsible, sober, dependable fatherhood."

Again I nodded in agreement, but I was already thinking about how to get around it. She asked me if I had family I could call on, someone who could help with caregiving for Annie. Hired people were okay but family was better. I thought about my mother in Miami, wondering if I could stand to have her under the same roof for any length of time. "Maybe," I said, and it was her turn to nod in agreement.

My lawyer ended our discussion on what she figured was a positive note. "She's going to have a hard time getting sole custody, Ted, or restricting your parenting time as she is asking. That's a very high burden indeed. They will rely heavily on the allegations of domestic violence and substance abuse. If what you have told me is true, you have nothing to worry about."

***

I was headed out of the parking lot, reflecting on Denise's last words to me and their implications, when my cell phone rang. I was so preoccupied that it took a couple of rings before it registered. I picked it up. "Hello?"

"Ted, it's Maxine Chrenshaw. Got some news on the Hart case."

"Hi, Max," I said as I turned the corner onto Magnolia. "You calling to say you're dropping the charges and prepared to proclaim my client's complete innocence?"

"I thought it was your client who was delusional." The soft chuckle on the other end made me smile. Maxine Chrenshaw was one of the lawyers I had most admired when I worked at the State Attorney's office. When I learned that she would prosecute the Rosenberg murder case, I had mixed feelings. She was smart, tough, and very effective with a jury. She would be a formidable opponent. On the other hand, she was very ethical and very fair. She really believed what others only professed, that her job was to seek justice, not just convictions.

"I take that as a no," I said, chuckling myself.

"But I do have some new evidence to share. I'll send you an updated discovery response in writing but thought you'd want to hear this now."

"Yes?" I prompted, knowing she would not have called me with good news.

"They've found what appears to be the murder weapon."

CHAPTER 9

*D*etective Walter Browning was bald and slightly overweight, with pink cheeks on a Pillsbury Doughboy face. What made it all the more unusual was that he wasn't sweating, not even a thin film of perspiration, though the room was quite warm. He fished a pack of gum from his shirt pocket and offered me a stick. I shook my head no. As the detective unwrapped one for himself, he motioned for me to have a seat on the other side of his desk. He sat himself, popped the gum in his mouth, and began chewing furiously, looking at me. Then he turned, took out a key from his pants pocket, and used it to unlock a two-drawer file cabinet behind him. From the bottom drawer he took a small paper bag, then pushed the door closed with his foot. He turned back to me and put the bag on the desk.

"One of the hospital gardeners discovered it," he said. "It was buried blade down in a flower bed less than thirty yards from your client's bedroom." He retrieved the object from the paper bag and placed it in front of me. It was a letter opener, gold plated with a pearl handle. "The wife identified it. Said she got it for him as a gift on a trip to Mexico. The secretary says he kept it on his desk."

I looked at Browning. Nothing in his demeanor hinted at the animosity that is sometimes the natural state between law enforcement officers and defense attorneys. When Maxine had suggested I go talk to him without her, I had been surprised. Prosecutors generally don't like defense attorneys talking to their witnesses outside the formal deposition setting, and even when they don't mind, the detectives usually do. Perhaps it was because I had once been a prosecutor or that a significant number of law enforcement officers had come to me over the years with their legal problems—contract disputes, real estate closings, divorces. Perhaps it was simply that they did things a little differently in Chattahoochee. Either way, I appreciated the courtesy.

I picked up the item and turned it over in my hand. The four-inch-long blade was not particularly sharp but was pointed and shaped such that it could make a nasty little weapon—primitive yet effective, especially if great force was applied. "Has the M.E. examined it?"

"He says the blade is consistent with the wounds."

"Any prints?"

The detective shook his head. "Nothing."

That's good, at least, I thought. Jurors liked fingerprints. They expected fingerprints and probably a little DNA evidence too, thanks to the popularity of the *C.S.I.* television shows. "What about the clothes found in the washer? You got the lab results back yet?"

"Not yet. Looks like somebody tried to destroy any DNA evidence by using bleach, but I'm pretty sure the stains on them were blood, probably the victim's."

"Anything to tie them to my client?"

"Don't know what the lab folks will turn up, but a couple of the cottage residents and the staff person said they looked like Hart's. The jeans are the same size as the others in his room. So are the shoes." He hesitated. "Not that there's anything particularly distinctive about them, except for that Yankees cap."

I frowned. "Doesn't look too good for the visiting team, does it?"

Browning shrugged.

"Any other possible suspects?"

The detective gave me a sideways look, surprised perhaps that I actually thought there might be plausible alternatives to my client's guilt. "You got someone in mind?"

"How about Andy Rudd? I hear he's facing an investigation on charges of sexual abuse of patients, and the victim had been the one pushing it. He was also the first person to report to the scene after the custodian called it in."

Browning shook his head. "Andy had reason to be pissed off at Rosenberg, sure." He swiveled in his seat, then leaned back. "And between me and you, this ain't the first time the smell of rot has come off of Rudd. Word is, he got and keeps his job 'cause he's got something on the hospital administrator. I don't know." He held out his hands, palms up. "But as to the murder, trouble is, his window of opportunity was pretty small. Not only would he have to kill the victim, he would also have to plant the clothes and the letter opener and get back to the scene in about two minutes. Not likely."

"Maybe he had help."

Browning pushed out his lower lip momentarily, then went back to chewing his gum. "Maybe," he allowed, "but if so, his helper was the brains behind it. Andy's just not clever enough to have planned the murder and frame your client."

"So you agree that my client's been framed."

He smiled. "Not so fast, counselor. That's your theory, not mine. And I guess it has to be, 'cause the only way your guy is innocent is if someone is framing him." I nodded. "And," he continued, "if that's the theory, you're looking for someone who is very clever."

We were both silent for several seconds, reflecting on that observation. Then I asked, "Any prints of value from the scene?"

"Some. The print guys haven't done all the comparisons, but we have some to work from, and I've got some preliminary reports." He pulled a file from the file cabinet, opened it, and began to summarize the contents. "Raymond Curry, the custodian. His prints were found on the doorknob and frame and on the phone. There were other prints of value near the desk, most of which belonged to the victim. There were more prints in the corner of the office that served as a sitting area, some on a glass coffee table, and one on the wooden arms of a wingback chair. These aren't considered particularly helpful since they were a distance from where the struggle took place, and it would be natural to find the prints of clients or colleagues there."

He leaned forward in his chair and tossed the file on the desk "We haven't matched any of those yet, but we're narrowing the field, starting with people we know were in the office shortly before the murder. According to his calendar, Rosenberg had sessions with a couple of patients, a Donnie Mercer and an Angela Watson, the week of the murder. He met with Dr. Barbara Hutchinson fairly regularly. She was like the second in command or something like that. And then there is the secretary, Isabella Martinez. I want to rule these folks out first." He looked at me then. "And, no, we haven't found any that match your client."

"Thank God for small blessings," I said and folded my hands in front of me. "Does Barbara Hutchinson have an alibi?"

Browning arched his eyebrows in my direction. "Home, watching television."

"Hmm," I said. "Alone?"

"She was with her husband."

"So they are each other's alibi."

"Yeah, I guess so."

"Hmm," I said again, then, after a long couple of seconds, I continued. "I heard that Rosenberg may have had more than a strictly professional relationship with Barbara Hutchinson." I watched the detective closely for his reaction but couldn't detect anything other than mild curiosity.

"Where did you hear that?"

Theo had not wasted any time testing the rumor mill at the hospital and had found that it was quite active. One of his main sources so far, he told me, was James Washington, who had turned out to be a real gossip. "Oh, just around," I said.

Browning decided not to push it. "Well, I wouldn't put too much store in those kinds of rumors. People talk. Doesn't mean there's anything to it."

"If it was true, though. . . ." I didn't finish the sentence. Didn't need to. Browning conceded the point with a shrug, then I went into what I thought might be a related area. "Walter, one of the items listed as taken from the crime scene was a cigarette lighter. I believe your report says it was located underneath the victim's desk?"

"That's right."

"You have it?"

"It's at the lab, but I have a photograph, actually several." He found the file he was looking for quickly and spread the photographs out before me. There were shots from different angles, close up and far away, showing its location at the scene. I chose one that was a close-up, showing its details. The lighter was slim, gold plated with black trim.

"It wasn't Rosenberg's, was it?"

The detective shook his head. "He wasn't a smoker and didn't allow people to smoke in his office, according to the secretary."

I picked up the photo again. "You have it dusted for prints?"

"Yes," he said, then, in anticipation of my next question, offered, "one partial of poor quality, not good enough to do a match."

"No?" I looked up at the detective.

"Of course, you're welcome to have your own expert examine the exhibit. Maybe you can find someone who feels more comfortable making a comparison."

I let the idea percolate in the air a little. "Any idea who the rightful owner might be?"

Browning folded his arms in front of him and leaned back in his chair. "You mean other than your client?"

"Indulge me."

He rubbed his chin with his thumb and forefinger. "The secretary doesn't smoke and didn't recognize the lighter. Both of the patients, Watson and Mercer, smoke, but they denied it belonged to them, and they both showed me their lighters when I asked them about it."

"They could have gotten another."

"Could have."

I noted that the size and style of the lighter suggested a woman, then asked, "Could the killer have been a woman?"

The man pursed his lips. "Could be but not as likely, given that there was a struggle and the victim was overpowered."

I nodded but said nothing. Although this was a logical conclusion, I thought a woman perfectly capable of committing the crime. Perhaps it was not a face-to-face confrontation. Perhaps the killer was waiting for the psychologist in his office, behind the curtain in the bay window. The element of surprise coupled with rage can be very powerful. I decided, however, not to share this theory with Browning.

"So," I said, "if we agree that the fingerprint on the lighter belongs to someone other than my client . . ."

He smiled again, shaking his head. "There you go again. I don't know that we agreed to that. The print examiner couldn't say for sure one way or the other."

I held my hands out. "I try." As we talked, I pictured Browning at trial. He would come across as a likable, dedicated public servant. He would refer to his notes now and then, just enough to suggest a desire to be accurate but not enough to imply that he did not remember the events. He would be a very effective witness, relating to the jury the evidence that had led him to my client. "Let me ask you something, Walter."

"Yes?"

"Does it make sense that this seriously mentally ill person could have so carefully planned the murder of his former psychologist, somehow knowing that the victim would be in his office at that date and time and that the door to the office building would not be locked?"

The detective pursed his lips neutrally but said nothing.

"Would this same person, who is careful enough to wipe all his prints from the crime scene and the murder weapon, clumsily hide the weapon where it would surely be found and, worse, put the bloodstained clothes in the washer down the hall from his bedroom? Would he then make an incriminating statement when security arrived at his room? How do you explain these inconsistencies?"

The detective looked at me for several seconds, as if trying to decide if I was serious or not. Finally, he said, "Maybe your client is not as crazy as you think—or not as smart as he thinks."

CHAPTER 10

I turned in my chair and surveyed the crowded courtroom. It was regular motion calendar day so there were several other lawyers present with their clients, waiting for their motions to be heard. The clients who were out on bond sat impatiently in the general audience section, irritated that they might have to wait all morning before their case was called. Those clients in custody, on the other hand, saw it as an opportunity to get out of jail for a while, a field trip of sorts with entertainment. They were quite content to sit in the jury box, cuffed and shackled with leg irons, and watch the show. For my part, I was glad to be first on the docket.

There were a couple of reporters there, one from the local weekly paper and one from *The Tallahassee Republican.* They were in the front row, just behind the prosecution's table. In the corner of the courtroom, a man stood behind a video camera, but I didn't see the TV news reporter to whom he was no doubt attached. Next to me was my client.

Nathan had not wanted this hearing, but he seemed resigned to it now, calm and relaxed. As he predicted, our psychologist had found him incompetent, and theirs, competent. I was a little surprised by Joe Jensen's finding of incompetence but understood his reasoning. Nathan had apparently not been as open with the psychologist as he had been with me.

Jensen had given me his report over the phone two weeks before: "Classic paranoid schizophrenic. Delusional thinking and reports of auditory hallucinations. Extremely distrustful. It took me several minutes to even engage him in conversation, and then it was begrudgingly. He acknowledged that he was, at the time, hearing voices, which he identified as coming from God, telling him that I was not to be trusted."

"Hard to argue with God," I observed.

I sensed his smile on the other end. "Yes, I suppose so." I heard the shuffle of paper, then Jensen continued, apparently reading from his notes. "He was oriented as to time and place. His memory capacity appeared to be generally intact, though difficult to assess because of his unwillingness to discuss details of his case or his past, and due to his delusional thinking."

"So far, doesn't sound too much different than most of my clients."

The psychologist ignored me and continued in that same sterile tone intended to project objectivity. He told me that, aside from the delusional aspect of it, Nathan was generally coherent and understandable, eye contact was good, mannerisms were generally appropriate.

"What about his understanding of the legal process, his ability to assist in his defense?"

The psychologist gave a small snort of a laugh. "No problem with his understanding the nature of the charge, the range of penalties, the role and function of the various courtroom personnel. His ability to display appropriate courtroom behavior would appear to be acceptable, though marginal."

"So what's the problem?"

"The problem is his paranoia and delusional thinking. You can never be sure if he is cooperating or misdirecting. It's a toss-up as to his ability to testify effectively in his own defense. He is likely to go off on some tangent about spies and talking to God."

On the question of sanity at the time of the offense, Jensen was unable to render an opinion. "Since he denies the act or can't remember it and because he refuses to talk to me about it, it's impossible for me to determine whether he was legally insane at the time."

Given my interaction with Hart, I thought Jensen would have found him, as I did, a little nuts but legally competent. What surprised me most, however, was my client's reported lack of cooperation, which seemed to be the biggest stumbling block for Jensen.

When I asked Nathan why he had not cooperated during the examination, knowing its likely effect on the examiner, he had seemed unconcerned.

"Jensen was a nice enough guy," he said, shrugging. "In another context, we could have been friends. But I mean, seriously, what did he expect? Anything I told him might later be divulged. He told me that. Of course I was suspicious and less than fully cooperative. What? Give the prosecutor my most intimate thoughts so she could use them against me at trial? Alert the real murderer to what I suspect and give him a chance to cover his tracks even more? That, I think you will agree, would not have been prudent." When I didn't respond, he added, "Besides, the lady psychologist for the State says I'm competent, though for the wrong reasons, I might add. That's all the judge will need."

I was wondering about that when the side door to the courtroom opened and the bailiff bellowed, "All rise. The Circuit Court in and for Gadsden County, Florida, is now in session, the Honorable Maurice Palmer presiding."

The judge walked briskly up to the bench, then climbed the two steps in one stride. He stopped momentarily in front of the large leather chair and looked out over the courtroom, then took his seat. "You may be seated," he said.

Maurice Palmer was a fifth-generation native of Gadsden County, the descendant of slaves and sharecroppers and the first African American elected to the bench since Reconstruction. He had come back to his hometown after a career in the Navy, law school, and three years as a prosecutor in Fort Lauderdale. He hung up his shingle at an office across from the courthouse in Quincy and for the next ten years built a small but successful general practice. He enjoyed a reputation as a capable and fair judge, learned in the law and with a keen understanding of human nature.

"Mr. Stevens," he said, "it's your motion, I believe."

"Yes, Your Honor. We call Dr. Joseph Jensen."

I didn't try to dress up his testimony for maximum effect. As I mentioned, I was ambivalent about his conclusion, and I knew my client's preference. Despite my less-than-inspirational presentation, however, Jensen made a pretty effective witness. Part of it was his appearance, which was very disarming. He was short and rotund, with a sandy beard and bald head. His ruddy face was open and friendly, and his eyes twinkled when he spoke.

I hadn't planned to do a vigorous cross of the State's expert either, but when it came to it, I couldn't help myself. There was just something about her that made you want to bring her down a peg. Dr. Judith Conn was an unsmiling woman of about forty-five. Her long, straight black hair, speckled with gray, was pulled back and tied loosely with some kind of ribbon. It gave her a school girl look, which, under the circumstances, seemed quite ridiculous. She spoke, as she wrote, with pomposity and arrogance.

"Mr. Hart is a man of high intelligence and an even higher opinion of himself. He exhibits some classic symptoms of paranoid schizophrenia, but they are symptoms that may very well be feigned or greatly exaggerated. He strikes me, rather, as a sociopath, a narcissistic, neurotic individual who can be very charming and very manipulative. It is my opinion that his symptoms are mostly for show, an attempt to manipulate the system and evade the consequences of his actions."

I took my time moving from the counsel table to the podium. I stood there several seconds, looking at the witness, a sarcastic half smile on my face "Let me see if I've got this straight, Dr. Conn. Mr. Hart, in your opinion, is faking his symptoms?"

"Or exaggerating." Conn seemed calm and polite on the surface, but I could sense the hostility underneath the thin smile.

"If he is faking, then he must be pretty good at it, right?"

"Not that good, obviously."

"'Cause he didn't fool you?"

Conn didn't respond, the answer obvious, as was her bias. I ended my cross by pointing out that she had virtually no clinical practice, that she was, in essence, a professional witness who testified almost exclusively for the State. I sat back down, satisfied, but then had a sickening feeling that I might have been too effective. My client said nothing, just looked straight ahead, but I could see the tight lips, the vein in his temple throbbing.

Apparently, my cross was not enough to destroy her credibility with the judge. Or maybe he just saw right through all the psycho mumbo jumbo on both sides. Judge Palmer asked Nathan a few questions, then cleared his throat and looked down at us from the bench. "I find the defendant competent to proceed." The judge hesitated a moment, then said, "Are there any other matters I need to address this morning?" Nathan raised his hand. "Yes, Mr. Hart?" the judge said, looking at my client.

Nathan stood. He looked at me briefly before turning back to face the judge. "Your Honor, now that you have found me to be competent to proceed, I would, at this time, like to discharge my attorney and represent myself."

***

A tense murmur rippled through the crowd, then turned to silence as all eyes were on the judge, waiting to see how he would respond. He looked at Nathan for a couple of seconds, then turned his attention to me. "Mr. Stevens?"

A trial lawyer never wants to appear surprised by anything that happens in court. The best way to accomplish this is to anticipate every possible variation. Sometimes, though, the unexpected happens, and you just have to fake it. Which was what I did.

"Your Honor, Mr. Hart had expressed dissatisfaction with my

decision to pursue a determination as to competency, but he has not, before just now, told me he does not want the benefit of my services." I had reverted to overly formal lawyer talk to mask my surprise.

The judge pondered this for a second or two, then let out a small sigh as he turned his attention back to Nathan. He began a series of questions intended to determine if Nathan understood the disadvantages and possible consequences of self-representation. Palmer listed some of the benefits of having an attorney: He knows the law, the rules of procedure and evidence, how to file and argue motions, select a jury, cross-examine witnesses, etc. Did he understand that the judge could not advise or help him? That if he made mistakes during the trial because he didn't understand the rules of evidence or procedure, he would not be able to complain about the result on an appeal?

All of these questions Nathan answered appropriately, which I think rather disappointed the judge. Whether or not he actually represented himself competently, Nathan had clearly demonstrated that he was capable of making an informed decision on the issue, which was all the law required. Palmer looked around the room. He leaned back in his chair and folded his arms as he studied my client. "Mr. Hart, you seem to be an intelligent, articulate person. You also say you understand the ramifications of your decision to represent yourself."

"Yes, sir."

"I'm just curious, then, why a smart guy like you would want to give up the advantage of having a lawyer represent you." He leaned forward in his chair, his hands clasped together and elbows resting on the bench. His face expressed what appeared to be genuine concern. "I mean, if I had a serious illness, I'd go to a doctor. That makes sense, doesn't it?"

It was a rhetorical question, and Nathan didn't answer. The judge continued. "Do you really want to represent yourself, or is it more that you have some problem with your attorney?" He hesitated, but still Nathan didn't respond. "Mr. Stevens is a very fine attorney. He will do a good job for you. Is there some particular problem with him we could address, a way to make you more comfortable with the arrangement?"

"Your Honor, you make some good points, and to be honest I don't really want to have to represent myself, but Mr. Stevens is not following my directions, as evidenced by his attempt to have me declared incompetent. I ended up at the hospital because my lawyer didn't listen to me, went against my wishes. I don't want that to happen again. This is my life, my freedom, and I need to feel I have some control over my own case." He turned and faced me.

The judge looked at both of us for a moment. "Mr. Stevens mentioned the disagreement over strategy concerning the competency issue. Is there anything else?" Palmer seemed to exude empathy, concern, a desire to be of assistance.

Nathan hesitated a moment, looked around the courtroom, then asked the judge if we could approach the bench. The judge seemed reluctant but motioned for us to step forward. Once there, Nathan lowered his voice and continued. "No offense to Mr. Stevens, Your Honor. I'm sure, as you say, that he is a fine attorney. But he also has personal distractions."

"Personal distractions?"

"Mr. Stevens' problem with substance abuse is hardly a secret, nor is the fact that his wife has recently filed for divorce—again—alleging all sorts of things that we need not repeat here. Needless to say, it's enough to distract anybody. I need somebody who can focus on my case."

No one said anything for several seconds. Maxine backed up and to the side a step, indicating that this was not her fight. The judge looked at me.

My stomach twisted in a knot. The anger washed over me, engulfing me, and I was in danger of saying something I shouldn't. So I took a moment, willed myself under control. I cleared my throat, looked first at Nathan, then at the judge. "Perhaps it would be better, Your Honor, if you appointed someone else as Mr. Hart's lawyer. It's obvious that the level of trust necessary for me to properly represent him is not present."

The judge shook his head. "Not so fast, Mr. Stevens. It doesn't work that way, as you well know." Turning to Nathan, he said, "Mr. Hart, here's the deal. You can decide to represent yourself or you can have a court-appointed lawyer, but you don't get to say which lawyer you get unless you hire your own. Only under certain circumstances could I give you a different lawyer, and none of what you have told me today would be sufficient grounds for me to do so."

Nathan shrugged. "I guess we're back to where we started then, with me representing myself."

Palmer looked first at Hart, then at me, then back at Hart. "There is another possibility, one you might find agreeable, Mr. Hart. You can be your own lawyer if you want, but you could have Mr. Stevens as standby counsel. He can advise you, assist you, and if you later change your mind about self-representation, he could step right in and take over."

Nathan stood there several seconds, as if carefully considering the suggestion. In fact, I realized then that he had no intention of representing himself. What he was angling for was control, the ability to call the shots when it mattered. And Judge Palmer had just made that possible. My client gave me a barely perceptible wink, then turned back to the judge. "That might be acceptable, Your Honor."

***

The field of psychology is at best an inexact science. Symptoms can be misinterpreted and a person misdiagnosed, each false assumption building upon the next until the ignorance and arrogance are impenetrable.

The fact that I hear voices, that I converse with God—they call this having auditory hallucinations. I don't care for the term because it implies that the experience is not real. It dismisses the possibility of transcendental communication with a being that exists in a form beyond our normal comprehension. An extremely limiting view, don't you think?

And what if it is real? What if, for some reason you can't imagine, you have been chosen? Why should you not embrace the possibility and all its potential? Why dismiss it out of hand? These are questions that never seem to be asked in the world I now inhabit. To suggest the possibility is to admit that you are insane. As a result, I seldom acknowledge the voices that, though quieted by the medications, have never been completely silenced.

I have been hearing the voices now for many years, at least since my early teens. Most of the time, even without the medications, they have been faint, like quiet conversations you might overhear in a restaurant—noticeable but only a minor distraction. At times, the voices are more intense, more insistent. Shouted demands rather than quiet suggestions. Hateful and vicious invective. These, I acknowledge, can be quite distracting and unnerving.

My mistake was not in listening and communicating with the voices, but rather in doing so out loud and in the presence of others. People naturally fear what they don't understand. It took me a while to fully appreciate this and to modify my behavior accordingly, but by then it was too late.

The other major symptom contributing to my diagnosis is what they call delusional thinking—in my case, that my father, my uncle, and I have all been operatives of the Unit at one time or another. Again, the leaders of the Unit are not gods, but they are very clever, very careful, and very powerful. They are masters of manipulation, operating under a cloak of secrecy so strong and pervasive that to most people they are invisible.

My inability to convince others of this truth has been frustrating—very frustrating—but it doesn't make it a delusion. It is said that the Devil's greatest evil is to convince people that he does not exist. I have learned, however, as with the voices, that the more I persist along this line, the crazier I am thought to be. To argue about it is pointless.

I ask that you consider the possibility that these "symptoms" are not really signs of mental illness at all, but rather of extraordinary abilities and experiences. Hearing voices is not necessarily a bad thing. Not everyone who sometimes drinks to excess must go the AA route and never have another drink. Some people can learn to control their drinking. Likewise, one can learn to control the voices, instead of vice versa. And just because something cannot be presently proven does not make it untrue.

***

The digital clock on the sign outside the bank reads 2:33 p.m., and the growl in my stomach reminds me that I have had nothing but coffee since I hit the road this morning. A minute later, I spot the Burger King sign and pull in, surprised to see, at this time of the day, several cars in the parking lot. I almost don't stop, wary of large groups of people.

But I now realize that I am very hungry, and my desire to eat something—and quick—has suddenly become quite compelling, counterbalancing my security concerns. I back into a space so the temporary tag is not readily visible. When I enter the restaurant, all of the customers and employees stop what they're doing to look at me, and I am thinking that this was not a good idea at all. But then they all turn back in their seats and continue their conversations.

I notice one man talking into his wristwatch, and I strain to make out the words to see if he is talking about me. But all the conversations in the room are a jumble of voices, blended together and at such a volume that it is impossible for me to focus on any one of them. By sheer force of will, I suppress the panic that threatens to paralyze me, determined not to show my distress. The buzzing noise decreases to a tolerable level as I approach the counter.

The young girl smiles at me and says, "Welcome to Burger King. May I help you?" I give her my order, pay, then stand back against the wall and survey the room again, looking for anything, anyone, out of place. Two teenagers in a back booth look over at me, then turn back to each other and whisper something. They look at me again as they both get up from their seats, empty their trays into the trash can, and then start walking toward me.

One of them heads for the bathroom, but the other keeps heading my way. He stops several feet away. "Florida State fan?" He points to the baseball cap on my head.

I nod. "You bet," I say, quickly recovering.

"That's where I want to play," he says. "My coach says I've got a good shot at it."

This is way more information than I needed to know, but I give him the appropriate words of encouragement and he seems satisfied. When his friend emerges from the bathroom, the boy says "Maybe I'll see you there next year."

"Good luck," I say as the two head toward the door. The ball player waves in response.

Well. That went pretty well, especially considering the alternatives. When the girl calls my number, I collect my burger and head outside. I had planned to take it with me, but it is a beautiful day, a little cool but sunny, perfect for lunch *alfresco*. I'm also thinking I can get some writing in. So I grab my notebook from the truck and head over to an outside eating area, away from the building, and plop myself down at a concrete table.

The first bite of the burger is heaven. My sense of taste is now quite enhanced, and I savor every bite, taking my time to make it last. The sun on my face feels warm and soothing. Except for brief bumps in the road, some mild distortions in my sensory perceptions at times, my transition off the drugs has been easy and most satisfying. My old confidence is returning. Yes, it is good to be alive and free.

I open the notebook and begin to write.

CHAPTER 11

Judge Palmer's ruling allowing Nathan to be co-counsel complicated matters considerably for the hospital, since it carried with it the right of reasonable access to information and witnesses. Nathan would have to be given some freedom of movement. The parameters had been the subject of much debate. The judge settled on a compromise: Nathan would be allowed access to phone and Internet services and whatever books and reading materials I brought him. He could participate in interviews or depositions of witnesses at the hospital, in which event he could be secured and supervised as the hospital administration deemed appropriate.

Shortly after the ruling, I was asked to meet with the hospital administrator, Karl Mathews, and other key staff to discuss security protocol. At least that's the way Frank Hutchinson put it when he called to arrange the meeting. I suspected it was more about PR concerns than security.

We met in Mathews' office, which was tastefully though not lavishly furnished and decorated. Present were Mathews, Frank and Barbara Hutchinson, Andy Rudd, and Rebecca Whitsen. We all sat around a large, oval-shaped oak table, which Mathews told me had been built twenty-five years before by some of the patients. The man was tall and thin, with a small paunch the size of a honeydew melon. He spoke with a measured cadence and seemed to choose his words carefully, a skill of many career bureaucrats. I decided early on that I didn't much like him.

He was, however, the only one in the assembled group who wasn't on Nathan's list of suspects, though I imagined that if I were to mention his name it soon would be. Not that any of the others were compelling alternative suspects, based on what Theo had been able to dig up.

Rebecca Whitsen, for example, had a connection to both victim and defendant, but I had no information that there was bad blood between her and Rosenberg, nor any other motive for murder on her part. And she had a good alibi. She had been reached by phone at her apartment in Tallahassee when one of the staff called to tell her about the murder.

Andy Rudd was a more appealing alternative. Big and broad shouldered, he had an air of arrogance about him often associated with people who try desperately to hide their intense insecurities. I was inclined to accept Detective Browning's assessment of his intellectual capacity, but I didn't want to underestimate the man. Meanness and corruption have their own cunning. The fact that he still had his job, much less was attending this meeting, while under investigation for sexual abuse of patients told me a good deal about him—and about his boss.

Did he have sufficient time to kill Rosenberg, plant the evidence, and reappear on the scene? It was a little tricky but doable, I thought, certainly if he had not acted alone. This latter theory, however, complicated things even more.

Barbara Hutchinson was hard to read. She was not an unattractive woman, but despite her best efforts, she had been unable to either stop or hide the effects of aging. The angular jaw and high cheekbones, once prominent features of her classic beauty, now made her look harsh and bitter. The hazel eyes that once sparkled with the optimism and promise of youth, captured in the photo I had seen on Frank's desk, now reflected the cynicism of a middle age that had come too quickly for her.

Theo had confirmed with some of the staff the rumor, as asserted by Nathan, that Rosenberg and she had been having an affair. But that was all he had confirmed: the rumor. There was no hard evidence of the liaison. But assuming it was true, it opened up possibilities as to both Frank and

Barbara Hutchinson. Maybe Rosenberg broke it off: the old hell-hath-no-fury motive. Maybe her husband found out. Maybe it was a little bit of jealously mixed with humiliation, if Rosenberg was rubbing his face in it. There was at least something to explore in the motive realm. And their alibi was mutual: They were at home watching television. Convenient.

All of them were polite, though I could feel the tension in the air. Of course, they all knew why I had been invited to their little meeting. They wanted me to help keep Nathan under control, to keep this from becoming more of a public relations nightmare than it already was. Wasn't going to happen, though.

Now don't get me wrong. I had my own problems with the little shit. He had played me, jerked my chain good. Nathan had outmaneuvered me, and I was pissed at myself for not having seen it coming. What was even more maddening, I could see his point, would probably have done the same thing in his position. My initial anger had subsided into a sort of cynical apathy. Let him hang himself then, if he insisted he knew better than his lawyer.

Somewhere inside me, though, that competitive urge to win and that pesky sense of professionalism gnawed at me. I realized to my chagrin that I didn't want off the case. For better or worse, I wanted to see it through. Regardless, I wasn't about to conspire with the hospital staff against him. I get pretty protective when it comes to my clients, even the assholes.

"Perhaps," I told them, "my client should be present if we're going to talk about security protocol. Indeed, if he knew I was meeting with you without him, he would probably consider it a betrayal." Which was why, of course, I didn't plan to tell him about it.

Mathews frowned. "That is what we wanted to avoid, quite frankly. We just need to figure out how to accommodate Mr. Hart and maintain order and security as well."

"We could increase his medication to a more reasonable level," Barbara Hutchinson suggested. She looked over in Whitsen's direction, perhaps looking for support, but it was not forthcoming.

"The man is housed in a secure facility," Whitsen said, "and already significantly medicated. I don't think it is appropriate to alter the patient's treatment for the convenience of the hospital. There is too much of that already."

The others shared a look. This was not what Mathews and the others wanted to hear, I was sure. So much for a united front. "Jesus," Rudd said under his breath.

"To the contrary," Barbara Hutchinson jumped in. "It is entirely appropriate to alter treatment based on the patient's change in circumstances." The woman touched her hair with her hand, smoothing it down. "He's looking at prison now, adjusting to a completely new environment."

When Rebecca asked if that meant they had concluded Nathan was guilty, they looked at her as if she had completely lost her mind. "You mean you haven't?" Barbara Hutchinson asked.

"He is entitled to the presumption of innocence."

"That's only in court, my dear," Barbara said. "Not in the real world." She looked at her husband for confirmation.

He obliged. "Look," he said, "I was a criminal defense attorney for years. Trust me: The evidence against him is overwhelming."

Trusting Frank Hutchinson was something Rebecca Whitsen was apparently not inclined to do. "Yes, that may be. Still, he has articulated some alternative suspects and theories to me." She looked over at me then, prompting the others to do likewise. This, of course, was just what they were afraid of.

"Yeah? What's he saying?" Rudd folded his arms and leaned back in his chair, looking first at me, then Whitsen.

"I'm afraid that is confidential communication that I am not at liberty to divulge." Rebecca was making a point to be very formal.

"Me either," I said.

"You can confer with a colleague, though, for the purposes of diagnosis or treatment," Barbara Hutchinson said, looking at Whitsen.

"Yes," Rebecca said, maintaining the formality, "although that would not be the purpose were I to repeat his words here."

"Oh, great," Frank said. "That's all we need. This freak is going to parade everybody from the hospital in front of the jury with some wild conspiracy theory. And even if Judge Palmer won't let him do it, he'll get plenty of press coverage with his ranting." He looked at her as if she were to blame.

Rebecca was having none of it, though. "I don't see how you can stop him from presenting his defense or why you would want to," she said. "He is, after all, a paranoid schizophrenic, right? Surely you're not concerned that he will be taken seriously. If you do try to muzzle him, it will confirm his suspicions, make him more determined to tell the world about it, and give him the credibility he would not otherwise have."

Karl Mathews looked around the room, giving the others a chance to counter the logic of the observation. No one said anything. After a few seconds he turned to Whitsen. "Rebecca, I understand your situation. I'm sure you will exercise discretion in the matter in the interest of both the client and the hospital." He waited for some affirming statement or nod from the psychologist but received none.

Realizing he had reached a dead end, he changed direction and asked Rudd to explain the proposed security protocol, assuring me at the same time that it was just a starting point. His main goal, he said, was the welfare of the residents.

I had my doubts but said that I appreciated his cooperation and flexibility. I assured him I wasn't looking to make things more difficult for him and the staff. I'm not sure he believed me either, but he expressed his appreciation for my cooperation as well. When Mathews announced the end of the meeting and thanked everyone for coming, I started to make my way to the door, headed to meet with my client.

"Mr. Stevens?"

I turned to face Rebecca Whitsen. "Yes?"

"Can you spare a few minutes? I'd like to speak to you about Mr.

Hart." She paused a couple of seconds. "It may be relevant to his case."

I looked around the room at the faces of the woman's colleagues, all of whom had stopped in their tracks, glaring at Whitsen. I felt like the student who has just been singled out by the teacher for some special recognition. "Sure," I said, and as we walked out of the building together, I could almost feel the daggers in my back.

We walked in silence for several seconds before the psychologist spoke. "Mr. Stevens . . ."

"Ted, please."

She gave me a small smile. "Okay, first names it is. I'm Rebecca." She hesitated a couple of moments, then started again. "So, Ted, you have heard about my unpleasant experience at St. Elizabeth's with a former patient?"

The reference was to her last place of employment in Washington, D.C., and to a patient who had stalked her, tried to terrorize her. I didn't want to admit that I had been snooping into her past, but of course I had and was sure she would assume as much. "Only the basics," I said, "though from what I heard, unpleasant experience would be a gross understatement."

She held her briefcase in both hands, pressed against her chest as she walked. "Perhaps," she said, "you should know some of the details, as it might have a bearing on the current situation with your client."

"I'm listening."

She smiled slightly as she looked down at her hands. "Cindy Sands was charged with the murder of her parents, apparently for their money. She cleaned out their bank accounts and took off before the police could implicate her in their deaths. She was arrested two years later, found incompetent to proceed, committed to our facility, and assigned to me. It became obvious to me early on that she was faking her supposed schizophrenia. And she knew I knew. Despite that, we got along well. She was, I think, just trying to string it out as long as she could, hoping for some opportunity of escape to present itself."

The psychologist brushed her hair behind her ear, then pulled on the ear lobe as she hesitated a moment. "In time, though, she became too attached to me, very possessive. Eventually, she grew more and more obsessive and increasingly aggressive toward me, prompting me to withdraw as her psychologist. Another psychologist was quickly assigned and in short order determined that Cindy had regained her competence. A hearing was scheduled for thirty days out."

"That's when she escaped?"

Rebecca held up her hand as to a child who is trying to get ahead of the reader of a story. "Cindy was both outraged and hurt that I had 'deserted' her, as she put it, and she began to send me messages via e-mail or with letters cut from magazines. At least I assumed it was her, though it wasn't clear how she managed to get past security. Anyway, two days before the scheduled competency review hearing, she escaped."

We passed through the entrance of the building in which Rebecca had her office. As we stood before the elevator, she continued her story. "Despite a massive manhunt, Sands seemed to have just vanished. Then, about a week after the escape, I spotted her one day on my way into work, standing underneath a street lamp as my taxi passed by. Cindy waved to me and smiled, and did like this." Rebecca made a slicing motion underneath her throat to illustrate.

"I reported the sighting to the police, as I did when the messages started to come again in my e-mail and regular mail at work and then the handwritten notes left on my front door. At one point they had a cruiser making regular passes by my home, but the police were never able to spot her, nor did I ever see her again."

The elevator opened, and I waited for the two occupants to exit. They both nodded a greeting to Rebecca, which she returned. Once inside with the doors closed, she gave me a tight smile, pushed the button for the third floor, and said, "About six weeks later, I got a call from the detective assigned to the case. He told me they had found a body burned beyond recognition in a mobile home fire, and they thought it might be

Cindy Sands. Apparently, they had an ID from the landlady who had rented it to her the month before, personal items in a car parked out front belonging to Cindy, and a ring on the body's finger that had belonged to her. The mobile home itself was completely destroyed in the fire."

"Those things go quickly once they start." The elevator doors opened and I followed Rebecca out into the hall. "Did they determine the cause, the origin? Was it arson?"

"Accidental," she said over her shoulder as she walked. "They figured she fell asleep in bed while smoking, aided in her sleep by the contents of a liquor bottle that was found empty next to the bed." She stopped at the entrance to her office and turned to face me. "Anyway, two days later the detective called back to tell me the medical examiner was able to make a positive identification of the body as Cindy's, based on her dental records on file with the hospital. Plus, he said the fingerprints in the car were a match."

I followed her inside her office. Rebecca hung her jacket on the rack in the corner, then sat behind the small oak desk, motioning me to the chair opposite her. I took a seat and looked around the room. The walls were institutional pale yellow. The paintings were generic, Impressionist landscapes. On the bookcase behind the desk were photographs, family mostly but some landscapes there too. The obligatory diplomas and certificates were grouped together, proportionally, on the wall on each side of a bookcase. A small area rug in front of the desk coordinated nicely with the paintings and the pale yellow of the walls.

I turned back to Rebecca and prompted, "So, did the messages stop?"

She nodded. "Yes. I took a leave of absence for a couple of weeks from the hospital and eventually decided that I needed a fresh start, a change of scenery. I read about an opening here, applied, and put the ugly experience behind me. Or so I thought, until I started receiving these."

She reached over and grabbed a file folder from the corner of the desk, opened it, and pulled out several e-mail messages, which she spread in front of me. I started reading the e-mails as she continued. "As you can see, each message says it is from CindySands521@yahoo.com."

I noticed the dates on the e-mails. They had begun a few weeks before Rosenberg was killed and continued about once every couple of weeks thereafter. The contents of the messages were juvenile, cliché-ridden tripe: "You can run but you can't hide!" "You didn't really think you could kill me off that easy, did you?" Some were quite short. Others, the more recent ones, were more lengthy. There were references to supposed details of conversations between Whitsen and Sands.

"I didn't think much of it in the beginning," Rebecca continued. "Plenty of people knew of the incident. And it wouldn't be difficult to learn my e-mail address. I thought somebody was just exercising his sick sense of humor. But these later messages contain information that only someone who has studied the case thoroughly would know. Someone has gone to a lot of trouble to try and harass me with these."

"Is there a way to trace these things, find out who is sending them?"

"I took them to our technology officer. He explained that a person who knows his way around computers can do what they call a spoof, where he routes an e-mail through various servers to conceal its actual place of origin. But, again, if you know what you're doing, you can eventually trace it back to the network and sometimes the individual PC in that network."

"Any luck?"

"Not yet. He says he may be able to narrow it down to a particular network and even the individual computer if the e-mails keep coming."

"You're thinking, though, it might be someone at Florida State Hospital, right?"

She looked at me, a hint of surprise on her face, but she nodded. "Perhaps."

"Which means it's either a patient or a staff person. Any likely candidates?"

She frowned. "I have not made a lot of friends among my colleagues,

I'm afraid. I have an independent streak that plays against the go-along-to-get-along mentality that generally pervades these places. Petty jealousy sometimes leads to petty efforts to sabotage another's professional career or just harass her for spite."

I waited to see if she might get more specific. She did. "Barbara Hutchinson seems particularly bent on pushing me out. She was against hiring me, I know, and for some reason she seemed to think I was her competitor, professionally and otherwise."

I arched my eyebrows. "Otherwise?"

"I think she had something going on with Rosenberg and thought I was making a play for him."

"Were you?"

She snorted a laugh. "The man was disgusting. He did make a move on me one day in his office, but I shut him down quickly and firmly."

That, I thought, would not be hard to imagine, but I didn't say so.

"Anyway," she continued, "I mentioned the e-mails to her the other day, just to see her reaction. If she knew about it, she did a good job of hiding it. Plus she professed her relative computer illiteracy. Her husband, she said, was the computer geek in the family."

I remembered the nice setup in Frank's office, the PC magazines on the credenza. "Anybody else?"

She hesitated for a couple of seconds. "On the other hand, Nathan is very adept with a computer and has always had access to one at the hospital. Indeed, it is one of the biggest carrots the staff has to keep him in line. "

"Hmm," I said, nodding slowly. "What makes you think it has some connection to Nathan or Rosenberg's murder?"

"I'm not at all sure it does, but there's something else."

"Yes?"

She began to rifle through the file again. "I understand the detectives recovered a cigarette lighter from the crime scene? Gold plated with black trim?"

"That's right."

She took a digital photo print out of the file and handed it to me.

I looked at the print. Though it wasn't a great copy, it was good enough for me to see that it appeared to be a photo of the lighter found under Rosenberg's desk. "Yeah," I said. "That's it. Did you get the photo from Browning?"

She shook her head. "This is not from the Rosenberg crime scene. It's from the crime scene of Cindy's parents."

CHAPTER 12

As soon as the ball went up, I was moving toward the basket on the off side. Perry, the player I was guarding, had been moving up the lane, looking for a pass, so he was out of position when his teammate threw up the jumper from the wing. I turned and placed my back against Perry, my arms out to the side. Then, as the ball moved closer to the basket, so did I. I bent my knees slightly, timed the jump perfectly, and pulled down the rebound.

I made the outlet pass to Frank, who in turn whipped it quickly to Kate, who had made it close to center court. Then Frank and I started running up the court on either side of her, leaving the slackers to bring up the rear. Two of the defenders had made it back and were positioning themselves to try to stop the fast break. The first guy had to come out to Kate, get her to pull up, denying her the layup. The other stayed in the center of the lane, watching Kate, ready to go either way, depending on whom she passed to.

Kate did pull up, but she kept her dribble, waiting as Frank and I got closer to the basket. She stutter-stepped, dribbled to her right, then pivoted, turned her back to the defender, and, while looking in Frank's direction, flipped the ball over her left shoulder, a perfect no-look pass that hit me in stride. The man near the basket had gone with the fake and was unable to recover in time. I laid the ball against the glass for an easy layup and the game.

"Great pass," I said to Kate as we exchanged high fives.

"Way to run the court," she replied, and we both headed for the water fountain.

Frank called out behind us. "You two staying for another?"

We both said no, and the others regrouped to begin the next game. I was dripping with sweat, like a leaky faucet, exhausted, and sucking wind badly. Kate, on the other hand, had barely broken a sweat and looked as if she could keep going for hours. I followed her and watched from behind as she bent to take a sip of water, admiring her form, hidden somewhat beneath loose-fitting shorts and jersey over a T-shirt.

She finished and moved aside for me. I wiped the sweat off my forehead with the back of my wrist band, feeling self-conscious. Kate had been playing ball at the Christian Life Center for several years. There had been some reservations at first from the guys—and some awkwardness—but the novelty of her gender had long ago worn off. The former college player obviously loved the game, and she was very good at it. She played hard but fair, and she wasn't afraid to bang it up with you under the boards either. She was a scrapper with finesse. Any contact on the court, though, while going for a rebound or a loose ball, was completely nonsexual. That was the only option. So I tried to put the thought out of my mind, only minimally succeeding.

Kate and I lingered by the water fountain, trading awkward pleasantries until I finally got around to asking her about her pending divorce. "How's it going?" I asked and immediately regretted bringing up what was surely a sore subject. But despite the small frown, Kate seemed eager to talk about it.

"It's going, which is a good thing," she said, looking down. "Greg is being a horse's ass about things, but we're talking."

The Waters family—Kate had kept her maiden name of Marston—was old-time Tallahassee, extremely wealthy and influential in business, political, and civic affairs in the community. They owned three automobile dealerships, two banks, and quite a bit of real estate, and they made up the core of one of the oldest and largest law firms in the city. Like his wife, Greg had played ball at the Christian Life Center for years until his knees refused to cooperate. But, unlike Kate, he played basketball the way he played life, with a sense of entitlement. Truth be known, I'd never much liked him. "Greg can be a horse's ass," I agreed, shaking my head from side to side. Then, in my Tony Soprano voice, I added, "You want I should get a couple of guys, work him over or something, get him to see reason?"

She gave me a small smile. "Thanks. I'll keep it in mind." After a moment's hesitation, she asked, "What about yours?"

"We're not—talking, that is."

And that was the most frustrating part of the whole thing. I felt as though if I could just talk to Beth, we could work things out, maybe even get back together. And, yes, I had been thinking that this was an option, as my lawyer had suggested, after I'd had time to cool down. We had been at this point once before, and she had come back. I still loved her, and I thought she loved me too.

Kate frowned. "She still has the restraining order?" I nodded. "What about visitation with Annie?"

"Not much progress on that front either." I knew that Kate was genuinely interested but was also sure she didn't really want me to unload either. I was engulfed in a constant melancholy, which at times became a sadness so deep and dark nothing could penetrate it, but nobody wanted to hear that weepy, wimpy stuff. She was just being polite, which I appreciated nonetheless.

She didn't say anything for a few seconds, perhaps thinking I would say more. "Listen, Ted, if I can help in any way, let me know. I know Beth, of course, and think she's a good mother. But you're a good father too. I'd be happy to testify to your parenting skills, your involvement in Annie's activities."

Our daughters were close in age, had attended the same school, and had played organized sports together—if you could call anything kids that age did organized—so she'd had plenty of opportunities over the years to observe me interact with Annie. I smiled at her and put my hand on her shoulder. "Thanks, Katie. I'm hoping it doesn't come to that, but if it does, I may take you up on your offer."

Looking into her large brown eyes, seeing the genuineness of her offer of help and support, the thought crossed my mind that perhaps I might ask her out. Nothing serious, maybe a bite to eat or something. See where it went. Misery loves company, right? A couple of times I started to say something, but it caught in my throat.

As if suddenly reading my mind and wanting to save me the embarrassment of the moment, Kate said, "Well, I better hit the showers. Greg's bringing Maggie to the house at eight. Who knows? Maybe he'll be on time for a change." Then she was walking off down the hallway with a "See you later, Ted" and a wave of her hand.

As I watched her disappear into the locker room, I could have kicked myself. What had I been thinking? While I would have no compunction about going out with another woman, Kate, unlike me, had class and discretion. Even if she found me halfway attractive, she would not want to give even the appearance of involvement with another man right now. Still, part of me chastised the other part for failing to act. Fear of rejection perhaps?

I had another chance when I walked out of the building some thirty minutes later and saw Kate putting her gym bag in the trunk of her car. I could've gone over to her, but I hesitated in the shadow of the entrance, like a voyeur, watching after her as she pulled out of the parking lot. Then I adjusted the bag on my shoulder and headed for the office. A vague sense of opportunity lost followed after me.

***

The Rose Building was empty when I entered a few minutes later and made my way up the stairs to my office. I plunked down my gym bag on the floor, got a bottle of water from the mini fridge, and stood for a few minutes at the bay window, watching the night traffic below. I finished the water, placed the empty bottle on the corner of my desk, then sat down and started going through my phone messages.

The first was from Dick Ervin, opposing counsel on the new construction case I'd picked up recently. I called the number, got the answering machine, and left a message. The next was from the mother of one of my criminal clients. I didn't really want to, but I called her back.

"Hello?"

"Hey, Ms. Johnson. This is Ted Stevens, returning your call."

"Why you trying to sell my son down the river? Rashaun says you told him to take the State's deal."

So much for pleasantries. "That's right, Ms Johnson. I did advise him that I thought it would be in his best interest to take the plea offer. I think it's reasonable."

"Ten years? You think ten years for my baby boy is reasonable?"

Her voice was sharp and getting louder. Experience has taught me, however, that it's generally best to let them get it all out without interruption. So I did.

"I paid you good money, Mr. Stevens. I had to go to every family member and friend I know to get up the money, but I did it 'cause Rashaun needed help. He didn't want no public defender, he said, and you had done right by him before. But now you take my money and you sell him down the river. Now that ain't right, and you know it. I can't have my baby go to prison. He a father now. He needs to be with his son."

The anger had been diffused a bit now with sadness, and I could sense the air releasing from her balloon. When it appeared she had said all she planned to for the time being, I responded in what I hoped was a calm and comforting voice, fighting back the urge to give her what she had given me.

"Ms. Johnson. I know it's not what either you or Rashaun wanted to hear, but sometimes a lawyer has to give a client bad news. Now, I could lie or gloss over things, give you and Rashaun false hope, but I've investigated the case, reviewed the evidence the State has, and it looks mighty bad for Rashaun. The truth is, he robbed that guy at the ATM machine. The State knows it. He knows it. And you know it. They got him on the surveillance camera. And it's a real good, clear picture. If he goes to trial, he stands a good chance of being convicted. And if he does, the State is going to ask for life. I know ten years is a long time, but considering what he's looking at if he goes to trial. . . ." I left the rest of it unspoken but clearly conveyed.

After a few seconds, she said, "Rashaun says that ain't him on that video."

I sighed. "You saw it yourself, Ms. Johnson. Tell me that's not your baby boy Rashaun on there."

She couldn't, of course, and so she said nothing for several seconds. "Can't you get him probation, maybe a little county jail time? He's only a boy, and he ain't never been in any trouble. Not like this."

I hesitated a moment before responding. "Yes, he's young, and yes, he doesn't have a bad record, but he's hit a home run on this one. The prosecutor wanted twenty-five years. I've got him to cut that by more than half, with the rest on probation. I know this guy. That's as good an offer as we're going to get. And that offer expires if he doesn't accept it by pretrial."

A long silence followed on the other end. I was about to say something to prompt her when she spoke again, the anger now completely gone from her voice, replaced by a sad resignation. "Okay, Mr. Stevens. I'll talk to him."

I knew I was right in my evaluation of the case. Her "baby" had stuck a nine millimeter in the face of a young college student, scared the shit out of him, and robbed him of not only his money but his dignity, his innocence, and his sense of security and well-being. Rashaun Johnson deserved what he would get, and he had no right to anyone's sympathy. But as I hung up the phone, I couldn't help but feel sorry for the young man who would have to face the consequences of his rash and stupid decision, and I grieved for his mother's loss.

***

I had gone through all my e-mails, drafted a set of interrogatories in a civil case, and was about to leave when I heard the front door open and close, then the sound of footsteps up the stairs. Thirty seconds later, Theodious Williams was standing in my doorway. I swiveled my chair to face him.

"Odious, I'm beginning to think you have absolutely no social life. Every time I come to the office at night or on the weekend, you're here."

"Funny, I was thinking the same thing about you." He looked over at the gym bag on the floor and said, "Been playing round ball?"

"Yeah, over at the church, and I am whipped. You should join us sometime."

"I'm not really a basketball player," he said.

I frowned.

"What?"

"Nothing."

"Oh, I get it. You never met a black man who wasn't a player?"

"No, you're just the first to admit it."

Theo frowned briefly, then gave me a small grin, shaking his head. "I guess I opened myself up for that one."

"I guess you did."

I opened the mini fridge behind my desk, took out two more bottles of water, then turned back to him, raising one of the bottles up in question. He nodded and I tossed him the bottle. We both took swallows. I motioned to him to take a seat, which he did, then I went right to the Hart case.

I told Theo about the meeting with the hospital administration, about Rebecca Whitsen's startling revelation. He was instantly intrigued. Something to explore but not to make public. A two-edged sword, he observed. "If there is some connection with the cigarette lighter and everything, it has possible blow-you-out-of-the-water potential. On the other hand, if Nathan is behind it . . ."

"Which could very well be the case."

"If he is behind it, then it will make him seem even more diabolical, more scheming, and more guilty."

"So," I said, "how we looking so far for more mundane alternative suspects and theories?"

"Not particularly promising. What makes it so difficult is we're looking for people who not only had a motive and opportunity to murder the victim but to frame our client as well. That narrows the field considerably." So far, most of the people didn't have an apparent motive or the requisite opportunity or, in some cases, either.

"You checked out Nathan's first case, the murder of his family?"

He nodded. "Read the court file, looked at all your notes, talked to the detective on the case. I couldn't talk to his lawyer since he's dead, but the PD's investigator is still around, and he was pretty helpful. Plus they let me copy whatever was in their file."

I nodded.

"Anyway, there was absolutely nothing to corroborate his story. There was no forensic evidence of other people in the house that night—no prints, no DNA, no empty shells, no bullet holes in walls, nothing. No witnesses who saw anybody skulking around or anything else unusual. I'd say his story about the Unit operatives attacking was creative but not at all believable."

"What about his injuries?"

"Either self-inflicted or the result of his family members trying to defend themselves."

"That was my initial conclusion too."

Theo hesitated a moment, then asked, "What do you mean, initial? You change your mind?"

"No, I still think he's a delusional killer."

Theo gave me a long look, frowned, then said, "On the other hand, it looks like nobody really explored the theory, including his lawyer. Everybody dismissed it as the fantasy of a crazy person. I mean, after all, that's what the shrinks were saying." He was silent for a few seconds. "There may be some secret espionage groups operating out there. Probably are. There're certainly a lot of wackos on the Internet who are sure of it, a lot of conspiracy nuts. But I haven't uncovered any evidence to support what appears to be a primary delusion for our client."

"So the uncle's not a spy?"

Theo shook his head. "Again, everything I've been able to learn about our client and his family suggests there is no connection to espionage except in Nathan's head. Robert Hart is what he appears to be, a college professor of international studies who does a little consulting work for the State Department on the side."

"How about the uncle personally? Any motive to want to see Nathan either behind bars or in the hospital?"

"Funny you should ask. There may be another motive, though not a particularly strong one, and it's kind of complicated. He's the trustee for the trust his brother, Nathan's father, established. Under the terms of the trust, the uncle decides what, if anything, to pay to the beneficiaries. And as trustee, the uncle has complete, unbridled discretion in handling the trust funds. The beneficiaries include Nathan, Nathan's deceased brother, and the uncle's three kids. The beneficiaries are entitled to their share, unfettered, when they reach the age of thirty, provided they can demonstrate competency and the ability to manage their own affairs."

"Kind of difficult if you're confined to a mental hospital."

"Indeed."

"I guess this would give the uncle incentive to keep him in the hospital?"

"Kind of." He took a swallow of water.

"How much principal is in the trust?"

"Don't know. It's sealed."

I arched my eyebrows at him. "That's unusual."

"All I know is, that's what the trust document specifies, and when I went to look at the file in probate, I was allowed to see the trust instrument but not the annual reports or other accounting documents. That, I am told, would take a court order."

I rubbed my chin with my thumb and forefinger and took another sip of water. "I'm thinking I'd really like to know how much money we're talking about."

CHAPTER 13

*R*obert Hart walked back and forth in front of the students with his hands clasped behind his back. His movements were easy and graceful, his voice powerful and confident. He was just concluding a lecture to a large group of undergraduate political science majors, all of whom were furiously taking notes as he spoke. I sat in the back of the classroom, observing Nathan's uncle carefully, trying to see him as the master spy my client insisted he was. He did have a James Bond look about him—an older James Bond. His thick, silver hair was professionally styled, and he wore a dark gray suit, white shirt, and conservative red tie. His ramrod-straight posture added to an air of formality that suggested former military.

I had been planning on talking to the uncle, but it had not been a priority. Now that the lunatic was in charge of the asylum, however, it had jumped to the top of my to-do list. It was why I sat there in Robert Hart's classroom, following up on my client's delusional paranoia, leaving open the possibility that he might be right.

When the buzzer sounded, signifying the end of class, the lecturer abruptly stopped and the students began to file out. As Nathan's uncle began to place his notes and other materials in his briefcase, I made my way down to the front of the classroom.

"Professor Hart?"

He looked up. "Yes?"

I extended my hand. "Ted Stevens, sir. We met during the prosecution of your nephew a few years back."

The man took the extended hand, gripped it firmly, and looked into my eyes, then gave me a quick once over. "Yes, Mr. Stevens, I remember. Nice to see you again," he said, then went back to putting his things in the briefcase.

"And you. I'm in private practice now and, as you may have heard, I've been appointed to represent Nathan on a new charge."

He looked up at me. "Yes, I had heard that." His expression suggested disapproval, but he didn't voice it. "What can I do for you?"

"I was hoping I could have a few minutes of your time, ask you some questions."

Hart closed his briefcase and picked it up. "I've got another class in fifteen minutes. Why don't you call my office and set up an appointment?" As he said this he started to move toward the door.

I began to walk along. "Well, actually, I tried to get an appointment, but your secretary wasn't able to fit me in on your calendar for quite some time. She suggested that I might be able to catch you between classes, maybe talk on the way."

Hart stopped and looked at me again. He figured either that I was lying or that he needed to have a little chat with his secretary. "Very well," he said, then started walking again, me at his side. "Ask away."

"First of all, let me apologize for bothering you at all." I saw his frown relax a little and knew I had chosen the right tack: respectful, deferential. "I wouldn't even be here except my client has insisted, and as you may have read in the papers, the judge is letting him be co-counsel. It's the worst of all possible worlds for me."

The other man nodded, still walking at a good clip. "You're still attorney of record and responsible for what happens, but your client gets to call the shots."

"Exactly. And if I don't explore every lead, every theory he gives me, and show there is nothing there, he can come back later in a post-judgment motion and claim ineffective assistance of counsel, maybe get a new trial."

The professor understood, saying, "What would you like to know?"

By this time, we had exited the building and were headed across Landis Green. It was a warm autumn day, and I was feeling a bit nostalgic as we made our way among the groups of students who were lounging on the grass, some throwing a Frisbee, but I stayed focused on the topic at hand. I started with an open-ended question. "What was Nathan like as a kid, from your perspective?" Hart pursed his lips but didn't answer right away. "As you can imagine," I added, "I never know if the information I get from Nathan is reliable."

The professor gave a small sigh. "Nathan was a bright, good-looking kid who excelled in both academics and athletics, though he was a bit peculiar in some things."

"Such as?"

"He was very religious, bordering on fanaticism, especially for a young kid. I blame that on his mother. Betty was a lovely person, but she was always a couple of cards short of a full deck. Thought she was some messenger of God or something. Didn't seem to have a big effect on his brother, Bobby, but, then, he was older.

"Anyway, Nathan began to go from slightly peculiar to really strange. And he became a control problem. There was underage drinking, pot smoking, discipline problems at school to go with slipping grades. He would improve for a while but then do something bizarre. When he announced a desire to join the Army right out of high school, at the age of seventeen, his parents consented. They hoped maybe it would straighten him out."

"It didn't?"

We paused at the street. Hart looked both ways, then started across, me right beside him. "I think this is where Nathan's delusions really began to take over. He was sent over to Kuwait just after the Gulf War, where he became an aide to the second highest ranked officer in the region. He was basically a secretary, but he imagined that he was privy to very sensitive information, that he overheard various high-level conversations by people who were, according to him, members of this worldwide secret organization."

"The Unit?"

The uncle nodded, still looking straight ahead while he walked. "I'm sure none of this is really news to you."

It was my turn to nod. "But I sure appreciate your perspective on it."

He resumed his narrative, relating that Nathan had seemed to improve, went off to college, and did pretty well for a couple of years. Gradually, he slipped back into a pattern of drugs, poor grades, and trouble with the law. It was obvious, he said, that the boy had real psychological problems, but nobody guessed it was as bad as it was—until he killed his parents and brother.

By this time we had entered the Bellamy Building, the location of his next class. He stopped just inside the entrance and turned to face me. "That's about it, the abbreviated version anyway. Is there anything else?" His body language and tone of voice suggested he assumed the conversation was at an end.

"I have just a few specific questions, if you can spare another couple of minutes."

The professor frowned and looked at his watch. He motioned to me with his head to continue walking with him, then he started off down the hall. "Go ahead. I still have a few minutes before class starts."

I repeated Nathan's claim that he was an operative in the Unit. The uncle snorted a laugh of disgust. Surely, he suggested, there was no need for him to respond to the delusional ravings of a paranoid schizophrenic. Surely, I did not take any of it seriously. I assured him that I did not and that he need not answer any question he didn't want to, at this time. But, I said, my client would probably insist upon a formal deposition in that event. I needed to be able to tell my client and the court that I had pursued all theories suggested by my client.

The man relented. He sighed deeply, then told me, "I am not a spy, nor was my brother. Neither of us ever worked for the CIA or any other covert agency of any kind, official or otherwise. My brother was once a mid-level State Department employee. He moved here in the late eighties to become a professor. I too am an academic."

I gave him a look of embarrassment that said I appreciated the absurdity of the line of questioning, and I assured him that what he said was supported by all the evidence I had. "Still," I said, "both you and your brother were also consultants for the State Department, which is often a cover for CIA types. Both of you made frequent trips out of the country, right? And somehow, this former mid-level State Department employee was able to arrange for his son, a lowly enlisted man in the U.S. Army, to be assigned as an aide to one of the highest ranking officers in the Middle East." I raised my arms and extended my palms.

The man gave me a small smile. "As I said, your client is delusional, and it sounds like you've been reading too many spy novels yourself."

I smiled back at him and decided to switch gears, asking him about the trust that Nathan's father had set up for him. Yes, he said, there was a trust. Yes, he was the trustee. And, yes, he had sought a legal ruling forfeiting his nephew's interest in the trust.

We had stopped now, just outside the classroom, and turned to face each other. "Of course, by the same token," I said, "Nathan is unable to claim whatever lump-sum distribution he may be entitled to under the trust or seek to have you removed as trustee until such time as he is released from the hospital and declared competent."

"That's correct."

"I understand there was a sizable amount of principal in the trust. How much exactly?"

"I don't know what you call sizable. At any rate, the amount of the principal is confidential under the terms of the trust. Those were my brother's specific directions." I arched my eyebrows but said nothing. Hart continued, responding to the unasked question or implication. "My brother trusted me completely, and no bond or judicial oversight was required. However, when Nathan started filing his multitude of pleadings,

I voluntarily submitted the trust document to the Circuit Court, under seal, for review in camera. The judge agreed with my interpretation but abated my action for forfeiture until such time as Nathan is released from the hospital."

"Where did your brother get such a large sum of money to put in a trust on his government salary?"

He smiled thinly. "There you go again. Who said it was a large sum of money?"

I held out my hands, palms up, but said nothing.

"Whatever amount my brother was able to put in the trust, he was able to because he worked hard, was frugal with his money, and was a wise investor. And I know Nathan says that I am stealing money from the trust." I started to say something, but he waved me off. "I live a modest lifestyle and have no need for extravagances. I'm not rich, but I don't need to steal from my nephew to live comfortably. And, contrary to his delusional conspiracy theories, I have no motive to keep him there. I want him out and legally competent so I can pursue my lawsuit, forfeit his interest in the trust, and see that it goes to more deserving beneficiaries. It has nothing to do with greed but all to do with principle."

"Is that what you were discussing with Dr. Rosenberg?"

"Excuse me?"

"When you went to see him." I pulled out a small spiral notebook from my pocket, thumbed through several pages, then looked back up. "According to Rosenberg's appointment calendar, you two had a meeting in his office on June fourteenth, which was just a few days before Nathan's conditional release hearing."

"Oh, that. Yes, that is one of the items we spoke about. As we have established, I have an interest in the mental and legal status of my nephew. Dr. Rosenberg was good about keeping me advised." He extended his hand to me. "Now, if you'll excuse me, I need to attend to my class. If you have further questions, it will have to be later."

I shook the professor's hand and thanked him for his time, then stood in the doorway, watching him walk down the aisle toward the front of the classroom. I noted the expensive clothes he wore, recalled the Rolex I had seen on his wrist. Perhaps he had no need for extravagances, but he certainly was not adverse to them either.

CHAPTER 14

I was outside on my deck that evening, smoking a cigar and drinking a longneck Bud. Bjorn was at my feet, chewing on a tennis ball. I was listening to the sounds of the neighborhood, putting some distance between me and my memories, and putting myself in the mood to make a phone call.

The hearing on the motion to change venue was held in the judge's chambers. Denise told me it wasn't necessary for me to attend, but I had wanted to go. I thought it might be harder for the judge to deny the motion if he had to look me in the face. Besides, it would give me a chance to visit Annie while I was in Panama City. I also hoped it would give me an opportunity to meet Beth face to face.

Didn't work out that way.

In the reception area outside Judge Ralph Simmons' chambers, neither Beth nor her parents were there, only the lawyer. He was a clean-cut man in his early forties with an insincere smile. His name was Barry Thompson, and I disliked him immediately. Nothing he said in the few minutes that passed as we waited for the judge changed this first impression—not the banal small talk he attempted, and certainly not the condescending suggestion for a compromise. Perhaps, he said, we could agree that Annie stay where she was until the Christmas holidays and then reevaluate the situation.

Something about the man's cocky manner, coupled with his sneer of a smile, made the offer seem not just hollow but insulting too. "Nice try,

Barry. You must think I'm a real fool. That's how I got into this situation to start with. The Petronises paying your bill, Barry? Pulling your strings? Well, I believed them before when they said they just wanted to help, while all the time they were plotting behind my back to set me up. No, I think I'd rather just kick your ass in court."

Thompson looked at me, momentarily made speechless by my venomous tone of voice. I looked at Denise, who rolled her eyes and turned away, as if symbolically washing her hands of her volatile client, but she couldn't suppress a small smile of approval. Thompson looked back at me and gave me one of those nasty smiles. "Yes, I've heard about that temper of yours. Never too far beneath the surface, is it?"

Denise stepped between us, facing Thompson, her back to me. "Why don't we talk later, just the two of us?"

"Sure," he said. "Let's see how the judge rules on your motion." There was that insidious smile again and patronizing tone, suggesting an overwhelming confidence. Despite my conviction that the law and the facts were on my side and despite Denise's reassurances that she had dealt with the judge on several cases and found him to be very fair, I was suddenly filled with uncertainty and dread when the receptionist announced that Judge Simmons was ready for us.

The judge was seated behind his desk when we came in. His office was large—large enough that his massive oak desk, a long conference table that abutted it, and a leather couch with two end tables on the opposite wall all fit comfortably within the space. The wood-paneled walls were dotted with photographs, some of family, some that recorded fishing trips, some with the judge next to various officials of note. There were also plaques and certificates. A framed copy of the Constitution of the United States hung on the wall behind him. Except for a small stack of files on the corner, a telephone, and a crystal pyramid paperweight, his desk was clean.

The judge was a small, thin man who seemed dwarfed by the large chair in which he sat. He parted his thin, gray hair in the middle and wore round, wire-rimmed glasses and a bow tie, all of which combined to give him an old-fashioned look. He motioned for everyone to take a seat, greeted the two attorneys of record by name, and then looked over at me, raising his eyebrows.

Denise answered the implied question. "Let me introduce my client, Your Honor. This is Ted Stevens. He is also a lawyer in Tallahassee." I would have offered my hand, but the expanse of desk and table was too great, so I just nodded in the judge's direction.

"Yes," the judge said. "Welcome to Panama City, Mr. Stevens."

"Thank you, judge, but to paraphrase W.C. Fields, all things considered, I'd rather be in Tallahassee."

There were a couple of moments of awkward silence as the others digested this rather risky attempt at humor. "Yes, well, I guess that's why we're here this afternoon," the judge said. He leaned forward in his chair, elbows resting on the desk and his hands intertwined underneath his chin. He looked over at Denise and told her he had read her motion and the response filed by Thompson, as well as the affidavits filed in support of and in opposition to the motion. "Is there anything else you'd like to add this afternoon?"

Denise quickly reviewed the undisputed facts and then summarized her argument. "The law is clear, judge: Venue is proper only where the parties last resided together as husband and wife. And that is Leon County. Residence is a question of intent, not just physical location. There is absolutely no basis to find that the parties ever intended to establish legal residence in Bay County. This was always a temporary arrangement. The last place the parties lived together as husband and wife was Leon County."

The judge nodded and then turned his attention to Thompson, who responded that the parties, indisputably, had been residing in Bay County as husband and wife when his client decided to file for divorce. "In fact, neither the wife nor the child has resided in Tallahassee since early summer. The husband did, however, reside with them sporadically during the summer in Bay County. And the law does not require that the parties establish legal residence, only that they reside there."

He hesitated a moment, looking at the judge. "Moreover," he said, "Bay County is clearly the most convenient forum to decide what is in the best interest of the child. The wife has a large extended family here. Her current teachers, friends of the family, doctors, day care workers—almost all the pertinent witnesses, except the father—reside in Bay County." He leaned forward in his chair slightly. "Isn't it better to inconvenience Mr. Stevens than all these other witnesses?"

Simmons looked over at Denise, giving her the last word.

"Judge, don't let Mr. Thompson take you down this rabbit hole of the most-convenient-forum argument. As you well know, that concept is only applicable if you are choosing between two legally permissible venues. We don't have that here. There is only one legally permissible forum, which is Leon County."

Judge Simmons looked down for a moment, then at both attorneys to make sure there was nothing more. "I'll take the matter under advisement and give you a ruling shortly," he said abruptly, then closed the file folder, signaling that the hearing was over.

I didn't like the fact that the judge had taken the motion under advisement. What was there to think about? It was obvious, wasn't it? Maybe the judge had decided to rule against me and didn't have the guts to tell me to my face. This, combined with the fact that my in-laws had refused to let me talk to Beth or visit with Annie while I was there, had made me anxious, distracted, and generally pissed off all the way back to Tallahassee. It had taken a good bit of time and a fair amount of alcohol before I felt like I could make the call.

I put down my beer, gave Bjorn a pat on the head, and then picked up the portable phone and punched in the familiar number. To my surprise, my wife answered. "Beth, it's Ted."

Silence on the other end for several seconds.

"Beth?"

"Ted, you know you're not supposed to have any contact with me. I don't want you to get in trouble."

Oh, that was rich. "Well, I'd sure hate to see what would happen if you did want to see me get in trouble."

"Don't start with me, Ted."

"Don't start with you? You're the one who got the injunction. You're the one who filed for divorce without even the courtesy of telling me you were going to, much less trying to discuss whatever problems you perceived." I realized my voice was rising and I toned it down. "Why are you doing this, Beth? Why can't we sit down like adults and discuss this? We can make it work."

"I can't, Ted. I just can't. I've tried, but it's like a broken record. It's the definition of insanity, doing the same thing over and over again and expecting a different result."

"Even if you don't want to work on the marriage, at least let's talk about Annie. I can't believe you're trying to keep her away from me."

"I'm not trying. . . ." She let it trail off, then said. "Seriously, we can't be talking."

"That's ridiculous. We are grown-ups. We can do what we want. What, you afraid you'll get in trouble with Mommy and Daddy?" When she didn't respond after a few seconds I prompted, "Beth?" Still nothing, though I could tell she had not disconnected. "Beth?" I said again.

"Ted?" The voice of my mother-in-law.

I cursed under my breath. "Liz, would you put Beth on the phone, please."

"She doesn't want to talk to you, Ted."

"Let her tell me that."

"That's what she was trying to do. And you are in violation of the judge's order by trying to contact her."

"How was I supposed to know she would answer the phone? I'm just calling to talk to my daughter. No law against that, is there?"

Silence on the other end for a moment, then "She's just getting ready for bed, Ted. This is not a good time."

I fought with all my might against the wave of anger that washed over me at her words. I knew that to express it would not be wise, would likely result in a termination of the call. But I also knew that to surrender to her power-seeking manipulation would only encourage her, make it worse in the long run. With great self-control, I took a pull on my cigar, exhaled, then said in a calm, neutral tone of voice, "Listen, Liz, it's only eight-thirty. Isn't it enough that y'all arranged to schedule her for a doctor's appointment this afternoon when you knew I would be there for the court hearing?" I felt the anger rising again and checked myself. "Bad enough you wouldn't let me see my daughter. It's going to look even worse in court if you don't let me at least speak to her."

More silence on the other end as the woman pondered her options. "Ted," she said finally, "the doctor's appointment was scheduled some time ago. We had no idea you intended to appear at the court hearing. And you didn't tell us you were coming until yesterday, and then it was too late to reschedule the appointment." Her voice had a tired tone to it that suggested the circumstances were just a variation on an old, repeated theme or pattern on my part. "There is not and has never been a conspiracy to keep you away from Annie, as you seem to think. We do expect, however, some common courtesy on your part. We have told you that it is best that you call Annie before eight o'clock in the evening."

There were plenty of things I wanted to say, but what came out was, "Okay, maybe you weren't trying to keep me from seeing Annie. It was just coincidence. But the fact is, I didn't get to see her when I was there, regardless of the reason. And I'm sorry I didn't call sooner, but I wasn't where I could talk. So come on, Liz, isn't it more important that Annie talk to her father than adhere to some rigid schedule?"

After a few seconds the woman on the other end surprised me by saying, "All right. Hold on. I'll get her."

I waited for perhaps a minute, then, "Daddy?"

The voice of my daughter, surprised but happy, was like a tonic, as effective as any drug I could buy in smoothing out the rough edges of my psyche. When I finally got to bring her back home, I would have no need for such self–medication, I told myself. "Hi, Pumpkin. How's it going?"

"Fine," she said without conviction. In response to my questions she related in detail what she had done that day, but it was all relayed without enthusiasm. I wondered if perhaps my daughter was not as eager to talk to me as I was with her, but then, after a couple of minutes, she lowered her voice almost to a whisper and said, "Daddy, I miss you. I miss my friends too. When can I come back home?"

Her words filled me with both joy and pain. "I miss you too," I said, then tried to think of the best way to answer her question, remembering the admonishment not to talk to Annie about the case.

"I mean, I like it here okay, but I'd rather be in Tallahassee with you and Mommy. She says y'all decided it was best that I live here. Is that true?"

I chose my words carefully. "No, honey, that is not true. I want very much to bring you and Mama back to Tallahassee. Mama and I just disagree on what to do. That's why a judge is going to decide what's best. It's not something you need to worry about."

"Don't I get to say what I want? I'm almost nine."

Tricky, I thought. I couldn't think of a better response than to tell her the truth. "I'm hoping that we can work it out before the judge has to decide, but if he does, I'm going to ask him to talk to you about what you want—just you and the judge, without me or Mama or Grandma or Grandpa there so you don't have to worry about hurting anybody's feelings."

"Good. I'll tell that old judge just what I want."

I suddenly had an image of my daughter, who was a miniature version of my wife—long, straight black hair, olive skin, and dark eyes that burned with intensity and determination. I was sure she would. When it was time to say good-bye, the dog gave a short bark at something in the distance, and Annie said, "Is that Bjorn?"

"Yes, it is. He says he misses you."

"Oh, I miss him too. Give him a kiss for me, Daddy."

I looked over at the Doberman. He was looking back at me, panting with his long tongue hanging out. "I think we'll wait and let you do it personally." I then promised to do everything I could to bring her home and said good-bye to my daughter. When Annie hung up, I thought I heard another click just afterwards.

CHAPTER 15

*N*athan smiled and waved to a couple of patients we passed. On the outside, he appeared calm and relaxed, even a little cocky, but I noted that the jittery eyes were back. I sensed an underlying tension, an anxiety about him as we walked down the hall of the General Forensics building toward the cafeteria. As per the established protocol, a security guard accompanied us but at a discreet distance.

In his room, minutes before, I had brought him up to date on our investigation, our efforts in building a defense. He had been rapt with attention, very interested in my impression of his uncle, eager for me to pursue the trust angle.

"That's a front for the Unit," he said, satisfied. "You check it out. You'll find he has millions in that account." He was sure that if I would just follow up diligently, I would become convinced of the man's sinister motives and conduct. It seemed to give him a real lift.

Then I told him about the e-mails to Rebecca, the former patient, and the cigarette lighter. I asked him if he had been sending them.

"Now who's paranoid?" he asked.

"Did you send them, Nathan?"

"There are ways to trace those things, you know," he said, evading my question. "The sender can route it all over the place to throw you off, but if you know what you're doing, you can find out what network and even what PC it came from."

"Did you send them, Nathan?"

He grinned. "Of course not. Why would I want to do that?"

"I don't know," I said, truthfully. There was no logical reason, only a sick and twisted one, which was what bothered me. "Just want to make sure you don't dig yourself a deeper hole."

"I'm telling you, it wasn't me." A hint of anger flashed in his eyes, then just as quickly it was gone, replaced by a mischievous glint. "But the whole thing does intrigue me." He rubbed his beard with his fingers. "I knew about Rebecca's past, of course, about Cindy Sands. It was part of her allure, really. And now this." He looked off into space for a couple of seconds before bringing his focus back to me. "Well, it's just too coincidental, Ted, don't you think?"

It seemed a rhetorical question. I simply shrugged.

"Like I say, you can trace those things," he repeated.

"The hospital tech guy is working on it. He thinks they're all coming from somewhere at the hospital," I said, fudging it just a little. "Just can't pinpoint the specific computer."

"Hmm. . . ," he said after a couple of seconds. "Not that I relish the anguish it must cause Rebecca, but I suppose we should hope our mysterious correspondent keeps at it so we can identify the culprit."

"I suppose."

Although I had watched my client carefully throughout this exchange, and though I pride myself on my ability to read people, I couldn't tell if he was lying or not. I had an uneasy feeling about it but couldn't be sure whether it was the situation or his reaction to it. Similarly, I was unsure of the accuracy of my impression of him now as we walked together.

Nathan looked over his shoulder at the guard, then turned back to me. "It's beginning to happen again," he said in a whispered voice.

"What is?"

"They're trying to poison me, slip me the hallucinogens. It's subtle but I can tell the difference, which is why I have to very careful about what I ingest. Vending machines have become my preferred source for food and drink."

I avoided his eyes lest he see the skepticism there, but I think he sensed it anyway.

"I know you think me unduly cautious, even paranoid, in this regard, but I need the full use of my faculties. I must maintain a certain vigilance. Don't you see?"

I didn't but said I did.

"My ability to mix with the general population now has been really helpful. The patients may have their deficiencies, but many are very attuned to their routines and notice when something is different. I've also been able to tap into the gossip grapevine. It might not be accurate, but it's useful just to know what people are saying."

"Uh-huh," I said. "And what are people saying?"

Something caught his eye then and he whispered to me, "Speaking of which, eleven o'clock, one of my sources." He stopped and turned to face me. "Name's Anthony Sims."

He bent his head in the direction of the man across the cafeteria. "Thinks he's God." The man he had indicated looked young, like Nathan, barely out of his teens. "Technically, he says that he is the Son of God rather than God, but if you believe in the Holy Trinity, we're just splitting hairs here."

We began walking toward Sims. "He's always spouting some amalgamated, new-age, populist form of religious doctrine that seems to draw its chief inspiration from the lyrics of the Beatles song, 'I Am the Walrus.'" I gave him a sideways look. "I know," Nathan continued, "but he does seem quite sincere. More importantly, he has his ear to the ground, and most of the time, he's pretty normal."

The phrase about the pot and kettle came to mind, but I kept it to myself.

Nathan approached Sims and made the introductions. Tony bowed slightly toward me as he took my hand in both of his. "I am called Jesus," he said, "the Christ, the Messiah, Prince of Peace, Lamb of God, Savior, the Alpha and Omega, the Way, the Truth, and the Light. . . ."

"He gets the idea, Tony," Nathan said, interrupting him. He turned to me. "He can go on for quite a while." Turning back to Sims, he said, "So, what do you hear, Tony?"

"About what?"

"Don't be coy. Any talk about the murder, about who might have done it?"

"You mean other than you?"

"Yes, other than me."

Tony then gave us a summary of what he said was going around. There were some, he said, including himself, who thought Nathan had been framed."

"So, who's behind it? Any ideas?"

Tony leaned forward and whispered his response. Most of it was obviously wild speculation, but it did corroborate the gossip I had already heard. He gave us the names of two patients who said they had seen Rosenberg and Barbara Hutchinson "making out," as it was described to him. I made a mental note to speak to them both.

"Also," he said, "you'll want to talk to Donnie Mercer."

"Yeah? You got something on Donnie?"

"All I know is that he has been looking for you. He told me he has information on your case, but he wouldn't say what it is."

There was a silence between them for a couple of seconds, broken by Tony. "To me, it looks like the Unit is still after you, Nathan. This is the kind of thing that requires coordination, planning."

I looked at Tony closely. Was he mocking Nathan? Had Nathan put him up to this for my benefit? He and Nathan spent the next couple of minutes discussing the possibilities as to how and through whom the Unit could have worked this evil plan. In the end, though, he returned to the hard reality that this was, no doubt, the view of the minority. Most of the patients, he said, thought Nathan had killed Rosenberg.

"And many are frightened of you, Nathan, or at least uneasy when you're around. You are an oddity among oddities, if you will."

"You don't appear to be frightened," I observed.

His smile was small but serene. "The Son of God knows not the fear of mortal men."

Yeah, I bet. I shrugged and looked at Nathan, who then turned to Sims. "Thanks, Tony. Peace be with you."

"And with you." He turned to me. "Mr. Stevens, a pleasure to see you again."

Again? I didn't want to ask. "Likewise," I said, and watched his back as he moved toward the lunch line. I turned to Nathan. "You want to get some lunch?"

"Not here," he said, with a little impatience in his voice. He pointed his chin in the direction of the adjoining day room. "Let's go where we can talk." I nodded and we walked over to a game table, one that had both a checkerboard and a chessboard painted on it. We took seats opposite each other. Nathan looked around the room quickly, then leaned forward. "I was hoping to see Donnie."

"They're not going to let us talk to him," I said, looking over at the security guards across the room." Frank Hutchinson had insisted that any witness who was either an employee or a patient was not to be questioned without his being present. "So as to protect their rights and those of the hospital," he said. He couldn't really enforce it, but in the interest of détente, I had agreed, knowing that it was Nathan he was concerned about and was sharing that concern to some degree.

Nathan looked at me then, his eyes opened wide, as Jimmy Carter used to do when he wanted to make a point. "Donnie's involved in this somehow. You find out anything on him?"

"I got Theo checking him out. I do know he has a criminal history but nothing significant."

Nathan waved his hand in dismissal. "Listen, let me tell you about Donnie Mercer—what you won't find in any official record. Donnie's in here based on a dual diagnosis of manic-depression and substance addiction. A more accurate description would be to say he's a drug dealer who is very moody and knows what symptoms to exaggerate."

Nathan then told me that, since his admission to the hospital, Mercer had committed several rule violations, even criminal acts—in part, Nathan was sure, just to see if he could get away with it. He routinely managed to get drugs and alcohol onto the grounds without getting caught. On one occasion, Nathan said, he severely beat one of the patients.

"Yeah, guy named Alfred Bushman. Happened after lights out. Alfred made two mistakes that night. One, he sneaked out of his room to smoke a cigarette in the stairwell, and two, he tried to blackmail Donnie for drugs when he saw him coming."

Nathan was silent for several seconds. I figured it was a dramatic pause. I was right.

"Before Alfred knew what was happening, Donnie had kneed him in the balls, put him in a headlock, and rammed his head into the concrete wall, then threw him down the stairs. He told Alfred to say he had been sleepwalking and had fallen down the stairs if anyone asked what happened to him. He told Alfred if he said anything different, he'd come to his bed one night and finish the job. And even though nobody bought it, that was the story Alfred insisted on selling."

"How do you know about it?"

"Donnie never acknowledged it to me directly. He just speculated on what might have happened in a way that said he did. Then he said something to the effect that it was an insignificant event in the life of an insignificant person."

"Well, we have his deposition set for next week. Maybe we'll get a bead on him then."

Nathan shook his head. "Not likely. He knows something, but he's not going to talk about it on the record."

"Hard to say," I said neutrally. As I pondered what my client had just told me, unsure what part, if any, to believe, I looked around the day room. It was moderately crowded, with a variety of activities going on around us. There were a couple of guys on one side of us playing checkers. On the far side of the room, two not-so-athletic patients were having a hard time getting the Ping-Pong ball over the net more than once. There were a couple of patients who just sat by themselves on a bench or chair, rocking back and forth, looking down at the floor. Several more sat in front of the large-screen television, expressionless, unengaged with the images in front of them or around them.

"Game of chess?" Nathan reached for a bag from the shelf under the table.

I looked at my watch. "I don't know. I need to be getting back."

"Trust me. It won't take that long."

I was tempted to take the bait. His arrogance, his assumption that I was no match for him, got under my skin. And Rebecca had mentioned this as a way to build a bond with my client. But I really didn't have the time. "Maybe another time," I said.

He gave me a small, smug grin. "Okay," he said, putting the bag back in its place.

My peripheral vision picked up the image of Nathan's psychologist crossing the room as I heard her name called out. Both us looked in the direction of the voice. One of the patients who had been next to us, debating the artistic value of the movie *Taxi Driver* with another patient, now walked quickly toward Rebecca, who was passing through the room. "I need to talk to you a minute, Dr. Whitsen."

Nathan leaned over to me and whispered. "That's Robert Henderson. His diagnosis is bipolar, though he also has substance abuse problems, as well as some significant physical health issues, all of which have taken a heavy toll."

I took in the image of Robert Henderson. He was exceedingly thin and frail looking with scraggly hair, and his personal hygiene left something to be desired. Rebecca looked at her watch, perhaps contemplating the time this conversation was likely to take. She checked her impatience, though, stopped, and gave the man a smile.

"Hello, Bob. How's it going?" She extended her hand to the patient, who took it warily. The psychologist then subtly wiped her hand on her pants leg.

"Can I ask you something?" the man said, pressing in close.

"Sure, Bob, but can you back up a little bit? Remember, we talked about giving people their personal space."

"Oh, sorry," he said, backing up a step.

"Little more," Rebecca said, pushing the air with the back of her hand. The man obliged and backed up a couple of more steps. Rebecca smiled again. "So, what did you want to ask me?"

Bob turned slightly and waved his hand around the day room. "How come some of these guys who have been here only a few months are getting to walk all over the place without a staff escort? I've been here for almost three years. I can't even go out of the building without an escort. That's not fair. It's not right." There was a hint of anger, a bit of righteous indignation in his voice, but he seemed rather calm overall.

"Now, Bob," Rebecca said, putting her hand on the man's shoulder and gently steering him over to the side a bit. "We've talked about this before. You can't worry about anybody except Bob Henderson. Everybody's different, and they go at their own pace."

Bob frowned. "But . . ."

"No buts about it. Now, I know you had a little bit of a slide a few weeks ago, got off your plan, but you've been doing real well lately, haven't you?" Bob nodded, glad for the praise. "We're going to have a team meeting next week and review your status in terms of privileges. You keep doing well and we can talk about a little more freedom of movement." She gave him another smile. "Okay?"

"Okay," Bob said, somewhat mollified but sure there was something else he needed to say. Before he could think of it, though, the psychologist had disengaged herself and was walking quickly across the room.

Before she reached the corner, though, she turned, paused, and looked back across the day room in our direction. I don't know whether it was intended for Nathan or me or both of us, but she gave a slight frown before she turned around again and disappeared from view.

***

The flashing school zone sign seems to come out of nowhere. Instinctively, I slow the truck, and my eyes go to the speedometer. Then I spot the cop, sitting in his car. There is no need to panic, however. No cause for alarm. This is, after all, a school zone. Not unusual for a police officer to monitor traffic to deter speeders. I feel him staring, though, as I pass by, and my heart skips a beat. My peripheral vision catches his movement, slight, bringing something up to his mouth. A radio? Is he signaling someone up ahead?

Now, now, take it easy. Don't jump to conclusions. You've done nothing wrong.

In my rearview mirror, I can see him watching me. But he doesn't start his car and follow me. One second. Two seconds. As I move down the road, I stare at the patrol car in my mirror, willing it to stay. And it does. I round a curve and lose sight of it.

See, I told you. Nothing to get all worked up about. He was not suspicious. He has not called ahead. There is no roadblock.

Or is there?

***

The sight of students leaving school after the last bell had triggered a memory that, with the threat of the law receding, I return to. It was a parent conference with Gerald Barton, principal of Leon High School. I can remember the details, though it has been several years. We sat in the outer office, my parents and me. It was a little after three in the afternoon. My father appeared calm, if a bit annoyed at having to wait, but my mother was tense. She held on to his hand. None of us said anything. It was like sitting in the waiting room at the hospital, but instead of grief and worry, it was embarrassment that my parents were responding to in their different ways. We were all relieved when the door opened and the principal came out of his inner office.

Mr. Barton had jet-black hair, thick and wavy, which he combed straight back and kept in place with generous amounts of hair gel. His jacket was off, his tie loosened and his sleeves rolled up. He was a tall, thick man with big, beefy hands. He extended one to my father. They shook and exchanged greetings, calling each other by their first names. He did likewise with my mother, but he called her Mrs. Hart. He called my name too but did not offer his hand. Instead, he used it to usher the three of us into his office. Then he closed the door and used his hand again to invite us to have a seat. He tightened his tie, rolled down his sleeves and buttoned them but left the jacket on the rack in the corner. He smiled wanly at us before sitting in his chair. Then he got right to the point.

"Larry, Mrs. Hart."

"Please, call me Betty," my mother said.

Barton nodded, but he didn't say her name. "I asked you to come in today because, quite frankly," and here he looked over at me briefly, "I've become very concerned about Nathan."

Mr. Barton opened the file folder in front of him. My parents looked briefly in my direction, then back at the principal. "Nathan has always been an outstanding student," he said, "a good athlete, active in school clubs and other extracurricular activities." He looked first to one parent, then the other, not sure who would be the foreperson of this jury. "He has never been a discipline concern in the three and a half years he has been at Leon."

We all knew there was a very big "but" coming. We had not been asked here so that I could receive some outstanding student award. This was the educator's standard technique of saying something positive before bringing up the negative, which was the point of the conversation. Barton looked again at something inside the folder.

"That's why it is so hard to understand this sudden turn of events, these actions that are so out of character for Nathan." He thumbed through the file. Neither of my parents said anything. "Let's see. Nathan has gone from getting straight As to Bs and Cs and two Ds this last grading period. He has been suspended from the next basketball game for fighting." He looked up at my parents, but still they did not respond, knowing that my principal was not finished. And he wasn't. He made note of the complaint by one of the cheerleaders that I had touched her "inappropriately," whatever that meant. "And then there is his appearance," he said, and the three of them looked at me. "Nathan used to be neat and well groomed, and now, well. . . ." There was no need to finish the sentence. Was it drugs, he wanted to know.

It was my father who finally spoke. "No, Gerald, it's not drugs. At least nothing showed up on the drug test I had him take after the school dance incident." He looked at my mother, who nodded. "I can also assure you that Nathan has been appropriately sanctioned at home for his misbehavior."

"We have all gone to a counselor," my mother added. My father gave her a disapproving look. No need to divulge everything, to air our dirty linen in public, he was saying with his eyes. I had to agree. Besides, we had not gone to counseling. I had gone to counseling. They just set it up. Like I'm going to spill everything to some hack who would repeat it all to my parents? Not likely. Our family physician had prescribed some medications to help me sleep. He thought I was just a little stressed, that I had spread myself too thin and the pressure had just built up.

This is what my mother told Barton, and my father nodded his agreement. "Doesn't excuse his conduct," Dad said sternly, looking over at me. "But," and here he softened his tone, "all teenagers have to challenge authority, sometimes do some stupid things to get attention. But we're over that now, aren't we, son?"

I nodded enthusiastically and looked in Mr. Barton's direction. I mustered my best conformist manner and tone of voice. "I'm sorry, Mr.

Barton. You won't have any more trouble from me."

Mr. Barton looked at me with a skepticism that was completely missing from the faces of my parents. But if he had doubts, he did not voice them. Instead, he said. "Good, Nathan. I'm glad to hear that. You have a lot of friends here at Leon, and I'm not just talking about students. We all want you to succeed and be happy. School is hard work sometimes, but it should also be fun. I want you to look back ten, twenty years from now and think of your years at Leon High as some of your best."

I nodded politely but was thinking that it was getting pretty deep in there on both sides of the desk. Wasn't I entitled to let off a little steam, to have a little fun, as my father had just suggested? What's wrong with a little vicarious or symbolic rebellion against authority?

The answer, from my father, was there's nothing wrong with any of it, as long as you are in control. You must control events and other people. They don't control you. The coded messages were becoming easier to decipher, the meaning more apparent. All I had to do was concentrate, and the pattern became obvious. Yes, my father and I were in direct, clear communication, but in a language only the two of us understood.

My mother's answer, on the other hand, was to pray fervently. She prayed for me and with me. If there was a church event for teens, I was there, even though it was clear to both of us by then that it was not working. I had expanded far beyond the confining dogma that she preached, its veil lifted from my eyes by the hypocrisy of its adherents. Notwithstanding her fear that she would lose me to Satan forever, I was by then beyond Satan, beyond the first principal, and beyond the arbitrary limits that some of us place on our relationship with God.

If I am to be objective—and I do wish to be—one could argue that these episodes were symptoms of the onset of schizophrenia. That's what virtually every psychologist who has looked at my records and taken account of my history has concluded.

None of us knew exactly what was happening back then, nor could any of us have foreseen the events of the next few years. I just remember that the conversation with Mr. Barton had ended on a positive note. When my parents and I stood to leave, I noticed that my father had been twisting a piece of paper in his hand. Some might have called it simply a sign of nervousness, but I knew better. I watched as he dropped the crumpled and twisted paper in the trash basket when he stood. He glanced sideways at me to make sure I had seen him. When we were back in the outer office, I made an excuse to go back into Barton's inner office. I went directly to the trashcan, retrieved the small scrap of paper, and unraveled it. It was a blank notepad sheet. The letterhead across the top read The Hotel Allegro.

***

I don't know how long the car has been behind me, as I have been lost in my thoughts, but when I look in the rearview mirror, I spot the police cruiser, closing the distance between us quickly. For one fleeting, hopelessly naive moment, I consider the possibility that he just happens to be going in the same direction in a hurry. But then he pulls up directly behind me and turns on his flashing blue light, and I am instantly in survivalist mode.

All right, still no need to panic. Control. Control. You must remain in control. Consider all the possibilities. You could try to outrun him.

Yeah, right. Outrun him in this piece of crap?

Now think. Consider the situation rationally. Leave yourself some options.

I search for a spot to pull over. A dirt road just ahead, off to the right. I turn and travel down it just enough to be out of easy sight of any passing motorist, then stop. The cop parks behind me. He leaves the blue light going, but he doesn't get out of the car for what seems a very long time. I use that time to calm myself, to still the churning of my stomach, to ready myself. He is calling in the temporary tag but probably won't get much info on that, as the dealer probably has not recorded it with the proper authorities. The question is, when he asks to see my driver's license, will he see that the photo doesn't quite match? If he runs it, will he discover that it has been reported lost or stolen? Will he see through my change in appearance and determine that I am the escaped mental patient from Florida he has heard about?

The officer exits his vehicle and begins walking toward my truck. It has become clear to me that I will have to make a choice based on one of two assumptions. Either the man knows, or will quickly learn, who I am. If so, and if I do nothing but sit quietly in my car, I will be caught. Thus, preemptive action is called for. On the other hand, if this is just a routine traffic stop and the officer has no reason to suspect that I am not who I claim to be, I will run a great and unnecessary risk by such preemptive action.

I will just have to go with my gut on this one.

Just as the officer makes it to the rear of the truck, I make my choice.

CHAPTER 16

*I*scheduled the depositions for hospital employees at the institution for everyone's convenience. We were in a small, musty-smelling meeting room in the administration building. A larger room would have been more comfortable, but I preferred the close quarters. To paraphrase Granny, aka the Big Bad Wolf, the better to hear, see, and smell you. Present were my client, the prosecutor, the court reporter, and Frank Hutchinson. Just outside the door was a security officer.

I tried to walk that fine line between finding out everything I could and not betraying our defense strategy, such as it was. Theo had done a good job of researching everybody and helping me prepare for each witness.

Raymond Curry was a very important witness. I needed to uncover some basis on which I could argue that he could have been mistaken in his identification of Nathan. Fortunately, he gave it to me. He readily acknowledged that it was dark in the office and that he didn't get a chance to observe the murderer for more than a couple of seconds before the person ran past him. His identification was based in large part, he said, on the size of the person and the clothes he was wearing. "Especially," he said, "the Yankees baseball cap, 'cause I knew Nathan wore one just like that."

I would have a hard time convincing a jury that the clothes in the washer, including the cap, were not Nathan's. The clothes, though nondescript, were the right size. The cap, which was fairly uncommon, had been tied to Nathan by several people who said he often wore such a cap, though no such item was found among his belongings. But that wasn't the point. If the person Curry saw was not Nathan, or at least if there was some doubt about it, then the theory that my client was being framed for the murder seemed at least plausible.

Andy Rudd, whose deposition was also taken that first day, was a bit of a pain in the ass. He was arrogant and evasive, a bad combination. It took much longer than it should have to get even the most basic information out of him. I asked some very pointed questions about his motive and opportunity to not only murder the victim but to frame Nathan as well. I wanted to stir him up a bit. And it worked.

After several questions about the allegations of sexual abuse of patients, he stood up, said, "I ain't got to take this shit," then stormed out of the room. We took a break, and Frank talked him into returning. I was determined, however, not to let his temper tantrum deter me. My questions became more pointed, more accusatory in tone and content. Whatever Frank had told him, though, seemed to have had the desired effect. I could tell that Rudd wanted to leap across the table and rip my tongue out, but he remained seated and answered all of my questions, albeit tersely and while glaring at me the entire time.

Twenty minutes later, during a break, Rudd decided to let me know how he really felt. I had just finished a Mountain Dew and was headed back to the deposition room when he approached me. I could almost smell the testosterone. I readied myself for something physical, but he stopped about three feet away.

"You think you're real clever, don't you?"

"Pretty clever."

I was still ready for a swing or something, as the anger coming from him was tangible, but he made no move toward me. He snorted, disgusted. "I'm going to tell you this one time and one time only: Don't fuck with me."

This time, I was the one who moved in closer, and he braced himself.

I started to tell him that I didn't respond well to threats and to offer to go toe-to-toe with him right then and there. But I decided I wouldn't take the bait. I smiled and said, "Don't worry. I'm not attracted to you in that way, or in any way really." Then I turned and walked away, leaving him, thankfully, speechless.

The last witness on the second day of depositions was Donnie Mercer. Frank Hutchinson made the introductions. "Hello, Donnie," he said in that condescending tone he used with the patients. "Have a seat." He indicated a chair at the head of the table, the only empty one. He introduced Maxine and me, then he waved his hand in Nathan's direction. "And you know Nathan, of course."

Donnie smiled and gave Nathan a small wave. "Hey, man. Long time, no see."

"Yeah," my client said simply.

I started with the preliminary questions: name, age, occupation, that sort of thing. Mercer seemed to grow more comfortable with the questioning as we went along and looked over at Nathan often. I established that his height and weight were similar to Nathan's, that he wore the same size pants and shirt, and that he wore his hair long, as Nathan did.

I then asked him about the circumstances of his removal from Sunrise Cottage two weeks before Rosenberg's murder and his placement in General Civil. Donnie confirmed that it had been the result of a rule violation, being caught with marijuana. I tried to make it into a motive, suggesting he was mad at Rosenberg as a result, but Mercer denied harboring any ill will toward the victim as a result.

"He was just following the rules. And, actually, he argued against the move, but the rest of my team overruled him. I messed up, plain and simple. I have only myself to blame." He also pointed out that he was back in Sunrise Cottage within a week.

At the end of the day, Nathan and I met in a small room in the General Forensics building. There was a lingering scent of vomit, which made me a bit nauseous, but Nathan didn't seem to mind. Donnie Mercer was the first topic of conversation.

"Donnie was lying about the lighter," he said simply but with a confidence that was compelling.

"He came across pretty well, though."

"You have to understand, Ted, that it's all an act.

I pursed my lips and managed a weak "Hmm."

"But he did give me a signal during the deposition."

I arched my eyebrows, "What are you talking about?"

"You remember he kept doodling on a legal pad during the deposition, and you asked him at the end to show it to you?"

"Yeah."

"Did you see the message?"

"There was no message. It was just crazy drawings, geometrical shapes."

Nathan smiled. "Maybe to you. But I could see it. Donnie had inserted and disguised within his doodling a one-word message: sex."

"Okay," I said, trying to keep a neutral tone.

"I don't know whether he was trying to help or throw me off, and I'm not sure what he was referring to, but you said, Ted, that illicit sexual relationships were at the core of many murders."

"That's true."

"I'm just wondering then if we have explored this theory sufficiently."

"Well . . . ," I began.

"What about Andy Rudd and his sexual escapades with patients, for example?"

I leaned forward in my chair, my forearms resting on the table. "As to Rudd, yeah, sure. He has apparently built himself a little fiefdom here that he is loathed to relinquish. The word is he uses intimidation, coercion, bribery, and blackmail to stay in power." Nathan was nodding in agreement. "The question is, would he use murder?" I hesitated a moment for him to consider the question, then added, "The job pays okay, and the power trip might be appealing, but cold-blooded murder is a big step up from bullying or using whatever dirt you may have on people to your advantage."

Nathan didn't respond. I then raised the points Browning had made to me. Was Rudd smart enough to have planned and executed both the murder and the frame-up? Was it even possible for him to have murdered Rosenberg, planted the clothes and the murder weapon, and then managed to be first on the scene?

And Nathan gave me the response I'd given Browning. "Maybe he had a helper, like Donnie Mercer." I nodded for him to continue. "Donnie could easily have taken my clothes, given them to Rudd, then retrieved them and the letter opener from him after the murder. While Rudd rushes back to the scene, Donnie plants the clothes and the murder weapon. Later, he perfects the frame-up by connecting me not only to the clothes but to the cigarette lighter as well."

I pointed out that Rudd was not of the same body type.

"Maybe it was the other way around. Donnie, dressed in my clothes, killed Rosenberg, and Andy helped him perfect the frame-up."

"And why would he do that? Why would he willingly assist Mercer? Or vice versa, for that matter?"

"Maybe it wasn't willingly," he suggested. "Donnie is working some angle all the time. He and Rudd are on a natural collision course in this place. Maybe they both have something on the other and have reached some kind of détente."

I shook my head. "Rudd could cause Donnie trouble, sure, but he couldn't get him out of the hospital, which I assume was his goal. And Rudd had some motive to want Rosenberg out of the way, but what about Mercer?"

"Perhaps Donnie was hired by the Unit. And if they think he is having second thoughts, he is in danger."

Internally, I was rolling my eyes, but on the outside I remained neutral. "Perhaps."

Nathan returned to the sex-angle theory for murder, suggesting different suspects. Was there any evidence that either Rosenberg or his wife was having an illicit sexual relationship? "Wouldn't that create a possible motive for murder?" he asked, "For example, a scorned lover, a jealous spouse?"

I told him that while I agreed with this theory in general, I found it less appealing here, where we had to explain not only a murder but also a frame-up. The jealous spouse or spurned lover is more likely to kill out of passion, and though planning isn't out of the question, it's not likely to be a very complex plan."

But, I told him, we had been pursuing that angle as well. "Bottom line, though," I said, "we've come up with nothing on the wife. Not even a hint of a rumor. And this is a small town. People talk. If she had something going on the side, she's done a hell of a job keeping it hidden. Besides," I added, "I've seen the lady, talked to her. She's petite, demure, not the type for murder, even vicariously. I can tell you I didn't win any friends even bringing up the subject, but she handled it with class. I could be wrong, but my gut tells me this is not a promising direction."

Nathan seemed unconcerned. "What about Dr. Rosenberg?"

"That's a different story, as you know. There are plenty of rumors but nothing concrete. No corroboration." I hesitated. "The names I've heard are maybe the secretary, Isabella Martinez, or maybe Barbara Hutchinson, but again, nothing corroborated."

"Maybe," Nathan suggested, "they were both involved with him."

"Could be," I agreed. "The thing is, though, Martinez has a good alibi. She was out of town on some family thing the night of the murder. Plenty of witnesses. And we've talked about Hutchinson's alibi. I've also checked out those two patients your friend Tony mentioned, the ones who supposedly said they saw Rosenberg and Hutchinson together."

"And?"

"Nothing. I couldn't get anything out of them. They were barely coherent."

Nathan considered this for a couple of moments, then asked, "What about Dr. Whitsen? Any evidence of a sexual relationship between her and Rosenberg?"

I shook my head. "Nothing."

"Any other motive for Rebecca?"

Again I shook my head. "She did have words with Rosenberg about a week before the murder, according to the secretary. Martinez said she could hear them arguing but couldn't make out what it was about. Anyway, Whitsen left in a huff. When I asked her about it, she said it was a disagreement over the treatment of a patient. She thought the medication dosage was too high."

"That sounds like Rebecca," Nathan said, smiling.

"And," I said, "she has a pretty good alibi."

"Yeah, you told me. She was forty-five miles away when the murder occurred, in her apartment."

I nodded.

"What about the cigarette lighter found on the scene? Any match on the prints?"

"The State's expert said the print was not of sufficient quality. I've got my own guy looking at it but haven't heard back yet."

"I can't help but think there is some connection to Rebecca's former patient. Any progress on who's been sending her those e-mails?"

I looked at him, trying to see beyond the neutral face he displayed. "I don't know," I told him honestly.

He stood suddenly and began pacing the room. "Are we sure this former patient, Cindy Sands, is really dead?"

"The medical examiner was sure," I said. "The dental records matched, plus there were prints at the place and her personal items. You read the materials I left for you, didn't you?"

He paced slowly, his hands behind his back. "You asked our fingerprint guy to compare the print on the lighter with Cindy Sands', as I instructed?"

"I did. But, as I said, he hasn't gotten back to me yet."

Nathan abruptly stopped his pacing and turned to me. "This has got Unit written all over it, Ted. They probably planted the lighter at the scene, got Donnie to lie and connect me to it. They're playing with me. And, mark my words, they will have planted some clue to suggest that I'm behind the e-mails too."

There was a long silence then as he looked at me expectantly. Up until this last observation, my client had seemed, well, rational, asking the kinds of questions that suggested a thoughtful, reasonable approach. Now he was back in fantasy land again. Even worse, I couldn't tell if he was really serious.

"I see what you mean, Nathan," I replied, but as I said it, I was wondering who was playing with whom?

CHAPTER 17

*T*he Low Country–style home sat on a meticulously landscaped lot and matched the description Maxine had given me. There were cars parked up and down the street for several hundred feet on either side of it, further confirming that I was in the right place. I found an open space in the line of cars and squeezed mine in.

Maxine's invitation had come at the last minute, an afterthought at the end of a long day of depositions in the Rosenberg case. "Say, Sam and I are having some people over tonight. It's a fund-raiser for the public library. There'll be some great barbeque, Sam and his group will play a little music, and we'll pass the hat. Should be fun. What do you say?" When I didn't answer right away, she continued, "We'd love to have you join us."

The prosecutor was probably just being polite, and my initial inclination was to decline. I had not been much for socializing lately, not for some time actually. "I suspect that, under the circumstances, I would not be the most popular guest there. I'm sure I am *persona non grata* in this community right now."

She smiled. "We're talking money here, Ted, for the library. We'll put up with a lot for money. Besides, several of the players will be there: Walter Browning, the Hutchinsons, Rebecca Whitsen. Maybe you can ply them with liquor, and somebody will slip up."

I admit I was intrigued by the possibilities. I might learn something in an informal setting that I couldn't through more official channels. And the idea of creating a little stir among the locals was perversely appealing.

When I thanked her and told her I would stop by for a while, Maxine had seemed just a bit surprised, but she immediately said, "Wonderful," and gave me directions to her house.

I spent about forty-five minutes with Nathan, going over the day's depositions and where we stood in preparing the defense. We seemed to be in a less adversarial position with each other these days, which was encouraging. Still, I thought it wise not to mention Maxine's party.

With time to kill before the event, I went down to the Corner Pocket, a little tavern on the outskirts of town. I had a couple of beers, maybe three—who's counting?—and shot a few games of pool with an old geezer who showed remarkable skill with a cue stick when he could keep his hands from trembling. I wondered if I was seeing myself in thirty years but decided that was silly. When I left, I purchased a pint of bourbon and sipped from it on the way over to Maxine's. Now, as I prepared to go up to her house, I took one last swallow and put the bottle back in the console, its contents about half gone. It was not enough to get me drunk but enough to take the edge off, to make me sociable.

I know what you're thinking. What about my promise of no booze or drugs and the UAs to back it up? Well, sometimes you tell your lawyer what she wants to hear. It was an unnecessary, unrealistic, and unfair requirement of me anyway. Besides, I had been pretty good. I was careful not to drink to excess in public and had stayed away from any illegal drugs completely. And I'd been around long enough to skirt any UAs. They say they are random, but they never check more than once a week. If you get called in unexpectedly, you make up some excuse. There would be nothing Beth's lawyer could use.

The front door was open so I walked right in. I searched the room for a familiar face, spotted the hostess across the room, and made a beeline toward her. She turned as I approached, following the gaze of the women with whom she had been talking. Maxine was wearing a sleek black dress with spaghetti straps, a different image entirely from her courtroom appearance. I liked it.

"Ted, I'm so glad you could make it." She leaned forward and gave me a small hug.

"Thanks for the invitation," I said after she released me. I looked over at the other women and smiled briefly. "Hello."

"Ladies," Maxine said, holding on to my arm and turning to face them. "Let me introduce to you Ted Stevens." I gave a slight bow. "He's a lawyer from Tallahassee." There was a moment of silence as the rest of the untold story about me filtered through their minds. There was obvious distaste evident on some faces but not all. Those who let their feelings show briefly quickly recovered and masked it with that Southern, small-town politeness, which is a lie. A kind lie but a lie nonetheless.

Still holding me by the arm, Maxine led me away from the group and toward the dining room. "Some snack food in here," she pointed to the table, "and serious food to be served outside soon. Booze and soft stuff outside as well, though there may be some beer in the fridge if you don't like the selection out there."

"I think I'll stick to the soft stuff tonight. Got to drive back to Tallahassee."

She wrinkled her nose, her sense of smell probably telling her that her guest had already been drinking, but she didn't contradict me. "Sure," she said. "What can I get you?"

"I can get my own. You tend to your other guests." I looked over toward another couple coming through the front door. She smiled again, nodded, then released my arm and went over to greet the newcomers. I made my way to the sliding glass doors that led to a pool and terrace beyond. Along the way my peripheral vision picked up Frank Hutchinson and his wife in the kitchen, talking with another couple. Frank spotted me too but neither of us acknowledged the other.

I stepped outside. People were milling about, some standing, others seated around the patio tables that dotted the terraced pool area. Others were gathered around a makeshift stage where two guys were tuning their acoustical guitars. I recognized one of them as Maxine's husband, Sam.

He was tall and thin with a bald head that made him look thinner. We had met a few times at office parties and events when I was still with the State Attorney. Nice enough guy, a pharmacist, as I remembered.

I made my way over to the bar, which was attached to a covered outdoor kitchen area. Several people were busy there, and the long table was laden with barbecued pork and chicken and all the fixings. At the bar, I got a Coke.

I moved over to the side of the bar, leaned back against a pole, and looked out over the crowd. I spotted, in short order, several familiar faces, including Walter Browning, who was talking to his boss, Sheriff Hank Friendly (who was not particularly) and County Judge Peter Toppler, a short, red-faced man who was seriously attacking a handful of chips. I noticed too that the Hutchinsons had moved outside and were sitting at one of the patio tables.

Then I saw Rebecca Whitsen step through the open doorway onto the terrace. She was dressed in a dark blue business suit over a white blouse. Her hair, which she usually pinned back, fell loosely around her face. She looked both prim and sultry at the same time, and I felt an unexplained twinge of disappointment when I saw that she was accompanied by a man, someone I did not recognize. Her date? A colleague from work? Maybe both? The man introduced her to a small group of people standing near the door, then left her and headed for the bar, where he retrieved two glasses of wine.

I began that awkward ritual of mingling, that social dance of polite lies that is an important skill for anyone but especially for a lawyer. If it's not work related, it's a dress rehearsal. It helps, of course, if you're actually interested in people, but it's not a prerequisite. Besides, there's only so much of you to go around, only so much interest you can have. Some of it—most of it, really—has to be faked. Unlike my partner, Paul, who is a natural, I have never been very comfortable in the role. Over the years, however, I have become, if not a master, at least competent in the art. At any rate, I managed to work the crowd pretty quickly and before long found myself standing in front of Rebecca Whitsen. She was seated by herself at one of the patio tables when I came by.

"Dr. Whitsen." I gave her a small, formal bow.

"Mr. Stevens." She waved her hand in the direction of the vacant chair. "Care to join me?"

"I'd be delighted," I said, pulling out the chair and sitting down. "Where's your date?" When she gave me a questioning look, I said, "The guy you came in with."

She smiled faintly and looked out over the crowd as if to locate the man. "That's Dr. James McDonald, one of our psychologists. He's not my date, though. We just happened to come in together, and he was kind enough to get me a glass of wine." She turned her attention back to me. "Nice of you to notice, though."

I had the feeling then that the psychologist had just read my mind, analyzed it, and reduced me to some Freudian cliché. What was more amazing, though, was that I was not embarrassed by it, nor was she. The icy coolness I remembered from our first visit was still there, but for some reason it seemed more of an affectation and thus less threatening.

We chatted for a few minutes, the usual inconsequential things, but somehow I ended up telling her about my divorce case, the custody fight. She found the right mixture of empathy and supportive outrage at my wife and in-laws, and there was an intensity in her eyes that made me feel as if she was focused exclusively on me. Damn, she was good.

I made a conscious effort to balance out the one-sided conversation, but she gave me only the superficial information. When I pressed her for details, she gave me that little half smile and said, "I imagine you have researched me thoroughly by now. Nathan would have insisted on it."

"If it was up to Nathan, I'd have a full dossier on everybody at the hospital."

She turned her head just a bit, surveying the crowd a moment, then turned back to me. "It's very important that you treat his suspicions seriously, Ted." She folded her hands in front of her. "It is the nature of his illness that he is prone to paranoia. You don't want to feed it, but if you brush it off, you will lose whatever trust you have been able to build."

"Point taken," I said, raising my glass to her. "And I do take his suspicions seriously, most of them anyway. Have you received any more of those e-mails?"

She shook her head. "No," she said simply. "Nathan told me you asked him about them. Maybe he has stopped so they can't be traced back to him."

"I don't think that would stop him."

She smiled. "I think you're beginning to understand how your client thinks."

I shrugged. "That may not be such a good thing."

She started to say something when Sam announced into a microphone that it was time to eat. He said a quick blessing, and everybody converged on the food table. I was disappointed when Rebecca ended up at a different table.

It was after the meal, as I was coming back from the bathroom, that Frank Hutchinson cornered me. "Ted, wait a minute," he said as I was passing by. I turned to face him. His facial expression didn't seem particularly friendly. I figured I knew why and braced myself for a confrontation. Hutchinson wasted no time in getting to his point, something I knew from experience was not an uncommon effect of consuming significant quantities of alcohol. Frank leaned in a little too close. "I understand you want to take Barbara's deposition." It was an accusation more than a question.

"That's right. It's scheduled for next week. But, of course, you know that, since I sent you a courtesy copy of the notice."

The man stepped back and considered me for a long couple of seconds. "Why?"

"Excuse me?"

"You heard me. Why do you want to take her deposition?" He leaned forward again, apparently thinking he was intimidating.

I was not impressed. "Could you move back a little, Frank? You're invading my personal space." I was calm, nonthreatening in my manner. Hutchinson frowned, but he stepped back again. "Now, first of all, you keep using the word 'want' in reference to your wife's deposition, as if there is some question as to whether I will. There's not. As for the reason, that should be patently obvious. Your wife worked closely with Rosenberg. They spent a lot of time together. She was one of the people who saw him in his office the day he was killed. She says she's quit, but she used to be a smoker. They found a cigarette lighter underneath Rosenberg's desk the night he was killed. Maybe she knows how it got there." Hutchinson's face was getting red, but he didn't say anything. "Put yourself in my shoes, Frank. What would you do?"

I had not mentioned the possibility of a romantic connection between his wife and the victim, but it was obviously on his mind. "I wouldn't try to ruin the reputation of a murder victim and the wife of a friend based on some unsubstantiated, vicious, and totally false rumors and innuendoes. I wouldn't try to imply something to a jury that I had no proof of just on the off chance it might confuse them into thinking there was reasonable doubt." Hutchinson's voice had a resignation to it that made it sound very sad.

Of course, you would, I thought, but kept it to myself. Instead, I asked, "Is there something out there to be found, Frank? If so, you might as well get it out on the table here, just between us. 'Cause if there is something to find, I'll find it. You know I will. But if you tell me now, I swear that if it's got nothing to do with the case, I will leave it alone. I won't use it."

We both knew it was a lie. The truth was, unless it could clearly be shown not to be helpful, I would use whatever I could. That was how the game was played. I softened my tone. "Listen, Frank, like I said, I'm not out to embarrass anyone if I don't have to. If there's nothing to find, then great. But if there is . . ."

"There's nothing to find, Ted. The problem is, it's impossible to prove a negative. So, in your search for what doesn't exist, you will end up giving credence to malicious gossip." And with that, Frank pretended to see someone he needed to talk to and excused himself. I watched after him for several seconds, contemplating the consequences that followed a vigorous defense. Without bothering to seek out my hostess, I quietly and quickly made my way to the front door and left the party, suddenly feeling as though I had overstayed my welcome.

CHAPTER 18

I sat in my car in the dark, drinking a beer and listening to a Rolling Stones CD. I was parked on a side street just off Tennessee, in the shadows of a large, vacant building. On the corner was the convenience store where I had purchased the six-pack. From my vantage point, I had a good view up and down the narrow street. At the intersection straight ahead, the prostitutes were strutting and posing, propositioning passing pedestrians and motorists alike. In the parking lot of the convenience store, drug dealers transacted business.

I looked at my watch. It was almost 8:30. Where was Wayne? I had called him right after my phone conversation with Denise Wilkerson. Could he score some cocaine for me? Colson had hesitated only a second before telling me, "Sure," and instructing me where and when to meet him. It was now fifteen minutes past the designated time.

Okay, yeah, you're right. Cocaine's a serious drug with serious penalties if you're caught. I should stick with the booze. At least it's legal. Or even pot, which is illegal but not as serious. Yes, all very true. But I wanted that mind-altering jolt. I needed it. And it was not like I was a crack addict or something. I did powder only, and I hadn't done any for almost a year.

I downed the last of the beer, crumpled the can and tossed it on the floorboard, then took a second beer and opened it. The shaken contents rushed out in a foamy mess, spilling over the sides of the can. I quickly stemmed the flow with a vacuumlike suction at the opening. I took a napkin from the glove compartment and wiped the can. I tucked the napkin between the seats, wiped my hand on my pants, then slid down in my seat a bit. I reflected on the call I had received earlier from Denise, when she told me of the judge's ruling on venue.

She tried to put the best light on it. "We knew this was a possibility, Ted."

"Yeah, I can smell the home cooking, and I'm the main dish."

"I don't think so. It could have gone either way."

"Yeah," was all I said in reply.

"Basically, he felt that since both Beth and Annie had been in Panama City for several months and you stayed there occasionally, based on your testimony that you had reconciled, he figured this is where the two of you had last resided as husband and wife. He also said Bay County was the most convenient forum since most of the witnesses are there." There was silence for a long time as I still said nothing. Couldn't. "The judge has set the final hearing for late November."

"November?"

"That's as soon as the judge could give us a full day."

My head knew this was pretty normal, but my heart couldn't understand. "This is just what they wanted. Delay things so that the judge will not want to disturb the status quo."

Denise didn't contradict me. "There is some good news," she said, diverting my attention.

"Yes?"

"The judge granted our request for expanded visitation while the case is pending."

"I get overnights in Tallahassee?"

"Every other weekend, and one day a week in Panama City."

It seemed ridiculous to be grateful for a small amount of time with my own daughter, but everything is relative, and in this upside-down nightmare I found myself in, I would take what I could get, which was considerably more than my wife had offered, after all. I just couldn't bring myself to express the enthusiasm I knew Denise wanted to hear.

"Ted, I know you're not happy with Judge Simmons' ruling, but he's a fair man, and I think our chances at final hearing are good, assuming you don't do anything to mess them up."

We both knew what she was referring to. "I'm fine. Don't worry."

"Just don't let this cause you to relapse."

"I said I'm fine, Denise."

She had let it drop then, and part of me had felt guilty and disloyal after I got off the phone with Wayne. Now, as every nerve in my body ached for the relief of self-medication, I wondered if my choice had not been a subconscious instinct to self-destruct. But why should I feel guilty? I could do without it, sure, but why should I?

Mick Jagger was just beginning "Sympathy for the Devil" on the CD when a sharp rap on the passenger-side window jolted me out of my seat, causing me to splash beer from the can and onto my pants leg. "Shit," I said, holding the can out away from my body and turning toward the hulking figure of Wayne Colson, who motioned for me to unlock the door. When I did, he quickly opened it and slid into the seat. He looked over at me and grinned as I wiped beer from my pants leg and the seat.

"A little jumpy tonight, are we?"

"Damn, Wayne, somebody's going to shoot your ass one day, you keep sneaking up like that, especially around here."

Colson's grin expanded into a big smile. "And irritable too. My, my. Must have been a bad day in court."

"Don't ask. You don't want to know." I took a swig of beer. "You got the stuff?"

He reached into his back pocket and pulled out a small ziplock bag of cocaine and placed it in my open palm. I examined it quickly, then wrapped it in a napkin from the glove compartment and placed it under my seat. "I'll take it off your bill."

Wayne frowned. He would have preferred cash but understood the advantages and the realities of the barter. "Hey, man, at this rate, I'll be forever getting even."

"You could always opt for the traditional method of payment: money. It's still popular with many people."

My client grinned again. "No, man, what you need instead is a more significant delivery. Maybe you got some of your lawyer friends might be interested. You could make a little profit yourself." I shook my head, smiling, but it didn't deter him. "Even better, the people I do business with are looking to retain legal counsel. I could recommend you. They need somebody who knows the area and the people, including the coastal communities. Somebody to act as liaison with law enforcement and others. It could mean a lot of money." He rubbed his thumb and forefinger together. "You know what I mean?"

I knew exactly what he meant. Wayne's suppliers were looking for someone to advise and act as a go-between to bribe certain law enforcement and other officials to look the other way or run interference for them with those who wouldn't. It would also be helpful to know how to influence a prosecutor or judge if somebody—usually a lower-rung seller—got caught. I shook my head. "Don't want to hear about it, Wayne. And I need to remind you that the attorney-client privilege does not extend to illegal acts you tell me you intend to commit."

"I guess supplying blow to your lawyer is an exception?"

"Good point."

"Besides, you misunderstand. I'm talking strictly legit here. I wouldn't get you in trouble. You wouldn't need to know any details, just what you felt comfortable with. The less you know, in fact, the better for everyone."

"Not interested," I said, closing the subject. Then, after a moment's hesitation, I reached under my seat, retrieved the cocaine, and handed it back to him. "As a matter of fact, I've changed my mind on this too."

"You're not pissed, are you, man? It was just an idea."

I waved my hand. "No, just changed my mind."

"Well, listen, Ted, I had to put out some money I didn't have for this."

I smiled. "I'll still take it off your bill."

"Okay, man, that's good. But, here, you should at least have a snort. This is good stuff."

I hesitated, then nodded as Wayne picked up a file folder from the floorboard and put it in his lap. From his wallet he removed a ten-dollar bill. He carefully laid out a line of the white powder, rolled the bill into a makeshift straw, and handed it to me. I used it to vacuum half of the line up my nose. I threw my head back and sniffed again several times, then I put the makeshift straw to the other nostril and repeated the ritual. When I was done, I rubbed my nose with my thumb and forefinger, brushed the remaining coke back into the bag, and handed it to Wayne. "Thanks."

He smiled. "Okay, man, no problem. Anyway, I guess I better run, earn some money to pay those attorney's fees." He opened the door and stepped out. "See you later, Ted. Be careful."

"You too," I called after my client, who was already headed back down the street. I started my car engine and prepared to pull out. I looked in the rearview mirror and caught sight of a car coming slowly down the street. I took another sip of beer and watched it approach. Something about it looked familiar. As it came closer, I could tell it was an early-model Chevrolet Impala, a '63. When the car pulled even with my parked vehicle, I looked over at the car and its driver, and I knew where I had seen both before.

I watched as the Impala pulled into the parking lot of the convenience store and stopped. It was immediately approached by a short, thin man who leaned down toward the open window on the driver's side, engaged in a few seconds of conversation, then produced something from his pocket and handed it to the driver in exchange for some cash. As the Impala prepared to exit the lot and the driver looked both ways for traffic, I saw again clearly the face of James Washington. I watched as the social worker steered the classic Chevy onto the street and up to the intersection, then turned right. I hesitated for a couple of seconds. Then, without knowing exactly why, I pulled out into the street, turned right at the intersection, and fell in behind the Impala.

***

I followed the car out of the commercial area, west on Tennessee Street, then north on Ocala Road, where Washington turned in to an apartment complex and parked. I did likewise at what I figured was a safe distance. I watched Washington walk up to one of the apartments and figured he was probably just going home to smoke his weed in private. Pretty dull. But then I remembered from Theo's report that Washington lived in Chattahoochee.

James hesitated at the door, not to retrieve keys from his pocket but to ring the doorbell. When the door opened, I strained to get a good look at the occupant. Across the darkened parking lot, with only the porch light for direct illumination and Washington partially blocking my view, I didn't have the best vantage point. There was no question, however, that I was looking at the face of Dr. Rebecca Whitsen. She looked past Washington briefly, as if checking the area, then stepped back, opened the door wider, and let him in.

For a good five minutes, I sat in my car, drinking a third beer and pondering the possible interpretations and implications of what I had just witnessed. Perhaps Washington had stopped by for something work related. Possible but not likely. He had not been carrying files or other documents when he walked up to the door. And what work-related matter would require a visit at night to the psychologist's home? Was there a romantic relationship between the two? I had seen stranger pairings. And the longer James remained in the apartment, the less strange it appeared. Perhaps the drugs had nothing to do with his visit. Perhaps they had everything to do with it.

I had just about decided to leave without the answers I sought when the door opened again. James stood at the threshold for several seconds, saying something to Rebecca, who held the door with both hands. Washington turned and started toward his car, and Rebecca closed the door. There was no kiss good-bye, no warm embrace. This, coupled with the relatively short time Washington had remained in the apartment, militated against a romantic liaison. I didn't want to acknowledge it or its implications, but I was relieved by this observation.

I watched as Washington got in his car, backed out of the space, and began to move toward the exit. As he did, though, he looked in my direction, pausing for several seconds. There was nothing about my plain Honda Accord that would draw his attention, and my windows were tinted so I couldn't imagine he could even tell there was someone inside, much less identify me. Still, I instinctively slid down in my seat so that I could barely see over the steering wheel. James stayed there for a couple of more seconds, idling in neutral as he continued to look in my direction. Then I heard the transmission click into drive and watched as the Impala pulled out into the street and accelerated away.

For the next couple of minutes, I struggled with the choice of simply leaving or going up to the apartment. Then, having made my choice, I spent the next couple of minutes building up the courage to do it. Finally, I got out of my car, walked up to the door, and rang the bell. For what seemed like a very long time but was probably no more than ten seconds, I waited, almost giving in to my second thoughts and walking quickly away.

Finally, the door opened and I was looking into the questioning face of the psychologist. There was no hint of alarm there or anger or even annoyance, only mild curiosity. She did not greet me or speak to me at all. She just stood in the doorway, looking at me expectantly.

"I was in the neighborhood. Thought I'd drop by." The extremely lame lie hung in the air between us. I half expected her to close the door in my face without saying a word, but instead she gave me a "hmmph" and a bemused upturn of her mouth. Then she turned and walked away from me but left the door open. I stepped inside and closed it behind me.

***

The first thing that struck me upon entering Rebecca's apartment was the air of impermanence. Unlike her office, her dwelling did not seem to reflect her particular tastes. It seemed temporary, generic. A couch and chair faced a stereo cabinet, sharing one end table. No television, no paintings or other decorations on the walls.

As she led me to the kitchen, I watched her from behind, admiring the shape of her underneath the loose-fitting pants and sweatshirt. She spoke without turning around. "I know what you're thinking, Ted, and it's not going to happen."

"What?"

She took a bottle of scotch from a cabinet and placed it next to a water glass located on a small round table in the breakfast nook. "I'm talking about sex between us. Not a good idea. Very unprofessional. If your client accuses you of banging one of the prime suspects in his murder case, I want you to be able to deny it."

I gave her a half smile. "I could lie. I've had some practice at it."

"I'm sure you have," she said, giving me a half smile in return, "but Nathan will know if you do. So, just wanted to clear the air on the subject."

My hands went up to indicate surrender, but I was thinking temporary retreat only. The psychologist took another glass from the shelf and placed it on the table. She motioned for me to take a seat, and she did the same. Then she began pouring the scotch into the glasses.

"I figure you for a bourbon man," she said. "But I also figure you for a person who's not too particular what he drinks, especially if someone else is buying. I assume scotch is okay with you?"

"Sure," I said, noting that the bottle was almost half gone. "Tough day?"

She hesitated a long time, then said, "Kind of a good-news-bad-news combination." She took a swallow from her glass. "I got another e-mail." She stood and walked toward the dining room. "Similar stuff," she said over her shoulder, "asking me had I gotten my affairs in order, telling me the judgment day was near, that sort of thing." She retrieved a file folder from the dining table, brought it back, and placed it in front of her. "This one, though, includes information that, to the best of my knowledge, was known only to Cindy Sands and me. Specifically, it contains details of sexual abuse she told me about during our sessions." She opened the folder, took out the top document, and handed it to me. "There's also a reference to Dr. Rosenberg and to Nathan."

I read through it quickly. It was in places a rambling, caustic diatribe but in others a sentimental, nostalgic remembrance. The short passage dealing with my client and his former psychologist read: "You don't have much time, Rebecca. Why do you waste it with that Hart character? He is a LOSER, LOSER, LOSER!"

I put the note down and looked at her. "Has your tech guy been able to trace the source more specifically?"

She nodded. "That's the good news, I guess. As I suspected, he's now narrowed it down to the hospital network but not the individual unit. He says the e-mails may have come from different computers in different parts of the hospital, not just one source."

I arched my eyebrows at this. "Doesn't that suggest staff rather than patient? Someone with general access?"

"The residents can use only certain computers, which are closely monitored so we know who used them and when. If you're staff, you can use your log-in name and password on any computer in the hospital. Moreover, many people don't bother to log off or shut down their computers at the end of the day."

"Or, if you knew someone's password . . ."

"Exactly. We're not real secretive about that either, in case a secretary or coworker needs to get to your files when you're gone. They are given out quite freely."

"Still, it gets us closer. One good thing, given Nathan's rather inflated opinion of himself: I doubt he would call himself a loser."

She gave a noncommittal shrug as she held her glass with both hands, staring at its contents. She looked up at me and frowned. "So, not the best of days for me but, then, no worse than yours, I'm sure." I could not have agreed more, but I felt it would be bad form to say so out loud, so I merely nodded. She looked at me closely then, the beginnings of a smile forming on her lips. "You know Ted, for someone with bipolar disorder, manic stage, cocaine is probably not the preferred self-medication for you."

"How did you . . . ?" I began before she put her finger under her nose in a wiping motion. I stopped and did the same.

She gave me a tired look. "The bipolar diagnosis is unofficial, but I'll wager accurate." When I didn't respond, she continued. "Sometimes you feel like you don't want to get up in the morning, like nothing matters anymore. Sometimes you feel like you can go all day and all night. You like to stay busy. You need to stay busy. The problem is, you lose your focus and become irritable easily. You do things you regret later."

I shook my head slowly, gave her a smile I wasn't quite committed to. "Sorry, doc. Misdiagnosis. Actually, I'm generally pretty even keeled. I have my ups and downs. Sometimes they're chemically induced, that's all."

She frowned, looked at her glass, then brought it up to her lips and took a sip. "What do I know?" She hesitated a moment, looking over my head at some spot on the wall behind me. "Booze has some advantages in the self-medication area, starting with the fact that it's legal."

"A real plus," I agreed, raising my glass.

"Of course, you never know when your mood will swing and how much. The alcohol, which is, after all, a depressant, can make that swing more rapid and the crash harder. It also slows your reflexes, affects your judgment—as witnessed by the fact that I have invited you into my apartment." She smiled, a bit larger now, and I smiled in return. "It also has been known to make some individuals more aggressive and belligerent, resulting in unfortunate incidents." She looked over in my direction.

I raised my hand. "Guilty as charged."

She smiled again and hesitated, perhaps weighing the pros and cons of what she was contemplating. "So, Ted, what really brings you to my apartment tonight? And don't tell me you were just in the neighborhood, since you should have no reason to know where I live. You been following James around? Or me?"

"Neither really." I took a swig of the scotch and grimaced a little as it went down. "What's the deal with you and him anyway? Boyfriend-girlfriend?"

She chuckled. "Hardly. He's just a friend."

"And your drug supplier?"

Her face grew dark. "I don't do drugs, and I have discouraged James in this regard." She hesitated a moment, a half smile on her lips, then raised her glass. "Illegal drugs anyway." She put the glass down. "You still haven't answered my question, though. What really brought you here?"

I grinned. "Should I lie on the couch, Dr. Freud?"

"If you want, as long as you answer my questions."

I frowned, told her about seeing James, following him there. "Curiosity, I guess." I hesitated a moment, then added, "Maybe I was wondering if the cool, aloof psychologist lets her hair down on occasion." She shook her head slightly in approval of this and took a sip of scotch, though she seemed to be waiting for more. "Maybe I just wanted to see you again."

She smiled at this, picked up the bottle of scotch, and refilled my glass.

CHAPTER 19

*T*he combination of booze and cocaine had the effect of impairing my judgment and motor skills, yet making me oblivious to it. It would have been prudent, given my condition, to take a cab home, as my hostess had suggested. I, of course, refused. So it was that I came to be navigating the streets of Tallahassee in the early-morning hours, making my way slowly toward home.

I was thinking about the off-the-cuff diagnosis of bipolar disorder the psychologist had made earlier. I first became familiar with the term when I was sixteen. It was used to describe my father's torment, to explain why he could be a loving husband and father one day and a sadistic bully the next. They said it explained why he had come home early one afternoon, sat down in a chair in the living room, put his 12-gauge shotgun in his mouth, and pulled the trigger. I had been the one to find him there, soaked in blood and surrounded by my mother's lingerie.

It was not a sufficient explanation then, and it wasn't now. Certainly not an excuse. It didn't explain the cruelty of it. It didn't explain why he had chosen me. The image has haunted me ever since, never too far below the surface, dark and desperate, like the illness. And with it comes the fear—never fully acknowledged but impossible to fully ignore—that despite my conscious efforts to the contrary, I could fall down the same deep, dark well.

I was doing my best to push these thoughts back into the subconscious realm when the headlights came out of nowhere, heading right toward me. I slowed and tried to get out of the way, but I couldn't seem to react quickly enough, couldn't focus. The oncoming lights swerved over then, and somehow both of us managed to stop, side by side at angles to each other. Inside the other car were a woman and a young girl, partially illuminated by my headlights. The woman looked both alarmed and angry. The child just looked alarmed.

For several seconds the woman and I sat there, staring at each other, neither of us quite comprehending what had happened. Then the woman rolled down her window and shouted, "Have a nice day!" That seemed rather sarcastic under the circumstances, I thought. It was then that I looked up and saw the sign, the arrow pointing in the opposite direction. I realized that what she had said was "One way!"

I gave the lady a sheepish look and mouthed "I'm sorry." She hesitated, perhaps weighing whether it was worth the time and trouble to call the authorities. Then she backed up, maneuvered her car around mine, and sped off down the street.

***

The image of the woman and child from that night seemed to have been burned into my mind. I know it seems like a cliché, but I think I took it as a sign, a message. And I know what you're thinking: Why didn't I get the message sooner? Lord knows there were plenty of opportunities. The point is, when that image and its implications were still gnawing at me a week later, I decided to swear off the booze. I also called to make an appointment with Christine Carter.

Theo had been giving me an update on the Rosenberg case when the return call from the center came in. "Yes, Mr. Stevens," the woman said, "Ms. Carter asked me to call you and see if you could come in this afternoon. She has a full schedule, but people often don't keep their appointments." The tone of her voice suggested I probably fell into that category myself and knew just what she was talking about. I thanked her and told her I would come right over. "You might have to wait a while," she warned.

The lobby of the Tallahassee Addiction Recovery Center was crowded, but I managed to find a seat in the corner where I could spread out my work. It had been quite some time since my last visit, but the place still had that same antiseptic, institutional look and smell about it, like a jail, just with more plants. There were the outdated magazines on the end tables, the same mix of clientele, from scared to sullen, and the same condescending, knowing look from the receptionist when I checked in.

I was glad now that I had brought something to work on as it appeared the woman had been correct about having to wait. I used the time to reflect on what Theo had told me and review my cryptic notes, perhaps fill in some of the gaps from his abbreviated oral summary. I made additional notes on a legal pad as I went along, trying to piece it all together. I started with the notes on James Washington, who I felt now warranted a closer look.

"Age 41 / born in Baltimore / mother: drug addict, in and out of prison / father: unknown / raised by grandmother / two siblings, both older sisters / juvenile record but nothing serious / adult criminal history / some misdemeanor marijuana possession charges, one simple possession of cocaine, one with intent to sell / honorable discharge from Army / never married but pays child support for a teenage daughter in Boston / AA degree in generic health care / worked as Certified Nursing Assistant at McClean Hospital in Belmont, Mass., for several years / then a Psychiatric Aide at Bangor Mental Health Institute in Maine for several more / started at FSH nine months ago / good evaluations so far / gets along well with staff and patients, described as easygoing, smart, and diligent."

I'd noted a two-year gap between his last job and Florida State Hospital and had asked Theo about it. "Apparently, he left his job to look after his grandmother, who was terminally ill. He was out of the mental health field for about two years. Worked a variety of part-time jobs: taxi driver, waiter, that sort of thing. After his grandmother died, he moved to Valdosta, Georgia, where one of his sisters lives, and stayed with her a short time until he got the job at Florida State Hospital."

"Social life?"

"According to the staff I talked to, he's taken a date to a couple of functions but has no steady girlfriend. He will hang out with the male employees on occasion, but they say he mostly keeps to himself. He lives alone in a small apartment near the hospital."

"Relationship with Whitsen?"

"He seems to be particularly loyal to Dr. Whitsen, but no one suggested any romantic involvement. No one knew of any particular problem Washington might have had with Dr. Rosenberg or any other information that might suggest a motive on his part to want the psychologist dead."

I made a note on my legal pad. "Motive? Didn't put the drug charges on his job application to FSH. Did Rosenberg find out? Would that be enough to get him fired? Did previous employers know?"

"What about his alibi?" I asked Theo.

"Fairly good but not rock solid. He was working that evening, within sight and hearing of several other employees during most of the evening. They couldn't swear he was there the entire time. He was with a group when they all got word about Rosenberg, which was not that long after the paramedics arrived on the scene. Logistically, it would have been difficult but not impossible for him to have committed the murder, planted the evidence, and gotten back to his post."

I jotted another note: "Not likely to be mistaken for Nathan. Could he have assisted? Not likely. No evidence of more than one murderer. No easy division of labor. Couldn't plant the clothes or the murder weapon until after the murder, so what would the second person do to help? Verify the two-year gap. Baltimore is close to D.C. and St. Elizabeth's. Could there be a connection to Cindy Sands? Is he sending the e-mails? Is he Whitsen's 'protector'? Are they having a sexual relationship?"

I pulled out my notes on Rebecca Whitsen.

"Age 39 / grew up in Portland, Maine / father: fisherman, died in

2005 / mother: in and out of mental health facilities most of her adult life, now has Alzheimer's / foots bill for mother; visits occasionally / no siblings / one uncle, her father's brother, who used to be in fishing business with him / allegations of sexual abuse / he moved, no address / no other family / full scholarship to Harvard; B.A. in psychology; masters and PhD from Duke / married and divorced after two years; one of her professors / no children / worked in North Carolina a few years, did some private practice, then took the job at St. Elizabeth's Hospital in D.C. / after the incident with stalking patient, took a little time off, then took position at FSH / mixed reviews from previous employers: extremely smart, innovative, and effective with her patients but aloof, with very few close friends." I circled the word Maine and made a note: "Is there a Maine connection to JW?"

Theo's most recent report was on Whitsen's infamous patient. I reread his narrative, hitting the highlights: Cynthia Sands was an only child from a wealthy family. She was kicked out of two private schools for misconduct, had early trouble with the law, which her parents hushed up. Quite smart, she ended up at NYU and did well, apparently managing to stay out of trouble. She majored in psychology, worked for a professor at his clinic, and did a stint as an actress in New York, without much success. She never married. She experienced escalating mental problems, prostitution, and drugs and was eventually hospitalized on two occasions, diagnosed with borderline personality disorder. She murdered her parents, cleaned out their bank accounts, and disappeared before the police could pin the murders on her. She was captured two years later.

Before I could finish reviewing the rest of my notes, I caught a glimpse of Christine Carter standing at the front desk. She followed the receptionist's gaze in my direction. Our eyes met, and I thought I detected both surprise and curiosity there. On her dark face there was a hint of a smile. She motioned with her head for me to come over. I packed up my files quickly and walked toward her.

"Teddy Bear," she said, giving me a little more of that half smile.

"Long time, no see." She held a clipboard in both hands and didn't bother to extend one to me.

"Hello, Christine. Thanks for fitting me in."

She motioned again with her head to follow her down the hallway. I did, watching her substantial rear end, like two beach balls moving in tandem underneath the dress, one more thing that hadn't changed since my last visit. In her office she gave me another good look and then said, "What's up, Ted? You get ordered here again?"

Christine had been the one to monitor my no-alcohol conditions while my DUI charge was pending and while I was on probation. She was a no-nonsense woman who had a finely tuned bullshit detector, and she had detected mine easily. I had managed to fool most of the people in the court system, but I had not fooled her.

"You remember what you said to me when I finally got off the alcohol conditions? I thanked you for your help, said I had gotten control of the drinking."

"I sure do. I said you were just lying to yourself. I told you that whenever you decided to get serious about your substance abuse to come see me."

I gave her the most earnest look I could muster. "Well, I'm ready to get serious."

She looked at me for a long time, seemingly smelling the air for the lie. Then she gave me that half smile again and said, "We'll see, Teddy Bear. We'll see."

CHAPTER 20

*P*aul and Anna Morganstein lived in Killearn Estates, an older but stable residential development just past I-10, off Thomasville Road. Paul had purchased a lot on Lake Jackson a few years back, on Brill Point, but they had decided not to build. They liked their neighbors, they explained, and the kids had friends there. Maybe when they were both off to college, Paul said.

I checked my watch as I pulled up in front of the Southern Colonial–style house. Six-thirty. Right on time. From the passenger seat I retrieved the bottle of wine I had purchased at the liquor store on the way, then crumpled the receipt and put it in the ashtray. Some would say it was risky for me to go into the liquor store, even if I was buying for others. The conventional wisdom was that one should avoid triggers: places, people, and situations you associate with drinking or other drug use.

And I had pretty much taken it to heart. I had stopped going to the Rajun Cajun and hanging out with the likes of Wayne Colson. Now don't get me wrong. Deep down, I didn't really believe that bullshit about not being able to have even one drink, but I'd been trying to do as directed, if for no other reason than to demonstrate my sincerity, my commitment, and my willpower.

I'd been doing pretty well too. Three weeks of sobriety and only one relapse, which Christine said was normal and not a real concern at this point. I'd been going to the AA meetings again, and I did try to avoid triggers. But, at the same time, I also believed that what doesn't kill you makes you stronger. It was a test of will and faith to some degree, as with Daniel in the lions' den, and every time I went in and came back out, I was stronger. This evening would be one of those situations to be avoided generally: a group of friends gathering to watch an FSU football game. Lots of food, booze, and a festive atmosphere.

Paul's elder son, Andrew, opened the door. He didn't make eye contact, did not greet me, just turned and shouted over his shoulder toward the kitchen. "Mom, Ted's here." He looked back at me. "They're back there," he said, pointing in the direction in which he had just shouted.

Andrew was a younger, thinner version of his dad, with significantly more hair. The thick, bushy mane was tied back in a short ponytail, and he sported an earring in his left ear. Very neo-hippy. "Hey, Andrew. How's it going?"

He took my outstretched hand and shook it, but his grip was limp. "All right," he said, then stood there a moment, anxious to leave, but before he could I asked another question.

"How's school going?"

"All right, I guess." He looked back toward the kitchen, as if hoping his mom would rescue him. He turned back to me. "Well, gotta go. See ya."

"Good to see you," I called out to his back as he shuffled on down the hallway. I turned to face Anna Morganstein, who had just turned the corner. My partner's wife was in her late forties and a bit heavy, but the Italian beauty was still one of the sexiest, most alluring women I knew. She frowned at the retreating figure of her son. "I must apologize for my socially challenged child." She gave me a big hug, her ample breasts pressing hard against me. She smelled of lavender and a hint of bourbon. It was the bourbon that I found distracting, disconcerting even, as if I was drawing its vapors from the air straight into the pores in my skin. It was such a positive yet scary feeling that I stepped back a bit. This might be harder than I thought.

"How you doing, Ted?" Anna, who exuded warmth and openness,

was a natural at her chosen profession: marriage and family counselor.

"I'm good," I said, offering up the bottle of wine.

She held me at arm's length, as if inspecting me for the truth of my last statement. I didn't know if she was satisfied but she smiled, took the bottle of wine, and thanked me for it, then locked her arm with mine and led me into the kitchen, where she introduced me to Theo's date, a petite woman with a plus-size smile. I repeated her first name in my head as I grasped her hand and squeezed gently in a semblance of a handshake. "Nice to meet you, Rose."

Her grip was more firm than I expected. "You too, Ted. I've heard a lot about you."

I winced. "I hope you will keep an open mind."

This is when the other person is supposed to say that what she heard was all good, but she just smiled and said, "I'll try."

I decided I was going to like her.

"Rose is a teacher at Sealy Elementary."

"Oh, really," I said. "What grade?"

"I'm teaching third grade this year."

"That's my daughter's grade."

"What school does she go to?"

I hesitated a moment. "Well, for the time being she's in school in Bay County, but she's zoned for Kate Sullivan."

Rose didn't say anything, didn't inquire further, which suggested that she knew the story. She just nodded and gave Anna an anxious look, as if apologizing for unintentionally touching upon a sore subject with one of her guests. That was even more embarrassing for me, though, so I pretended she didn't know and that discussion of the subject did not bother me. "I'm in the middle of a divorce," I offered. "We haven't resolved custody issues yet."

Anna, correctly intuiting that a conversation on the subject was a good thing under the circumstances, asked, "How is Annie, Ted? She was over here with you last weekend, wasn't she?"

I smiled. "Yeah. I did the typical weekend Dad stuff. You know, mini vacation, a flurry of activities to fill up the time, book-ended by the trip over and back to Panama City, which left us both exhausted. Had all her friends over for a sleepover. She had a good time, but it's not really what you would call a normal parenting situation. I know that's the reality for thousands of fathers, but it sucks." I hesitated a moment. "Annie's doing well, though, under the circumstances."

There was an awkward silence for a few seconds, then Anna put her hand on my arm and assured me that everything was going to work out. With a lot more confidence and conviction than I felt, I said I was sure it would. I quickly excused myself and headed for the deck, where Paul and Theo had gathered around the grill and where the subject of conversation was apt to be less painful.

"Smells good out here," I said as I approached.

Paul was dressed in jeans and a long-sleeve polo shirt, over which he wore an apron inscribed with the words "Master Chef" underneath a stitched likeness of a pig's head wearing a chef's hat. Hands were shaken all around and greetings made, then Paul opened the grill to display a large quantity of chicken and ribs. He picked up a small basting brush and bowl and began to slather the meat with sauce.

"I didn't know you were dating Halle Berry," I said to Theo, who blushed but didn't respond right away.

"She is lovely," Paul said.

"We're just friends," Theo finally said. "We go to the same church."

"You and Halle Berry go to the same church?"

"Rose."

"Rose and Halle Berry go to the same church?"

Theo shook his head, giving me a half smile. "Who's on first?" he said.

"That's what I said: Who's on first?"

"You two are like children," Paul said, closing the lid on the grill. He turned to me. "And you're the worse."

I ignored him and turned to Theo. "Seriously, y'all been dating long?"

"We're not dating," he said. "We're just friends."

"Uh-huh. What? She married?"

Paul slapped me on the arm with his grill mitt. "You are incorrigible. Leave the man alone."

I turned back to Theo. "Odious knows I'm just kidding. See, he's smiling." And he was, though not a big smile. "Really, Theo, I'm sorry. She seems like a very nice person."

"She is," was all he said.

The conversation shifted then to the upcoming game. Paul had hooked up one of his TVs out on the deck, running the cable through the window. One of the strings of games broadcast that day was on with the sound muted. We talked about who had won and who had lost big cases locally, which lawyers were leaving which law firms to go where or with whom. Eventually we got around to Nathan Hart's case, with Paul wanting to get an update. Anna did not like to hear shop talk around the dinner table, he said, so best to discuss such matters now.

I deferred to Theo with a wave of my hand. He concisely summarized our defensive posture at that point and listed all of our alternative theories and suspects. As he did so, Paul listened intently, nodding his head occasionally, but did not interrupt. When Theo finished, my partner, in typical fashion, zeroed in on what he thought was our best angle: point the finger at Donnie Mercer. "Were you able to confirm what the client told you about his drug use and sale, his intimidation of patients? Any ties to this Rudd guy?"

"Actually," I said, "Nathan's description of Mercer differs substantially from that of the staff." I nodded to Theo again.

"According to the people I talked to," Theo continued, "Mercer gives them very little trouble and doesn't have a history of violence, before or during his stay at the hospital. He's a druggie, that's all. The stories Nathan told Ted about Mercer beating up a patient and slipping something into another's food, well, the staff suspects that was Nathan. He's the one the other patients are afraid of, not Mercer."

"Still," I said, "Mercer remains a good person to point the finger at."

Paul stepped back to the grill for another round of basting. Without looking up, he said, "This possible connection to the psychologist's former patient is weird." Both Theo and I nodded. "You say she got another e-mail. Any luck in tracing it to a specific computer in the hospital?"

"Not yet," I said. "Whoever's doing it is pretty computer savvy. But the hospital's tech guy is working on it. Just a matter of time, he says."

There was a lot said in the silence that followed.

***

Later that evening, after I got home from the Morgansteins' house, the Hart case was still on my mind. Neither Theo nor Paul had seriously considered our client's theory that the Unit had manipulated events and was somehow responsible for setting him up as the fall guy for Rosenberg's murder. I didn't really take it seriously either. On the other hand, I was not quite ready to dismiss it.

So, there I was, planted in front of my laptop, surfing the Net, reading about worldwide conspiracies. Bjorn was sprawled out on the floor next to me, sleeping the sleep of the dead. I had recently been investigating my client's delusional world of spies and counterspies, of secret, powerful organizations that may exist only in the minds of crazy people, many of whom were not in mental institutions. Indeed, the number of Web sites and blogs dedicated to the subject was quite astounding. Some of the entries or postings were very similar to the rambling journal entries Nathan had shared with me. It was probably a case of mutual delusion, each supporting and encouraging the other bloggers. But, as strange as it seemed and despite Theo's assurance that there was nothing to it, I somehow felt compelled to follow up.

I was curious about Robert Hart. Could he be associated with some secret spy organization? As Nathan directed, I had tried to cross-reference several major international incidents in which Nathan suspected Unit involvement—including the first Twin Towers bombing and 9-11—with the professor's travel. I put in a public records request for his travel vouchers to the university and the State Department. The university was forthcoming. The State Department was not, which was frustrating since the cost of much of his travel, especially overseas, would have been billed to the State Department. I had been getting the runaround on my request for a month now.

What I got from the university in terms of travel vouchers, though, was not inconsistent with Nathan's assertion. For example, the records showed that Robert Hart had been in south Florida, then at Logan Airport, on dates and times associated with the travel of several of the hijackers on 9-11. Of course, the fact that Robert Hart had been at those places on those dates didn't prove anything. Thousands of others were there too. There were other things, though. The professor, who had told me of his frugality and lack of need for extravagance, had villas or homes in Italy and Hong Kong. His explanation for his visit to Rosenberg the week before he was killed was plausible but a bit suspicious.

There was, of course, the mysterious trust, the terms of which remained a secret. The fact that Hart had taken such pains to ensure it remained sealed also made me suspicious. Finally—and this will seem the most strange, touching on paranoia—I had the feeling that I was being followed, watched. I had nothing to confirm it, just a vague, intuitive sense that came upon me from time to time. I am not superstitious, but I have learned over the years to trust my gut on such things. Of course, even if my sense was correct, there was nothing to prove that Hart or this mysterious organization, the Unit, had anything to do with it.

Perhaps it was all just coincidence. Perhaps I was letting my client's delusions cloud my objectivity and spur my imagination. Perhaps, as Hart had suggested that day on campus, I had been reading too many spy novels.

Before I closed my Internet connection, I opened my e-mail program to check my messages. About halfway down the list I saw it, a message from someone called Cindy. I clicked on it and it opened. An involuntary shiver escaped from me as I read the message: "Don't get too close to the psychologist, Ted, or you might get BURNED!!!" I stared at the screen and reread the message several times.

I suddenly had that strange feeling again of being watched, but when I looked around the room quickly, I noted that the blinds were pulled shut on all the windows. I shook my head side to side once, as if shaking away the notion. Then I closed the e-mail and the program, stood up from the chair, and headed off to bed.

***

It is 6:30 when I reach the outskirts of Petersburg, Virginia, just south of Richmond. They would expect me to choose one of the cheap motel chains, one that was right off the highway. So I eschew the bypass and follow the direction of the sign that reads "Downtown Business District." I am feeling more relaxed now, less tense. The encounter with the cop did much to restore confidence in my instincts and my judgment.

The way I saw it at the time, I had to commit one way or the other to a plan of action before the officer reached my car door. There were risks associated with each path. I knew that. And contrary to popular opinion within the law enforcement and psychiatric communities, I am not a violent person by nature. I act only if and when absolutely necessary. This time, I chose to wait. It was the right decision.

"May I see your license and registration, please?" the officer said. I gave them to him quickly, without fumbling. He was polite, told me he had stopped me for "going a little fast coming through the school zone back there."

Though I had not exceeded the speed limit, I did not contradict him. "Oh," I said. "I didn't realize I was going so fast."

He looked at me closely, perhaps weighing my response, perhaps looking for some sign of nervousness. He would find none, unless it was in his imagination. The man asked me where I was headed, and when I told him, he wanted to know why I had not taken the interstate. "That would have been a lot quicker," he said.

Yes, I agreed, but I was in no hurry and preferred the more scenic route. I also volunteered that I had spent time in the area as a boy during the summer with my parents.

The officer seemed to like this response. "Well, Mr. Coxwell," he said, looking at the license once more before handing it back to me. "We are glad to have you visit with us. Just slow it down a bit, okay?"

And that was it. No command to exit the vehicle with my hands raised, to lie facedown on the ground. No arrest. Not even a ticket. Just a warning. And I was on my way. No, Danny Coxwell had not yet discovered that his license was missing and might not for several more days. How often do people really use their driver's license anyway? I had not been linked to the truck purchased in Thomasville. Probably no one in regular law enforcement knew where I was or was heading.

About four blocks from the main business district, my peripheral vision catches a glimpse of the sign, and I abruptly turn down the side street. I park in front of the three-story, red brick building, underneath the sign that identifies it as the Hotel Allegro. I told you there are no coincidences. Though I have no memory of ever being here before, the place looks familiar. And somehow I had known where to find it. Somehow my father's implanted message those many years before in Principal Barton's office had maneuvered the space-time continuum to lead me here. Surely, there was divine direction at work.

Without hesitation, I grab the small duffle bag from the seat and head up the steep concrete steps. Just inside the heavy wooden door is a very small lobby area. To the right is the registration desk. An elderly woman smiles at me. "May I help you?" she asks. I tell her I would like a room for the night. She tells me what is available and the rate. I ask to see the room. This does not seem to bother her in the least. She grabs a key from among many that hang on the wall behind her and takes me up the stairs. The room she shows me is on the second floor. It is small but clean.

It has a small desk in the corner.

"This will do nicely," I say. The woman says I can come back down when I get settled to check in officially. She smiles at me again, and in that instant she looks like an older version of my mother. I take the key from her, thank her, and close the door. Without wasting any more time, I retrieve the notebook and pencil from my bag, sit down at the desk, and begin writing.

***

Three days after his deposition, I had a brief encounter with Donnie Mercer. It was lunchtime and, as usual, I had a security escort to the cafeteria. Now, wherever I went, I felt the eyes on me as I passed down the corridors. Patients stared unashamedly. Some of them giggled to themselves. I had always felt alone there but never so much as when I was the center of attention.

Mealtimes are laden with stress in a mental hospital, and I could feel the simmering caldron of psychic energy when I walked inside, each individual coloring his or her own picture, and each coloring outside the lines. That's how I saw them mostly, as children who try their best to make the picture match the reality, getting close sometimes but unable to stay within the lines. On occasion, when I'm feeling down, it is how I think of myself as well.

As I waited in line, I heard the familiar voice. "Don't look around. They're watching you."

I complied, looking only at the security officer seated in the corner. He was looking our way but seemed unconcerned. I took a carton of milk, a sealed container of strawberry Jell-O, and a packaged honey bun and put them on my tray. "I need to talk to you about your message," I said under my breath, not looking at Donnie. "Was it a reference to Rudd or to Rosenberg?"

I could feel his smile though I could not see it. "No, man. You're not even close. But never mind that. I've got something that will blow your mind, my friend." He took a plate of roasted chicken, mashed potatoes, and green beans from the line worker and put it on his tray. "But not now and not here. They're watching you like a hawk. I'll get away somehow at night, visit you in your room." And then he was off to the corner of the room, joining a group of patients. I dared not initiate additional contact, and despite my attempts during lunch, I was never able to make eye contact with him. He said he would come to me at night, so I figured he would.

Several days later, though, Donnie had yet to visit me in my room, nor had I seen him in the cafeteria or any other common area. I had to consider that I might never get the information he had promised. Even if I did, there was no guarantee that it would be helpful or reliable. And though he had told me "never mind" about the sex message, I simply couldn't forget about it. Perhaps that was what he was counting on.

***

I can hear the soft hum of the electric clock radio on the nightstand across the room. It reads 1:13 a.m. I put down my pencil and stretch my arms and legs, then sit motionless for a full minute, my arms folded across my chest, taking in the sounds of the small hotel: the door closing to a room down the hall; the drip in the bathroom sink; the swish of the owner's cat as he pauses outside my door for a moment, then passes on down the hall; the ticktock of the grandfather clock in the lobby downstairs; the creaking of the bed in the room next door as a restless lodger tries to get comfortable. Just as I begin to reach for my pencil again, I hear something else.

The sound is very slight, a scraping of antennae against wood, but it is compelling. In my peripheral vision I spot the cockroach extending its head out from the small space beneath the baseboard. I remain motionless as the dark-bodied insect boldly steps out into the room. The small lamp at the desk is the only light, and it casts a strange shadow of the cockroach against the floor, creating the illusion of something much larger. Slowly, I turn to face the intruder.

Does she sense my presence? Yes, it is a female, laden with eggs. I don't know how I know this, but I do. Roaches are not unfamiliar to me. Florida State Hospital is, after all, dotted with older buildings surrounded by large live oak trees and other vegetation. This, together with the hot, damp climate, makes it virtually impossible to keep them away. Don't really bother me. After a while you get used to them. I took a live-and-let-live attitude toward my insect friends. Rarely did an encounter end tragically.

Something is telling me, though, that this will be different. Whether it is symbolic or an actual threat, it doesn't matter, as I can sense the evil that has just entered the room. It fills my nostrils with its stench, so strong I can almost taste it. If I don't act quickly, I am sure it will possess me, consume me. No, this is not something to be ignored. I must act.

Slowly, almost imperceptibly, as I have been processing the stimuli, analyzing the information, and formulating a plan, my shoe has found its way into my hand. I rise quickly from the chair and move toward the enemy. She hesitates momentarily, startled by my quick movement. Does she realize I'm there? Maybe not.

The moment's hesitation by the cockroach, her indecision, is a fatal error. She scurries back toward that small space under the baseboard, but it is too late. Just before she can reach the security of her home, only a nanosecond away from safety, my shoe finds her and flattens her against the old oak floor.

From the nearby wastebasket, I take the thin advertising flyer for a local pizza parlor and use it to scrape the insect from the floor. Its antennae are still wiggling. I bring her up close to my face, studying her. Suddenly, I am filled with remorse. Steeling myself, I struggle to get beyond this weak sentimentality. I bend the flyer in two, the roach inside, like a funeral shroud, then squeeze it around her body, feeling and hearing the crushing of whatever life remains. Then I fold the flyer one more time and toss it into the wastebasket.

Now I sit motionless, completely silent at the desk, my breathing controlled, shallow. I listen, watching the door, then the window. Was the roach a drone, a scout, a feeler to scope out the situation?

Don't be ridiculous. It was a roach. Nothing more, nothing less. This is just the kind of thinking that got you in trouble to start with.

I'll bring them out into the open. I put on my coat and start for the door.

Stop it! That's just what they would expect.

I nod in agreement with the voice and choose the window instead. I quickly open it and ease myself out. Grabbing the drainage pipe with both hands I shimmy down to the ground and within seconds I am headed toward downtown.

***

I couldn't understand why Donnie had not come to me as he had promised he would. Security at the hospital was laughable. An occasional foray out of one's residence after curfew was not an unusual occurrence, especially for Donnie. Regardless, I decided that if he wouldn't come to me, I would go to him.

That night I waited until everyone was asleep, then quietly made my way to the bathroom. The window there had a thick metal screen over it, secured in place to discourage residents from trying to crawl out. I removed the screws with the help of the small screwdriver I had taped behind the toilet. I placed the screen against the wall, then carefully and quietly slipped out the window and onto the ledge.

Someone should tell the administration that, although architecturally pleasing, the concrete ledges outside each window, the protruding concrete accent borders around them, and the recessed mortar between the bricks were not the best features from a security standpoint. It was fairly easy for me to find sufficient footing to climb from the third floor to the ground without having to jump.

The sky was overcast that night, the air was heavy with humidity, and it was eerily quiet. In the distance a dog barked. As best I could tell, no one else was about, but I stayed close to the buildings and to the cover of trees and shrubbery as I made my way to the building designated as the Civil Unit.

As with all of the residential buildings on the hospital grounds, the Civil Unit's doors were locked at night but only as a safety precaution against intruders. Unlike General Forensics, where I was housed, there were no metal screens on the windows. The second window I checked was unlocked. I eased it open and crawled inside.

I took off my shoes and stood there for about twenty seconds, listening. Except for the hum of the electric clock on the desk against the far wall, all was quiet. There were a couple of night-lights, which illuminated the space sufficiently for me to navigate. On my first step, the wood floor under me creaked and I stopped, frozen, listening for any signs that I had been heard. Nothing. I continued, consciously making my steps as light as possible.

I made my way quickly but quietly up the stairs to the second floor. I opened the door onto the hallway and stood there for several seconds, listening. So far, so good. Fortunately, Donnie's room was the second closest to the stairs. I stood at the doorway for a couple of seconds, looked up and down the hallway, then slowly eased the door open. On the far side of the room, a figure appeared to be sleeping on the single bed, face turned to the wall.

For obvious reasons, I didn't want to startle the occupant. I moved a little closer to the bed, gradually adjusting to the darkness. "Donnie?" My voice was a whisper, and when I saw no movement from the figure, I said it a little louder. "Donnie." The thought occurred to me then, What if I have the wrong room? What if they moved him recently?

Now I could see a little more clearly, and as I moved closer to the bed, I saw neither head nor arms outside the covers, just a lump underneath. As I stopped right next to the bed, I knew, even before I pulled back the covers, that the bed did not contain Donnie Mercer or any other person. Someone had placed pillows under the bedcovers to make it appear as if someone was sleeping.

I cursed silently to myself and looked around the small room as if its occupant might be hiding in a corner or something, though I knew I was the only one there. Quickly I checked the room and confirmed, by the documents, photographs, and other items, that I was in the right place. Then I thought, What if he has chosen this night to fulfill his promise to visit me? Wouldn't that be ironic? Should I wait for him to return? Maybe he wasn't coming back. Maybe he had escaped. Maybe it was just another one of his drug runs. *I cursed again to myself. I couldn't afford to wait for him. No telling when he might return. Nor did I know where to search for him. He could be anywhere.*

I decided to retrace my route back to General Forensics. Maybe our paths would cross if he had, in fact, gone to see me. Carefully but a little more quickly, I made my way back down the stairs, out the window, and back to my residence. I looked carefully for Donnie but saw no sign of him or anyone else, for that matter. I climbed back up to the bathroom window and crawled inside, replaced the metal screen, and headed back to my bed.

Some of the patients were tossing and turning in their beds, and one was talking to himself, but no one was awake. There was no sign of Donnie, nor was there a note or anything that looked like a message from him on my bed or among my personal belongings. The time was 2:45.

At 3:30, I still had been unable to go to sleep, thinking that maybe Donnie would show up. I considered going back out and over to Donnie's building. Perhaps he was back now. But I didn't want to press my luck. When I finally surrendered and drifted off to sleep, I had a series of weird dreams. In one of them, Donnie Mercer was an owl, perched above my bed.

"Donnie, you're here. I knew you'd come. So, tell me, who was it?"

"Whoo," he hooted.

"Yes, that's what I want to know. Who killed Rosenberg?"

The owl cocked his head to the side, looking at me as if studying an alien creature. "Whoo." When I reached up to touch the bird, it bit my hand, and blood began to flow from the wound, a trickle at first but steadily increasing. As I looked up at the owl, I saw that the face was no longer that of Donnie Mercer but Rebecca. The owl looked at me impassively for a few seconds, then flew out the window.

When I awoke later that morning, I was gripped by an unease that I couldn't shake as I made my way to the bathroom. My head was pounding. My stomach was in knots, and I couldn't figure why. Looking in the bathroom mirror, I saw scratches on my face around my left eye. I touched it lightly with my finger. My hands were also scratched, the wounds appearing fresh. I knew I had not had them before last night. Had I done this to myself in my sleep?

When I stepped back into the dorm-style room, most of the other residents were waking up. Many of them seemed uneasy, the ripple of tension in the air almost palpable. It was a phenomenon I had noticed from time to time during my stay at the hospital. Say what you will about those whose minds do not work in conventional ways: They often have sensory and intuitive powers greater than those of what we call normal people. They know when something is amiss, even if they cannot adequately articulate the feeling or identify the cause of their unease. This air of tension and anxiety portended something unusual, something bad, and I thought I knew what it was.

CHAPTER 21

*M*y head pounded with each stride, as if my brain had been dislodged and was rattling loose up there. My breathing, at first shallow and labored, had grown deeper, expanding my lungs. The blood was beginning to flow more freely, redistributed throughout my body, loosening the joints and muscles. The bruised ribs still hurt but not as badly as when I'd started.

You'd think that a good, brisk run would not be the best cure for a hangover. You'd be right. But it works. It works in the same masochistic way that physical therapy works after surgery. And, yeah, you're right. I fell off the wagon last night.

But I had my reasons.

Bjorn moved beside me effortlessly. There would be no Frisbee today, no opportunity to run at full speed, and he knew it. This was a sympathy run with his master, and he did his best not to rub it in. This was unequivocal, nonjudgmental friendship. Just what I needed.

The decision to follow Beth last night had not been planned, more a spur-of-the-moment type of thing. I'd just dropped Annie off at my in-laws after my stingy, bimonthly weekend visitation and was filling up at the gas station just outside the entrance to Bunker's Cove, when Beth pulled up to the traffic light in her Volvo S80. As she waited at the light, she looked at herself in the rearview mirror, turning her head from side to side, running her fingers through her jet-black hair. Even from my vantage point, I could see the streetlight reflecting off her perfect olive skin.

It was obvious she had not seen me. Just as well. I was very much aware of the continuing restraining order that allowed contact with my wife only for purposes of child care issues, and only then through a third party. I didn't need that kind of trouble, especially right now. I was prepared to chalk it up to coincidence, to stand there and watch her drive off, then head on back to Tallahassee. But when she was still there as I was putting the hose back and tearing off my receipt, I was thinking maybe fate had something else in mind. So when the light changed and Beth turned left, headed toward the beaches, I got quickly into my Accord and pulled out after her.

She stopped at the bank about a half mile up the road. From a safe distance, I watched as she slid out of the seat and walked up to the ATM. She was dressed in a black silk party dress and high heels. This was not, I suspected, a trip to the grocery store. As she left the bank, I followed her onto Thomas Drive, my doubts flying out of the open window of my car and into the night air.

Three or four miles down the road, she pulled into the parking lot of the Moon Spinner, a large, popular night club. I took a space at the opposite end of the lot and watched as she approached the entrance. Was she meeting someone? Should I follow her inside, try to keep out of sight? It would be dark in there. It might work. Or should I wait out here to see if she left with someone? That might be hours from now though.

My questions were answered and my dilemma solved when she waved at someone waiting near the entrance. Even in the dimming light of early evening I could see the flash of her smile, the one that had pierced my heart the night I met her. The man who returned her wave was of medium height and had an athletic build and short dark, curly hair. He looked vaguely familiar.

At the entrance, they embraced and kissed. The blood drained from my head, replaced by ice, and the sharp blade of betrayal twisted in my gut. As I got out of my car and moved toward them, my mind was working through the rational, logical, and prudent options, pointing out the reasons to stop, turn around, get in my car, and leave.

There was not only the practical, very real problem of the restraining order; there was the hypocrisy, the egocentricity of my sense of betrayal. Who was I to judge, to take the moral high ground on the issue of marital fidelity? Why make a scene, embarrass my wife and myself, and make matters worse? But logic and rationality deserted me in the face of the emotional storm raging inside me.

"Hello, Beth," I said as calmly as I could, affecting a nonchalance I didn't feel. I had closed the distance between us and now stopped about six feet away.

For a brief couple of seconds, her face registered a mix of shock and guilt, which, when all things were tallied and put on a scale, might have been worth it. It was quickly replaced, though, by anger and righteous indignation. "Ted, what are you doing here? Have you been following me? Spying on me?"

Of course I had, which was pretty obvious from the circumstances, but I denied it. "Just thought I'd relax a little before I went back to Tallahassee, maybe spend the night on the beach. Imagine my surprise at finding you here with your boyfriend."

I looked at the man beside her again, realizing why he was familiar. It was Michael Okalidis, the guy who worked in the family restaurant, the guy Beth had dated throughout high school, the one her parents adored and assumed she would marry—until I came along. He stepped forward, standing between Beth and me, puffing out his chest.

"I understand you're a real tough guy with the women. You want to try something with someone your own size?"

"I don't know," I said, looking around the lot. "You got somebody in mind?"

It was not a prudent response. He had baited me and I had responded in kind, ratcheting up the testosterone level. True, he was smaller than I was, about four inches shorter and twenty-five pounds lighter. Still, he looked ready for a fight, and I had made it difficult for him to back down.

I watched his eyes, readying for the attack I figured was coming. But Beth stepped between us, her back to me, inches from his face. She grabbed his wrists.

"Mike, don't. Let me handle this."

He looked over her at me, fire in his eyes, then back at her. "I'm not going to leave you alone with him."

"Please, Mike. I'll be okay. Give us a minute."

"Yeah, Mike, all I want is a little private chat with *my* wife," I said, "if that's okay with you."

He looked back and forth again between Beth and me, then finally grunted and backed away a few feet. "I'll be right over here if you need me," he said to Beth but looking at me. Then he walked to the south side of the parking lot, within sight but not hearing. When he was a safe distance away, Beth turned to me.

"What are you thinking, Ted? You realize that I could have you locked up for violating the injunction? "

I ignored the questions, which were really a threat. "Now I understand why you didn't want to come back to Tallahassee, why you didn't want to work on our marriage anymore, why you lied to me about it, and why you wanted to keep me away. When did you and Mike get back together? Have you been with him all summer?"

"Not that it's any of your business, but it's not like that. We're friends."

"Yeah, that looked like a real friendly kiss."

"I'm telling you, it's not like that."

"Then why are you sneaking around?"

"We're not sneaking. . . . Listen, I don't have to explain myself to you," she said, but then she did anyway. "Mike was there for me when I needed somebody. You weren't. And that's how it's been with us for too long. I'm tired of the roller-coaster life with you, Ted. I need something—someone—I can rely on."

The words were like knives plunged into my heart. They made me sad and angry, but I tried to keep my face neutral. I lit into her, telling her she was full of shit, laying out the weeks of frustration. Why, I asked, had she not said anything before? Why did she not have the guts, the respect, to tell me to my face before? Why did she want to take away from me the most precious thing we shared, our daughter? I told her she was a selfish, spoiled brat who has to have her way in everything.

As I rattled on, Beth said nothing, which was the worst response I could have received. In her eyes, I saw the simmering anger and resentment, the brooding of a teenager forced to listen to a scolding by her parent but not required to pay it any attention, prepared—even anxious—to ignore it at the first opportunity. And she was not listening. Not really. I realized that there was nothing in those eyes for me except maybe contempt or pity. Not love, certainly. Ten years gone in the blink of an eye. An overwhelming sadness washed over me. Without another word, I turned and headed for my car, hearing her call my name as I walked away.

About halfway across the lot, I noticed Mike out of the corner of my eye. He was walking toward me, and he had two friends with him. I looked at the three men, then at my car, calculating distance and time, weighing my options. Mike called my name. I turned and faced the men, wishing I had a tire iron or other equalizer but resigned to the inevitable. "Yes, Mike," I said, my voice tired. The three men approached to about eight feet away and fanned out to surround me. "I see you invited more guests to the party," I observed.

"The more the merrier." He gave me a sinister smile.

"Funny, that's what your mother said last night when me and the guys came over."

"Very funny, asshole."

I focused on Okalidis. The other two looked able to deliver a pretty good blow. One was about my size, the other short but built like a spark plug. This was Mike's fight, though. I figured he would be the one to throw the first punch.

I figured wrong. The first blow came from the right, from the taller man. And he was fast, delivering a glancing blow to the top of my head as I barely ducked enough to avoid a full hit. The smaller one came at my legs then, intent on bringing me down to the gravel lot. I was able to deflect his charge, though, and throw him into his taller buddy. I turned just in time to catch Mike in full swing. I blocked his punch with my forearm, stepped inside the swing, and hit him, hard, directly on the nose. I heard the sound of bone and cartilage collapsing, followed by a scream of agony. I hit him again, a quick jab in the face, then another as he tried to cover up and reeled backward from the blows. I had not started this, but I was prepared to finish it.

Out of the corner of my eye, I saw it coming but couldn't react quickly enough. The big guy caught me on the side of my head with his fist, and I went down. I found myself on my knees, my vision clouding. I tried to get up, but my legs felt like rubber. Then somebody kicked me hard in the gut, and I doubled over.

Mike was over me now, his breath hot and stinking. "Where's that smart mouth now, motherfucker?" He stood up then and kicked at my head. I was able to put my hand up in front of my face, but the force of the blow knocked me on my back. I rolled over on my side and tried to push myself up, but another boot caught me in the midsection. Then another and another as I went into a fetal position, covering up as best I could.

"Okay, that's enough. We better get out of here before the law comes." It was the short guy, a gruff, gravelly voice. Another kick to the gut, for good measure, then footsteps walking away. I rose up on my elbows, then sat up. My breath was shallow, and I wondered if maybe I had a broken rib. "Hey, Mike," I called out. The three men turned around. "Fuck you."

Okalidis started toward me but was restrained by his two friends. They got into a late-model Ford Mustang and sped out of the lot. I sat there a minute, checking myself for injuries. My stomach and sides hurt like a mother, but I thought my ribs were just bruised. I could taste blood from a busted lip, and my head was aching, but, all in all, I thought, it could have been worse. A guy with a Moon Spinner polo shirt was standing in the doorway. How long, I wondered, had he been there? He walked over to me and offered a hand. I took it and let him pull me up. He held on to me for a few seconds while I steadied myself.

"You okay, buddy?"

I nodded. He looked at me, apparently satisfied that I was, then said, "You'll have to leave. We have a no-fighting policy here."

I looked at him and gave him a crooked smile. "Good policy. I was just leaving." I looked at the entrance where Beth had been standing, then around the parking lot to where she had parked. The Volvo was gone.

***

When Bjorn and I got close to the edge of the yard, he bolted for the door. He stood on the porch, turned, and looked at me impatiently, then scratched once on the door. When I opened it, he rushed in and headed for the kitchen and his water dish. He put his full face in it, slurped up a mouthful, then looked up at me, water falling down the sides of his mouth and onto the floor. Not the daintiest of drinkers.

I opened the fridge, grabbed a bottle of water, and slugged down half of it. I took a breath or two, then downed the rest of it. I looked over at my phone and saw that the red message light was blinking.

On my drive back to Tallahassee the night before, I had assessed the possible fallout from the incident at the Moon Spinner. I had to figure that Beth had probably gotten her lapdog attorney on her cell phone within a minute of leaving the parking lot, getting advice on how to handle things. Thompson would have put together a quick motion and woken the judge up to address the "emergency" of my willful conduct. So I was half-expecting a call from Denise, telling me that the judge had issued an order to show cause why I shouldn't be held in contempt for violating the restraining order, or maybe even that a warrant had been issued.

I could say that running into Beth was coincidental, but that was pretty lame. And even if anyone believed me, I still had the obligation to leave once I realized we were at the same public place. The fact that I had acted in self-defense against Okalidis would not matter either if he and his friends were prepared to lie, which I assumed they were. He would display the photo of his broken nose and swollen face, and my purported history of violence would do the rest.

I walked over and pressed "Play." The automated voice told me I had one message, delivered at 8:17 a.m. "Hello, Ted. It's Theo. Got some news on the Hart case. Give me a call at the office, unless you're headed here now, in which case I'll see you in a few."

I stared at the phone a few seconds, surprised and relieved it had not been from Denise. I followed the directions to delete the message, then punched in the number. He picked up on the second ring. "Hey, Theo. What you got?"

"Maxine Chrenshaw called this morning. You weren't here, so she asked for me."

When silence didn't prompt him I said, "Yes?"

"Donnie Mercer is dead."

CHAPTER 22

Nathan studied the chessboard, his brow furrowed in concentration. The last three moves had been made rather quickly on both our parts, but now he hesitated. We were in that small, glassed-in room near the security station in the General Forensics building. Without looking up, he asked, "Any news on Donnie's unfortunate demise?"

I shook my head. "No witnesses. Staff just found him dead out in front of the building. There will be an autopsy."

He made his next move—bishop F8 to D6—then looked up at me. "Jumping off a three-story building is not your classic suicide," he observed.

"Agreed. Could have been an accident." I countered with bishop F1 to D3.

"I think he was murdered," he said, looking at the board.

"Maybe." After a moment, I added, "If so, you have to know you're the prime suspect."

"Of course I am. That's the plan." Nathan looked at me for a long time as if considering whether to tell me something, then went back to studying the board. "I know who did it, Ted. I know who killed both Donnie and Rosenberg." He looked up from the board. "It was Rebecca."

"Oh?" I managed to keep my face passive.

"Well, I say 'Rebecca,' but in reality, the woman who calls herself Rebecca Whitsen is really Cindy Sands." He moved one of his pieces on the board.

My usual poker face dissolved. "Come again?"

"She killed the real Dr. Whitsen and has assumed her identity."

I didn't say anything for several seconds. I moved one of my pieces in response to his move and asked, "What makes you think so?"

His eyes lit up then, as if excited just thinking about it, and then he affected a calm detachment as he laid it out for me. The cigarette lighter and the e-mails to Rebecca were just too coincidental. There had to be a connection, he reasoned. What if Cindy Sands had not died in that fire? What if she had staged her death in order to create a new life for herself? The body was burned beyond recognition and had been identified from Cindy's dental records. But what if she had switched her dental records with those of her psychologist?

"So the person who died in the fire was really Rebecca Whitsen?"

"Exactly. She gets the jump on the psychologist, surprises her somewhere, overpowers her, then drugs her. She takes her to this mobile home, places her in the bed, and then starts the fire, making it look like she had fallen asleep while smoking in bed."

"And the difference in appearance? I've seen the news photos of Sands. You couldn't mistake her for Whitsen in a dark room."

"Plastic surgery," he said. "It's amazing what can be done these days. And it was six weeks or more after her escape that she was supposedly found dead. Time enough to have healed from such a procedure."

I could only stare at him. The whole idea seemed ludicrous. But, then again, I have learned to never dismiss out of hand any theory in a criminal case. Truth is indeed sometimes stranger than fiction. And I remembered from Theo's notes that Whitsen's father was dead, she had no siblings, her mother had Alzheimer's and wouldn't know the difference, and her only other family member, the uncle, lived on the other side of the country and had little contact with her. To her colleagues here she was a stranger. They didn't know Rebecca Whitsen until she showed up nine months ago. Cindy Sands had a background in both psychology and acting. Still . . .

"Think about it," Nathan said. "It was a perfect alter ego for her to start a new life. She would have loved the irony. Rosenberg must have found out or gotten too close, and Cindy killed him to protect her new identity. And that's probably what happened to Donnie too. He must have known something or suspected it, and he was going to tell me, so Cindy had to kill him too."

We both fell silent as I processed what he had said. After a few seconds, Nathan moved another piece.

I could see his strategy now: Advance the pawn to H4, then exchange pawns, thus extricating the bishop. Nice try, but there wouldn't be time for it to develop. "I'm intrigued, Nathan. Interesting theory, but . . ."

He held up his hand, then retrieved an expandable file folder from the floor next to his chair and placed it on the table next to the chessboard. "Here, let me show you," he said, opening the folder. "As you can see, the two women were similar in size and physical features, judging by these photos I was able to obtain off the Internet." He placed the grainy images on the table.

I leaned forward to get a better view. "You're kidding, right?"

He ignored my sarcasm. "It's not a striking resemblance, I'll grant you, but you cut and dye the hair and put some fake glasses on Cindy, and she starts to look more like her psychologist." I continued to shake my head, looking at the photo images. "And, as I said, they're doing amazing things with cosmetic surgery these days. It's not so unusual for people to go under the knife just to look like their favorite movie star. And I'm sure a discreet, willing surgeon could be found in the D.C. area, for a price."

I considered my next move and his statement for a few moments, then advanced my knight. "I don't know, Nathan. I haven't looked really close, but Rebecca's glasses seem real enough, and I've seen no tell-tale signs of cosmetic surgery."

"That might simply be a reflection of the skill of the surgeon," he offered.

Still looking at the board, I said, "Even if Cindy Sands were able to make her face look like Whitsen's, cut her hair, and get a pair of glasses, I seem to remember—somewhere in all that information we have obtained at your request—that Sands was a good three inches taller than Whitsen." I looked up at him then. "Now, cosmetic surgery has gotten quite advanced, but you still can't make a tall person short."

He thought about this for a few moments. He didn't have an answer to this observation, he said, not yet. "But I do have an answer to your last move," he said, lifting his piece from H5 and placing it on H4.

I quickly moved to counter, on the board and in our discussion. "Other than the fact that she has a great alibi, there's another flaw in you theory, Nathan."

"What's that?"

"Why do you think she would frame you for it? That doesn't make much sense, does it? Why would she pick someone clever like you, someone who would figure things out, as you have apparently done?"

A flash of anger crossed his face. "Are you mocking me, Ted?"

I was, a little, but said, "No, of course not. It seems like a reasonable question."

He looked at me closely then, trying to see beyond the mask perhaps. After a few moments, apparently satisfied with what he saw or didn't see in my face, he said, "Isn't it obvious? She wanted to match wits with me. She framed me for the murder in order to bring me into her game."

He moved his bishop from H2 to G3, taking my pawn. I immediately took his bishop. Two pawns for a bishop—not a bad trade. Nathan frowned and cursed under his breath.

"Don't feel too bad," I said. "Bobby Fischer made the same mistake in the opening game of his nineteen seventy-two match against Boris Spassky. He ended up losing the game," I added.

Nathan regained his composure and gave me that sly grin again. "You are a worthy opponent, Ted. I will concede this game," he said, laying down his king. "But you must also remember that although Bobby Fischer did indeed lose that opening game in nineteen seventy-two, he ended up winning the match."

He grinned and began to gather the chess pieces. When he had finished, he leaned forward and whispered, "I know you don't fully accept this theory, Ted, and I'll admit there are some holes that need to be filled, but I know in my marrow that she's the one." He looked around the room quickly and leaned in a little more. "I know because God told me so."

CHAPTER 23

*T*he holding cell at the Gadsden County Courthouse Annex was about twelve by eighteen feet in size. It had a toilet, a sink, and stainless steel benches. The floors and walls were relatively clean, even though the cell was often filled with prisoners, many of whom had serious personal hygiene issues. When I came into the area, I saw Nathan sitting serenely on the end of the bench in the lotus position, his eyes closed. His companions were giving him plenty of space.

"Hello, Ted," he said as I stopped in front of the cell. Then he opened his eyes and smiled in my direction. As if in answer to my silent question, he said, "I knew it was you. I could smell the familiar odor of your sweat."

Nice, I thought. I stood there a moment or two, my right hand in my pocket and my left wrapped around the handle of an old, soft leather briefcase. I looked over in the corner where a deputy sat on a stool by the back entrance door. "Carl, can I talk to my client over there? A little more private?" I pointed with my chin toward an empty holding cell on the other side of the room. It was the one they used for female inmates, though there were none present that day.

Carl looked over in our direction for a couple of seconds, shrugged, then walked over. He didn't say anything, but he opened the cell door and motioned for Nathan to come out. My client stepped outside and quietly followed Carl and me to the other cell. The deputy seemed surprised when I asked to be inside the cell with my client, but he just shrugged again, said "Suit yourself," and closed the door behind us.

I waited until Carl returned to his position by the back door, out of earshot. "Have a seat," I said as I sat down on one end of the metal bench and spread my files out in the middle. Nathan sat on the other end. "The proceeding today is called the pretrial hearing." I put both hands on my knees and leaned back against the wall, looking sideways at Nathan. "It is the last case management conference we will have before the trial. The judge will hear any pending motions . . ."

"Yes, yes," he said, interrupting, impatience in his voice. "What have you to report, counselor, as to the imposter?"

I sighed inwardly and picked up one of the files, opened it, and began to summarize the information I had obtained so far. I had scoured the Internet and other sources for some evidence to support his supposition. I had read newspaper articles and reviewed police files and archived television news broadcasts. I was even able to get a copy of a taped interview with Cindy Sands, which I studied carefully for any signs or clues as to how she might have transformed herself into the Rebecca Whitsen I had come to know. I'd come up with nothing. There was also still the problem, I reminded him, of her alibi.

"How do we know she was at her home when she was called? Maybe they called her cell phone."

I shook my head. "Nope. We asked. They called her home phone, landline."

"Who was it who called her?"

I looked at my notes, told him the name of the staff person, a Darlene Croft.

Nathan shook his head. He had never heard of such a person, he said. "Are you sure this person really exists? Maybe Cindy made it up."

No, I told him, Theo had actually talked to the person.

"Maybe she is mistaken or lying."

"Maybe," I conceded, "but as of now, that's her statement, and it is consistent with what Rebecca says. We have nothing to contradict it."

He looked past me for several moments. "And the police were sure of the identification of Sands as the person killed in the fire?"

I sighed. "No question. There were the dental records, of course, but there were also the fingerprints in the car parked in front of the trailer that matched up with Sands and the ID by the landlady."

"Of course they were Cindy's prints," he said. "She drove the car. And of course the landlady recognized Cindy's photo, because she's the one who rented the place before the plastic surgery. And if Cindy switched the medical and dental records, that would explain the misidentification by the medical examiner."

I suggested the logistical nightmare of exchanging all of the records. "Certainly she would have made some slip."

He gave me a look of pure exasperation. "Of course. That's what I've been trying to tell you. That's why we should dig deeper into the background of both women, pull as many records as we can, go back to high school if you have to, but you have to find the one thing that has been overlooked." He also noted that if the Unit was involved, it had the resources and the expertise to pull it off. "And the print on the lighter? Any luck with a match?"

"I asked our expert, as you requested, to double-check the findings of the State's expert. The prints on the lighter were checked against the prints of every person who might have been in Rosenberg's office."

"And?"

"He agrees with the State's guy. The print is not of sufficient quality to make a match with anyone." He looked over at me and frowned. "One more thing, Nathan, and I think it pretty much shoots down this imposter theory. I had him specifically compare Rebecca Whitsen's fingerprints to those of Cindy Sands." I hesitated a moment, then said, "They don't match. Not even close."

There was a long silence between us as Nathan seemed to consider this last bit of information. Finally, he asked, "Where did our expert get the prints of Whitsen and the others for comparison?"

"From the hospital files, same as the detectives. All employees are fingerprinted when they first start work there."

Nathan was not so easily convinced. "Maybe Cindy substituted someone else's prints." I was shaking my head slowly, preparing to speak, but he kept going. "What we need to do is get a fresh print from Rebecca, compare it directly to that of Sands. I've got a friend with the FBI who I'm sure has more expertise in this than your expert and a larger database. I'll bet you we'll find that the print on the lighter and the fresh print we get from Rebecca Whitsen are a match for Cindy Sands."

Yeah, right. He had a friend at the FBI. "Listen, Nathan. We have limited resources to throw at this thing, including my time. Now, I will get you whatever information you request if it's within my abilities, pursue whatever leads you tell me, but I have to say I think this is not your best bang for the buck."

Nathan looked at me closely then for several seconds. "Funny you should use that term. Freudian slip?"

"What?"

"You're banging her, aren't you?"

"What?"

"Rebecca . . . or Cindy. You're having sexual relations with my psychologist. Maybe that's what Donnie was trying to tell me."

I had not told Nathan about my visit to Rebecca's apartment. Both of us had agreed to this. Now I was wondering if Rebecca had said something. Or was Nathan just guessing. "Don't be ridiculous," I said

"That would be a serious ethical breach, I would imagine, not to mention a personal betrayal."

"I'm telling you, it's not true."

He studied me for several more seconds. I don't know if he was satisfied or not, but he relaxed a little, then shifted gears. "What about James Washington? Any connection to Sands?"

I ticked off the pertinent information, the pros and cons for this theory. Physically, he was taller and heavier than Nathan, not to mention a different skin color. It's unlikely Raymond Curry could have mistaken him for Nathan. He had lied on his application about his past drug charges, but there was no indication Rosenberg knew about it or that anything would have come of it if he did. "Theo did find a little hole in his story about his grandmother."

"Yes?"

I was hesitant to feed his paranoia, but I had to tell him. "Yeah, he did have a sick grandmother in Baltimore, and he did go back to care for her. But she died within six months of his arrival, which leaves eighteen months when he supposedly did a series of part-time, low-paying jobs. Now maybe he was just taking off extra time, but it did make me wonder if he could have been working at St. Elizabeth's, which is not that far from Baltimore."

He rubbed his chin, nodded. "And?"

"Working on it."

"Did you file the motion for continuance?"

"It's prepared but not filed," I said. "I figure I'll file it directly with the judge this morning."

"I'm telling you, Ted, we need to explore this fingerprint evidence thoroughly. This may be key. We can't go to trial without having nailed it down."

I could sense the anger in his voice, tried my best not to react. I turned to face him more directly. "This way, the prosecutor is thrown off guard a little bit."

It was hard to argue with the logic, and he didn't, though he looked at me for a long few seconds, trying to decide, perhaps, whether to believe me. My peripheral vision picked up Carl standing up from his stool and beginning to walk our way. "Okay, Stevens, need to wrap it up."

I put up my hand in acknowledgment and looked back at Nathan expectantly. He was still looking at me. Then he sighed and said, "I know she's the one, Ted. You need to find the proof."

***

Judge Palmer sat up straight in his chair. He looked annoyed. I had just suggested to him that we may need to postpone the trial date. "What's the problem?" the judge asked, leaning forward.

I hesitated, looking around at my client, then back at the judge. "I don't want to divulge our defense strategy, but what I can say is that we are pursuing certain evidence that could be extremely helpful to the defense."

The judge leaned back in his chair. "It's difficult, Mr. Stevens, for me to evaluate your request for a continuance based on such a vague and general statement."

"That's right, judge," Chrenshaw said, as if on cue. "The State is not interested in the secrets of the defense, but we oppose any continuance unless Mr. Stevens can articulate something a little more specific and compelling. Mr. Hart is the one, as you recall, who insisted on getting to trial quickly."

The judge looked at Nathan as he said, "Yes, I recall."

"Our subpoenas have gone out, and we have coordinated with the schedules of our expert witnesses."

Nathan stood and faced the prosecutor. "With all due respect, Maxine, if you folks had done your job properly, I wouldn't need to do it for you."

Maxine turned to the judge, ready to respond, but the judge raised his hand to stop her, then looked at Nathan, his eyes boring through him. His voice was not raised but his displeasure was obvious from his tone.

"Mr. Hart, in court you refer to persons, including attorneys and witnesses, by their last names. You will not address the prosecutor by her first name. Do you understand?"

"I meant no disrespect, Your Honor."

"The other thing, Mr. Hart, is that when you are asking the court for a ruling on something, you address your remarks to me, not to the other attorney."

Nathan nodded. Personally, I thought Palmer was being more than patient with my client. The judge sat for a few seconds. Then, apparently satisfied, he continued. "Now, either you or your lawyer is going to have to give me something a little more specific as to why you cannot be ready for trial as scheduled."

Nathan mulled this over for a few seconds. "Perhaps, Your Honor, it would be permissible for me to tell the court in private. Then you can evaluate the legitimacy of my request. Surely, Ms. Chrenshaw trusts Your Honor."

Maxine started to say something, and the judge again raised his hand to stop her, then looked in Nathan's direction. "I'm sure she does, but it doesn't work that way, Mr. Hart." He leaned back in his chair. "Ms. Chrenshaw gets to hear anything you tell me, just like you get to hear anything she tells me."

Nathan looked over at me. I leaned over and whispered in his ear. "We've got to give them something, Nathan."

"Okay," he said. He then turned and faced the courtroom crowd. I followed his gaze, which came to rest on Rebecca, who was seated in the back row next to James Washington.

I turned back to face the judge. "Very well, Your Honor. To be frank, my client is less than satisfied with the forensics investigation conducted by the State and with the expert I have retained, whom he sees as having too close ties to the FDLE. He wants what he calls a truly independent examiner to compare the fingerprint lifted from the cigarette lighter found at the scene to the known prints of several people, including Frank Hutchinson, Barbara Hutchinson, Rebecca Whitsen, James Washington, and Andy Rudd. He has a person in mind to do the comparisons."

Although we were focused on Rebecca, I wanted to hide this target in a crowd of names. I started to wonder if some of my client's paranoia was beginning to rub off on me. "We're not asking for the prints of every resident and employee of the hospital, judge, as I think we are entitled, but only of those with access to the victim, a questionable alibi, and a motive."

Judge Palmer looked at me for a couple of moments. He recognized the potential for an appeal if Nathan was not allowed to pursue his theories of defense, no matter how lame they might appear. And everybody knew my client could generate a mountain of paperwork if he had a mind to. Then he looked over toward Maxine, who had remained standing.

"Judge," she said, "all of these persons have their fingerprints on file with the hospital. You have already provided the defense with the money to hire an independent fingerprint examiner. They could have done these comparisons by now. In fact, they still have time before trial to do so if they want."

"The problem is, Your Honor, we believe that the fingerprint cards on file at the hospital might not be completely accurate, may have been altered."

"What makes you think that?' the judge asked.

I told Palmer I had a source at the hospital. I didn't tell him the source was my client. The judge considered this for a few seconds. He looked over toward Maxine again. She said that what my client was requesting would be an unnecessary imposition on these people, that we should have to show some reasonable basis to believe the fingerprint cards had been altered, and she urged the judge not to let the defense turn the trial into a circus. She didn't seem the least bit embarrassed by her cliché either. "Mr. Hart's paranoia," she said, "should not be what motivates or drives these proceedings."

The judge decided to give us a crumb. He said that he would not require anyone to provide new prints. If anyone volunteered, that would be fine. But, he said, we would have to do whatever we were planning by the time of trial. If further investigation provided a need for more time, we could ask for it then.

At this, I turned to the judge and said, "I noticed earlier, Judge Palmer, that some of these same people are in the courtroom this morning. Apparently they are interested in the proceedings. I'd like to pose that request to them now. Your bailiff could do it. It would be very convenient. That is, if they have nothing to hide." I turned then toward the audience, searching for Rebecca, but as I looked in the direction of where she and James had been sitting, I saw that both seats were now empty.

CHAPTER 24

I pulled into the parking lot of the Waffle House near I-10 and Thomasville Road a little after 6:30. It was still dark outside and a slight rain had begun to fall, which somehow seemed fitting for the day of my divorce hearing. I had asked Theo to meet me for breakfast before I got on the road, to talk about the Hart case, which was scheduled for trial the following week. I started to search the lot for his car before realizing that I didn't know what he drove. As I made it to the entrance, though, I could see him through the glass walls of the restaurant. He was sitting in a booth near the door. I took off my blazer and hung it on the rack, then joined him.

"Coffee, hon?" The waitress was already starting to pour before I could answer.

A little presumptuous, sure, but I admired the efficiency of it. I uttered the unnecessary "Yes, please," as she was pulling out her order pad.

She didn't exactly smile but her face seemed friendly when she said, "Whatcha gonna have?" suggesting that I needed no time to peruse the menu. I looked over at Theo, who shook his head and pointed to the coffee in front of him. Before the waitress could start scribbling down something she assumed I wanted, I said, "I'll have the All-Star Breakfast, eggs over easy, bacon, crisp, and hash browns."

She nodded appreciatively. Here was a regular, someone who knew what he wanted. "Juice?"

"Orange."

"Regular or large?"

"Large."

And with that, she tore off the ticket, flipped her pad shut, and put it in her apron. Then she turned and called out the order to the rather grungy-looking cook standing six feet away who, with his back to her, nodded in acknowledgment as he tended to the items on the grill in front of him. Less than sixty seconds from walking in the door, I had a cup of coffee in front of me and my breakfast on the way. There was something very reassuring about that.

I turned to face Theo, who was frowning in a friendly way. "Man, how can you eat all that crap so early in the morning?"

"Most important meal of the day, Odious. The body needs fuel. And I mean something substantial, not just a cup of coffee." He shook his head slowly from side to side but said nothing. I pulled a file out of my briefcase and placed it in front of me. "So," I said, "you ready?"

"Me? Yeah, I'm ready. But the spotlight's going to be on you. The question is, are you ready?"

"As ready as I'm going to be, I guess. By the way," I said, patting the briefcase, "thanks for putting all this together for me." Theo had prepared a trial notebook with separate sections for opening statement, expected legal arguments, witnesses, exhibits, and closing argument. There was a separate file on each witness containing an outline of possible questions and a digest of his or her deposition testimony. It was indexed and tabbed so I could easily find appropriate text for possible impeachment if the witness said something different at trial. "I've never been so organized."

This was perhaps a lie. Aside from virtually every other aspect of my personal and professional life, I am probably the most organized when I am in the thick of preparation for a jury trial. Indeed, I had supplemented and modified Theo's notebook to make it more to my liking. All in all, though, I had been comforted in the knowledge that our approach to trial was similar, that we both put a premium on preparation. And though

Theo shrugged off the compliment, I knew it would boost his confidence and make him an even more effective and committed team member. "So, you say you've got something on Rosenberg and Barbara Hutchinson?"

The waitress came by to top off our coffee. Theo waited until she had moved on before responding. "I obtained the voucher records from a conference on forensic psychology the two attended in Daytona Beach last year. Both Rosenberg and Hutchinson were signed up as attendees, the only ones from the hospital to go or at least to turn in vouchers. Nothing unusual there, given their positions at the hospital. But here's the thing. I pulled their voucher forms for the trip. Rosenberg had expenses for lodging, food, and mileage. Hutchinson only requested reimbursement for food and lodging."

"So? They rode together. Nothing unusual about that either."

"No, and their receipts show they had separate rooms for the conference too. The interesting part is, the conference was over on Friday, and though he didn't bill the State for it, Rosenberg's hotel receipt shows he stayed an extra two nights, came back on Sunday."

Still not so unusual. People often took advantage of the reduced rate to stay an extra night or two. Maybe he had a meeting.

Maybe, Theo conceded. "Hutchinson's hotel bill, however, didn't have a charge for the extra nights." Theo waited a few moments to let this sink in. "There could be a logical and innocent explanation. Perhaps she caught a ride back with someone else, though as I said, they were the only ones coming from Chattahoochee. Maybe her husband came and picked her up. Maybe she stayed with relatives or a friend."

"Or maybe she paid for the extra two nights with a different credit card, to separate personal from business expense, also not that unusual," I suggested.

"On the other hand, perhaps she stayed with Rosenberg and was too cheap to try and cover her tracks by keeping a separate room when she wasn't going to get reimbursed for it."

"The implication's there anyway."

"You want me to follow up? I can ask her about it directly, try to get her credit card receipts."

I shook my head. "Follow up, see what you can find, but don't ask her anything and don't let her know what we have. I'd rather surprise her with it at trial, not give her a chance to think up something." I hesitated a moment as our waitress set my breakfast in front of me. I surveyed the food with satisfaction, picked up a piece of greasy bacon, and took a bite, then looked back at Theo and said, "I've got another dart of suspicion to throw her way as well."

Theo's eyebrows arched in a question over his coffee cup as he took a sip, and I continued. "Barbara Hutchinson told Rebecca Whitsen that she was barely literate when it came to computers and e-mail. She said her husband was the computer geek in the family. But when I asked Frank a few days ago about spoofing and how one might trace an e-mail of unknown origins—being intentionally vague, of course—he assured me that his wife was the computer-savvy one in the family."

Theo's eyebrows arched even higher at this information. "So one of them is lying."

"Maybe both of them."

"And," Theo said, "if they're working together in some cover-up, they sure aren't coordinating things very well."

I nodded, then changed the subject. "What about James Washington? Any word on whether he worked at St. Elizabeth's?"

He shook his head. "They had no record of a James Washington working there, at least not within the past five years."

"Meanwhile, our client's obsession with his psychologist-as-imposter theory has continued unabated. He's become more and more irritable, irrational, and unreasonable in the last couple of weeks. Last time we talked, he told me he had managed to lift a print of Rebecca's from a glass. I didn't bother to ask him where he had obtained the tools or the knowledge to do so. He said he had sent it to his friend at the FBI. He handed me what he said was the e-mail message back from his friend, confirming that the print did indeed match that of Cynthia Sands."

Theo raised his eyebrows. "Really?"

I shook my head. "It was an advertisement from U.S. Airways for discount flights. When I point this out, Nathan gives me this look of complete disdain. Well, of course it's in code, he says. The friend was doing him a favor. If he got caught he would lose his job. He says he thinks he can convince him to come forward at trial, if necessary, but it shouldn't be if we can just get the judge to make Rebecca give a fresh sample in court and have our expert compare it."

"'Cause her print on file at the hospital is a forgery?"

"That's right."

"What'd you say?"

"I told him we would need something other than a coded message to convince the judge to change his ruling. Unless Rebecca was willing to give the sample, it wasn't likely that Judge Palmer would require it. He frowned and pondered that for a bit, then said he would think of something."

Theo gave me a sympathetic shrug and shook his head. "What are you going to do?"

"I'm not sure," I said, then shoveled some more food into my mouth. "I'm still working on it."

"Is he still bent on testifying?"

"That's the way he's leaning," I said, "but I haven't given up on that either. At least he's agreed to hold up on a final decision until the State rests its case. We'll just have to play it by ear."

Theo and I spent the next few minutes confirming who would question which witness. I had taken the lion's share of this but didn't want Theo to look or feel like a potted plant in the courtroom, so I had given him a few of the noncontroversial witnesses to handle. We discussed the theme of our defense and the key points to bring out in cross-examination and tried to anticipate the counterpart from Maxine. When our waitress swooped in to clear my plate away, seconds after I put the last bite of food in my mouth, I looked at my watch. "Well, I better get on over to Panama City."

As we both stood, Theo snapped his fingers and said, "Oh, I almost forgot. I went through Donnie Mercer's personal belongings as you asked. The hospital finally gave the okay, though I had a security guard with me the whole time."

"Find something useful?"

"Maybe." He pulled a piece of notepaper from his shirt pocket. "In his wallet he had a scrap of paper with a phone number on it. I was curious so I jotted it down and called it later."

"And?"

Theo pulled out his cell phone, punched in the number, and handed the phone to me. I put it up to my ear and heard it ringing. After the fifth ring it went to voice mail: "You have reached the office of Professor Robert Hart. Please leave your number and a brief message so that I may return your call as soon as possible. Thank you."

CHAPTER 25

*D*enise Wilkerson leaned on the podium and looked at me. She paused for a few seconds, then asked her question. "Mr. Stevens, you have heard the testimony of your wife as to why she thinks it is in Annie's best interest that she stay primarily with her, here in Panama City. You've heard her suggestion of the parenting arrangement. You have opposed this. Why?"

I looked around the small courtroom, collecting my thoughts before answering. My wife sat demurely next to her lawyer, refusing to make eye contact with me. She had been a good little actress, tearing up at the appropriate times, telling the judge of her growing concerns during our marriage that I was drinking more and more, turning violent at times. Life with me the last few years, she said, had been an emotional roller coaster. She testified about my putting my hand through the wall of her parents' guesthouse the past summer. She told the judge about the Moon Spinner incident. Of course, she made it sound worse than it was. And, let's face it, it was already bad enough.

Her lawyer had paraded a host of family, friends, doctors, teachers, and others to say what a wonderful parent she was, what wonderful people her parents were, how Annie was thriving in school and with Beth. Their expert witness opined that my child was comfortable in the present arrangement and had a supportive extended family in Panama City, and that to move her to Tallahassee at this point, in the middle of the school year, would be particularly stressful for her.

The evidence had not been all one sided, however, as Denise had done a pretty good job of parading witnesses in front of the judge too. We did our best to concentrate on quality rather than quantity. Paul's wife, Anna, was one of my best witnesses. A marriage and family counselor herself, she came across as an unbiased professional who happened to have a wealth of firsthand knowledge of the situation. She did a great job of laying out our position—not only was I completely capable of caring for Annie, but that to continue with the present arrangement would be detrimental to my relationship with her. Annie may have made the adjustment to life in Panama City, and it was true that she had extended family there, but she had lived in Tallahassee all her life. She had longtime friends, a network of doctors and a dentist, and others who were supportive.

One of the primary factors in considering who should be the primary residential parent was which parent was more likely to encourage and facilitate a good relationship between the child and the other parent. So the questions Denise posed with her evidence were these: What kind of parent lied to the other about her intentions? Who unilaterally decided to yank her child out of the only home and school she had known since birth? Who had used questionable claims of domestic violence to severely limit the other parent's contact with the child?

I was thinking about all of this as I considered my attorney's question. Finally, I began my answer. "I have been an active parent of my daughter from the day she was born. Beth did the bulk of the caregiving duties. That is true. But I changed diapers, fed her, rocked her to sleep, read bedtime stories to her as she got older, took her to the doctor, to daycare, and otherwise did everything my wife did, except for breast-feed."

I looked over at my wife for a couple of seconds, then back to the judge. "She wants you to believe that I'm a drunk, a drug addict, that I'm irresponsible and pose a threat to my child. That's ridiculous. While it is true that in the past I have abused alcohol, it never has affected my ability to care for Annie. My wife, in the several years that we were together, never hesitated to leave our daughter in my care. But now that she has decided she doesn't want to stay married to me, suddenly I can't be trusted to properly care for my daughter. I love Annie very much, Your Honor, and I would never do anything to put her in harm's way."

Denise let the echo of my words fill the room. She figured she could do no better than this, so she said, "No more questions, Your Honor."

The cross-examination was intense, but I had prepared for it well. Thompson asked me about my use of alcohol and drugs. I acknowledged moderate alcohol use up until recently but denied use of any illegal drugs.

"Never?"

"I did some marijuana and cocaine in my younger days, but not in quite some time." I pointed out that all of my UAs had been negative for the past two months.

"When was the last time you used any illegal drugs?"

"It's been so long I don't remember."

"Certainly not within the past, say, six months?"

"Certainly," I said, confident that he had no proof to the contrary.

And, you see, that's the trap people fall into when they are afraid of the truth or the consequences of it. It would have been far better to admit to the recent use and abuse of alcohol and other drugs and explain why my recent sobriety was solid.

"Do you frequent an establishment in Tallahassee called the Rajun Cajun?"

I guess I should have seen it coming then, as the question suggested a detailed knowledge of my comings and goings. "Occasionally," I said.

"Do you know a man named Wayne Colson?"

I shifted in my seat, the sweat beginning to bead up on my forehead. I willed my face to remain impassive as I assessed the situation. "Yes. He's a client."

"Have you, within the past six months, used or had possession of any illegal drugs in the presence of Wayne Colson?"

Now I was beginning to perspire freely as I did a quick review of the possibilities. It was most likely a bluff. Wayne would not have told these people about any drug use on my part, not because of any loyalty to me, but because he would have had to incriminate himself in the process. After all, he had been my source. And even if I had been watched, it was unlikely they could have seen or photographed anything in sufficient detail. Besides, I had already committed to my lie. "No," I said.

"You are sure?"

This time, having committed myself, I did not hesitate before answering, "I'm sure." I tried then to suppress the second thoughts that kept rising to the surface as the lawyer shuffled through his papers. Eventually, he looked back up at me, smiled briefly, and said, "No further questions, Your Honor."

Denise decided to leave well enough alone and opted to not ask any additional questions on redirect, and we rested our case. I returned to my seat, convinced that I had successfully called Thompson's bluff. But when the judge asked him if he had any evidence to present in rebuttal, he said, "Just one witness, Your Honor. The petitioner calls Wayne Colson."

***

You have heard the lies about the deaths of my parents and my brother. You think you know what happened, but you weren't there. Neither were those who accused me of this most heinous of offenses. They were murdered, all right, but not by me. This is what happened—the truth.

I was in my senior year at Georgetown University when I began to hear the voices on a regular basis again. My senses, already sharpened, became enhanced dramatically. At first it was great. Everything was brighter, more vivid. Sounds were more distinct, as were smells. It was fall then in Washington, and the golds and reds of the surrounding hills were the most beautiful, warm, glowing colors you could imagine. I felt energized, strong, and smart.

Gradually, however, the colors became too bright, the sounds too loud, the smells too strong. My ability to sort and to screen the stimuli around me deserted me at times. As a result, I found it increasingly difficult to concentrate on whatever task was at hand. The voices, which had been at first an aid to enlightenment, to inner peace and self-knowledge, became taunting, insulting, slanderous tirades.

The tide of stimuli ebbed and flowed, however, and I found that I could make defenses, compensations. For example, the voices seemed to come mostly at night and mostly through the light fixture on my bedroom ceiling. I removed the light and I taped over the hole. That seemed to work for a while. Eventually, though, it seemed that the voices followed me. They announced themselves intermittently and unexpectedly.

Things got worse. I couldn't sleep. I found myself becoming very agitated. I was being watched, followed, everywhere I went. It was at this time that I finally began to piece things together, began to see the pattern, connecting the dots. I realized that the organization I had been working for was a consortium of business and military interests that had created a shadow government worldwide, a group of ruthless and powerful people who had, for years, manipulated everything from stock markets to wars. Rulers were assassinated, governments were infiltrated and overthrown. They controlled, through bribery or coercion, countless governments and businesses throughout the world. I naturally felt betrayed.

I wrote a paper. It was more than two hundred pages, detailing all of the work that I had done, the information I had gathered, and the knowledge and facts that I had deduced about the Unit's work. I called my paper "The Invisible Hand" (apologies to Adam Smith) and attached to it documentation to back up everything. I secreted several copies of it in locations throughout the country with instructions to my lawyer what to do if anything were to happen to me. I informed my contact that I was discontinuing my association with the Unit and warned him to leave my family and me alone.

This is when they started slipping me the hallucinogenic drugs, started setting me up to destroy my credibility. I was arrested shortly after that one evening for aggravated assault and battery and disorderly conduct. This was the result of a confrontation with an operative who had been following me. He was about to kill me with a poison-tipped umbrella so I took him down *with a blow to the throat that almost killed him.*

At any rate, I found myself in the psychiatric center diagnosed with schizophrenia, paranoid type, and had my first introduction to psychotropic medication. My parents were called. The next thing I knew, the charges had been dropped, I was withdrawn from school, and by early December, I was back in Tallahassee.

The voices had stopped, but my thinking was fuzzy, my coordination limited, unfortunate side effects of the drugs they gave me. The week before Christmas I started cutting back on my meds. A couple of days later, I stopped altogether. I realized it was risky, but I also knew that I needed all of my senses intact. By Christmas Day I was doing pretty well. I had none of the symptoms and none of the side effects either.

My father was acting very strangely, though. He wanted to know about "The Invisible Hand" and where I had secreted my paper. The problem was that I had not told anyone other than my lawyer and my contact about the paper. I began to suspect my father's participation. There were obvious breaches in security all around the house. His nonchalance about the danger was very disturbing. As the days passed, I found myself becoming more and more agitated, nervous, certain that some action by the Unit was imminent. Then, in the early morning hours of New Year's Day, it happened.

I did not sleep that night. I lay in my bed, tense, listening for any sound that might be unusual. I found that I could hear even the slightest sound throughout the house: the ice maker in the refrigerator, the drip of the faucet in the bathroom, the constant hum of the electric alarm clock.

Then I heard it: the sound of a window opening. I got out of bed and crept down the hallway as quickly as I could, picking up a baseball bat along the way. In the kitchen, I noticed the door was not locked. I grabbed a butcher knife from the drawer and slipped it into the waistband of my gym shorts.

As I made my way down the hall, I caught a glimpse of a black-hooded figure just stepping into my brother's room. I waited several seconds, then I burst in, oblivious to my safety. The intruder had a gun with a silencer. I had time only to react, and I did so quickly, swinging the bat as hard as I could.

He was just bringing the gun around to face me, but it was not quick enough. He managed to get off two rounds, but he was off balance and the gun made a spitting sound, putting two bullets into the wall near my brother's bed. My bat connected with his head, buffered by the arm that held the gun. It was enough to put him down, probably for good. My brother awoke and looked up at me, his eyes wide with terror. I put my fingers to my lips and held my hand up, mouthing, "There may be more."

I took a look down the hallway. Nothing. I listened. No sound. Then I made my way to my parents' room. I hesitated outside for a moment and then quickly opened the door and slipped in. My mother was there alone! I bent down to wake her and noticed, out of the corner of my eye, movement. Suddenly, someone was on my back, choking me. I grabbed for the knife, and the two of us struggled for it. Then there was another assailant.

Somehow I broke free and grabbed the bat. I couldn't get a good swing because of the close quarters, but I managed to knock one of them back. As I turned, though, the other had gotten the knife. I swung the bat as hard as I could, catching him right on the wrist. The knife dropped. I grabbed it quickly and stood up, facing the two assailants. One of them called my name. The other one circled around to my back. I turned to face the one circling, and the other one made his move. My mother, in the meantime, lay still in the bed. Certainly she would have been awakened by the noise, but still she lay there.

I sensed the movement behind me just in time. I wheeled and thrust the knife into the man's chest, the blade plunging deep, to the hilt. I drew it up and to the side and then withdrew it just as the other figure moved toward me. I started to turn, but I was not quick enough. I felt the red-hot flash of pain in my shoulder, then my neck. I saw the blade of the knife. Then there was a blow to my head, and almost instantaneously I lost consciousness.

When I awoke I was in the hospital. Both my parents and my younger brother had been killed. I told the police what had happened, but they wouldn't believe me. They had found no bullet holes in the wall, no other bodies, no blood in the house other than from my family. They said my wounds had been self-inflicted or the result of my family trying to defend themselves.

Perhaps the police had been in on it. Maybe the operatives had just done a good job of cleanup. They had the time and the resources. The point is no one looked past the easy answer: The crazy kid had gone berserk. He had killed his family during a delusional episode, and his mind couldn't accept the truth. That's what the psychiatrists concluded.

I was heavily sedated, turned into a walking zombie, and committed to Florida State Hospital for months until I was finally found to be competent to face the charges. All the while, the evidence that would have cleared me was lost or destroyed. My paper exposing the Unit had been destroyed, as had all the copies. They had gotten to my lawyer, who denied even knowing me. Though I could reconstruct the substance of my essay, I no longer had the documentation to back up my assertions or the credibility necessary to give it credence in court.

Objectively, intellectually, I understood the disbelief of others. It was, after all, quite a fantastic story. But emotionally, it was the hardest time of my life. You can't imagine the frustration, the utter despair that weighed me down at this time. No one would even take me seriously.

My court-appointed lawyer, a short, fat man who sweated a lot, told me one day he had negotiated a deal. I would plead no contest and be placed on probation for life. A condition of the probation was that I be committed to Florida State Hospital. As soon as I was cleared by the doctors as not a danger to myself or others, I could be released. I went along with it. Remember, despite attempts to paint me as a monster, I was just a kid. And I was all alone, abandoned. My immediate family was dead, and my extended family wanted nothing to do with me. My uncle had seen to that. You can't understand the complete emotional devastation I experienced, the overwhelming depression. So I relied upon the advice of the only person who seemed to be on my side. I trusted my lawyer. He said the State's case was very strong. Yes, I took the deal.

And I have regretted it ever since.

***

I give the reflection in the mirror close scrutiny, pushing my freshly shaven face up close to the glass, turning from side to side, then back up a few steps to get the full-length view. I tuck in my shirt and straighten it. I frown, then give myself a smile—first a small grin, then a big one full of teeth. I turn sideways, checking my profile, then turn back to face the reflection again.

You're so vain. You probably think this song is about you. The tone is teasing, playful, as the voice sings a line from the Carly Simon tune.

"It's not vanity," I say, still looking at the reflection, smiling again. I smooth the short hair with my hand, tuck the shirt in a little more. "Just checking the parts. Got to make sure I can blend in."

Well, just make sure you don't get overconfident. That's a short fall to complacent, sloppy, and careless.

"Don't worry. I've got things under control."

Yeah, that's what you said last time.

"This is different. You'll see." As I move toward the kitchen area of the small efficiency, I hear no response. There is only silence in the room as I sit at the table on which I have spread the fruits of my research. There are stacks of papers on the small table, as well as on the other chair, the counter near the sink, the compact refrigerator, and even the bed. All of it is, however, neatly arranged and logically organized.

And, yes, the voices are back, like long-lost friends. But this time they are more reasonable, more helpful and respectful. I control them, not the other way around. Physically, I feel great. I am focused, energized, and able to go at full throttle with hardly any sleep. And these last two days have been quite eventful and informative.

I made it to Washington, D.C., two days ago and went right away to St. Elizabeth's Hospital. Once I located it, I searched for a suitable residence within walking distance but quickly realized that I would stand out in the sea of black faces that surrounded the area. So I took a room several blocks away. It was in a run-down building, and parking was hit or miss along the street, but it was close to the metro line, was cheap, and had a kitchenette so I could eat in.

My cover was that I was a graduate student from Florida doing research at the psychiatric facility just up the street. The landlady, an elderly woman with poor hearing, seemed pleased to have a nice, clean-cut young man to rent the small room.

Once I settled in, I walked down to the hospital, sat on a bench across the street from the entrance, and just watched the comings and goings for a while. I then did a 360-degree reconnaissance of the entire hospital property, making notes of other entrances, parking areas, security features, that sort of thing. At around 4:30, I observed a white van arrive near the employee and service entrance. The lettering on the side read "Eagle Cleaning Service," and the image of an eagle in flight was emblazoned just above it. Three men dressed in blue jumpsuits stepped out of the van, removed some equipment and supplies from it, then went inside the building. I was waiting for them four hours later when they came out. I approached the man who appeared to be in charge. He was older and was the only one not carrying either supplies or equipment.

"Excuse me, sir."

The man turned toward the sound. He was a big man, thick but not fat, with a walrus mustache. He looked at me warily, then, quickly assessing the situation, decided I was not a threat and relaxed. "Yeah?"

"Hi. I'm Danny Coxwell." I stuck out my hand to him and he gripped it firmly, then released, but he didn't give me his name. "Just started as a student intern at the hospital, and I'm looking for a part-time job to help make ends meet. I was wondering if maybe you could use some help in the evenings at the hospital."

The man—Albert was the name on his jumpsuit front pocket—looked me over for several seconds, then he gave a look toward the other two men. "Well," he said more to them than to me, "we are spread a little thin right now." Both of the other men nodded slightly in acknowledgment of the truth of his observation. He turned back to me. "I can only pay minimum wage, no benefits." I nodded, and that seemed to seal things.

He told me I would need to get a badge from security, which would require a photo ID, preferably a driver's license, "to make sure you're not some terrorist," he said, and we all chuckled. He said he would call in the morning to set it up. Could I start tomorrow evening? The sooner the better, I assured him. He said he would have a uniform for me the next day as well. "It might be a little big on you," he said, sizing me up, "but it will have to do for the time being. We all wear 'em. Looks more professional and all. And everybody knows who we are that way. Don't want to get mistaken for one of the patients when you get ready to go." He and the boys chuckled again. I didn't think it was too funny but I managed a smile.

So, after securing a job and a way into the hospital, I paid a visit to the public library, got my card, got oriented, and continued my research. I had gotten some information from the computers at Florida State Hospital, but the problem was that it cost money to get the complete article online, something I had very little of while confined. Besides, the small amount of stuff I had been able to view and copy I had had to leave in my room when I escaped.

Not that I've got a lot of money now. I don't. But I also know that all the money in the world won't do me any good if I can't prove my innocence, convince everyone of the validity of my theory. So I have spent the necessary funds to make copies of what I have found, and I have been painstakingly reviewing the materials, looking for patterns, clues, and organizing them in the most logical fashion. I know that a persuasive argument is one part content and two parts presentation.

I also know that old news articles will not be enough, just a starting point. So today I also tracked down all of the police reports concerning Cynthia Sands, including the files on her stalking of Dr. Whitsen. I did the same thing for any court files that were opened in the cases. The court information was very easy to obtain. The police files were a little more tricky. In order to get what I needed, I had to play the role of a news reporter. I told the woman on the phone, the fourth person I was referred to, that the angle was to feature the psychologist, where she was now, what had happened to her, that sort of thing. She had agreed to pull the necessary files for me. She even let me view the videotape of Cindy's interview with the detective. I had spent the rest of the afternoon organizing and poring over everything I had received.

I stop writing and stretch my hands out in front of me. I sharpen the little stub of a pencil with the hand sharpener. Waste not, want not. Then I pull the legal pad over to me. Just as I am about to begin again, I detect the very slight sound of footsteps outside my door. I hold my breath and listen. The footsteps stop, and someone knocks on the door. A jolt of adrenaline rushes through my body, and I am instantly alert. It is not the loud, insistent knock of police officers, readying themselves to force open the door, but it is just as alarming, maybe more. It might be Unit operatives or someone subcontracted for the job.

No, not likely. Why alert me, give me a chance to consider the situation? If the Unit was involved, they would simply burst in. Probably. I will myself to remain calm, but my heart is pounding as I approach the door, arming myself with the frying pan from the stove. Not much of a weapon perhaps, but better than nothing. I stand to the side of the doorway as the person just outside raps again lightly.

"Mr. Coxwell?"

I recognize the voice of my landlady instantly, and my heart slows a bit.

Don't trust that bitch. Are you crazy?

"What, the little old lady?"

What do really know about her? Maybe she's supposed to seem nonthreatening. Maybe she has someone with her, someone who has convinced her or forced her to knock on the door.

The voice is urgent, insistent. Maybe he has a point.

Yes?" I say, still standing to the side of the door.

"Mr. Coxwell, it's Mrs. Wiggins."

"Yes," I say again, without opening the door.

"I made some brownies and thought you might like some."

Tell her to just leave the plate on the floor outside the door.

"Don't be ridiculous! How very strange that would seem. I'm pretty sure I heard only one set of footsteps at the door. Let's not overreact." I wait a moment but there is no response, and I confidently open the door and smile. "Hello, Mrs. Wiggins," I say, looking first beyond her and up and down the hallway, then at the plate of brownies. "How nice of you. Those look delicious."

I hold out my hand for the dish, but the woman doesn't release it. She looks behind me. "Do you have someone in there with you?" I shake my head. "I thought I heard voices." She looks again into the room, not quite sure whether to believe me, but she relinquishes the plate and says "Well, I hope you enjoy them."

I thank her and close the door as she turns to leave.

CHAPTER 26

*T*he courtroom was crowded, standing-room-only crowded. The news coverage had been extensive so most everyone in the small community knew what case was being tried. And to many, this was considered high entertainment. The extra bodies seemed to make the space that much hotter, and I was beginning to feel a little nauseous. I also realized, to my dismay, that I had a strong urge to find a bottle of bourbon.

Theo and I had avoided the press by coming in a side entrance to the courthouse. We had met briefly in the holding cell area with Nathan, who seemed relatively calm and compliant. In fact, he seemed unreasonably calm and unconcerned, even docile. He had quit pestering me about his imposter theory, about fingerprints, about getting a continuance.

I didn't like it.

The three of us walked in together, greeted by a noticeable drop in the volume of conversation. Theo and I shook hands with Maxine, who had no one else at the table with her—strategically a good move, I thought. Before we could take our seats, the bailiff called the room to order and announced the entrance of the judge. Maurice Palmer quickly traversed the distance to the bench, sat down in the large leather chair, and directed us to be seated. The trial of the State of Florida versus Nathaniel L. Hart had begun.

Palmer was polite and courteous, but he wasted no time in having all potential jurors sworn. He asked the necessary questions to assure himself that the potential jurors were citizens of the county and were otherwise legally qualified to be jurors. He listened to and denied the few requests for excusal. Then he seated the requisite number in the jury box and asked a series of preliminary questions designed to get some basic information and weed out those people who were obviously unable to be fair and impartial. He then turned over the questioning to the lawyers.

Maxine started off with an advantage over me. She was a local. She knew a lot of the people on the panel or at least their families. She looked and sounded like she was one of them, which she was. By contrast, I was from Miami, and though I had lived in Tallahassee for several years, it just wasn't the same. I had trimmed my hair and tried to spruce myself up for trial, but I am by nature and habit a little scruffy looking.

My client's appearance was not likely to comfort the potential jurors either. He had refused to shave his scraggly beard or cut his hair, a matter of principle, he said. Theo's suit was a little too flashy in my opinion, given the venue, but he was a handsome man with a nice smile, well groomed and with a clean-cut look about him that I felt would be reassuring to the jurors, especially the women.

Maxine spent a good deal of time questioning each individual juror: occupation, family, background. In addition to the useful information obtained, it allowed her to seem like a gracious hostess who was very interested in her guests. She explained to them their job: Listen to the evidence and determine what the facts were, apply the law to those facts, and decide if the defendant committed a crime. Could they do that? All agreed they could. She asked them if they could do that without letting sympathy influence their decision. And here she looked over at Nathan. "Neither sympathy for the defendant, who admittedly has a sad history, nor for the victim's family," she said, looking then at Rosenberg's wife and their two sons seated in the first row behind the prosecution table. The jurors all lied and said they could.

Going second is a real disadvantage in *voir dire,* especially when the prosecutor has been very thorough. There is very little that hasn't been covered with the jurors, and they are generally getting pretty tired of questions. Your best bet is to hit the few key points you need and win their approval by being brief, but not so brief they think you're not interested. This is the course I tried to follow.

During jury selection, Nathan made detailed notes about the potential jurors and passed them to me. Remarkably, his instincts on this corresponded to Theo's and mine. Maxine too seemed pretty satisfied with the potential jurors, and by 12:30 we had selected the panel that would try the case, including two alternate jurors. Palmer had them sworn in and gave them the preliminary instructions about not discussing the case or obtaining information about it outside the courtroom, then sent them to lunch. Opening statements, he said, would begin at 1:30.

***

When Palmer called the lunch recess, Theo headed for the restroom and I stepped outside, pulled out my cell phone, and called the office. While I was waiting for someone to pick up, I noticed Robert Hart and Frank Hutchinson having a conversation. They were standing near the side of the courthouse. I found this quite interesting as Frank had told me several weeks earlier that he had never met Nathan's uncle. The two men were too far away for me to see them clearly, but it appeared that it was a conversation Hart was not interested in having, because he turned and walked away as Frank continued talking. Frank looked after the man for several seconds, then turned and walked in the opposite direction. Neither seemed to have seen me.

Although I had tried to find a factual basis to tie Hart to some secret spy organization, it remained beyond my grasp. Having finally gotten the voucher information from the State Department, the records had not matched the specific events, places, and times suggested by Nathan. Perhaps that was because, as Nathan said, its members were very good at concealing their work and even the group's very existence, hence the term "secret" organization. Perhaps it was because its existence was only in the mind of my delusional client. Regardless, I had no proof to back up the theory.

Jan came on the phone before I had time to ponder the matter further. She gave me my phone messages from that morning. One of them was from Denise Wilkerson, whom I called back first. I figured she was calling to tell me the judge had ruled, and I was both anxious to hear from her and dreading the call at the same time. In general, things had gone pretty well, I thought, at my hearing, until Wayne Colson made me out to be not only a cokehead but a liar as well.

No, that's not fair. What he did was tell the truth. I had recently used cocaine, and I had lied about it. I had no one to blame but myself. There was a reason I felt like I was being followed, being watched. I was. An investigator hired by the Petronises had photos of Wayne and me, snorting coke. They threatened him with violation of probation. Sure, they couldn't really prove it, not just with the photographs. He should have come to me. But I couldn't really blame him.

Thompson was smug, Denise was embarrassed and pissed, and I was severely depressed. My lawyer didn't even ask for a recess to talk to me about it. She just recalled me and asked me to comment on Wayne's testimony. I guess I could have denied it still, let the judge decide whom to believe, but I decided to leave the lies behind and accept the consequences of my actions. So I told the judge the truth, the whole truth, including my near accident and subsequent trip to see Christine Carter and why I had not been forthcoming before. It was not the finish I had hoped for. I could only pray that I had been able to salvage something with my belated full confession. For what it was worth, it had helped to soothe Denise's hurt feelings, and she had later put as good a face on the situation as she could. Now, I held my breath as Denise came on the line.

"Hey, Denise, it's Ted. Got your message." I braced, not wanting to ask her directly but wanting her to get right to the point and put me out of my misery.

Perhaps sensing my anxiety, she told me right off that no, the judge had not entered his order. "What he has done, however, is to request that Annie be brought to his chambers so he can talk to her, with just the court reporter and the bailiff present. No parties or attorneys." When I didn't respond, she added, "That's good news, Ted."

Annie was only eight years old, and the judge would not give her preference much weight, but I was not about to look a gift horse in the mouth. At the very least, it suggested the judge had not made up his mind. "Yeah, that's great," I said, though I instantly began to wonder if it was. I thought that Annie would say she wanted to come back to Tallahassee. She had expressed that to me. But I also knew from years of doing these types of cases that parents were often unaware of how their children really felt, refusing to accept that their kids might just be telling them what they thought their parents wanted to hear.

For all I knew, Annie was telling Beth something completely different. Moreover, the judge might ask her about specific things she had witnessed, and without knowing it or meaning to, she could damn me with her youthful, innocent perceptions. Denise opined that the judge would probably reach a decision very soon after he talked to Annie. I thought she was right. "Thanks, Denise. Keep me posted, will you? I want to know as soon as he rules, for good or bad."

"It will be good, Ted," she said with a confidence that for one brief moment enveloped me as well. I thanked her again. But when I hung up, the knot in my stomach twisted a little tighter.

CHAPTER 27

*R*aymond Curry was the first witness for the prosecution and was both excited and nervous to be the center of attention. The dark blue suit was worn and ill fitting on his thin frame, but the black shoes were shined to perfection. The white hair on his head was in sharp contrast to the dark chocolate color of his skin. I could see the old man's Adam's apple move up and down as he swallowed hard and said, "I do," before the clerk could finish administering the oath. He sat with his hands folded tightly in his lap, as if afraid they would betray him if allowed to move freely.

Maxine stood at her table and hesitated for a couple of seconds. "Would you state your name for the record, please, sir?" She moved from the prosecution table to the podium next to the jury box. Now the witness would naturally look at both her and the jury while answering the questions.

"Raymond Curry."

Maxine spoke in a soft, Southern accent, and her smile seemed at times ironic and wry, as if she were amused by something that only she understood. Her movements, like her smile, suggested an open and easy confidence.

"And what is your occupation, Mr. Curry?"

"I'm the custodial supervisor at Florida State Hospital."

"Were you so employed on July fifteenth of this year?"

"Yes, ma'am. Been there for thirty-two years now." He was beginning to relax just a little. The prosecutor helped by gently taking him through some more routine questions: What were his general duties? What hours did he work? How many staff did he supervise? What was the standard operating procedure for cleaning the buildings after the normal business day? The prosecutor then asked him about the night of July 15th and where he was at approximately 9:45.

In painstaking detail, the prosecutor guided him through every step. Maxine was a masterful stage director. As Raymond figuratively got closer to opening that office door, she had moved from the podium to stand in front of the prosecution table. She leaned back against it slightly with her arms folded in front of her. She had a legal pad on the table behind her, but she rarely glanced at it. She was not the type to rely upon a lot of detailed notes. The case would be presented to the jury as a story, in a natural, even homey, manner, as if to a neighbor sitting on her front porch after supper. She stood straight then, walked a few paces toward the jury, then turned and faced her witness. "Now, Mr. Curry," she said, "tell us what you saw when you opened that door."

Raymond's Adam's apple went up and down again. He put his hand to his mouth briefly, wiped away a bit of perspiration, then returned it to his lap. He looked first at the jury, then back at Maxine. "Well, the first thing I noticed was that the lamp on the desk was knocked over, but it was still on, throwing a weird angle of light across the desk and the room. There were books and papers and other stuff all over the floor. It was a mess. And I could make out what looked like drops of blood on the desk."

"Did you, at that time, see Dr. Rosenberg or any other person in the room?"

"Not right away, I didn't. But just as I stepped into the room, after a couple of seconds, Nathan all of a sudden stood up from behind the desk."

Maxine had him clarify for the jury that Raymond meant my client, had him point to him. She then hesitated for several seconds, again letting the tension build, creating the desire in the jury to hear what came next. She took a few steps toward the jury, stopped, then turned back to Raymond.

"Let me ask you this: Did you notice anything unusual about the defendant?"

"Well," Raymond said, his nervousness forgotten, "he had blood all over him. His eyes looked real wild, and he was holding what looked like a knife in his hand."

Maxine walked over to the clerk's table, retrieved the gold-plated letter opener with an ivory handle. She placed it in front of the witness. "Mr. Curry. I am showing you what is marked as State's exhibit number one and ask you if you recognize this item?"

He took the object in his hand, turned it over, then said, "This looks like the knife—or letter opener is what it really is—but I thought it was a knife that night." Raymond then described how Nathan had just stood there for a couple of seconds, then bolted past him out the door and down the hallway.

"Did you try to stop him?"

Raymond paused, looking at Maxine as if she were as crazy as any resident at Florida State Hospital. Then he shook his head slowly from side to side. "No, ma'am, I sure didn't. Nathan's a young man and a good sight stronger than me. Plus he had that knife or letter opener or whatever it was. It wouldn't have been a smart thing for me to do if I had thought about it, and I didn't."

A few snickers rippled through the audience. The judge looked up sternly and silenced them.

"What did you do after the defendant ran past you?"

Raymond told the jury about finding Rosenberg on the floor and calling it in. "Then I knelt over Dr. Rosenberg, took my shirt off, and tried to stop the flow of the blood." Raymond looked down, then continued softly. "But it just kept coming." Maxine hesitated, not asking another question. Then Raymond added, "God, there was so much blood."

Maxine wisely finished her direct here. "Your witness," she said, then walked over to her table and took a seat.

I stood at the table, not approaching the podium, suggesting that my questions would be brief. The custodial supervisor had been a likable witness—unassuming, sincere, with just the right amount of nervousness. I would have to make sure I made my points but also be careful not to rough him up too much and thereby lose the goodwill of the jury.

First, I got Curry to reiterate that the only light in the office was from the lamp that had been knocked over and that the whole thing had been very traumatic. As in his deposition, he acknowledged that his identification of the person as Nathan was not with 100% certainty, that it was in some part based on the clothes and the cap worn by the person. Then I took him back to the beginning.

"Mr. Curry, when you approached Dr. Rosenberg's office, could you hear people's voices, someone shouting or talking?"

"No, sir."

"Could you hear signs of a physical struggle, a lamp being knocked over, papers or books being pushed off a desk, that sort of thing?"

"No, sir."

"In fact, you heard no sound coming from inside that office when you approached, did you?"

He thought about it a second. "No, can't say I did."

"Did you see this person stab the doctor or strike him in any way?"

"No, sir."

"Mr. Curry, you say that this person had blood all over him. Is that correct?"

"Yes, sir."

"Isn't it true that the blood that you saw was mostly on his shirt sleeves and his pants legs?"

Raymond thought about it for a couple of seconds, then said, "Yes, sir."

"When you bent over Dr. Rosenberg to check his pulse, to see if he was still alive, and when you tried to stop the bleeding, did you get any blood on you?" I was standing now next to the jury box, my arms folded.

"Well, yeah, there was blood all over. It was hard not to."

"So, Mr. Curry, you are standing there in the doctor's office, understandably shaken, covered with blood. If someone had come in on you at that point, it wouldn't look too good, would it?"

Raymond answered, "I guess not," just as Maxine voiced her objection to the question. The judge sustained it and instructed the jury to disregard Raymond's answer. The bell, however, could not be unrung.

***

If I had been reluctant to give the custodian a hard time on cross, I had no such hesitation with Andy Rudd. I started by establishing his motive, the complaints of sexual abuse of patients. He was evasive and defensive, pointing out that the complaints had been determined to be unfounded. Indeed, each patient had recanted, no doubt in fear, but Palmer wouldn't let me go behind the findings, making this motive much weaker.

I asked about the lack of any control over ingress to and egress from the hospital grounds—no fences or gates, no guards posted at the entrances—and the relative light security for many of the buildings, including the one that housed the victim's office. He acknowledged the report at about 9:30 of an unknown man on the grounds who had run when approached by security. It wasn't much, but I hoped it might raise questions in the minds of the jurors. Having made my second point, I moved on to the third.

"Now," I said, "let's talk about the circumstances under which you came into contact with my client that evening." Just about everyone in the room, it seemed, shifted in his seat with this shift in focus. "You testified that Mr. Hart was sweating profusely."

"Yes, I thought that was unusual."

"This occurred on July fifteenth. It gets pretty hot in July around here, doesn't it, Mr. Rudd?"

"Sometimes. It generally cools off in the evening, though."

"It was quite warm that evening, though, wasn't it?"

"Not that I recall."

I looked around the room. Everyone there knew that it is almost always warm in the summer, even at 10:00 p.m. I turned my attention back to the witness. "Sunrise Cottage, where Nathan was residing, doesn't have central heat and air, does it?"

"I'm not sure. I think there's a couple of window units there."

"Do you know where those window units are in relationship to the defendant's bedroom?"

"No, not really. I never figured that was part of security." Rudd gave a little smirk.

Those window units were, in fact, in the living room and in the kitchen area, away from Nathan's room, and I had documentation to establish that. And as Rudd's report noted, Nathan's door had been closed. Maxine stood up and said, "Your Honor, the State will stipulate to the location of the air-conditioning units and that it was hot and humid that night."

Judge Palmer looked at me, and I nodded. "Very well," he said.

I turned back to a frowning Rudd. "Do you know whether my client normally sweats a lot?"

"I don't know. Your client may be a real sweat hog, but most people don't sweat like that just lying in a bed." He looked in the jury's direction, a smirk on his face.

"Now, Mr. Rudd, you also said that you thought it unusual that my client was lying on his back with his arms straight down by his sides."

"Yes."

"Have you ever observed the defendant sleeping before?"

"No, I can't say that I have."

"So, you don't know whether that is a usual sleep position for my client."

Rudd's face was beginning to turn red, but he did his best to act unaffected by my questions. "In my experience, it seemed really strange. That's all I'm saying."

"Do you know whether Mr. Hart is normally groggy when he wakes up or is one of those people who get out of bed wide awake and ready to go?"

Rudd waited a few moments before answering, perhaps finally recognizing the pattern but unable to do much about it. "Like I said, it didn't seem that he was asleep at all."

I looked at the jury. "Yes, that's what you said." Then I turned back to the witness. "Do you know what medication Mr. Hart was on at this time and what dosage?"

"No, Mr. Stevens. That's not something I keep up with."

"So you don't know whether my client might have been displaying the effects of some type of medication he had taken."

The witness shrugged. "I don't know any of that. I just know what I saw, and it didn't seem right to me."

"Indeed, Mr. Rudd. Don't you think it would be quite unusual for someone who has just committed a heinous murder to be so incredibly calm, as you described Mr. Hart, when security men burst into his room?"

"Objection. Calls for opinion." Maxine was on her feet.

"Well, Mr. Rudd has been pretty generous with his opinions up to now," I said, looking up at the judge. Palmer nodded, overruled the objection, and directed Rudd to answer the question.

Rudd turned back to me. "Some people are just cold blooded."

"So, then, your opinion is that Nathan was extremely calm because he is simply a cold, calculating murderer?"

"That's the most logical explanation, yes."

"Let me lay this out then and see if it is consistent with your theory. Mr. Hart devises a plan and sneaks out of his room one evening, somehow knowing that his victim will be in his office, that someone will have left the door to the office building propped open, and that the victim's office will also be unlocked. He knows also that there will be a letter opener that he can use as a murder weapon on the psychologist's desk, that the victim will not press the security button within easy reach when he enters his office and approaches his desk." I paused a moment. "All this making sense so far?"

"Objection," Maxine called out. "Compound question and calls for speculation."

I gave a deep sigh and waved my hand dismissively toward Rudd while looking at Maxine. "She's right, Your Honor. There's been more than enough speculation from this witness today. I'll withdraw the question."

The judge's frown told me to watch myself, but what he said was, "Very well."

"I'm done with this witness," I said with what I hoped would seem like extreme distaste, then took my seat at the counsel table.

CHAPTER 28

*H*aving started off with the more dramatic evidence in her case, Maxine then began to systematically establish the foundation on which it rested. She called the EMS folks to corroborate the scene and the victim's dire condition, as described by Rudd and Curry. Similarly, the two security guards who accompanied Rudd to Nathan's room confirmed his account of the encounter with Nathan, including what was and was not found in the residence. They also testified to securing the scene of the murder as well as Sunrise Cottage, pursuant to Rudd's direction.

Browning was, as expected, a very good witness. Maxine led him carefully through his investigation of the crime, from his arrival on the scene to the processing of the physical evidence and his consideration of alternative suspects. He identified the clothes removed from the washer and the other evidence collected. He explained the photos of the crime scene and of Nathan's room. He told the jury about the cigarette lighter found at the scene.

Maxine no longer had Donnie Mercer as a live witness to tie the lighter to Nathan, and both his statement to Browning and his deposition were inadmissible hearsay, which I was able to have excluded. Score one for our team. Still, she did pretty well with what she had.

"You have shown the jury the photo depicting the defendant's nightstand and the pack of cigarettes on top. Let me ask you, Detective Browning, whether you searched inside that nightstand for matches or a cigarette lighter that might accompany those cigarettes?"

"Yes, ma'am, we did. We searched the entire room."

"And did you ever find any?"

"No, ma'am, we did not."

After presenting a few witnesses to link Nathan to the clothes in the washer, Maxine brought on the FDLE crime lab analyst who had examined and tested them. She had the witness explain the scientific basis for the testing, how it was conducted, then asked about the results. The witness confirmed that the reddish brown stains on the pants, shirt, and shoes were made by human blood, but the sample had been degraded to the point that DNA testing was not productive.

Maxine acted surprised. "Was the sample too old?"

"No. The stains appeared to be recent."

"Well, what caused the degradation, if you know?"

"Someone put a large amount of bleach in the wash. Bleach is very effective in destroying any trace of DNA on an item."

Maxine let this last bit of testimony linger in the minds of the jury as she willed them to look in Nathan's direction. It was, in fact, a very damaging piece of evidence, in part because it made it hard for me to argue that the clothes were planted there to implicate my client. Why, Maxine would ask, if you were trying to frame a person for murder, would you try to destroy the evidentiary value of what you were planting?

It was a good question. The only answer I could come up with was that it made the frame-up all the more convincing and it destroyed the real killer's DNA. It seemed pretty lame even to me. When the judge denied my motion for directed verdict after Maxine rested her case and adjourned for the day, I could feel my cautious optimism slipping a couple of notches.

***

Theo was driving us back to Tallahassee, both hands on the wheel, eyes on the road, doing just below the speed limit. A black man learns early, he said, not to give the police another reason to stop him. I took a bite of my honey bun and washed it down with a swig of Mountain Dew. Theo gave me a quick glance, then trained his eyes straight ahead again. He shook his head slowly.

"What?"

"How can you eat that crap?"

"Hey, I didn't complain when you took me to that vegetarian place at lunch."

"Yes, you did."

I took another bite of the bun. "Well, but I ate it. Problem with that kind of stuff is it just doesn't stay with you."

"You mean the way flour, sugar, and lard do?"

"Exactly."

He shook his head again and gave me a small smile. "Whatever. Just don't get crumbs in my car."

"Yes, sir," I said, giving him a mock salute with the honey bun in my hand. Theo kept his car, a Chrysler 300, immaculate. I turned to face him. "So, how do you think it's going?"

He reached over and turned down the volume on the radio, then, still looking straight ahead, he pursed his lips and said, "I think you've made some points on cross, built up some credibility with the jury. We just want to make sure we don't lose it by trying to give them something they're not ready for, something we can't back up."

What he meant, of course, was that we should not alienate the jury with the delusional fantasy theories advanced by our client. I agreed, and I think even Nathan realized this, as much as he didn't want to. When we met after the trial had been adjourned for the day, he seemed resigned to it.

"If only Judge Palmer had given us more time," he said, his voice trailing off. "I felt certain that Hal would have come through on the print comparison. I don't know why he hasn't responded to my e-mails. Maybe the Unit has intervened." Nathan had seemed to be talking to himself then, and I didn't interrupt. He looked back at Theo and me. "Okay, we'll follow that route: Go for the acquittal first; then we'll uncover the full truth."

I finished my honey bun and put the wrapper in the paper bag it had come in. I looked around but saw nowhere to put it, so I held it in my hand. "If Nathan testifies, it won't be good for us," I said finally.

Theo nodded. "He will come off as arrogant and defensive at the same time. Maxine will rip him to shreds on cross."

"Yeah, it's going to be ugly, but what can we do? He's insisting on it. And to be honest, if I were in his shoes, I'd probably do the same thing. Jurors always want to hear the accused say he didn't do it."

Theo was silent for a long couple of seconds. "Maybe so. Still, he's just going to dig his own grave."

We talked then about the witnesses we planned to call, confirmed who would handle each, the major points to make. The overarching theme of our defense was to point the finger at the recently deceased Donnie Mercer, whom we considered our best alternative suspect, but we also had the Hutchinsons and Rudd as possibilities. Essentially, the plan was to muddy the waters and hope it created a reasonable doubt in the minds of the jurors.

We discussed whether to introduce, through Rebecca, evidence about the e-mails she had received, the lighter, and their connection to the infamous Cindy Sands.

"It's got a lot of jazz to it," I said, "but it's just not worth the gamble."

"Yeah," he agreed. "First, it's doubtful the judge will let it in. We don't have any evidence to connect it to the victim or his murder. More importantly, by tracing the e-mails to the hospital, to areas Nathan might have had access to, we leave it open for Maxine to suggest it's Nathan who's been sending them, especially with the cigarette lighter being linked to him. It would make him appear even more sinister, more diabolical."

"And that we don't need."

***

Nathan was not a good witness. He did okay on direct exam, but, as Theo predicted, Maxine made him look not only like a liar but a bad one at that. She also managed to get him to lose his temper, thus demonstrating effectively to the jury his potential to become angry and dangerous. I did a very short redirect to minimize the damage; then we began calling our other witnesses.

I decided to let Theo handle Barbara Hutchinson. Part of it was to distance myself in the eyes of the jury from what would probably be some unpleasant mudslinging. Part of it was he had earned it. He had worked hard gathering the evidence to implicate her in Rosenberg's murder. He had prepared for her questioning thoroughly, and I knew he would be effective.

He was.

The psychologist was dressed in a conservative, dark blue dress. When she walked to the stand, she held her head high, and as she took the oath, she made brief eye contact with me, a bit of a challenge there in her eyes. When Theo rose from the counsel table and approached the podium, she seemed a bit surprised, apparently having expected me to conduct the questioning.

Theo started out with nonthreatening questions about the victim and his habits, establishing their working relationship, her knowledge of his management style, his schedule. He asked how they got along, whether they ever had disagreements.

"Of course, we didn't always see eye to eye, but we respected each other's professional opinion and had an excellent working relationship."

Gradually, very subtly, Theo began to hint at a different relationship. It was risky because if we couldn't at least create a real inference of its existence, the jury would be sympathetic to her and not too happy with us for suggesting it. Barbara knew, of course, that Theo would eventually head in this direction and had prepared for it. She was calm and composed as she emphatically denied any relationship with the deceased that was not strictly professional, tossing in with her answers just the right amount of righteous indignation.

Yes, she was doing quite well—until Theo asked her about the conference in Daytona Beach. This she had not prepared for. Although she maintained her composure, I could see the beginning pricks of panic in her eyes as Theo became more and more specific with his questions, and she painted herself into a corner with her answers.

"Let me show you what has been marked as defense exhibit number three. Do you recognize this document?"

She studied it for several seconds, then looked up. "Yes, this is my travel voucher form for the conference."

"And the reason you fill out this form and submit it to the hospital is so you can be reimbursed for the expenses you incurred while attending the conference, correct?"

"Those that are reimbursable, yes."

"The cost of transportation is one such expense, correct?"

"Yes."

"But on this voucher," Theo said, raising the document aloft, "you did not seek reimbursement for the cost of transportation, did you?"

"Apparently not."

"Is that because you rode with someone else?"

Maxine rose from her seat. "Your Honor, Mr. Williams may be fascinated by Dr. Hutchinson's travels, but it doesn't appear to be remotely relevant to this case."

Judge Palmer looked over his glasses at Theo. "Counsel, do you have a point to make with this line of questioning?"

"Yes, sir."

"Try to make it soon, please." He looked at Maxine. "Objection overruled for now."

Theo turned back to the witness, who no doubt had been collecting her thoughts during the brief legal skirmish. "So, my question was, did you ride to the conference with someone?"

"I must have."

"You would have asked for reimbursement otherwise, wouldn't you?"

"Yes."

"Isn't it true that you rode to the conference with Dr. Rosenberg?"

"Could have been. May have been another of our staff. That was over a year ago."

Theo paused a moment, letting the incredulity of her suggestion that she could not remember drift through the room. And this is where she really blew it, because in and of itself it was not that big a deal that she rode with a colleague to the conference, but she had made it seem more suspicious by not admitting it right off. Perhaps it was because she realized now where Theo was going. "Would it refresh your memory if I showed you the list of attendees of the conference?"

She shrugged. "Perhaps." Theo handed her the document, and she made a show of looking it over. After several seconds she looked back up. "It does refresh my memory, and you are correct. I rode to the conference with Dr. Rosenberg."

"Did you ride back with him?"

"Yes."

Again, Maxine rose to her feet. "I'm sure we're all glad to have solved this mystery, but, Your Honor, I still don't see the relevance."

The judge's look was a bit more stern as he said, "Nor do I, Mr. Williams."

"If you'll give me just a little more leeway, judge."

"Very well, but only a little."

Theo then retrieved another document from our table and showed it to Maxine. As she was looking over it, he said, "Your Honor, I offer defense exhibit three into evidence, and in addition, exhibit four, which I am showing to counsel. It is another voucher form, authenticated as a business record of the hospital by the affidavit of the records custodian."

The judge looked over at Maxine. "Any objection, Ms. Chrenshaw?"

Maxine gave the document back to Theo. "I still don't see the relevance of the line of questioning, but I have no objection to the authenticity of the documents."

"Subject to tie-up, they will be admitted."

Theo placed both documents in front of the psychologist. He pointed to the fact that Rosenberg had claimed mileage for the trip, corroborating that she rode with him. Then he pointed out that while the supporting documentation for his lodging expense, his hotel bill, showed a charge for an extra two nights, hers did not. "Can you explain that, Dr. Hutchinson?"

Now, it is always risky to ask a witness a question you don't know the answer to, but we felt we had no choice here. If we had tipped our hand earlier by asking for her credit card records, for example, we would have lost the value of surprise. We were depending on her reaction to the question, rather than whatever explanation she came up with, to tell the true story.

She did not disappoint. First, there was a deer-in-the-headlights look, then much too long a pause as she looked up and to the right, as if searching for a plausible lie. "I don't have to explain myself to you," she said finally. "Like I said, it was over a year ago. Maybe I stayed with a friend. Maybe I put the extra nights on a different credit card. I don't remember." This time, her tone was tinged with way too much righteous indignation, which, unlike before, now tended to make her all the less believable.

Theo bore down then, asking a series of leading questions that began, "Isn't it true that . . ." and concluded with each element of our theory of her guilt—that she and the victim had been having an affair; that he broke it off; that she was furious, humiliated; that she exacted her revenge that night, covering her tracks by making it look like one of the patients had done it.

She denied each one, of course, but she had lost all credibility with the jury. I could see it on their faces. As I watched her on the stand, the more I thought about it, the less of a stretch it was to imagine her as the killer. If Rosenberg had ended things, she had motive and certainly opportunity. She was similar in size to Nathan, could have been mistaken for him in the dark, her hair tucked up under a ball cap. Did Donnie Mercer know something and try to leverage it with her? Did she lure him to the roof, then push him off when he was off balance and under the influence of the drugs she had slipped him? Were the e-mails coming from her? Was she computer illiterate, as she had claimed to Rebecca Whitsen? Not according to her husband. And the lighter? She could have left it at the scene by accident or on purpose.

Of one thing I was certain. If she was the killer, her husband was covering for her. He was her alibi. It was possible they had planned everything together, but I doubted it. It was one thing to lie for your wife out of loyalty but quite another to plan the murder of two people and the frame-up of another. It was a difference I emphasized to Frank during the recess, planting the seed that I hoped might produce a reconsideration of his alibi statement. Did he really want to go down with her?

Apparently, he was willing to take the risk. Or maybe the alibi was the truth. I didn't know. Either way, he did not budge. He insisted that both he and his wife were at home watching television when they received the news of Rosenberg's death. When I asked about the inconsistency of telling me he didn't know Nathan's uncle and the conversation I had witnessed during a recess, he denied ever having told me that. He knew the uncle, he said, and had talked to him on occasion as the man was interested in the medical and legal status of his nephew.

Robert Hart was also unflappable. He expertly handled every attack I could muster, and I doubt I gained much credibility pointing my finger at him as a possible alternative suspect. I purposely steered clear of any reference to the Unit or other such motive and instead sought to suggest the trust dispute as a reason to want Nathan to stay inside. Trouble was, I had been unable to get the probate judge to open up the file. I could only imply something more sinister, suggest that Rosenberg had been paid to ensure Nathan's continued commitment and had been killed because he got greedy. It was incredibly weak, but it was all I had on him. His explanation for his contact with Rosenberg seemed reasonable, even to me.

As for why Donnie Mercer had his phone number, he did not fall for my bluff. "I have no idea. I do not know the man, nor have I ever spoken to him." Perhaps, he speculated, he was planning to call him with information on his nephew, hoping to get paid for it. I tried to tell myself that at least I had given the jury a taste of his frostiness, his undisguised hatred of his nephew, and had clouded the waters a bit more, but as I watched the faces of the jurors when Hart stepped down from the witness stand, I was not comforted.

Still, even though it hadn't gone as well as I had hoped, when we rested the defense and Palmer recessed for the day, announcing that closing arguments would be in the morning, I still felt like we had a decent chance of an acquittal. I had no idea my client was about to really put the nail in his coffin.

***

Right to the end, I had held out hope that the jury would do the right thing. Ted and Theo did a pretty good job attacking the State's evidence. And I made a great witness too. I was calm, detached even, gave a very reasonable account of my actions, and explained away all of the circumstantial evidence. Maxine and I got into a little spirited give-and-take during her cross-examination, but I never raised my voice or lost my cool.

I was watching the jurors, however, reading their faces, their body language, and I began to acknowledge cognitively what my gut already knew. There was one juror in particular, a young woman who worked at the bank in Quincy, with whom I had connected psychically during the trial, who let me know what was going on. At the close of the evidence, when I looked into her eyes, it was as if she was mentally holding up a large poster with the word ESCAPE! on it.

***

I used a heating pad pilfered from the nurse's station and blankets from my

room to raise my body temperature. I forced myself to throw up. When one of
the aides came in, I seemed appropriately ill, justifying a trip to the on-site
hospital. I told her I didn't want to go, begged her not to take me. I was sure,
I told her, that they would put me under, drug me, then implant the radio
transmitter in my brain again.

This was exactly the right approach. The aide gave me a tolerant half
smile. She told me not to worry. She would have Anthony, another aide, stand
guard and watch everything closely.

They put me in a room with another man named Francis. He told me
he was there for a heart transplant. I didn't believe him, of course, and I
discouraged any kind of conversation. Finally, he left me alone. Anthony did
stay outside my door, at least for a while, but eventually he went back up to
the main nurse's station, as I knew he would. I could hear them talking and
laughing down the hall.

Feigning sleep, I waited, listening. A little after 3:00 a.m., the place was
dead. All of the other patients were sleeping. Anthony was snoring loudly, and
the medical staff, down to a minimum, hovered around the central nurse's
station. I eased out of my bed and paused at the doorway, making sure that
Anthony was still out, then I made my way quickly but quietly down the
hallway. Unlike the General Forensics unit, the doors at the medical clinic
were not locked, nor did the opening of them set off any type of alarm. In less
than thirty seconds I had left the building, and within a minute more I was
off the hospital grounds.

***

Maxine Chrenshaw's house was only about a ten-minute walk from the
hospital. I made it in five. I knew where it was from checking the phone
book. This target, you understand, was planned ahead of time as well. Surely
you can appreciate the perfect irony of it.

It was quiet on the street. A dog a few houses down barked but only a
few times, then was quiet. I checked the front door, which, not surprisingly,
was unlocked. Small towns—you gotta love 'em. Slowly, carefully, I opened it,

stepped inside, and closed it just as carefully. I stood just inside the doorway for at least a full minute, waiting patiently, listening. I took in the smell of the place: the burned cigars of her husband, air freshener, an undefined mustiness common to old, wood-frame houses, the lingering aroma of fried pork chops. The dominant sound was the ticktock of a large clock on the side wall.

My eyes adjusted to the dark, and I took in the red print sofa and matching chair, the blue velour recliner. A cat, black and white, sitting very still on top of the TV, watched me without alarm. Photos on shelves and side tables depicted a younger Chrenshaw with her husband and kids, sufficiently long ago that I made the assumption that the children had long since left their parents' home.

I waited until the heating system kicked in again before I moved. Then I cut quickly but quietly in the direction of the master bedroom. The bedroom door was open about six inches. I stood looking in for several seconds, watching the prosecutor and her husband sleeping on the king-size bed.

I stepped just inside the door. My eyes took in the rest of the room quickly. I soon saw what I was looking for. On the nightstand, by her husband's side of the bed, lay his wallet, small change, and his truck keys. The flooring underneath the carpet creaked as I took a step. I stopped, waited. No movement. The man was snoring softly.

I tried to slow my breathing and step without making a sound. I was aware of the swish of cloth touching as I took the first step and consciously widened my stance. The floorboard creaked again as I moved, just three feet away from my adversary. I studied her closely. The hair was thin and in disarray, and even in the dark, I could see the age spots on her face. The husband snorted, but he didn't wake. Then he turned on his side, toward his wife, dropping an arm over her. I picked up his wallet and gently retrieved the set of keys, making sure they didn't clang together. Holding them tightly in one hand, wallet in the other, I eased back out of the bedroom, across the living room, then slowly, carefully, I closed the front door behind me. All in all, it had taken me less than ten minutes.

The old Chevy pickup was parked behind the newer model Buick in the driveway. With the same care exercised in the house, I eased open the driver's side door, leaving it ajar. Once inside I found the appropriate key on the chain and put it in the ignition but did not start the engine. I put it in neutral and let it roll, gently, out into the street. Then I coasted down the small, hilly street. Two houses down I popped the clutch to start the engine, then accelerated smoothly away.

CHAPTER 29

*I*t was about 6:45 a.m. when I got the call. I was still half asleep when I picked up the receiver and mumbled, "Hello?"

"Ted, this is Walter Browning."

I was suddenly wide awake and sitting on the edge of my bed. An uneasy feeling grew in the pit of my stomach.

"Your client has escaped from the hospital. Sometime in the early-morning hours." I barely had time to process the information when the next shoe fell. "Looks like he broke into Maxine's house, stole some cash and her husband's truck."

The calm, almost monotone delivery made it all the more chilling. I fell into a numbing silence as Browning gave me the rest of the story— Nathan's feigned illness and trip to the medical clinic, the staff finding him missing, the burglary of Maxine's house and theft of her husband's truck. "We found the truck a few minutes ago in Tallahassee, near the bus station, where a man fitting your client's description purchased a ticket to Tampa early this morning. The bus left around six-fifteen."

The uneasy feeling in my stomach was becoming a stone that seemed to grow larger with each new revelation. "Did you intercept the bus? Have you caught him?"

"Has he contacted you, Ted?" When I didn't answer right away, he said, "Is there someone there with you?"

"No," I said finally, recovering somewhat and realizing what he meant, and also realizing that I was probably under suspicion, not for any particular reason other than my association with Nathan.

"You haven't heard from your client?"

"No," I said simply.

There was silence on the other end for several seconds, then a small sigh. "If he hasn't contacted you, he probably will," he said, then asked me to call him if that happened. It was more a direction than a request.

"Of course," I said, though I was thinking it through even as I spoke. The attorney-client privilege was sacrosanct. I could not divulge information my client gave me without his consent nor use it against him, including, perhaps, his location.

When I hung up with Browning, I called Theo and gave him the news. I told him to go to the office and wait to hear from me as to what was to happen. Then I quickly showered, dressed, ate breakfast, and drove over to Gadsden County.

It was a little before 9:00 when I walked into the courtroom. Apparently news of the escape had spread quickly as the room was crowded and abuzz with excited conversation. The bailiff told me the judge and Maxine were waiting for me in chambers and escorted me back.

Palmer's office had an old-fashioned feel about it, with the wood floors, antique furniture, and several black-and-white photos on the walls, depicting people and places of an earlier time. The judge was seated at his desk, Maxine in one of the two antique oak chairs in front. I took his silent invitation and sat in the other one, quietly exchanging greetings with them both. We were all silent for several seconds until Palmer finally said, "This is a damn mess." Neither Maxine nor I sought to contradict him. "A damn mess," he repeated.

I turned to Maxine. "Sorry about all this. Are you okay?"

She gave me a wry smile. "I'm afraid to go to sleep, but other than that, I'm fine." After a couple of moments, she added, "He was in my bedroom, Ted. He took the keys and wallet right off my nightstand."

I didn't know what to say so I just nodded and looked toward Palmer.

Thankfully, he plunged ahead. "Well, what do you propose we do at this point, lawyers?"

He looked first at me. I cleared my throat. "I hate to have to try it again, but I think a mistrial is the only sensible option, judge. News like an escape can't be contained, not in a small town like this. The jurors probably already know it. It would be very prejudicial to continue without him present. Besides, I think it has been a very trying morning for everyone, especially Ms. Chrenshaw. It would be difficult to finish the trial under these circumstances."

Palmer nodded, then turned to Maxine.

"I disagree," she said. "I can assure the court that I am fine and ready to proceed. As to the defendant's absence from his trial being prejudicial, I should hope so. But it is not an unfair prejudice. Rather, it is the natural result of his own choices, his own actions. Now, I will stipulate that the fact that he burglarized my house and stole my husband's truck is not something the jury should hear, and I won't get into that. But the fact that he has escaped lawful custody is something we have a right and an obligation to present to the jury."

Maxine, having obviously anticipated the issue, pulled open the notebook on her lap and read to the judge the pertinent provision of the Florida Rules of Criminal Procedure. "If the defendant is present at the beginning of the trial and thereafter voluntarily absents himself or herself without leave of court, the cause of the trial shall not be delayed or postponed, but shall proceed thereon in all respects as though the defendant were present."

It was hard to argue with her logic or her authority, but I tried. "Your Honor, nothing will prevent Ms. Chrenshaw from arguing the inference of guilt because of the flight of the defendant, but in all fairness to him, he should have a chance to explain it, to rebut that inference if he can. Issue a *capias* for him. When he is captured and the case is tried again, she can present that evidence. But to do it now will ensure he is unfairly convicted."

The judge seemed to be weighing his options as he sat there for several seconds, nodding gently. He looked over at me. "If Ms. Chrenshaw were to request it, under the circumstances, I would grant a mistrial, but she says she wants to go forward, and I think that's what we should do." He hesitated a moment. "But I'll tell you what. We will take a recess for the rest of the day. Maybe they'll catch him and have him back by the morning. We will start back up at nine tomorrow."

***

It was about 9:20 when I left Judge Palmer's chambers and headed across the street for a cup of coffee at the Bean There Café. I checked in with Jan at the office and discovered I'd received a call from my bank, deemed important, and with a request that I call a Mr. Sherman back ASAP. I obliged and was put right through to his office.

"Mr. Stevens," the voice on the other end said, "this is Fred Sherman at Sun Bank. Sorry to bother you, but there has been some unusual activity on your account, and, as a precaution, I thought I should contact you."

"What do you mean 'unusual activity'?"

"Well, there were several ATM withdrawals from your account early this morning at our various branches around town. The first was at the Tennessee Street branch at four-oh-six, the last at four forty-six at the Betton Hills branch. All were for the maximum amount allowed for any one transaction."

"There must be some mistake, some computer malfunction." But as I said it, I was thinking otherwise. I pulled out my wallet and began searching for my bank card.

"You did not withdraw the funds then?"

"Why would I say there must be some mistake if I had, in fact, withdrawn the funds?" I instantly regretted my sarcasm. It wasn't his fault. "No," I said, "nor have I given anyone my card or my PIN." There was a brief silence on the other end as if he expected what was coming next. "But I've just turned my wallet inside out searching for my bank card, and it's not here."

The man said he would have the video of the transactions pulled. Would I be available to review them with security, see if I could identify the person? Did I have any idea who it might be? I answered yes to both questions and suggested a meeting in about forty-five minutes. I got my coffee to go and headed back to Tallahassee. On the way I dialed up the Gadsden County Sheriff's Office. I thought Walter Browning might want to meet me at the bank.

***

It was no surprise when an undisguised Nathan Hart was pictured on the videos. He even smiled into the camera on a couple of occasions. Browning, of course, wanted to know how Nathan got possession of my bank card, how he knew my PIN, and I didn't have a good answer. Maybe, I said, he lifted the bank card from my wallet without my knowing. I had written my PIN on a business card in my wallet, and maybe Nathan had seen it. Or maybe he just guessed right.

This latter theory, as improbable as it sounded, was supported at least in part by the security man, who said the time taken at the first transaction and Nathan's actions at the keypad suggested three tries at the PIN before the machine responded. Three tries were all you got before the machine, for security purposes, would presume fraud, keep the card, and tell the user to check with the bank during regular business hours. Browning, who was watching the monitor, smacking away at his gum, didn't look up when he said, "Damn good guesser," in a tone that suggested disbelief. Then he turned to me. "What is it, your PIN?"

I hesitated a moment, not really sure why since the security had already been broken, then said, "It's my wife's name, Beth."

CHAPTER 30

*M*y client had not been captured by the next morning so, pursuant to Judge Palmer's ruling, the trial continued. Maxine quickly put on the pertinent evidence. I had very little cross. I tried to imply by my questions that maybe Nathan just wandered off, disoriented by his illness, that nobody really knew his motivation. It was pretty pathetic, but it was all I had. Then it was time for closing arguments.

Maxine quickly summarized the case against my client, then addressed the suggestion, "popular over at the defense table," as she put it, that someone else had killed Rosenberg and framed Nathan for it. She went down the list and analyzed the evidence, or lack thereof, to make a case against each one of the alternative suspects we had thrown out—and found it wanting. She mentioned the escape but didn't dwell on it. There could be no reasonable doubt, she told the jury, that Nathan had been the one to kill Dr. Rosenberg. The only thing that was even subject to debate, she suggested, was what degree of homicide was appropriate. But even here, she said, the answer was obvious if they carefully considered the evidence.

"This was no accident. This was not a situation where the defendant just lost it during a session with his psychologist. The man was stabbed seventeen times. The evidence shows that Mr. Hart knew exactly what he was doing, and he knew it was wrong." She folded her arms in front of herself and rocked slightly, then began to pace slowly in front of the jury box. "True, Mr. Hart is mentally ill. But that does not excuse his act, legally or morally. He may be mentally ill, but he is also a calculating, cold-blooded killer, and you should find him guilty of first-degree murder." Maxine lingered there for just a few moments after she finished, looking each of the jurors in the eye, as if to assure them that she meant every word.

I stood in front of the jury for several seconds before beginning, building the anticipation. "If Raymond Curry could happen upon the scene while the victim was mortally wounded but still alive, why couldn't Nathan Hart?" I put my hands in my pockets, turned and walked slowly in front to the jury box a few steps, then stopped and turned back. "What was his motive? That he got turned down for conditional release and blamed the victim?" I hesitated a moment. "But this was the third time he had been turned down. Why exact his revenge now? Sure, he made threats, but that wasn't the first time for that, either."

Then I pointed out what I thought had been our best argument: the inconsistency of the State's theory. It had never made sense to me, and I was hoping it wouldn't to the jury. "This was a pretty sophisticated plan of murder. The State had just determined that Mr. Hart could not function in the outside world. This is the person the State suggests planned this elaborate murder? And if the prosecution's theory is true, then you also have to believe that this same person, despite the careful and elaborate plan of murder, was so careless and sloppy that he disposed of the murder weapon steps away from where he sleeps and put the bloody clothes in the washing machine at his own residence. Does that make sense? Does it make sense that such a careless person would not leave a single fingerprint at the scene of the crime or on the murder weapon?"

I suggested to them that Raymond Curry may have been mistaken and that he had admitted as much on the stand. Finally, I spoke to the fact that my client was not there in the courtroom. Guilty conscience was one explanation, I agreed. But, I added, so was innocence. "An innocent man faced with the very real prospect that a jury would not give him the benefit of the doubt—who was convinced that he must find the evidence that would prove his innocence—might conclude that he must take matters into his own hands."

There was, I said, reasonable doubt as to my client's guilt. The evidence was consistent with guilt, but it was also consistent with a number of alternative theories of innocence. The law, I told them, required that under those circumstances, a verdict of not guilty was the only proper verdict they could render.

The jury apparently disagreed. They deliberated less than an hour before returning a verdict of guilty as charged.

***

I was sitting in the recliner, asleep, when the call came in. The ringing of the phone was faint and distant in my mind, background to the drama being played out in my subconscious. My sleep had been fitful but insistent, and it now refused me easy escape from its surrealistic realm. On the third ring, my mind began to bridge that murky ravine between sleep and wakefulness, and I identified the source of the noise. On the fourth ring, the machine kicked in, and I listened to my disembodied voice tell the caller to leave a message.

"Hello, Ted. It's me, Nathan."

I was fully awake then. I reached in the dark for the portable phone I usually left on the end table next to the chair but grabbed only air. Quickly, I turned on the lamp, adjusted to the light, and looked around. Where was that phone?

"Okay. I guess you're not there or, as the message says, can't come to the phone right now. I'm sure you're not screening your calls, avoiding me. Not after all we've been through."

I was out of the recliner then, heading toward the kitchen and the wall phone. I stubbed my toe on a bar stool in the semidarkness and stopped momentarily to curse.

"Anyway, just called to let you know I'm okay. Actually better than okay. Didn't want you to worry."

It seemed to take me forever to cover the width of the kitchen.

"When I've gotten the proof I need, I'll get back to you. Until then, be careful."

I picked up the phone. "Nathan, I'm here. Nathan?" I heard the click. "Nathan?' I said one more time, holding the phone to my ear for a few more seconds. "Damn," I said and slammed down the receiver.

***

An hour later, I sat in the office of Detective Walter Browning, having exchanged brief greetings and having declined his offer of a cup of coffee. The huge man on the opposite side of the desk brought his hands together in front of him, intertwining the fingers. "You got the recording?"

I produced the small disk from my pocket and shoved it across the desk. Browning took it in his hand. "Not sure it helps you or me," I said. Nathan's words had been ambiguous, subject to different interpretations. "I wish I had been able to talk to him directly."

The detective seemed to consider this for a moment, then said, "Still, it might give us something to use to locate him. I'll turn it over to the boys in the lab. It's amazing what they can get off those things, background noise and stuff."

"Where do you think he's gone?" I asked. Browning looked around the room, not answering. There was silence for a long couple of seconds. Then I leaned forward, my hands on the desk. "You don't really think I had anything to do with this, do you, Walter?" It was more a statement than a question.

"Nah," he said after a moment's hesitation. "Though I'm probably in the minority." He leaned back in his chair. "Some say Hart could have somehow managed to lift your bank card without your knowing it, but they find it hard to believe he just got lucky and guessed your PIN. Just a little too coincidental."

"You don't agree?"

"I think you've sailed a little close to the wind at times and can be a little antiauthority in your attitude." His tone did not suggest disapproval. "But you wouldn't knowingly help a murder suspect escape. And if you did, you wouldn't be so stupid as to leave a trail leading right to you. I figure Hart stole your bank card, probably sometime during the trial, and you didn't miss it. He got lucky and guessed your PIN, like you said. It's usually something obvious."

When it appeared that he was finished, I repeated my earlier question. "Where do you think he's gone?"

He looked directly at me. "We're not sure he's gone anywhere. He may still be in the area."

"What? I thought the prevailing view was that he was headed to Tampa."

"Yeah," he said, leaning forward a bit. "It looks like he bought a bus ticket to Tampa, but we don't think he actually went. We intercepted the bus this side of Ocala and he wasn't on it. Now, he may have gotten off along the way, then taken another bus. But the driver didn't remember him, nor did any of the passengers. We're thinking maybe he got spooked, possibly saw a police car at the station and decided not to get on. Or maybe he just wanted us to think he has left the area. At any rate, there's no evidence that he took any other mode of public transportation out of the area."

"What about stolen cars?"

The detective smiled. "Very good. Yes, there were a few of those that night and in the few days thereafter, including Maxine's, and one motorcycle. But all have been recovered in this area, with the exception of the motorcycle, and there is no physical evidence to tie him to any of them, with the exception of Maxine's."

"You sure it was him then, at Maxine's?"

"Oh, yeah. His prints and DNA are all over the truck and in their house." He pursed his lips, then nodded."

"So, you think he's still around here?"

"Don't know, but I do know that you're not the only person getting messages." He hesitated again. "Your friend, the psychologist."

"Whitsen?"

He nodded. "'Cept hers wasn't by phone. Somebody left a handmade note on her dining room table. Found it when she got home last night."

"What kind of note? What'd it say?"

The detective turned in his chair to the side, opened up a file drawer in his desk, and took out a document. "I made a copy. Gave the original to the lab folks to process, see what they can find." He pushed the paper toward me.

It was letter size, and the message on it had been made with letters and words cut from a magazine. It read:

"Every move you make, every breath you take, I'll be watching you."

"The Police," I said, identifying the band to which the lyrics belonged.

The detective pursed his lips again. "I'm impressed."

"And you think Nathan left it?"

"Well, we don't have any prints or other physical evidence yet to tie him to it, but who else?"

I didn't have an answer. I wondered if I should tell him of Nathan's imposter theory. It certainly provided a motive for Nathan to want to go after her. On the other hand, they already thought that Nathan was after the psychologist, so the specific motive was irrelevant. Rebecca herself had apparently not passed along this information to Browning. Why should I? And surely they were taking all necessary precautions for her safety. "Why would he do that?" I asked finally. "Why stick around? Seems like he would want to get as far away as he could."

Browning began to place the document back in the drawer. "Maybe he feels he has unfinished business here."

***

Rebecca opened the door to her apartment and ushered me inside. It seemed like years ago that I had been here, sharing a bottle of scotch. There was still the familiar coolness and nonchalance about her, but the pale, drawn face and the bags under the eyes suggested the anxiety that she hid just underneath the surface. The smell of stale cigarette smoke permeated the air, corroborated by the mountain of cigarette butts in the ashtray on the end table next to the couch.

"Thought we should compare notes, so to speak," I said.

"What a terrible pun," she said, but she smiled just a little when she said it, then turned and headed toward the living room. "Come on back." She retrieved a cigarette from the pack on the end table. Her hands trembled slightly as she lit it. She offered me scotch again and I declined, noting the half-empty glass on the table. She gave me an inquiring look, then just shrugged and took a sip from the glass.

"I noticed the police cruiser in the parking lot when I came in."

"Compliments of our local sheriff's office, at the request of Walter Browning. They ride by every so often. Sometimes they park for a few minutes."

"Browning told me about the note you received," I said.

"That's 'notes,' plural. I received the second one this afternoon." She retrieved a paper from a file on the end table and placed it in front of me. It was a piece of regular copy paper with words and letters clipped from a magazine. The message read: "Murderer! Prepare yourself! The day of justice is upon you!"

"He left it on my desk at the hospital."

"You think it's Nathan?"

"Who else?"

"Maybe they're from the real killer, who wants you to believe they're coming from Nathan, make you think he's still in this area."

She considered this for a couple of moments. "Possible, but that seems like a whole lot of trouble for nothing. Everybody already assumes Nathan is the killer anyway."

"Maybe that's just what they want you to think."

"You're beginning to sound like your client."

I ignored the taunt. "At one point, you thought Frank or Barbara

Hutchinson might be behind the e-mails."

She shook her head. "No, this goes way beyond petty workplace harassment."

"Got another one for you. What about James Washington?"

"What about him?"

Point by point, I laid it out for her. He had lied about caring for his grandmother, at least the time frame. He came to Florida State Hospital about the same time she did. He had befriended her. He spoke of her in glowing terms, bordering on adulation, obsession. He had a solid knowledge of drugs, both institutional and street. What did she really know about this man she had let get so close to her? How did she know he didn't have some connection to Cindy Sands? Could he have drugged Donnie Mercer, lured him to the roof of that building, then pushed him off? Did he have a key to her apartment?

Rebecca took a deep draw from her cigarette, then blew the smoke up toward the ceiling. She began shaking her head slowly. "Interesting, for sure. It's true that what I know about James is what he has told me, and I have no idea whether it's the truth or a lie. I don't know the answers to the questions you pose, except that he does not have a key to this place." She hesitated a moment, took another drag on her cigarette. "But I have to say, James is such a gentle person. I can't imagine he's a killer."

I didn't disagree with her assessment, I told her. "Just thinking," I said. I switched the topic back to Nathan. "You think he may have headed for D.C.? Maybe he figures that's where he'll find the evidence he needs to prove you're Cindy Sands."

She shook her head. "That would take a level of planning and commitment I don't think he is capable of right now. Remember, he's off his medications and is probably having auditory hallucinations. He'll think he's fine, but every day he goes without his meds, his symptoms will get worse. He'll become more controlled by his delusions. He may imagine he's on some great quest, dodging police and spies, but all the while he's stalking me and maybe you too. I think he may believe that we have both betrayed him in our own way."

I considered this a moment. I did have the feeling someone was following me, watching me. Maybe it was just my imagination. Or maybe it was Beth's private investigator, still on the job. I doubted that, though. "We should tell Browning about Nathan's imposter theory. If he's headed to D.C., it would help find him."

She pulled on her earlobe. "I guess it couldn't hurt."

I looked up at Rebecca and noticed something for the first time. "You're not wearing your glasses," I said, realizing I had never seen her without them. "Contact lenses?"

She had a look of surprise on her face for just an instant, but then she smiled. "I only wear them when I want to see what I'm doing, and I've never been able to stand contacts." She reached over, retrieved the pair of glasses on the end table, and put them on. "Better?"

I shrugged, but her comment about not being able to wear contact lenses triggered a memory of my first visit here, of being in her bathroom and noticing the contact lens solution and the lens container, open and empty. I looked at the woman again and saw that she was looking closely at me.

"So," she said, breaking the silence that had somehow become tense, "I understand you heard from Nathan too?"

"By phone. And I haven't really talked to him. He called and left a message on my voice mail." I gave her a summary. "You haven't received any phone calls?"

"Not yet."

And then, as if on cue, the phone rang. Both of us were paralyzed for several moments. When it rang again, I said, "I'll get it." I picked up the receiver and spoke into it. "Hello?" No response. "Hello?" I said again. Still no response.

I was about to speak a third time when the voice on the other end said, "I'm very disappointed in you, Ted." But before I could respond to my client, I heard the click and then the dial tone as he disconnected.

***

People bundled up against the cold; garbage cans overflowing; hundreds of conversations; gasoline exhaust fumes; colored lights; dirty, grimy windows; broken bottles; urine and alcohol odors mixed with sausage, onions, and peppers. Car horns in staccato against the steady roar of the engines, the sting of the wind against my face. My breath as steam. Coffee brewing, pizza baking. In the distance, sirens. Beggars and whores; kids on bikes and skateboards; booming, blasting rap music.

The sun has descended behind the tall buildings, creating an amber, pinkish effect in the polluted sky above the city and large shadows on the street. I am craving a cigarette, and as if a sign, I come upon a small tobacco shop. The lettering on the window spells out an advertisement for exotic tobacco products from all over the world. The subliminal message, the anagram, says "They are watching."

I hesitate momentarily and use my peripheral vision to check up and down the sidewalk. I use the reflection in the store window to survey across the street. Nothing out of the ordinary. Nothing to verify the message. Giving one more casual glance around, I open the door and step inside.

"Good evening, sir." The man's physical features identify him as Middle Eastern, perhaps from Iran but educated in America, judging by the slight but noticeable accent. He is polite but not overly friendly. I nod in greeting and then look around the store quickly. He appears to be the only other person in the place, though I note the door that leads to a back room and the darkened plate glass window high up on the back wall.

"May I help you find something?"

"I'd like some cigarettes. I saw your sign outside. I have received the message." I look closely at the man for some acknowledgment of the connection, but his face registers nothing other than mild curiosity and confusion. "I thought you might have a suggestion."

"You said that you saw our sign, that you received the message?"

"That's right. That's what I said."

Continuing to look at me, a smile frozen on his face, he asks, "Is there a particular brand you are interested in, or perhaps a particular region of the world whose product you wish to sample?"

It occurs to me now that he is speaking in code. An incorrect answer could be dangerous. The voice, quiet but insistent, tells me to say "Iran," but another voice, more convincing, also has my ear.

You don't have time for this. Others will take care of it. You must focus on your mission first. Get your cigarettes and get out.

"Something European," I say.

The man frowns slightly. "I have just received a shipment from France." He reaches behind him and retrieves a single cigarette from a container inside the glass cabinet. "It is more bold than American cigarettes but not so dangerous as some others."

I take the sample, place it between my lips, then bend to the flame from the man's lighter. I can't help but notice that it is slender, gold with black trim. I inhale, hold it briefly, then exhale. I raise the cigarette up closer to my face, examining it. "This is nice," I say, taking another drag. "I'll take a pack." With the cigarette in my mouth, I pull out my wallet. The man gives me the price and a smile that is indulgent of the American whose tastes are undeveloped. I pay him, then step outside. Maybe it was not a front for a terrorist cell after all.

I am still thinking about this incident thirty minutes later as I sit on the bench across from the hospital, waiting for my shift to begin. At about 5:20, I put out my cigarette and head toward the rear entrance. Albert is right on time.

Yesterday, we went over the entire building, and he showed me what we did and where. All I cared about was that our areas of responsibility included the administration offices, more specifically the offices where the personnel records and the administrative files on all patients were kept. I made careful note of each location, the security measures or lack thereof in each.

It's amazing how much effort is put into keeping people out of certain areas during the day, but they think nothing of giving the cleaning crew run of the place at night. They leave cabinets unlocked, files on desks, sensitive materials out in plain view.

It took me a while to figure out the filing system, but once I did, I easily found Dr. Rebecca Whitsen's personnel file and, with not too much difficulty, the complete administrative file on her notorious patient, Cindy Sands. I will need copies or the originals to document my findings. I have decided that originals are better, as copies could easily be faked. The problem is I haven't yet found what I need.

After a while, Albert and I separate and I am able to get back to the place where I stored the files from the previous night to take another look. Earlier today, I had sorted through back issues of the newspaper, trying to verify my hunch about plastic surgery. Cindy could have found someone willing to do it quickly and discreetly. After all, the woman had money from her parents' bank accounts that she had hidden prior to her arrest and had refused to say where afterwards. Assuming she was able to access it after her escape, which seemed likely since she was able to effectively hide from the law during this time, she would have been able to buy the skill and silence of the right plastic surgeon.

Only I figured she wouldn't want to depend on the good faith of such a person to keep quiet. So I looked through the obituaries during this period of time, and I found the death notice of one Henry P Caswell, who had a private practice in cosmetic and reconstructive surgery. The obituary didn't mention the cause of death, but his age was forty-six. There has not been time to follow this up, but I am confident that there is a connection.

There was, of course, one major problem with this theory, as my lawyer had pointed out early on. Cindy Sands' records listed her as being five-seven. The woman who called herself Rebecca Whitsen was no more than five-four, if that. The only thing I could think of was that Sands must have found a way to alter these records, as she had the dentals.

Tonight, I have brought a magnifying glass with me. I lay the pertinent documents on the desk, side by side, and examine them. With the aid of magnification, I am able to observe that, in fact, the entries for height for both women have been altered. There are slight markings underneath the final digits, what look like erasure markings, and the faint outline of the transposed numbers underneath. It is subtle, but to me, unmistakable. "Yes," I say in a whisper and pump my arm once, my hand in a fist. Finally, something I can use! Certainly, an expert will be able to verify this. Plus, there are no doubt other records on both women that Cindy has not thought to change or been able to, records that would be inconsistent with those from the hospital—school records or other medical records perhaps, driver's licenses.

Their respective fingerprint cards I place into my bag. I can't tell anything without an expert, but again there appears to have been an alteration of the names. And this is even more obvious because it was the entire name that had to be altered.

I am so focused on the files spread out in front of me that I don't hear Albert when he comes down the hall. It is only when he approaches the entrance to the office that I sense his presence. I quickly close the files and lean over my vacuum cleaner just as he walks in.

"Hey, man, what's going on in here? You should be halfway down the hall by now. What's taking you so long?"

"There was a bad stain in the carpet, and I was trying to get it out. Now I can't seem to get the vacuum cleaner to work."

Albert frowns. "No, man, you don't try to clean the carpets. That's a whole 'nother job. We get extra for that. You just vacuum. That's all. I told you that."

I look down at the floor sheepishly. "Sorry, Albert. I just forgot."

Still frowning, he walks over to the vacuum cleaner. "What's the matter with it?"

"Don't know. It just died on me."

Albert leans over, bends down, and picks up the end of the cord.

Holding it up at face level, he says, "It helps if you plug it in."

I give him a face that says I have been completely humiliated. He shakes his head as he plugs the cord into the wall socket, then motions me to turn on the machine. I do, and it roars to life. Albert stands next to me and knocks my cap with his finger, moving it a half inch. His smile suggests good-natured ribbing more than aggression. "You better speed it up, man, if you want to get out of here on time with me." I straighten my cap, touch the bill lightly in acknowledgment of his message, and start vacuuming as he walks out the door.

***

Carefully, I push the aluminum foil into the crease of the baseball cap and adjust it, pulling down on the bill so that it covers more of my face. I don't really think they're monitoring my movements by satellite, but I have to cover all the possibilities. They could have implanted a tracking device somewhere inside my body—maybe underneath the skin on my forearm or in the back of my head or in one of my teeth perhaps. I know it is a cliché, but I've seen it happen too many times to ignore the possibility. If they have, it would be impossible to detect without some very sophisticated equipment, which I don't have. And I am certainly not going to start pulling out my teeth or digging holes in my arms like some lunatic looking for it. No, the best bet is to assume the existence of the device and take steps to jam or interfere with the signal.

Hence the cap and the aluminum foil. I know it's so stereotypical, but it works. It is why I never remain stationary for more than six hours, why I chew a lot of gum, and why I purchased the digital underwater wristwatch, which doesn't conceal my location but alters the time frame reference they can utilize. I keep it set three hours ahead.

For similar reasons, I bought the duct tape. I don't know why really, but it seems to work fairly well in keeping the voices out or at least keeping down the volume. As of late, especially at night, they are a little too active, too rambunctious, coming out through the spaces around the electrical outlets and light fixtures. It's a cacophony of voices, noise really, like a radio that is constantly going up and down the dial. I get little snatches of conversations coming through on occasion. Sometimes I lie there in the dark, concentrating, trying to decipher the code, to unveil the hidden messages.

Some of them are deep, spiritual or religious in tenor. Others are more mundane. The point is they can be quite distracting. And they represent a security risk as well. Just last night, my landlady knocked on the door. She wanted to know who I had in the room. She had heard voices again, she said. She was sure of it this time. I assured her there was no one else there, opened the door, and let her see. She didn't find anybody, of course, but she began to look at me with a good deal of suspicion after that, and she has been watching closely as I come and go.

So I have put tape around all the light fixtures and electrical outlets in my room, sealing them as best I can. It seems to be keeping the voices at bay, though nothing can stop them if they get really insistent. That's just the way it is.

They're going to take you out, Nathan.

Not if I keep one step ahead of them. Not if I can anticipate their every move before they make it. For example, the cigarette smoke drifting up from the door up ahead. It's dark there, just the glow from the cigarette. Two men, standing in the doorway, pretending to be talking, smoking. The man across the street, twenty feet to the rear. The woman by his side has her arm locked in his, looking up at him, smiling. The man is talking into his lapel. One of the men in the doorway grunts an acknowledgment and looks my way briefly. They probably have another team up ahead as back up.

You know their plan, don't you?

I'm about fifty feet away now. I notice the panel van with darkened windows just past the men. "Ah, yes," I say aloud.

No response. I go deeper into myself. Yes, one of the men in the doorway will step out as I approach. "Hey, pal," he will say, "you got a light?" or maybe "Can you spare some change?" The idea will be to distract me for just a moment. His companion will have the weapon, a knife or maybe a club of some kind. Nothing exotic. They will want it to look like a common mugging.

I am almost to the doorway now. One of the men steps away just a bit. The other man in the doorway throws his cigarette butt to the ground and puts his hand in his pocket. Before he can pull it out, though, I cross the remaining few feet in an instant. In an instant more, I have jammed the extended fingers of my right hand hard into his exposed throat. His hands go instinctively there, trying to locate the air that has just escaped. I bring my left hand across and with the heel of my palm deliver a blow to his nose that smashes the cartilage and sends it straight up into his brain. He collapses on the pavement.

The other man, startled, unable to react quickly enough, watches in horror as I take the knife from my pocket and plunge the blade into his stomach, then pull it upward and to the side. He falls back, clutching futilely at the gaping wound with both hands. There is a look of profound confusion on his face as he crumples and falls next to his companion.

I walk quickly away. The couple across the street have stopped to stare. They are momentarily confused, unsure of what to do. If they come to the aid of their colleagues, they will blow their cover. Besides, they can do them no good now anyway. They don't want to make matters worse by chasing after me, creating a disturbance. Same with the folks in the van. And before they can decide what to do, I have turned the corner, hailed a cab, and sped off. Looking out through the back windshield I whisper, "Not tonight, dear friends. Not tonight."

"Excuse me?" The cabbie looks at me in his rearview mirror.

"Sorry. Just talking to myself."

This seems to satisfy the man and he returns to concentrating on his driving. I continue, however, to look at his reflection in the mirror, comparing it to the photograph on the license hanging from the dashboard. The thought occurs to me that he may be in on it. Maybe he was part of plan B and had been waiting for me, planning to drive by just as I rounded the corner.

The voice comes from the overhead light. *You stupid shit. I've told you. There is no such thing as the Unit. There is just the Devil, and he has fooled you again into committing acts of evil. Those men meant you no harm. They were just common vagrants.*

"That doesn't mean they weren't dangerous."

You miss the point, Nathan.

"What is the point?'

The point is you're losing focus. This is not some silly spy game. This is a battle between good and evil. You must not draw attention to yourself. You must not be caught. You must not fail. Do you understand?

"Yes, Lord. I'm sorry." Then I notice that the cab driver is looking at me again in his mirror, and I wonder if I have been talking out loud.

"This is good," I say. "You can pull over here."

It is still two blocks from the address I gave him, but he is happy to be rid of me. He takes the fare and quickly drives off, muttering "psycho" under his breath.

"Yes, Lord," I say to the rear of his car as it disappears from view.

***

I dart in and out of the shadows as I make my way along the street, trying to gauge my situation, consider my options. I need to prove that Rebecca is not who she says she is. I have some pretty damning stuff, but what I need, given my lack of credibility, is the proverbial smoking gun. It has become clear, however, that my continued presence here has become too much of a risk.

The doubts and second thoughts have been hanging around for days now, dogging me, clawing at the door of my subconscious. Is it possible that I killed Rosenberg and don't remember it? Was my dream, my vision, the reality?

At night, when I try to sleep, I am plagued by another vision, a replay of the night my parents and brother were killed. But this time, it is my brother and my father who are attacking me. It is a nightmare too horrible to endure, but it comes just about every night now. My only defense is to stay awake. But that has its negatives too, as I'm sure you can imagine.

I pass the window of a photography studio and something pricks the back of my mind, a memory of passing a photograph on a wall. It is a nagging thought, a sensation that suddenly takes shape and comes into focus. I stand and straighten myself with new determination, then head in the direction of the hospital.

When I get there, I hesitate, retreating into the shadows of a building across the street to survey the area. I am glad to see that the guard on duty is the same one who was there when I left work a couple of hours earlier. He looks up as I approach.

"Hey, Jimmy," I say.

The guard looks up at the large round clock on the wall, then back at me. "What are you doing here, Danny?"

I look at him directly, satisfied that I display no sign of the nervousness I feel. "I realized that I didn't empty the trash in several rooms in the forensics section."

"What's the big deal? I'm sure they're not overflowing. They can wait 'til tomorrow."

I shrug. "Al says the hotshots in the offices complain if they come in and their trash hasn't been emptied. Al gets in trouble. I get in trouble. And I just started this job. I don't want to start out on the wrong foot."

Jimmy frowns, but it's hard to argue with the logic. He speaks into a walkie-talkie–looking device to a man named Clyde, tells him I'm coming his way to finish up some janitorial services and to just make sure the forensics wing is open. Satisfied that he will not have to move from his seat, he then motions me through the metal detector. When I'm on the other side of it he says, "You're just a little too dedicated, kid, but be my guest. See you in a few."

At a normal pace I make my way down the hallway. It is not bedtime yet, and there is still plenty of activity. The sights, sounds, and smells bombard me, blending with the internal voices. It is all I can do to screen out the extraneous and let the most beguiling voice guide me. I ignore the patients and avoid eye contact with the staff as I pass by.

The image of the photograph, the one I had recalled as I looked in the gallery window, is becoming more sharp and vivid in my mind. I'm pretty sure that it was in the forensics section, but I can't remember exactly where. The cafeteria? The break room? One of the offices? I slow my walk, hoping for a sign, something to trigger my memory.

Murderer! You must be punished. The voice is shrill, piercing. Then several other voices break in. *Die. Die. Die!*

"Shut up!" I say, much too loudly. Then I quickly look around to see a few patients look my way but no staff. A couple of the patients smile.

Relax, Nathan. Don't listen to them. You are not a murderer. You were trying to protect your family, not harm them. Don't let them play with your mind, Nathan.

"Do you know where that photo is?"

Yes. And so do you. Just follow your instincts.

I move down the hallway, up the stairs to the second floor, past the cafeteria and the break room, all the way to the entrance to forensics. The reception area is empty and it is eerily quiet. I stop and look around the room. On the wall, across from the staff station, is the photograph. I walk over and stand in front of it.

It is a group photo of some of the staff from the previous year, according to the notation at the bottom. I scan down the rows, looking for the face I had remembered. I find it, next to the last row, on the end. I get up real close for a better examination. With my fingers, I frame the face, blocking out the hair, imagining the person with and without glasses. I can almost hear the click as a vital piece of the puzzle locks into place, old assumptions knocked away in an instant.

"Of course," I say under my breath. "Of course."

CHAPTER 31

I took the stairs two at a time and was a bit winded when I reached the second floor. Jan was on the phone when I walked in. To my silent question, she shook her head. I went into my office, plopped my briefcase by the side of the desk, and sat down. I was staring off into space when Jan poked her head in a minute later.

"You okay?"

"Yeah, just thinking."

"Looks like hard work."

I looked up at her. "Theo in?"

"I think he's downstairs in Paul's office."

Back down the stairs I went and down the hallway to my partner's office. "Hey, Kathy," I said upon entering. "Theo down here?"

"They're outside," she said, jerking her thumb like a hitchhiker toward the rear of the building. I went through Paul's office and out the French doors that opened onto the terraced courtyard just beyond. They were seated at a wrought iron patio table. Both had coffee cups in front of them. Paul was puffing on a cigar.

The Italian-style courtyard was one of the nicest features of the building. The floor and walls were brick with marble accents to match the front of the building, adorned with plants and sculptures. It was open aired but covered by a plexiglass roof three floors above. Accessible from the library and conference room as well as from Paul's office, it was a great place for holding office parties and entertaining clients, and, since Kathy didn't allow smoking inside, it was a nice retreat for Paul when he wanted a cigar.

"Hey, Ted," my partner said, looking at his watch, "nice of you to come in today."

"I've been here all night. Just went out for breakfast."

"Well, it does look like you slept in that suit." He took a drag from his cigar and blew the smoke upward.

"That's because I did."

For a moment he looked at me, not sure if I was serious, deciding I was but mistaking the reason.

"Hear anything on the case? They find Nathan yet?"

I shook my head, looked over at Theo. "Not yet, but they think he's in the area." I told them about Rebecca's most recent message, about the new e-mail I had received the night before, the one that read, "Traitor! You have taken something from me and now I will take something from you. Then I'll come for you."

Paul leaned forward in his chair, the concern obvious on his face. "What do you think it means?"

Without hesitating I said, "I think it's a reference either to Annie or perhaps to Rebecca Whitsen."

Both men stared at me but didn't contradict me. They knew about Nathan's earlier threat against my family and me. They also knew about Nathan's accusation that I had been involved sexually with Rebecca. Finally, Theo said, "Have you told your wife?"

I shook my head. "I didn't want to be paranoid or alarm everybody unnecessarily."

Theo took a sip of coffee. "You tell Browning?"

I nodded again. "That's where I went this morning. I told him everything I knew—the imposter theory, confidential client information, everything."

If either lawyer was concerned with the ethical issues, neither voiced it. I also told them that I thought I was being followed. "It could be the private eye working for the Petronises or maybe just my imagination, but it also could be Nathan. Anyway, I've taken to checking my peripheral vision a little more, raising my alert level."

Paul frowned. "I think all of us in the office need to be on alert as well for any sign of our paranoid client."

I nodded my approval and took a seat at the table. "There's something else I want to run by you. I'd like us to reconsider Nathan's imposter theory."

Both of them looked at me as if I had lost my mind, and maybe I had. Neither said anything, though, and so I told them of my encounter with Rebecca, about her apparently doing okay without her glasses and her comment about not being able to wear contacts. "Yet I'm pretty sure I saw a lens case and contact lens solution when I was there before. And what's more strange, now that I'm thinking about it, the case was open but she was wearing her glasses that night."

Theo frowned. "What's it matter?"

"Why would she lie about it?"

My associate frowned. "Maybe you misheard her. Maybe she misspoke."

I shook my head. "I don't think so."

"So the idea is she wears contacts so she can see with the prescription glasses over them? All so that she can pretend she's Rebecca Whitsen?"

"I know it's a stretch, but . . ."

"That's more than a stretch," Paul said.

"Yeah," Theo agreed. "Like I said, you probably just misunderstood her. Maybe she wears contacts from time to time but just doesn't like them. It's not that she can't wear them."

"Maybe," I said, doubtful.

We were quiet for several seconds. Paul puffed on his cigar and exhaled smoke into the air. Finally he spoke. "So if this woman is a killer disguised as her previous psychologist, why is she sending herself and you harassing e-mails and messages? If she killed Rosenberg because he got too close, why leave behind the one item that might tie her to the murder and reveal her identity? And how did she manage to get one of her patients to show up at the scene at just the right time so he could be the fall guy?"

All good questions, and I didn't have good answers, but I tried. "As to your first question, because she's crazy. As to the second, because she's arrogant. As to the third, she dressed up as Nathan, just in case somebody saw her."

Both lawyers shook their heads, still skeptical.

"Okay," I said, shifting gears, "let's say Rebecca is not an imposter. But what if the real Cindy Sands didn't die in the fire? What if she has come here to continue stalking Whitsen?"

Paul leaned forward in his chair. "Listen, Ted, you're under a lot of pressure right now. You've been up all night. Why don't you go home and get some rest? Theo can follow up. We'll call you if anything comes up."

Before I could respond, Kathy stuck her head out of the door to Paul's office and said, "Ted, you have a call on line two, a Dr. Whitsen. She says it's important."

I shared a look with Paul and Theo, then went into Paul's office to take the call. I picked up the phone and punched the blinking button. "Hello?"

"Ted, this is Rebecca. Our tech guy has traced the origin of the most recent e-mails."

"Yes?"

"They're coming from the hospital, the administration building."

***

I was standing at the window in my office, looking down on the traffic on College Avenue, trying to sort through the new developments in Nathan's case. Rebecca had been pretty convincing on the phone. Perhaps she was an imposter, a very good actress, but she had seemed truly frightened. And if Rebecca was not Cindy Sands, if she was receiving e-mail messages from someone in the hospital, I had to consider the possibility that they were from my client. Perhaps he had, as Browning suspected, remained in the area. On the other hand, the e-mails and other messages may have nothing to do with Nathan or Rosenberg. And any of our alternative suspects could easily have sent them as well.

I tried to take my mind off Nathan's case, as well as my own, by busying myself with other work. Immersing myself in the troubles of others was generally a reliable way to take my mind off my own problems. But not today. I was feeling anxious and slightly morose, unable to concentrate on much of anything. I had drunk two twenty-ounce Cokes and smoked half a pack of cigarettes as I tried to work on an appellate brief due in ten days. I would read several paragraphs, then realize I hadn't a clue as to what I had just read. Finally I gave up and started going through my e-mails. I spotted one from a person calling himself Special Agent Harold Martin. The name sounded familiar. I opened and started reading.

Dear Mr. Stevens,

I hope that this message finds you well and that it comes in time to be of assistance in your representation of Nathan Hart. I have tried to reach Nathan by e-mail without success and thought I should pass on the information to you.

Nathan worked at the Bureau when he was in school several years ago. I know he has had his share of problems since, but he was a good kid and smart. He did me a real favor back then, and I owe him. The print he asked me to examine does have certain similarities to the known print of one Cindy Sands. It's not enough for a positive identification, but it's my opinion, unofficially, that the prints are from the same person. You may reply to this

e-mail or call me at the number listed above if you have
any questions or wish to discuss the matter further.

Sincerely.
Harold Martin

I read the last few lines again, then studied the e-mail address and
phone number provided. I looked in the phone book and confirmed
that the area code was for the Washington, D.C., area, then dialed it.
The recorded message said that Special Agent Hal Martin was unable
to take my call right now but if I would leave my name, number, and a
brief message, he would get back to me. I did so, then disconnected and
buzzed Theo. He didn't pick up. Neither did Paul. Kathy said both Paul
and Theo were at a deposition in a civil case. I thanked her, put down
the phone, and read the e-mail again as I printed out a copy, considering
the implications. I left it on my desk with a note to Jan to make a copy
for Theo.

Was it possible? Was Cindy Sands alive and pretending to be her
former psychologist as Nathan insisted? It had seemed preposterous—
until now. On the other hand, maybe Sands had changed places with
whoever died in that fire, but it wasn't Rebecca Whitsen—meaning she
was alive and stalking her former psychologist again. This theory was, in
fact, much more logical. It would explain the e-mails and other messages.
It would explain the murders of Rosenberg and Donnie Mercer and the
frame-up of Nathan. It fit the pattern of Sands being both her protector
and her tormentor. And it also meant that Rebecca may be in real danger.
I needed to call her immediately.

Of course, there was reason to suspect the legitimacy of the e-mail.
It had already been demonstrated to me that one can send an e-mail and
make it appear to be coming from someone else. There may actually be a
Harold Martin in Washington, D.C., whose computer had been used as
a decoy. If so, he would be wondering who I was and why I had left him

the message on his recorder. If and when he called me back I would know.

Figuring better to be safe than sorry, I phoned both her home and cell numbers, getting voice mail both times. I didn't want to frighten her with a message out of context so I just asked her to call me back. I was contemplating whether to call Walter Browning with this new information when Jan called out from her desk. "Ted, Denise Wilkerson on line two."

I had been waiting impatiently for this call all afternoon, but now I felt paralyzed, unable to move from the window. She had told me she expected a ruling from Judge Simmons by the end of the week. That was today. I had been subconsciously preparing myself for the worst, analyzing the situation with an objective, critical eye, listing in my mind all the reasons that the judge might not rule in my favor, why I didn't deserve a favorable ruling. As usual, I had no one to blame but myself.

"Ted, did you hear me?" Jan's voice brought me back to the here and now. "Denise Wilkerson for you on line two."

"I got it," I said, then forced myself to turn and walked toward my desk. I hesitated a moment, then, with a mixture of hope and dread, picked up the receiver. "Hello?"

"Ted, it's Denise. I know you've been anxious to hear something, but it was difficult to coordinate everyone's schedule." In the moment's hesitation before she continued, I thought to myself that the calm, even tone to her voice foreshadowed bad news. "The judge has made his ruling."

CHAPTER 32

*I*t was approximately 5:45 when I pulled into my driveway, already starting to get dark and cold. The yellow light from the street lamp blended with the dusk, producing an eerie, filtered look. It was as if I was watching some *film noir* version of myself approaching the house. Though it was still in the mid-fifties, the temperature was falling quickly and the lady on the radio had said that it was predicted to go below freezing overnight. I punched in the number of Beth's cell phone again and waited in the car while it rang, replaying in my head the conversation with Denise.

"The judge has made Beth the primary residential parent," she said, and my heart began to collapse in on itself. "But only if she agrees to live in Tallahassee."

"What?"

"Otherwise, Annie is to live with you primarily."

"What?" I said again, still not believing what I was hearing.

"Annie's coming back to Tallahassee, Ted."

"When? When is this to take place?"

"Beginning on the first of the year."

I made her repeat it twice. My heart, which had been in my stomach, soared with joy. Pure joy, followed almost immediately by the fears and concerns of someone who can't believe and doesn't feel he deserves the good fortune. What if Beth fights it? What if she appeals? What if Beth just refuses to live in Tallahassee, and I actually get what I had asked for?

Could I handle it? No. No way would Beth allow that to happen.

No reason to be concerned, Denise had said. If she appealed, the judge would probably be affirmed, as he had a lot of discretion in such matters and he certainly was unlikely to grant a stay of his order pending an appeal. She would have to comply. The judge was emphatic. Her lawyer had asked for a longer transition period, but the judge said he wanted Annie in school here by the beginning of the next term. Moreover, he wanted her to begin an adjustment period of more extended parenting time with me, starting tonight, "if the father so desires."

"He most certainly does," I said.

Beth was directed to do everything in her power to make it a smooth transfer or someone would be spending some time in jail. When I got the details confirmed, I raced out of the office to the house to put a few things together and get on the road in plenty of time to make the scheduled exchange at the place and time agreed to by the lawyers while the judge was still on the line: the McDonald's on Highway 90 in Marianna at 7:30. I had been trying to reach Beth to confirm that she and Annie were on the way.

She picked up finally after the fourth ring. I could imagine her reading the incoming call number and trying to decide whether she could bear to talk to me just now. "Hello?"

"Beth, it's me." I decided it best to skip any introductory pleasantries. Easier for both of us to get right to it. "My lawyer told me about the judge's ruling and the agreed time and place for the exchange. Just wanted to make sure we were on the same page and you and Annie were on your way out. It takes about an hour and a half to get there from your folks' place."

There was silence on the other end for several seconds. "Beth, you there?"

"Yes." Another hesitation. "Ted, listen, there's a problem. Annie's not here."

"What? You've got to be kidding. This is a new low, even for you."

I could feel the anger rising within me and struggled to keep my voice calm. "Well, where is she?"

"She's supposed to be with her friend Robyn Starks. She went over to her house after school. She was going to spend the night with her. I called when I heard about the judge's ruling, but I haven't been able to get in touch with Robyn's mother. They must have gone out somewhere. I've called her cell phone and Annie's cell, but I keep getting voice mail. Maybe they went to a movie."

"Maybe they did," I said, ratcheting down my voice, seeking calm. But the icy cold of terror began to grip me, to shake any calm right out of me. This could be just a ruse to keep Annie away from me for at least one more night, but it didn't feel like an act. I sensed the unease, the anxiety in a mother's voice. Should I tell her? She had a right to know what she was up against, the possibility of real danger. But I didn't want to panic her. I fought then for control.

"That's probably it," I said after a couple of moments. "Listen, I'm going to head out in a few minutes. You keep trying every person who might know something. Keep me posted. Call me on my cell phone. If you haven't found her by the time I reach the halfway point, I'll just come on to Panama City and help you look."

Though I tried to hide it, I think she sensed the hint of alarm in my voice, but she simply said, "Okay," and promised to let me know as soon as she knew something.

I was still thinking about the conversation as I got out of the car and headed for the house. As I got closer to the back door, the faintest tinge of concern, of uneasiness, caused me to pause. But it was only a moment's hesitation. My mind was too restless, rushing through the many things I needed to consider, to do in preparation.

Perhaps it was because I was preoccupied that I didn't pay sufficient attention to my surroundings. I didn't notice, for example, that the lights in the house were all off even though I usually left one or two on for security purposes. I didn't notice that Bjorn was not there with his nose in the fence to greet me, as was customary when I got home.

Nor was he waiting for me just inside the front door, as was his other modus operandi. It was only when I put my keys on the counter in the kitchen that I sensed a presence. I was on full alert then, holding my breath and listening, searching the room with my eyes. And then I saw his outline in the semidarkness of the family room, sitting in the recliner. Although the hair was short now and he had no beard, I knew who it was even before I flipped the light switch.

"Hello, Ted."

Reflexively, I moved back a step and brought my hands up, having caught sight of the pistol in his hand. My heart was pounding and a thin film of sweat formed involuntarily under my arms and on my forehead. Intuitively, though, I knew that I must remain calm. I willed myself to take a step forward and bring down my hands. Nathan stood abruptly from the chair and moved into the light.

His clothes were dirty and disheveled, as was the short blond hair. His eyes were those of a beast, the hint of which I had first noted at our initial meeting. They were now a mixture of intensity and vacancy that led me to think of one descriptive word: deranged. "Nathan," I said, "what are you doing here?" It was lame but the best I could come up with at the time.

He held his arms out to his sides, palms up. "Ta- da. You like the new look, Ted?"

I did a quick survey of the room, beginning to weigh my options. It was then that I saw my dog, sprawled out in the corner of the room. He wasn't moving. "Bjorn," I said, but he didn't respond. I looked back at Nathan, gave him a wordless stare.

He had followed my gaze, knew what I was thinking. "Don't worry about your dog," he said. "We got along fine. I just gave him a little something to make him sleep for a while."

I looked back over at Bjorn, saw his side move out slightly, then in. He was breathing. Then I turned back to Nathan. "What about my daughter? What have you done with her?"

He cocked his head to one side, looking at me. "What would I want with your daughter? I mean, she is a cute little thing, but you and I have business not appropriate for young children."

I tried to read my client, gain some sense of whether he was lying. I couldn't tell but sensed that I must stay as calm as I could. I repeated my initial question. "What are you doing here?"

"Waiting for you, of course." He was still pointing the pistol at me, and I found it difficult to look at anything else. He seemed to notice this, looking first at the gun in his hand, then back at me. "It's a twenty-two. It was all I could get on the street on short notice. Thought I might need some protection or persuasion. Might not even kill you if you took a slug, but then again. . . ." He left the implication out there.

"I almost went to your office. Wasn't sure you would come home in time. Saw you in your window, you know. But it was too risky. Too many other people." Nathan was pacing now, seemingly searching the room, for what I didn't know.

"Listen, Nathan, you need to turn yourself in. I can help you. I've got new information. It's important that . . ."

"Shut up! Shut up!" He was screaming and pointing the gun in my direction. I put my hands up, told him it was okay. Just as quickly, he calmed back down. "Not you, Ted. It's the others. They won't leave me alone. Sometimes I have to be very assertive with them. Sometimes logical discussion is not enough. They have to know who's in charge."

He looked down at the gun again, then at me. "And don't worry, Ted. I'm not going to shoot you unless you do something stupid. Though you'd deserve it. You betrayed me, for sure. I trusted you, man. I told you my secrets. How do you think I felt when I called Rebecca's phone and you answered it?"

"I can explain that, Nathan."

He waved me off. "It's not important anymore. What's important now is that I have the proof I need to show I am innocent of the murder of Rosenberg."

"What is it?"

He smiled. "Come on, let's go. We'll take your car."

"Where are we going?"

"To Rebecca's, of course."

Watch him. He may try something.

"Don't worry. I got things under control."

***

Ted pulls out of his driveway, puts the car in drive, then looks at me in the rearview mirror. "So, Nathan, what's this proof you have?"

He's just trying to humor you, to distract you.

When I don't respond, Ted says, "Come on, Nathan, you can trust me. We've got to work together."

"Yeah? Is that why, after I told you of my suspicions, pointed out the evidence of Rebecca's guilt, you were banging her behind my back?"

"Listen, Nathan, you've got it all wrong. I . . ."

"Don't even try, Ted. I can handle it. She's an attractive woman. I understand. But don't lie to me now. Don't insult my intelligence."

He's been in on it from the beginning. Kill him. Kill him now, before it's too late.

Ted looks in the mirror again. "What?"

"Nothing," I say, willing the voices into the background.

"Nathan," Ted says, "I got an e-mail today from your friend Hal Martin with the FBI. He says the print on the lighter belonged to Cindy Sands."

I smile at him in the mirror. "You didn't believe me, did you?"

"We can use this to get a new trial, to clear you. Let's let the police handle it."

"You still don't understand, do you, Ted?"

"I want to understand, Nathan. I'm listening."

I shake my head. "Let's wait 'til we're all together so I don't have to repeat myself."

We travel mostly in silence the rest of the way. By the time we park and start walking to Rebecca's front door, Ted appears resigned, maybe even welcoming the unfolding of events. I move to the side as Ted knocks on the door. When Rebecca opens it, I walk in right behind Ted.

Interestingly, she seems neither surprised nor alarmed to see us. She has a drink in her hand, which she waves at us. "Gentlemen, won't you come in." She makes a broad sweep with her other hand as she steps to the side and bows slightly. It is then that I note in her eyes the look of heavy medication. We follow her into the living room. I motion with the gun for them to sit on the sofa. I pull the matching chair up closer to the coffee table, place the duffle bag on the floor, take out a file and place it on the table.

Rebecca puts her glass down on the end table. "So, Nathan, have you found the proof you were looking for, the evidence that proves I'm Cindy Sands?"

"I'm sorry about that, Rebecca. I thought that you were not who you seemed, that you were an imposter. But I was wrong."

"Oh?" Rebecca doesn't seem surprised, but Ted does.

I turn to him. "I now know who killed Dr. Rosenberg and the others and who has been sending the messages to you and her. It all makes sense now, as you will see."

Neither Ted nor Rebecca speaks, perhaps not sure what to say, perhaps busy trying to weigh their options, thinking of possible means to disarm me. Neither makes a move, though. They just look at me neutrally. I pull out the photo and place it on the coffee table in front of them. "Look familiar?" When they still don't move, I say, "Come on, take a look."

They both lean forward, studying the group photograph and specifically the man I'm pointing to. "Isn't that . . . ?" Ted begins.

"James Washington," Rebecca says. She looks a little closer. "And this was taken at St. Elizabeth's in D.C. I recognize the background."

I nod. "That's right. At first I thought you must have known him, that you were in it together, but then I saw in his personnel file that he was there for only a month before Cindy Sands escaped, after you removed yourself as her psychologist. It's a large facility. Not unreasonable that your paths would not have crossed or that, even if you had seen or met him in passing, you wouldn't have recognized him later at Florida State Hospital without his dreadlocks and glasses."

Both of them sit back on the sofa, seemingly receptive now to what I have to say.

"Some of the reports of Cindy's escape speculated that she might have had inside help. That same someone could have helped her hide out and stalk Rebecca. That was James. That's why he didn't list his employment at St. Elizabeth's on his application for Florida State Hospital."

Rebecca nods slowly. "He must have been devastated when Cindy burned up in that fire. Either way, he would have blamed the person who was the object of Cindy's obsession, the one person with whom he couldn't compete for her attention. He would have wanted revenge."

Rebecca leans forward and looks at the photo again, nodding her head. "Who else," she says, "would know the intimate secrets of the relationship, the details of Cindy's crimes? Who better to compose the e-mail messages to me, enjoying the psychological torture? Her lover would know about the trademark cigarette lighter, wouldn't he? Maybe even have one lying around with Cindy's fingerprint on it."

"Yes," I say. "Rosenberg must have discovered James's indiscretion and confronted him. Maybe he knew everything. Maybe he was just getting too close for comfort. Either way, he had to go. And what a good patsy I would make. Easy for him to get my clothes, plant them in the washer. I don't think he planned on Raymond happening along, but it actually turned out even better. I know James is of a different race, but in the dark, with the cap and dark clothes, Raymond could have mistaken him for me."

As I go through the scenario, Ted begins to join in, answering some of the rhetorical questions I pose. Rebecca, however, has grown quiet now, taking it all in as she sips her drink. As I watch Rebecca, I notice her brush her hair over to the side with her hand and curl it behind her ear. Then she pulls on her earlobe. She does this ritualistic adjustment twice in a row. When she looks at me and smiles, I remember where I have seen this same idiosyncrasy recently—on the videotaped confession of Cindy Sands.

I am so absorbed in this realization and its implications, sorting it out in my mind, that when I catch the movement to my left, my reaction is too slow. Before I can pull my gun from behind my back where I had placed it in my waistband, James Washington has come down the stairs and is pointing a pistol in our direction.

Pull your gun. He won't shoot. And even if he does, you are smarter, faster, more accurate. He won't know what hit him. The voices are insistent, but I pay them no mind. I want to play this out, more curious than anything, my suspicions having come full circle in the last thirty seconds.

"You shouldn't be telling such lies, Nathan. You'll have them believing you."

My psychologist frowns as she stands and moves to the other side of the table. "He can be rather convincing if you accept his delusional basis. And I think he just about had Ted believing him, though I could have handled it. There was no need for you to show your face." She moves over to me, reaches behind my back, and removes the gun. "But I think our friend Nathan has finally figured it out, haven't you, Nathan. What was it?"

I push an imaginary strand of hair behind my ear, mimicking her, and she smiles slightly.

"How careless of me." Rebecca is now standing between James and Ted, who is still seated on the couch. She looks at Ted, then me. "So, care to revise your theory?"

I nod, but it is Ted who speaks. "Everything Nathan just said is how it happened, except that Cindy didn't die in the fire. It was, as he originally thought, a carefully executed plan to kill Rebecca Whitsen and assume her identity. James was your willing helper. He would have had access to the records to make the switch, made arrangements with the plastic surgeon, arranged for the necessary security breaches to make the escape itself possible. And since the plan had the markings of something in the works for longer than the month James was at the facility, I suspect there was some previous connection." He looks over at James.

"Yes," James says, smiling, "Cindy was a guest at our facility in Maine for a while. We got to be friendly—real friendly."

"But what's the story with the e-mails? How does that tie in?" Ted looks over at Cindy, but it is James who answers.

"Cindy fancies herself an actress, you know. She just got a little too much into her part. She sent them to herself." He chuckles. "There was a time when I thought she was beginning to believe she *was* Rebecca Whitsen." He moves over and puts an arm around Cindy.

Cindy carefully moves his hand from her shoulder, and James backs away a step as she frowns at him. She looks at me. "I don't know, Nathan," she says, twisting her hair behind her ear, "I kind of liked your first story better, with James as the grief-stricken lover bent on revenge in the most vile manner, following me to Florida, tormenting me with threatening messages, taking over where his girlfriend left off. I think that plays a lot better."

As she says this, she places the barrel of the gun—my gun—to James's temple and fires. There is a surreal moment as James stands there as if nothing has happened. Then he collapses to the floor. And before either Ted or I can react, she has aimed the gun at the head of my lawyer and fired. I watch in horror as a small hole appears in his forehead. Ted looks at Cindy, then me, before he falls over gently on the couch, as if preparing to take a nap.

I fully expect Cindy to turn the gun on me, but instead she leans down and takes the gun out of the hand of her dead lover. Then she stands and tosses the gun she has just used to kill two people at me. I grab it instinctively. With the other gun in her hand, pointed at me, she says, "You have two choices, Nathan. You can try to raise that gun at me and hope you can fire quickly enough and accurately enough to stop me from shooting you. And given that your gun is a twenty-two and this is a nine-millimeter, we can see who can do the most damage. Or you can tuck that gun into your waistband, very slowly and carefully, then leave out my door and keep going. Neither is a great choice, but for my money, the second is your best."

"Why not just kill me now?"

A smile comes over her face. It is a cruel, vicious smile. "Oh, Nathan, that would be too easy. It would spoil our little game." When I give her a puzzled look, she gives me a sneer. "You think you're so clever, such the chess master. Did it ever occur to you that I was playing you, setting you up, in more ways than one?" She waved the gun for emphasis. "So, as I say, you have two choices. And you have to be thinking, at least the second choice gives you a chance to tell your story. Maybe someone will believe you."

I reflect on the matter for only a couple of seconds, then I tuck the gun into my waistband and turn toward the door. "Oh, Nathan?" I turn back, half expecting a bullet to be coming my way, realizing that I don't care. But she just smiles and says, "Checkmate."

***

It is hot, very hot, in the small office. I wipe the sweat from my brow with the sleeve of my shirt, the handcuffs rubbing against my jaw in the process. The stenographer looks over at me, fingers poised over the keys. I continue.

"Of course, as you know, I barely made it out of the parking lot. I don't know whether the gunshots alerted a neighbor, who in turn called the police, or whether they had people watching the apartment. At any rate, they were waiting for me when I came outside. I could probably have eluded them but not without the cost of more human life. So I allowed myself to be captured."

I look at the detective, whose face is expressionless, a sign for me to keep going. "Now, Cindy has no doubt destroyed the photograph and other documentation I brought back. You won't find it in her apartment, of that I'm sure. But at least you know it can be obtained. If I did it, so can you. And I will have to depend on your good faith in this, detective, that you will sort this all out and establish my innocence."

I appreciate the fact that the detective has not had me shot up with drugs. I had accepted a mild sedative before the interview, however, as it was to our mutual advantage for me to be both calm and coherent, the voices muted. My statement is being recorded electronically and by a stenographer.

Walter Browning nods at me, then looks over at the other detective for a moment, the one he calls Scranton. She has said nothing during my entire statement. I can tell by the glance the two exchange now that neither believes me. Scranton speaks for the first time. "That's quite a story, Mr. Hart."

I look at her briefly, then back at Browning. "It's the truth and easily verifiable."

"Oh, we'll be checking it out." Scranton again, her tone unmistakably sarcastic.

"If you wait too long, she'll escape and you may never catch her again."

"No immediate concern about that, Mr. Hart." Browning this time. "You see, she's been here at the office too for a while. She's given us her statement." He pauses to pop a stick of gum in his mouth, then sits back in his chair. Despite the heat in the small room—he must have the thermostat up to eighty—he seems quite comfortable.

"As you can imagine," he says, "she's telling a somewhat different version of the events."

"I can imagine."

"What she says is that you went to her apartment in a very agitated state, having kidnapped your lawyer. You told them you had proof that this guy Washington was the one who killed Rosenberg and framed you for it. You made her call him up and get him to come over. Then, as you started to tell them why Washington was the murderer, you suddenly switched to saying Dr. Whitsen was an imposter, that she was really this mental patient. . . . What was her name?"

"Cindy Sands," I say. Good grief, has the man not been listening to me? Is he dense? Or is he just playing with me?

"That's right. Cindy Sands. Except that the photo you showed them was a picture from a magazine, and the records you showed them, the ones you say you got from the psychiatric facility in Washington, were just cut-up pages from a magazine as well. You had it all in this large duffle bag. That's what she provided us."

"Of course, she did. You didn't expect her to just hand over the evidence of her guilt, did you? If you search now, you'll probably find the very magazine she used to make all that stuff, to try and set me up again."

The detective shrugs. "Anyway, Dr. Whitsen suggests that you apparently see yourself as her guardian angel or something, like this Cindy Sands did before. When James showed up, she said you started talking to yourself, laying out what you called your evidence. She said you were hearing voices apparently, talking to people who weren't there."

"Are you hearing voices now, Nathan?" Scranton leans forward in her seat, studying me closely, as if I am some kind of bug under a microscope.

I am, of course, hearing voices. It is a din of noise inside my head as they blend together, an occasional shout to separate from the others. But I am also smart enough not to say so. Besides, I've decided I really don't like this woman detective, this Scranton. I ignore both her and the voices and turn my attention back to Browning. Surely he can see by my calm demeanor, my rational narrative of the events, that I am not the lunatic Sands has described.

"Then, without any warning," Browning says, "you shot Washington in the head. When your lawyer made a move toward you, you shot him in the head as well. You said something to Dr. Whitsen about an invisible hand or something like that, then just left."

"What about the gun James had?"

"There was no other gun in the apartment." Scranton, for some reason, feels like she has the right, the obligation, to pipe in again.

I give her a hard stare and again speak to Browning. "It was there."

Again, the man shrugs. "At any rate, the two of you certainly don't agree on the facts. The difficulty for you, I would say, is that she's a respected psychologist and you're a mental patient. Plus, none of the physical evidence so far supports your version. You see the problem, don't you, Nathan?"

It is my turn to shrug. I can see where this will end up, and, quite frankly, I'm not sure I really care anymore. I sigh. "As I said, detective, I will have to rely on your good faith and your diligence in investigating the evidence I have provided."

Browning gives me a rather sad look. Perhaps it is simply resignation. Then he motions with his head to Scranton. She goes to the door, opens it, and motions for the two deputies outside to come in. "You can take Mr. Hart back to his cell." The men stand on either side of me as I stand. "And, boys," Browning says, "be careful with him." They both nod and lead me out the door.

For several seconds, while the stenographer packs up her equipment, Browning looks down at the manuscript on his desk—my complete account of the strange and sad events that have led us to this point—and considers my oral supplementation of that account just now received. Finally, with the stenographer gone, he looks over at Scranton. "What do you think?"

"Bullshit," she says without hesitation.

Browning nods in agreement. "Interesting perhaps, even fascinating, but bullshit nonetheless." He picks up the manuscript. "I mean, there are passages in here that seem logical, that make sense. Then you come across some rambling pages of outright gibberish." He puts the manuscript back on his desk, still looking at it. "Still . . ."

"Do I detect some lingering doubt in your voice?" When Browning shrugs, she says, "You don't really think there's anything to it, do you?"

He doesn't answer her directly but instead asks, "Where are we on the physical evidence?"

"Too soon for ballistics to confirm a match of the two bullets in the victims with the gun we took from Hart, but the entry wounds suggest a small caliber, maybe a twenty-two."

"'Course that wouldn't be inconsistent with Hart's explanation."

"Aw, come on, Walter."

"I'm just saying, we have to consider it, if only to rule it out with the totality of the physical evidence." He pauses, looking at her, and she gives him a reluctant nod of agreement. "How about Stevens? Any word on his condition?"

She shakes her head. "Still in a coma. I would say he's lucky to be alive, but I don't know that's the case. Even if he lives, he'll probably have permanent brain damage."

The detective nods his head. "Well, let's work it up. Don't let them get sloppy on this, Scranton. And ask the hospital to keep us posted on Stevens."

She gives him a mock salute, then closes the door behind her. Alone, he picks up the manuscript and begins reading it again. After a while, he puts it down and starts to go through his mail. He begins to reply when the door opens after a perfunctory knock and Scranton steps in. Her face is flushed, her eyes wide.

"Walter, just heard from the hospital," she says. "The lawyer's come out of his coma, and he's talking."

CHAPTER 33

*I*t was early January but mild enough to enjoy a game of chess out in the courtyard, which is what Nathan was doing when I went to see him. He was concentrating on the board with such intensity that he didn't notice me until I was almost right upon him. He looked up and smiled.

"Hello, Ted."

"Nathan."

He looked back at the man on the other side of the chess board. "Pete, this is my lawyer, Ted Stevens."

Pete looked up then, sizing me up, but said nothing. I moved my cane to my left hand and offered my right to the man. Pete took it. "Nice to meet you," I said, suddenly conscious of the stroke-induced rigidity of tone.

"Yeah, you too," was Pete's response. Then he shifted his attention back to the board.

Nathan held up his finger for me to wait a minute. "Pete thinks he's on the verge of victory. Best not to break his concentration." After a couple of seconds' hesitation, Pete moved his knight but left his finger on the piece, studying the board. "Sure you want to do that, Pete?"

He lingered there for several more seconds, surveying the board. A tentative smile slowly formed on his face. He took his finger away. "Checkmate."

"Right you are, my good man." Nathan immediately laid his king

over on the board and stood. "You have taken my title of champion
. . . temporarily. I do, of course, demand a rematch, Sir Darby, at your
convenience."

Pete, still sitting, took Nathan's extended hand. "Of course."

"But now I must meet with my attorney, so I will beg your leave."
He gave him a bow, then left him sitting, wondering, as Nathan walked
off with me to a concrete table and benches a short distance away. He
looked back over his shoulder at his opponent, then to me. "Pete's an
airline pilot. He suffers from chronic clinical depression. During his last
flight, he had a powerful urge to put the nose of the plane straight down
and dive—not a good thing when you're thirty-five thousand feet in the
air with a plane full of passengers. That's when he decided to commit
himself. I won't name the airline he works for, as it might unduly damage
the public's confidence in the company and get me sued."

"I understand."

"He's a pretty good guy and not a bad chess player, though he's no
match for me. I've enjoyed his company, and I think our games and
conversations have been very therapeutic for him, especially on those
rare occasions when I let him win. He is rightfully suspicious, but I'm
sufficiently skilled that I'm able to make it appear legitimate. I set that
trap for myself several moves back. Though his moves weren't brilliant,
he at least saw the bread crumbs I left on the board for him and followed
them home."

When we were both seated, he said, "You're looking good, Ted."

I gave him a sideways glance that said I knew it was bullshit, then I
shrugged. "I'm getting there, slowly if not so surely. Still have a bit of a
balance problem. Bullet damaged the inner ear." He raised up the cane
slightly. "Hence the assistance. But the doctors think I'll get back close
to normal. Same with the droopy eye. The short-term memory loss will
probably stay with me for a long time, though, maybe forever. But, hey, I
was never too good in that category anyway." I smiled.

"You're lucky to be alive, my friend. Very few people get shot in the head and live to tell about it."

I smiled again. "People have always said I'm hard headed. Maybe they're right." I paused. "And maybe it's good you couldn't get anything bigger than a twenty-two. But at any rate, contrary to popular belief, my doctor tells me that getting shot in the head is not necessarily fatal, thankfully. Just beneath the skull is this tough fibrous material, harder in some than others, that can actually deflect an object like a bullet of small caliber, depending on the distance and the angle of entry. Any way you look at it, though, I was lucky."

"Well, I'm sorry, Ted. It was my fault for putting you in that situation. I feel really bad about everything."

I waved him off. "I know you do, Nathan, but it wasn't your fault. I got a pretty good look at the person who shot me, and she didn't look anything like you."

We let a few seconds of silence close the subject. "And your daughter? That all working out?"

I folded my arms against the cold and leaned back slightly on the bench. "Yeah, ironic as it may be, when I was laid up in the hospital, when I was most vulnerable, my wife let it lie. She didn't try to take advantage. She could have filed to reopen the case, but she didn't. She brought Annie to visit me in the hospital. We had a heart to heart." I hesitated a moment. "We won't be getting back together or anything, but she's moved back to Tallahassee, and we're working together to see that Annie gets the best of both of us. There are no pending appeals. The case is closed."

I had been looking off into the distance as I talked, and now I brought my gaze back to Nathan.

"I see you're back on the booze," he said, his eyes searching mine for a reaction.

The abrupt change of subject and the uncanny accuracy of his observation threw me momentarily, but I resolved not to give him the confirmation he sought. "Nope," I said as neutrally as I could. "Still sober."

But it was like being hooked up to a human polygraph machine. I could feel my heart rate quicken, a film of perspiration forming under my arms. Nathan was shaking his head, smiling slightly. "You were drinking last night—and not just one or two drinks. I can smell it on your sweat, Ted. No big deal, mind you. I never bought into that complete sobriety thing either, but the curious thing is why you have chosen to deny it, especially to me."

Damn, the guy was good. Yeah, I'd had a few the night before. It hadn't been the first time either, in the last couple of weeks. But so what? Nathan was right. It wasn't a big deal. I could control my drinking. I wasn't one of those fools who couldn't have a drink without getting drunk. So why had I lied? Perhaps I didn't want to feed his arrogance. Perhaps I just figured it was none of his business. I gave him a shrug but said nothing in direct response. Whether he took that as confirmation or continued denial, I don't know, but he didn't persist on the subject.

"Well," I said, "enough about my soap opera. Let's talk about yours. I bring you good news this morning."

"I'm being released tomorrow?"

"Not exactly, but you've been officially cleared of the murder of Aaron Rosenberg. The judge granted our unopposed motion to set aside the jury verdict and enter a dismissal of the charges. Cindy Sands has been charged with it, as well as with the murders of James Washington and Donnie Mercer."

"That's great, Ted," he said, though without the enthusiasm I had hoped for. I guess from his perspective it was long overdue and hardly unexpected.

And, indeed, once I regained consciousness and told Browning what happened at the apartment, he quickly began to put the puzzle together. He called Harold Martin to confirm that he was who he said he was and to confirm his opinion on the fingerprints. After that, it was pretty much downhill for Cindy.

She held out for about a week after she was arrested, but when she realized it was just a matter of time, she summoned Browning to her jail cell, where, despite a strong admonition from her lawyer, she gave him a full confession. She was, after all, quite proud of her clever plan. She was really anxious, I think, to tell Browning every detail. It was one of the most chilling interviews he had ever conducted, he told me. And it filled in the gaps, answered some of the lingering questions about the case.

Cindy confirmed that she and James had begun their relationship when she was a patient at the facility in Maine. He became a willing helper in her subsequent criminal behavior, though he never was an active participant. "Didn't have the stomach for it" is how Cindy put it.

When Cindy was at St. Elizabeth's, she developed a very symbiotic relationship with Whitsen. She denied that it was ever an obsession, though she confirmed that she studied everything about Whitsen, knew just about every detail of her life, could imitate her mannerisms and could anticipate her words and actions. She admitted to "punishing" patients or staff who gave Whitsen trouble. It wasn't much of a leap to go the rest of the way with plastic surgery after she escaped. Then she killed the surgeon with a drug overdose.

And, as Nathan had theorized, they abducted Whitsen as she walked toward her front door. They took her to the mobile home Cindy had rented, drugged her, poured booze down her throat, then set the bed on fire. Cindy then began playing the role of her life, that of psychologist Rebecca Whitsen.

They both got jobs in Florida, and everything was going well. Too well. As the pressure of maintaining the false persona increased, Cindy became so engrossed with playing her part she occasionally blurred the line between reality and pretend. She began sending herself e-mail messages, playing the part of both tormentor and tormented. The Cindy inside her sought to protect the Rebecca facade. Patients or staff who were seen as threatening to Rebecca were targeted by Cindy.

It was in this context that Rosenberg was killed, not just because he had begun to suspect something wasn't quite right about the new psychologist but also because he had threatened Cindy with discipline for her insubordination. Cindy saw him as disrespecting Rebecca, causing her trouble.

She had James steal Nathan's clothes, but it was she who wore them when she sneaked into Rosenberg's office, hid behind the curtain in the bay window, and stabbed him to death as he sat in his chair. And the lighter? She couldn't help herself. Cindy had to assert her identity. It was James who then put the clothes in the washer at Sunrise Cottage and plunged the letter opener into the ground in the garden nearby while Cindy sped away in her car. Raymond Curry coming on the scene and his mistaken identity were an unplanned fortuity.

How, you might ask, could Cindy have been at her home in Tallahassee at 10:15, thirty minutes after the murder, to receive the phone call? It was so simple I don't know why I hadn't thought of it. She had a call-forwarding device on her home phone so that calls were transferred automatically to her cell phone.

Another mystery was Donnie Mercer's connection. We may never know why he had Robert Hart's number, but it was probably that he was simply trying to work an angle to get either money or influence to get released. Cindy did resolve the mystery of Donnie's disguised, one-word message to Nathan: sex. Donnie had apparently happened upon Cindy and James having sex in one of the storage closets at the hospital. This was about a week after Rosenberg's murder.

When he tried to leverage this information into an early release, he signed his death warrant. Cindy went along with him, made a deal that if he would say he had seen Nathan with the cigarette lighter, she would make sure he got out within a matter of weeks. But as soon as Mercer was on record with his statement about the lighter, he was killed. James lured him to the roof of the building after having ensured that he ingested the drug cocktail through his food. Cindy surprised him, easily overpowered him, and knocked him unconscious. She then dragged him to the edge of the roof and dropped him over.

Sands enjoyed the little cat-and-mouse game with Nathan and with me. She correctly anticipated that Nathan would guess her secret but that he wouldn't be able to prove it. She also correctly predicted Nathan's escape. The chances were good that Nathan would be killed, but either way, Cindy figured, she remained in control of the game.

The good news was that Nathan apparently didn't kill the two men on the street in Washington, as he had thought. There were no reported homicides or even assaults in that area. Fortunately, he was deep into his delusional world by then and only imagined the deadly encounter. He had probably just brushed past a couple of homeless people panhandling.

The press had fun, at the expense of the hospital, with the story of a mental patient who passed herself off as a psychologist for almost a year with no one the wiser. But the way I see it, they were throwing rocks in a glass house. None of the reporters who covered the story in D.C., none of the folks who interviewed the poor "victim" of the stalking and murder attempt, had a clue she was an imposter. And I guarantee you, if Cindy had decided to pose as a news reporter, print or broadcast, these folks wouldn't have made her as a fake. The woman is a horrible, evil person, but she's smart—scary smart—and a natural-born actor.

Nathan nodded. The irony, he said, was that she had made a pretty good psychologist. "I mean, I think it was her unusual therapy style that resulted in my breakthrough. She gained my trust with her us-against-them alliance. Then, with her increasingly confrontational approach, she began to plant the seed of truth underneath that protective shield I had erected to keep it out. It festered there, taking root and creating cracks in the delusional world I had created, eventually bursting to the surface and exposing to me my own self-deception."

"I hear you've been making real progress," I said.

He shook his head slowly. "Dealing with the truth, the awful reality of my actions, has been the hardest thing I've ever done. When I finally realized that my world of spies, secret codes, and missions was one of my own creation, that I was the one who killed my parents and my brother, the guilt and shame were overwhelming. Had I not been watched closely during this time, I would probably have found a way to end my life.

"And I can't blame Uncle Bob for how he feels. Sure, he's worked every employee at the hospital in order to keep tabs on me, to keep me away from that trust money. But the thing is, I don't want it. As soon as I'm declared competent, I'll sign it over.

"The guilt is still there, will always be with me, but I have also come to accept that I was at the time consumed by an illness just as debilitating, just as real, as any physical ailment. It doesn't excuse the act in my mind, but it helps to understand it. I don't deserve to live, but I'm thinking that God has spared me for a reason. As I have said to you, I don't believe in coincidences. I have to have hope that I can control this terrible illness, learn to live with it, and atone in some way for what I've done."

"That's good, Nathan."

"That's what my new psychologist has been telling me, anyway. His name is Thomas Spencer. And, yes, I've checked him out thoroughly to confirm that he is who he says he is." He smiled. "I call him Undoubting Thomas because of his unflinching optimism in my full recovery and ultimate release from the hospital."

I gave him a skeptical look, which he ignored. "They've got me on this new medication," he said. "I don't like it, of course, but it seems to be working. The voices are gone. I have fresh insight into my condition. I understand that I'll always have to take medication. I'm not only resigned to it but am committed to making sure I'm continually monitored, because I never want to put myself or others in jeopardy again. I know it will be quite some time before I have convinced the powers that be of this, but I can wait. This time I'm serious."

"Yes," I said, smiling, "I think you are."

"Got a letter this week from an agent. She wants to sell my manuscript to a publisher and maybe the movie rights too. I'm thinking of calling it 'A Beautiful Mind.'"

"I think that's been done, Nathan."

"Anyway, I haven't decided what I'll do when I get out of here. I'm thinking maybe psychology." I gave him a look of surprise, and he shrugged. "It seems that I have an innate ability to relate to many of the patients, to help them work through their problems or issues. It's very satisfying." When I didn't comment, he continued. "Of course, I'm still thinking law school too. I'd make a great lawyer. Maybe we could practice together someday."

I couldn't help but wince. "I don't know that the practice of law would be enough of an intellectual challenge for you."

"I am inclined to agree," he said. "Anyway, I'll be getting out of here pretty soon." I arched my eyebrows but said nothing. Nathan looked around, then leaned in close and whispered, "Yeah, God told me last night. He was quite clear about it. And God has never lied to me yet."

Here are some other books from Pineapple Press on related topics. For a complete catalog, write to Pineapple Press, P.O. Box 3889, Sarasota, Florida 34230-3889, or call (800) 746-3275. Or visit our website at www.pineapplepress.com.

Conflict of Interest by Terry Lewis. Trial lawyer Ted Stevens fights his own battles, including his alcoholism and his pending divorce, as he fights for his client in a murder case. But it's the other suspect in the case who causes the conflict of interest. Ted must choose between concealing evidence that would be helpful to his client and revealing it, thereby becoming a suspect himself.

Privileged Information by Terry Lewis. Ted Stevens' partner, Paul Morganstein, is defending his late brother's best friend on a murder charge when he obtains privileged information leading him to conclude that his client committed another murder thirty years earlier. The victim? Paul's brother. Faced with numerous difficulties, Paul must decide if he will divulge privileged information.

Doctored Evidence by Michael Biehl. A medical device fails and the patient dies on the operating table. Was it an accident—or murder? Smart and courageous hospital attorney Karen Hayes must find out: Her job and her life depend on it.

Lawyered to Death by Michael Biehl. Hospital attorney Karen Hayes is called to defend the hospital CEO against a claim of sexual harassment but soon finds she must also defend him against a murder charge. The trail of clues leads her into a further fight for her own life and that of her infant son.

Nursing a Grudge by Michael Biehl. An elderly nursing home resident, who was once an Olympic champion swimmer with a murky background in the German army, drowns in a lake behind the home. Does anyone know how it happened? Does anyone care? Hospital attorney Karen Hayes battles bureaucracy, listens to the geriatric residents ignored by the authorities, and risks her own life to find the truth.

Seven Mile Bridge by Michael Biehl. Florida Keys dive shop owner Jonathan Bruckner returns home to Wisconsin after his mother's death, searching for clues to his father's death years before. He is stunned by what he discovers about his father's life and comes to know his parents in a way he never did as a child. Mostly, he's surprised by what he learns about himself. Fluidly moving between past and present, between hope and despair, *Seven Mile Bridge* is a story about one man's obsession for the truth and how much can depend on finding it.

Secrets of San Blas by Charles Farley. Most towns have their secrets. In the 1930s, Port St. Joe on the Gulf in Florida's Panhandle has more than its share. Old Doc Berber, the town's only general practitioner, thought he knew all of the secrets, but a grisly murder out at the Cape San Blas Lighthouse drags him into a series of intrigues that even he can't diagnose.

Secrets of St. Vincent by Charles Farley. Things are not always as serene as they seem in the little Florida Panhandle village of Port St. Joe. When bluesman Reggie Robinson is wrongly arrested for the gruesome murder of Sheriff Byrd "Dog" Batson, old Doc Berber and his best friend, Gator Mica, mount a quixotic search for the real killer on savage St. Vincent Island. If they survive the frightening adventure, they'll return with the shocking secrets that will shatter the town's tranquility forever.

Death in Bloodhound Red by Virginia Lanier. Jo Beth Sidden is a Georgia peach with an iron pit. She raises and trains bloodhounds for search-and-rescue missions in the Okefenokee Swamp. In an attempt to save a friend from ruin, she organizes an illegal operation that makes a credible alibi impossible just when she needs one most: She's indicted for attempted murder. If the victim dies, the charge will be murder one.

Mystery in the Sunshine State edited by Stuart Kaminsky. Offers a selection of Florida mysteries from many of Florida's notable writers, including Edna Buchanan, Jeremiah Healy, Stuart McIver, and Les Standiford. Follow professional investigators and amateur sleuths alike as they patiently uncover clues to finally reveal the identity of a killer or the answer to a riddle.

CPSIA information can be obtained at www.ICGtesting.com
Printed in the USA
BVOW07s1153300713

327129BV00002B/6/P